THE TREACHERY OF TIME

Also by Anna Gilbert

The Wedding Guest
A Walk in the Wood
The Long Shadow
Miss Bede Is Staying
Flowers for Lilian
The Leavetaking
Remembering Louise
A Family Likeness
The Look of Innocence
Images of Rose

ANNA GILBERT
THE
TREACHERY
of TIME

ST. MARTIN'S PRESS ❧ NEW YORK

Library of Congress Cataloging-in-Publication Data

Gilbert, Anna.
The treachery of time / by Anna Gilbert.
p.   cm.
ISBN 0-312-14055-X
I. Title.
PR6057.I49T74   1996
823'.914—dc20   95-46799   CIP

First published in Great Britain by Transworld Publishers
Ltd

First U.S. Edition: April 1996

10   9   8   7   6   5   4   3   2   1

PART ONE

WOOD ASTON

CHAPTER 1

Esther Aumery's first direct encounter with the darker side of life took place on a summer morning when she was thirteen years old. The experience was brief, its effect momentous. For the rest of her life, when moral issues arose and were seriously discussed, she had first to clear her mind of the memory of evil as she had first seen it in actual physical shape, come to contaminate the freshness of morning. Even then – perhaps only then was it possible – she had recognized it instantly for what it was.

Of wickedness in the abstract she had, of course, been long aware. It figured prominently in the Bible; its temptations beset the unfortunate Fairchild family with every breath they drew; but so far it had remained safely within the covers of books. Wickedness was not a thing one went in for at Lady Green.

Enlightenment came appropriately at daybreak. The low room was still dark; only the looking-glass reflected a glimmer of light from the window. Neck rigid on the pillow, she strained her ears to catch again a sound less familiar than the rustle of sparrows in the ivy or the creak of ancient floorboards. It was strange, adding to the strangeness of the early hour, to hear the quiet babble of the stream, so constant that normally one didn't notice it. It lulled her back to the edge of sleep.

Then, with a startled clatter of wings, a pair of wood pigeons rose from the nearest elm. Someone was coming along the lane from Wood Aston. Wheels rattled, hooves thudded, a whip cracked. Throwing off the covers, Esther sprang to the window in disbelief. No-one ever drove along the back lane, a narrow riverside track often flooded and leading nowhere. The cart road went past Keeper's Lodge. Though steep, it was wide enough even for timber wagons, and the ruts were filled twice a year from the Aumerys' own quarry.

She leaned out into the mysterious half-light and instantly drew back. Coming at full tilt round the bend to her left there dashed into view a brown-and-white horse between the shafts of a rickety cart. The driver was a man in a black coat with a black cap pulled down over his brow. He was bending forward, his eyes fixed on the way ahead with a concentration so fierce that he might have been driving for his life in a race against time itself. Behind him in the cart, a carpet bag and various bundles jostled and tumbled against one another.

Just by the gate the horse faltered and almost stumbled. The man half rose, reached out and lashed the poor beast with such ferocity that Esther winced. He was a thin man, pale-cheeked in spite of his exertions. He looked neither to right nor left, so that she saw him chiefly in profile, but as she leaned out again for a last look before the next curve in the lane took him out of sight, he glanced back over his shoulder and she saw his sick desperate face, its pallor tinged with green from the overhanging trees. Then he vanished in a cloud of dust and a scatter of pebbles.

The leaves, stirred by his passing, composed themselves. Presently the wood pigeons came back. The stream murmured on as if nothing had happened and that was reassuring. The incident had been disturbing in more than the usual sense of having roused her from sleep. The flying stones, the foam at the horse's mouth, the man's white face and black clothes, above all his mad haste – had burst upon the pearl-grey morning like screams from some unimaginable world of wildness and distress.

8

Her every sense freshened by the onset of a new day, Esther knew, with a child's directness of perception, that the man was in torment. He was fleeing from some terror of which he was not only the victim but the cause. It was terrible and sad. She feared and pitied him. One would have thought he knew that – Esther hesitated over a word not commonly said aloud and to be avoided even in thought – that the devil was after him.

The revelation, vivid as lightning, passed as quickly. High drama cannot be long sustained. Esther had not at her disposal the vocabulary in which to describe him as a man possessed. Instead she pulled down the ruffled cuffs of her nightdress with a sense of seemliness restored and condemned his behaviour in all its aspects as not quite the thing. People simply didn't drive like that in Wood Aston. The pace of village life was slow, slowest of all here at Lady Green, where no-one worked except the servants, who were reproved if they appeared to hurry. No ill-bred bustling must agitate the calm surface of life in the Aumery household whose leisurely routine had evolved in response to the somewhat passive inclinations of her father and the refined sensibilities of her mother.

However, Esther recollected, all things work together for good, according to Matty the housemaid who attended the Primitive Methodist Chapel in Unnerstone. Every trial, setback and disappointment must be seen as a test of faith and, if accepted with resignation, could well prove a blessing in disguise. Pouring water from ewer to basin and responding bravely to its cold sting, Esther saw Matty's stern doctrine in a new light. The man in the cart had been neither a trial, a setback, nor a disappointment, merely unpleasant, but he had served the useful purpose of waking her long before the usual time. She had wanted to get up early and, without his help, might easily have overslept.

Mindful of the wet grass, she dressed suitably in her outgrown green merino, a pair of darned stockings and the oldest of her three pairs of boots, so shabby that they were almost ready to be passed on to one of the village families, but still watertight. The parcel and envelope were ready in her lidded basket. They had been there for three days.

It was a quarter of a mile to Keeper's Lodge by way of the drive, but a path across the fields brought her in a few minutes to the foot of the green bluff, known as Scaur Crag, and to a steep path in the lee of a stone wall dividing rough pasture from meadow. Climbing quickly – though there was plenty of time – she arrived at the Godwains' gate. Prince knew her too well to bark and came out of his kennel to greet her with no more noise than the drag of his chain on the flagged path.

With the mingled misgivings and satisfaction that attend the delivery of a present, she laid the parcel on the right-hand seat in the trellised porch, that being the utilitarian side. On the opposite, decorative side, fixed high on the wooden beam, a fox's mask snarled down on a pair of inoffensive conch shells adorning the seat beneath.

For the last time, unable to resist, she opened the unsealed envelope and read the message on the lace-fringed card:

To Daniel from Esther, wishing you many happy returns of the day, 24 July 1914.

There had been no need to put the date except as a gentle hint that so unusually beautiful a card was meant to be kept, not carelessly thrown away. If, in years to come, Daniel should find it among his most treasured possessions, he would know exactly how long he had had it. By that time it would have an almost historic value. The phrase was Daniel's own.

Carefully lifting the gilt-edged flap, she took a final peep at the rustic scene framed in green leaves, tucked the card back in its envelope, laid it beside the parcel, tiptoed down the path, soundlessly closed the gate and hurried home across the dew-soaked grass, avoiding, wherever possible, the daisies.

Having shed boots, stockings and dress, she slid into bed again – the half-tester where her Great-Aunt Aumery had slept, and before her several earlier Miss Aumerys. Her face, pink-tinted in its cloud of dark hair, relaxed. Below the smooth brow blue lids closed upon eyes of deeper blue. In untroubled security she slept.

High in the crown of the Aston oak, Daniel contemplated the sky. The climb had been easy: he had done it scores of times. Wide-spreading branches provided footholds as safe as the rungs of a ladder, save for one rotten lightning-struck limb fifteen feet from the ground. Once past the last fork he could lean against the great trunk, his spine against the spine of the tree, his feet supported by a strong lateral branch, could stretch his neck and see nothing but the sky.

That is, he chose to see nothing but the sky. To the south-west stretched a hazel coppice, to the north an ancient oakwood, to the east the daisy-studded pastures of Lady Green. Daniel knew them too well to waste a glance on them; nor did he turn his eyes towards the church tower and roofs of Wood Aston or the belfry of the schoolhouse where, in less than half an hour, he must begin the day's work.

The sky was his domain – ever-changing, uncharted, unmarred by human intrusion, tinged now with the milky blues of morning and hung with white clouds still formless, like his aspirations. His brown, long-sighted eyes were raised in quest of the infinite. His imagination burned with undirected fervour. His heart swelled in response to vague but splendid promptings, intimations of greatness to be achieved through dedication to a mighty Cause.

What cause? No immediate answer came. It would have been unfair to demand one of a boy still awkward of limb, his features not yet grown into harmony, though his narrow cheek-bones and high forehead gave him a look of hungry intelligence, and his firmly curved thin lips promised eloquence.

A woodpecker, approaching the tree, found it occupied and veered away. Holding on to a branch, Daniel leaned to watch its flight, looked down and saw Esther coming along one of the broad rides between the trees, a neat figure in her summer dress, a stiff-brimmed hat perched firmly on her curling hair, her basket now filled with books. She was studying history, French and music with Miss Angovil at Wood Aston and was due at Priest's House at nine o'clock. She was never late.

'Esther! Wait a minute.'

She heard him without surprise. He was always somewhere about. But for her clean dress she would have sat down on one of the oak tree's anchoring roots, strong and broad enough to make a comfortable seat. Instead she put down her basket in the hollow between two of them and stood quite still, aware as always of the tree's immense, sheltering presence. It was hundreds of years old, nearly as old as the church, Daniel said. She laid a gloved hand on the rough bark and felt in the tree a quality she had never felt in church: a secret power awesome yet comforting, like the presence of an aged being, not a relation exactly nor even a person at all, but something one could in every sense look up to.

And looking up through the branches, she saw the soles of Daniel's boots as, with the ease of practice, he came down to earth, and not before time. He was cutting it very fine this morning, Esther thought with disapproval. But more important, had he found . . . ?

Daniel saw the appeal in her eyes, knew what he must say and said it promptly. 'Thank you for the present. It was a surprise.'

'You guessed who it was from?'

'At first I wondered – before I opened the envelope. It was too early for the postman. I couldn't think how it had got there at six o'clock.'

'It was there ever so much earlier than that. Do you like the card?' she couldn't help asking.

'I certainly do. It's just like you somehow. And thank you for the stockings. I needed them. You didn't knit them yourself? You did?'

'Yes, of course.' She had been knitting on four needles since she was a mere child, but this pair, as it happened, had turned out particularly well. Ought she to mention . . . ? 'Matty helped me to turn the heels. She actually did most of one of the turns.'

'They both looked the same to me,' said Daniel, this time with perfect truth.

'I was rather worried about the size. They do fit?'

'Er . . . I haven't tried them on yet.' He was suddenly conscious of the time and of his old knockabout breeches and jersey. 'I'll have to go home and change – and I'll wear them today. Walk slowly and I'll catch you up.'

'He'll be lucky,' Esther thought as he tore off between the trees, 'if he isn't late and Mr Horner will have something to say if he is, birthday or no birthday.'

She, on the other hand, had nothing to fear. Even supposing that by some unlucky accident she should ever be late, Miss Angovil was incapable of uttering a word of reproof or of feeling the least obligation to do so. It was this lack of challenge in their relationship that had long since roused Daniel's suspicions. More than once he had denounced Esther's so-called lessons as a farce, an utter farce. It was high time her parents woke up to the fact that she had had no education at all. Criminal, he called it. He often used the word.

'Without education,' he had told her, 'human beings are no better than beasts of the field,' and then had burst out laughing at the unsuitability of the comparison in this particular case. 'Well, most of them.

13

But I tell you there can be no progress towards a better world unless mankind . . .' He often spoke of mankind, and Esther would listen, without the slightest harm to her self-confidence, while he enlarged upon the present uncultivated state of the human mind and the wretchedness of ignorance.

'I don't feel wretched,' she had once interrupted him to say, 'and I like going to Miss Angovil's. Besides, where else could I go?'

'If you'd been sent to the village school like everybody else, we might have taught you a few elementary facts. As it is you'll learn no more from old Angovil than you would learn from a ruminating sheep, apart from harmful out-of-date notions of social superiority . . .'

Neither hurrying nor loitering, Esther continued along the woodland path until it joined the road, which led down past the mill, over the bridge and up the hill on the other side. Skirting the churchyard, it brought her to the village as the fingers of the green-faced church clock pointed to five minutes to nine.

Wood Aston consisted of the Coach and Horses Inn, three rows of cottages, four or five solidly built houses of a superior kind and, opposite the inn, a school and schoolhouse – all casually disposed about a central green with the air of having grown out of the surrounding hilly fields, and remaining as much a part of nature as is possible for a human settlement dating back ten centuries.

Of the larger houses, Miss Angovil's was the most imposing. With its white railings and porch and bay windows commanding a view of the entire village, it appeared to preside over its humbler neighbours, though in the long history of Wood Aston it was a comparative late-comer.

Esther paused with her hand on the latch of the gate and looked across the green. For the past few minutes Prissie Merridon, Mr Horner's maid, had been ringing the bell for morning school – for the last time before the summer holidays. Most of the children were already gathered at the school gate though not, Esther thought, in their usual haphazard fashion. They had become an attentive group, united in some common interest, something to do with the thorn hedge between the green and the school yard. A late lamb? A broken-winged bird?

The bell stopped ringing. In the sudden silence Prissie ran up the steps and came out to join the children. A moment later, with dramatic suddenness, Daniel burst upon the scene. He had obviously run all the way, but, arriving under the church clock with two minutes' grace, he slowed down and with the dignity becoming to his position as pupil-teacher, strode to the school gate. He wore his best knickerbockers, a Norfolk jacket and stiff white collar and his new black ribbed woollen stockings.

The children stood aside unwillingly, exclaiming and pointing to the nearest thorn bush. Daniel stopped, bent lower. Intrigued, Esther ran across the green.

'Whatever is it?'

Daniel didn't answer. He had gone down on one knee and, with some awkwardness on account of the thorns, was reaching under the bush to pick up a bundle wrapped in a blanket. For a moment he remained kneeling, then he lifted the blanket and its contents and stood up. The children moved aside as Esther went nearer. She had known by the blanket that it couldn't be a lost animal, and half expected to see an abandoned baby. If only it had been a baby! But the limp object cradled in Daniel's arms was the body of a girl.

She lay motionless, a dead weight: a mere shape tightly swathed in the dirty blanket, so that her identity could only be guessed at. To Esther, striving to feel the reverence one was supposed to feel for the dead, she seemed as uninviting an object as one of the dubious bundles left under a hedge by departing tinkers. Indeed, that was what she could be. Taking a cautious step forward, Esther saw a face or part of one: a nose, a mouth half open, and under the chin a thick tress of hay-coloured hair wound round her neck like a noose.

'Put it down,' she urged as Daniel adjusted his burden so that it lay more evenly. 'Aren't you going to put it down?'

It was as if he hadn't heard. His half-smile expressed some feeling more complex than surprise or interest – a mingled awe and exaltation that Esther recognized as a special kind of feeling, one that she ought perhaps to share.

'I've never seen a dead person before,' she said by way of excuse.

'She isn't dead.'

It must be true if Daniel said so. Esther gave no more than a glance at the girl. It was Daniel's face that her eyes explored. She was well used to taking her cue from him: he was older, cleverer, aware of so many things she knew nothing about, that her failure to respond to this astonishing situation as he was doing made her uneasy.

Prissie felt no such pangs of conscience. 'Miss Esther's right. Put her down. She might have something catching,' she said and hurried off to fetch Mr Horner.

And at last Daniel carefully laid the girl down on the grass, threw open the gate and ushered in the children. Having stood in awestruck silence with barely a nudge, they broke into an excited babble as they went down the steps, but Daniel let them go as if they didn't matter and came back. He knelt down and loosened the blanket with as delicate a touch as if undoing the ceremental cloths of a long-entombed mummy, and fearful of finding nothing but desiccated bones which a whiff of air might reduce to powder. And there she lay, inert as the dead, her skinny legs barely covered by a short-sleeved, mouse-coloured frock: her arms, thin as sticks, glued to her sides, her legs and feet

16

stretched out as if she had been packed for storage like a poorly stuffed doll, and not yet painted except for blotches in varying shades of pink on her limbs and neck.

But she was certainly alive. The passive body pulsated lightly. From the half-open mouth came audible breaths, like the faintest of distant snores.

'Why doesn't she wake?' Esther whispered, adding dutifully, 'Poor thing,' and turned with relief as Prissie ran up the steps followed by Mr Horner.

'Dear me!' The schoolmaster pushed up his spectacles and peered at the occupant of the blanket as if to study a rare specimen of the natural world, an interesting moth or mollusc perhaps. 'I was expecting to find an abandoned infant, but this is a grown girl. Alive? Ah yes.'

'Drugged, I should think, sir.' Daniel had bent low to smell her breath.

'Godfrey's Cordial very likely,' Prissie said. 'A double dose and they sleep like the dead. Unless . . .' She drew aside her clean apron and knelt to take a closer look. 'Pooh! She stinks of spirits – and not only spirits. She hasn't been washed since goodness knows when, and she's riddled with flea bites. You be careful, Daniel. There'll be bugs in that blanket.'

'What's to be done with her, Prissie?' Mr Horner asked. 'It's rather outside my usual . . . er . . . sphere of duty.'

'She'll have to go to the workhouse in Hudmorton. That's where she'll have to go.'

'I suppose so, if we can find some means of getting her there. There should be a cart of some sort.'

'Nobody'll take her on any kind of cart until she's been scrubbed and carbolicked,' Prissie said. 'Her things'll need to be burned, what there is of them. Once they're got off her there'll be no putting them back. In fact from what I can see—' she investigated, turning her back to the others as a screen, 'she hasn't

17

a stitch on under that frock and she's not just a little girl either. It's a disgrace. Left here to die and not even clean and covered if her call should come.'

'Scandalous,' said Mr Horner mildly.

'It's criminal,' Daniel said. 'But I don't think she was left here to die, although she could have died and might still for that matter. Whoever left her chose a school gate in the middle of a village where she was sure to be found.'

'I think I know,' Esther said, astounded to find herself in so authoritative a position, 'who it may have been.'

'Would you recognize the man?' Mr Horner asked when she had told her story.

She hesitated. The sweat-drenched horse, the yellow-painted, open four-wheeled cart, the black cap and jacket, the forward thrust of their wearer's body – these she could see as vividly as when they had flashed upon the grey screen of early morning, and these she could describe. But of the man himself as distinct from his mad haste, she could give no clear account; and of her own awe-stricken sense of having seen, or almost seen, or just missed seeing wickedness unleashed, she could not speak at all. They were waiting, Daniel, Mr Horner and Prissie, to hear what she alone could tell.

'Very pale,' she said, 'and cruel and in a terrible hurry. Not to go anywhere.' Where could he go? The back lane led nowhere. 'To get away.' She tried to imagine the girl in the blanket as having been one of the bundles in the cart: saw it lurch and leap and fall over the side unnoticed as the horse galloped through the village. But it couldn't have happened like that. This particular bundle had been placed under the thorn bush deliberately.

'There were other things wrapped up in the cart. Do you think they were all . . . ?' A cartload of drugged

children? Her flesh crept. 'There may have been others
. . . like her.'

She was still reluctant to recognize the unmoving
form on the grass as a girl like – and even more unlike
– herself. She was sorry for her of course, but with
an instinctive shrinking from such unknown regions
of human experience as could spawn so undesirable
a situation as this.

It was Mr Horner who understood some at least of
her anxiety. 'Others? Not at all likely. A man engaged
in the grisly trade of selling children would know how
to dispose of them profitably in secret. Otherwise why
should he take the risk? The man was a scoundrel no
doubt, but his aim was evidently to get rid of the girl
in all possible haste, and with as little risk to himself
as possible.'

'But why?' Esther asked. 'And who is she?'

'There's likely something wrong with her,' Prissie
said. 'She doesn't look up to much.'

'How can we know who she is or why she's here?'
Daniel had flushed as if in annoyance. 'We don't even
know that the man Esther saw was the person who
brought her here.'

'I suppose you're going to tell us she dropped from
heaven,' Prissie said. 'If that's where she's come from,
you'd think they'd have made her decent first and given
her some underclothes. That blanket!' Her glance was
one of deep disapproval. 'It's plain to see she comes
from the lowest of the low.'

'Then we must raise her up.' Daniel's stern voice
vibrated with such energy that the others stared. 'I
mean,' he added hastily, 'that in a way she has been
left in our charge. Isn't it our duty, sir, to take care of
her?'

'To help her, yes. To take care of a person is a
longer and more serious commitment.' Mr Horner
gave Daniel a keen look and took out his watch. 'And
as for duty, at this moment yours is in the schoolroom.

19

There are twenty minutes of your scripture lesson left. "With whom hast thou left those few sheep in the wilderness?" Eh? Samuel I, Chapter 17.'

It was typical of their relationship that Daniel smiled and left at once – or almost at once. 'I was thinking of Matthew 25, verse 35, sir. "I was a stranger and ye took me in; Naked and ye clothed me."'

'Well done, lad. A good answer.'

'Here is an outcast, sir, a human soul in distress, and we can think only of fleas and the workhouse.'

On this high note and with a distinct flourish, he departed.

'She doesn't look distressed to me,' Prissie whispered when Mr Horner had seated himself on the low wall and was stroking his beard in thoughtful silence, 'any more than a piece of lardy-cake looks distressed. It's all very well for them two to recite the scriptures, but they won't be the ones to clean her up and comb the lice out of her hair.'

By this time interest in the new arrival had spread. Aproned women, having taken in the situation from their windows, appeared at their gates.

Prissie's mother, who kept the Coach and Horses, opened the inn door and called out, 'What's up, Prissie? What've you got there, for goodness sake?' Crossing the green, she caught sight of Mr Horner and adopted a less robust manner. 'Well, I don't know. Where's this come from?' and after a closer look, 'She doesn't belong to anybody hereabouts, I'll tell you that for sure.'

'It's what to do with her till she can be got to the workhouse,' Prissie explained. 'She can't be left here. But I've just done the back kitchen and even if I hadn't, I don't fancy having her in it, nor in the bath tub that's wiped every day and scrubbed once a week for Mr Horner.'

'It wouldn't be fitting,' her mother agreed, 'and him a widower.' She looked speculatively at the various cottages and at the silent spectators at their gates.

'What about Gladdie Cotts? She's got a scullery and nothing much to do. Have you a minute, Gladdie?'

But Gladdie, the middle-aged daughter of the parish clerk, recollected all of a sudden that her bread would have risen and went indoors. Following her prudent lead, the other women also withdrew. Doors were closed, windows resumed.

'It'll have to be you and me, Prissie, as usual. We'll take her into the wash-house at the Coach. You can be lighting the fire under the copper while I finish in the Tap. If that's all right, Mr Horner.'

'Yes, indeed. It's like you to come to the rescue, Mrs Merridon. I can spare Prissie for an hour or two, and a slice of cold bacon will do nicely for my dinner.'

In evident relief he took refuge in the schoolhouse. Prissie and her mother each took a side of the blanket and carried its occupant round to the back of the inn, where she was lowered to the wash-house floor until a makeshift bed could be contrived from a sack and clean straw. Prissie lit the boiler, unhooked a heavy zinc bathtub from the wall, put a towel and a clean worn blanket on a clothes horse . . .

'She can't still be asleep.' Mrs Merridon put her head round the door when these preparations were nearing completion. She came nearer. 'Well, I don't know!' Released from her swaddling bands, the visitor looked less doll-like. She lay on her back on the straw pallet, still motionless, but in a more natural attitude. The snoring had ceased. 'It's the queerest thing I ever saw or heard of.'

Mrs Merridon's voice had dropped to a lower pitch. The thick eyelids sealing the girl's eyes gave to her mask-like face an unnerving secrecy. 'She fair gives me the creeps. You're right. There must be something wrong with her or she'd never have been cast away like a poisoned cat.' She recovered herself. 'We'll give her another ten minutes, then into the tub with her, awake or asleep. The water'll likely wake her. She can

21

have some bread and milk and we can find out who
she belongs to and where she's come from. After that,
the sooner she's got away the better.'

'I was thinking – there's a chance Barney Trisk might
turn up tomorrow.'

'That's right. They were saying in the bar last night
that he was at Unnerstone. Would he take her, do you
think?'

'He'd want something for doing it. Catch Barney
doing anything for nothing. But who's going to pay
money for having her taken away?'

'Happen them at Lady Green could find half a crown
for once.'

'That's something they'd be glad to find and lucky
if they could.'

'Is it as bad as that? Bertha Godwain's been saying for
a long time that the Aumerys were heading downhill.
Well, you could have a word with Barney. If anyone
can get round him, you can. He's got his eye on you,
has Barney.'

'He's got a nerve,' said Prissie who was walking
out with Jim Burdle at the forge. 'He certainly has a
nerve.'

'I'll tell you what. Let's have that old red chair out of
the Snug. Her ladyship can be sat on it when she's had
her bath. It's on its last legs anyway, and the stuffing's
coming out.'

The two women pattered off across the cobbled
yard. Their footsteps died away. When all was quiet
again, the girl on the pallet opened her eyes. The
lard-pale face remained expressionless, but the eyes
made a difference. Considering the long drugged sleep
from which their owner had just awakened, they were
more alert than might have been expected. There was
not much to be seen in the drab wash-house, ill-lit
by one small window already misted over with steam
from the boiler. Nevertheless the girl's eyes travelled
slowly over the upper walls, the ceiling and as much

of the room as could be seen from her recumbent position.

Footsteps approached – and voices. From the yard came a scraping sound as Prissie and her mother alternately pushed and dragged the heavy chair. As they came nearer, the eyes closed.

'She's still asleep,' Prissie said.

CHAPTER 2

Fascinated, repelled, yet unable to tear herself away, Esther had watched the scene enacted at the school gate until everyone else had gone. From the schoolroom came the subdued murmur of children chanting the seven-times table. With a pang, she remembered the time. For the first time in her life she was late.

From the events of the past half hour Priest's House alone had remained aloof. Neither Spedding, the housekeeper, nor her mistress had put in an appearance. There was no need. From her bay window Miss Angovil enjoyed a panoramic view of Wood Aston. Her knowledge of its goings-on was intimate, comprehensive, complete. It supplied the yawning gap which often threatened Esther's lessons when other branches of knowledge failed. There was nothing the two of them enjoyed more than a good gossip.

Normally Esther's account of both the man in the cart and the girl in the blanket would have fallen on willing ears, but this morning Miss Angovil was not herself. Her pale blue eyes were heavy, her brows puckered from a headache after a wakeful night. Apparently she, too, had been disturbed in the early hours.

'All this talk about war. Does your father think it will happen, Esther? The dread of it has quite got on my mind. The suffering there would be! I keep on thinking of Roland.' Her beloved younger brother had been killed in the Boer War. 'It was foolish of me, but I got out his letters again and was reading them until I went to bed – far too upset to sleep. I didn't close my eyes until long after midnight and was just dozing off when I heard a cart . . .'

'It was him,' Esther breathed.

'He, dear. It must have been. Whoever it was drew up on the other side of the green. Naturally I was on the alert at once, thinking of burglars. But by the time I got to the window the cart had gone – into Church Lane, I think.'

She yawned. Esther fetched a pad soaked in eau-de-cologne and applied it to her brow; and as Spedding was in one of her frequent crusty moods and un-approachable, made a pot of tea, then copied out one of the fables of La Fontaine in her best handwriting while Miss Angovil dozed in her armchair. The morning lagged until the church clock striking twelve brought release and she sped to the stable yard of the Coach and Horses in the hope of further developments.

She was met by Prissie, who was on her way back to the schoolhouse. 'Yes, she's still there. She came to when we put her in the bath, but she might as well still be asleep for all the difference it's made. There's not a word passed her lips. It's like what I said – she's deaf and dumb and a half-wit as well. That'll be why she's been got rid of. The wickedness of folk is past belief. You can go in if you want.' The wash-house door was open. Prissie had taken no pains to lower her voice from its usual hearty pitch. 'There's no knowing. You might be able to get something out of her.'

A powerful reek of carbolic soap, Condes Fluid and quassia chips bore witness to Prissie's efforts, as did the girl herself. Vigorous scrubbing had left her limp. Against the shabby red plush of the chair from the Snug, her face looked paler than ever. Her hair, still wet, hung over her shoulders in lank locks darkened by washing to the colour of straw but growing lighter as they dried. She sat with drooping head, her eyes downcast; but at least they were open.

'Are you feeling better?' Esther glanced at the empty bowl and spoon on the floor by the chair. 'You've had some bread and milk. Did you like it?'

Unconsciously she had assumed the tone and manner appropriate when coaxing a child to speak; but there was nothing childlike in the impassive face, nothing even youthful apart from its smallness, matched by the skinniness of the arms and legs and of the bare feet dangling in front of the boiler fire.

Discouraged by her unbroken silence, Esther turned to go and was confronted in the doorway by Daniel. He had arrived so swiftly and towered so purposefully in the low doorway that she backed away, half persuaded that he had grown taller since she had last seen him little more than three hours ago. He had certainly changed. She felt in him a new vigour and energy she couldn't have described. Her impression was that he had grown older. After all, he was sixteen.

'She can't speak. Prissie thinks she's deaf and dumb. Or perhaps – ' Esther's low voice dropped to a whisper, 'she's not quite . . . you know . . .'

Daniel paid no attention. He went over to the girl and said quietly but with authority, 'What is your name?'

The girl looked up. A faint colour tinged her pallid cheeks. Her lips parted. Her eyes widened and were lit by a sudden inner brightness. But no answer came.

'Don't be afraid. You can trust me. I want to help you. Tell me about your family and where you come from.'

A shadow passed over her face. With no more force than that of a flower stem leaning towards the light, she put out a thin hand. Daniel took it in a firm grasp, then gently released it and turned to Esther.

'She isn't deaf, but it's no use urging her to talk. She was in no condition to know how she got here. You'd better go.' He followed her as far as the door. 'Heaven knows what's been done to her and whether it can ever be put right.'

26

Again, with sadness, she felt the change in him. For all his failure to draw so much as a word from the girl, he seemed unaccountably elated, as if holding in check a strong flow of energy. In the tiny room his voice had seemed to ring. He held his head high as he looked past her at the blue sky above the grey stable roof. And because he could do nothing without affecting her, because to every note he sounded she instinctively responded with the sensitivity of a delicate instrument, because he had changed, she changed too. Having known him from infancy, she had had no more idea of his separate identity than exists in one of two saplings growing side by side and differing only in age and height. Now, for the first time, she saw him as a distinct person separate from herself, an individual who could not only move unpredictably but also move away.

'I'm going now,' she said.

He only nodded but as she crossed the yard he called after her, 'I say! Can't you find her something respectable to wear? You've got all sorts of dresses, haven't you?'

'Oh! Well, I don't know . . .'

It wasn't true that she had all sorts of dresses, and those that she had were made to last until they had been let out, lengthened several times and even turned. People thought the Aumerys were as well off as all the Aumerys before them had been. It suited them to have people think so. The families of the two or three prosperous farmers in the neighbourhood would have been surprised to know how simple life had become at Lady Green.

Consequently Esther was taken aback by Daniel's unexpected demand on her charity. She still hesitated. Above his stiff white collar his mouth was severe. Her eyes moved down from the collar to the revers and then the belt of his tightly buttoned Norfolk jacket, and would in time have reached the floor had they not come to rest between the kneeband of his breeches and the top of his well-polished right boot, where a great hole gaped in his new black stocking. There were dropped stitches in three of the ribs.

'Oh, Daniel! Your stocking.'

He glanced down. 'Yes. It'll have to be mended. I must have caught it on that thorn bush. See what you can find, Esther. Anything warm and decent will do.'

Other people were coming, among them the rector. The general opinion was that there wasn't much they could do. Folk had troubles of their own, and what was the workhouse for if not to take in foundlings? Say what you like about the Poor Law, it came in useful at a time like this, and wasn't that what people paid their rates for? Daniel Godwain seemed to think the village should be responsible for the girl. Seemingly he'd heard or read in a book about people struck dumb by an accident or shock. If they were properly looked after they would get better – in time. This scheme of his for finding a home for her and getting up a subscription! If he'd been a bit older he'd have seen that it couldn't be done. Where was the money to come from? He was a clever lad, but his head was always in the clouds.

Daniel was not easily discouraged. When the school had closed in the afternoon, he combed the village and its surroundings in an attempt to find a temporary home for the girl, beginning with his own parents. His arguments cut no ice with them: they were used to his crack-brained ideas.

'Folk would think we were as soft as balm,' Bertha Godwain said, 'as we would be sure enough,' and she gave her whole mind to the cutting up of rabbits for a stew.

Thomas, her husband, walked down to the Coach and Horses that evening to look into the matter for himself. As bailiff, gamekeeper, gardener and forester ror the Aumerys, sole survivor of their outdoor staff, he made it his business to know what went on in the district. The Merridons, already accustomed to showing off their exhibit, took him to the wash-house. Daniel arrived there, hot and footsore, just as his father was leaving.

'Well, lad?' and when Daniel's only answer was a resigned shrug, 'It's no good, Dan. You mean it for the best but you're on the wrong tack. There are people whose job it is to look after the poor and homeless. You can't expect ordinary folk to open their homes to strangers. Human beings aren't like stray dogs and cats.' He had already observed the girl closely. He looked at her again. 'To be honest, I wouldn't let such as her past my doorstep. You don't know what's in her, either what was born in her or put in after.'

'Whatever it is can be changed; and who's to say that it's something bad?' Daniel broke off. The girl's face had changed. He went nearer and again she put out her hand. Again he took and held it.

'That's enough.' Godwain's slow voice had become brusque. 'We'll be off home now, Dan, so look sharp about it. You've better things to do and so have I. You'll have time enough for good works when you've passed your examinations and made a schoolmaster of yourself.'

So ended Daniel's crusade, his first: there would be others. He said no more and set off with his father, but left him at the stile and went home through the wood, feeling the need to be alone.

The unknown girl might have remained indefinitely at the Coach and Horses, to the vexation of the Merridons who felt obliged to take her indoors for the night to sleep on the kitchen sofa. But, luckily, Barney Trisk turned up the next day. He was a traveller in household wares and secondhand goods, whose round covered the surrounding dales as well as the outskirts of Hudmorton. After some persuasion, together with half a crown from the rector's Benefit Fund, he agreed to take the girl provided he could also take the chair she sat on.

Those who had felt obliged to stay indoors when help was needed turned out in force to watch the departure. The cart was drawn up on the cobbles in front of the inn, the tarpaulin hood folded back and the passenger hoisted aboard, dumb, passive, entirely lacking in youthful appeal. And yet, enthroned once more in the high-backed chair, she somehow took on an aura of dignity. The red plush combined with the green of Esther's merino to give a medieval touch to the equipage, its central figure resembling the wooden image in one of the pageants enacted by earlier villagers, now lying a stone's throw away on the other side of the churchyard wall.

Their latest descendants crowded round or climbed on walls to enjoy a spectacle even more rare than a funeral; but Daniel watched in lofty isolation from a boulder halfway up Cat Hill. The episode just concluded had brought him to a turning-point. It had been an experience in the same category, if not of the same historic significance, as Paul's revelation on the road to Damascus. When he had held the helpless form in his arms, knowing nothing about it except that it was human, he had been miraculously filled from top to toe with pure compassion like the dawning paternalism of a young father holding his first child. A new depth of feeling had flooded his being. His spirit had taken wing. The common thorn bush had been irradiated with a visionary light.

The vision faded. The primal instinct quickly modulated into an emotion less personal, but with all the ardour of an active imagination he saw the direction his life must take. He had found his mission. The lost creature in his arms had been sent as a reminder of all lost and helpless human beings. The world ignored them; he would espouse their cause. To fulfil their needs was his vocation. The decision to dedicate his life to suffering humanity was not his alone, it was heaven-sent. He had raised his eyes from the evil-smelling blanket to the limitless sky. Its morning blue was high and clear.

Earthly voices had intervened. 'Put it down,' one of them had said. By the time he had put aside the folds of the blanket, the heartfelt tenderness had almost left him. No mere girl, however pitiable, could compete in interest with the splendour of his own future. It was the thought of suffering in the mass that inspired him. Cruelty, neglect and greed defiled the earth. He saw it as a globe dripping with blood and tears. The healing remedy lay at his very hand. Education. Only by education could indifference be overcome, imagination nourished, sympathies awakened, cruelty purged.

Recollecting the incident, with lessening frequency and increasing vagueness, Daniel was to interpret it as a sign, an epiphany, a showing forth. But from his vantage point halfway up Cat Hill he looked down on houses and cottages, diminished like the church and inn, to the scale of a toy farmyard. Midgets clustered round a child-sized cart until a miniature horse moved in response to a whip-crack he was too far away to hear. He saw them not as individuals whose names he knew but as figures in a pattern. In the pattern there was meaning, and it was part of a wider pattern of deeper meaning still, if only he could find its key . . .

Esther, whom wild horses could not have dragged from the scene, watched Barney drive away and continued to watch even after the hood of his cart had disappeared into Church Lane. In spite of herself, she regretted the green merino. It had been useful, though only just presentable.

Matty had made no bones about the folly of parting

with it. 'Especially to the likes of her. Encouraging gypsies and such like is what we're warned against. There's no knowing what it might lead to. Not gratitude, that I can tell you. You needn't expect her to be grateful. More likely the opposite.'

Questioned as to what the opposite of gratitude might be, Matty had not minced her words. 'They don't like you having it to give to them. It stirs them up in funny ways. Ways that ordinary folk don't understand.'

'Rubbish.' Daniel had been terse when the gist of this discouraging conversation was passed on to him. 'She needs the dress and you don't.'

With pain she remembered the last time she had worn it, only yesterday, and on what errand. The stockings had turned out so well, without a snag or a reclaimed stitch. Daniel hadn't even noticed that one of them was torn and the pair ruined, and even when obliged to notice, he hadn't cared. He hadn't cared about the stocking, and she knew that he wouldn't keep the card either, beautiful though it was. It wasn't the sort of thing he cared about.

The cobbles felt hard under her feet. The church clock reminded her that it was time to go home. Everyone else had gone indoors or back to work or into the fields to play. After the excitement Wood Aston was itself again. She had not realized how quiet the village could be. Even the school bell, silent in its belfry, would not be rung again for a whole month.

Familiar landmarks asserted their continuing presence: the chestnut tree with its encircling wooden seat on the green, the stone horse-trough by the signpost pointing to Unnerstone, the mauve lupins in Mr Cotts' garden. She had never really looked at them before: had seen but never noticed how the windows on this side of the green glittered back at the morning sun, how dark it was under the stone canopy of the well, how steep Cat Hill with the sun behind it glowered across at Long Rake's longer slope, silver-green and patched with yellow gorse.

She, too, turned into Church Lane and, passing the stile, went home by the road which led down to the bridge, up the hill on the other side and on to Hudmorton. Already Barney and his mysterious passenger, and the cart with its clattering pans and clinking pots, had lost the clear outline of reality and were fading into a realm akin to that of fairytale, with the same lingering power to haunt the imagination and to change the everyday world to which mortals must return. As if the reality they had lost had been transferred in heightened form to the summer scene into which they had vanished, Esther saw it with newly awakened perception: the brown river between overhanging trees was mottled with pearly light, a wagtail bobbed and ran on a flat stone frilled with white foam, the cornfield was bordered with scarlet poppies.

With a sudden thrill of recognition she felt the beauty of the day – and with triumphant joy that she had found it for herself. No-one had told her. She was to remember for the rest of her life how air and earth and water had fused with the sun's fire to give her a brief moment of rapture – and to teach her how quickly such moments pass. Looking back in later years, she would see it as the last moment of childhood, which must end as it began – in ecstasy and pain.

She had stopped in the dusty lane, breathing almost suspended, ears intent, though there was no breeze to rustle the bracken, no sound but the midsummer murmur of flies. A cloud came, not in the sky, but in her memory. People could change. Places, too, might change. The whole world might change. Of the events threatening such a change and the fearful machinery that would bring it about, already rumbling into action, Esther had no conception. She could not know, not then, how treacherously time can break its promise; but her trust in the permanence of things had been shaken for the first time. She understood that beyond the sunlit fields and quiet hills existed other scenes: dark rooms and unlit passages, dirt and squalor, cruelty and pain.

CHAPTER 3

Barney Trisk enjoyed his roving way of life as a pirate might enjoy his swashbuckling adventures on the high seas. Billowing fields under a wide sky, foam of hedge parsley athwart his wheels in summer, spray from brimming puddles in winter, the freedom to change course at will – all these appealed to the romantic side of his nature as well as to his business acumen for, though priceless, they cost him nothing.

Wood Aston was one of his favourite ports of call. He was always sure of a homely welcome at the Coach and Horses. In fact, if he'd been the marrying kind, Prissie Merridon would have been his choice, but after an earlier experience which had all but wrecked him he had vowed never to think seriously of a woman again. What a rotten mess that had been! It had taken him years to get over it and back to plain sailing, and even now there were times when he woke in the night drenched with sweat from dreams almost as horrible as the thing itself. No, never again would he get himself involved with a woman. All the same, it was a shame about Prissie.

Meanwhile the morning was fine and warm; he had a promising round ahead, an unlooked-for half-crown in his pocket and the gratifying knowledge that he was doing somebody a bit of good. As they passed out of the shadow of the church Barney broke into song. He had a good voice and was sometimes persuaded to render a solo in public houses or at social evenings. 'Speak to me, Thora,' he now urged in his pleasant tenor, unaware as yet of the aptness of his choice.

From her red throne, his passenger commanded an uninterrupted view of the surrounding countryside: the low-lying mill, the stone bridge, the clear stream it spanned. She also commanded a view of such contents of the cart as lay between her chair and the driver's seat. It was on Barney's regular stock-in-trade – crockery, glassware, saucepans and haberdashery – that her eyes lingered, naturally enough; the discarded clothing and bits of old carpet were stacked behind her or wedged between the sides of the cart and her chair to keep it steady.

'Hold on,' Barney called over his shoulder as he put his horse to the long climb, and she gripped the chair arms as they laboured up to Keeper's Lodge on the crest of the hill where Bertha Godwain was waiting, drawn to her gate by curiosity rather than the need to dispose of two of Daniel's outgrown nightshirts and a bed cover. Owing to her bad feet she was the only person in Wood Aston who had not yet seen its latest arrival.

'I hear you've got company,' she said as Barney got down to take her offering, and, raising her eyes to the red throne, 'My stars!'

Though tactless, the exclamation was not unsuitable. Daniel's account of the foundling had not prepared his mother for the sight of her in the flesh, not that she had much flesh, and her stick-like legs were now covered by grey woollen stockings and the green dress had long sleeves. Barney had lent her an old purple curtain to serve as a travelling rug, and someone had contributed a red-and-white spotted handkerchief which she wore tied under her chin. It left exposed thick swathes of hay-coloured hair a shade darker than the cheeks they framed.

But Bertha, having swiftly taken in the curious blend of raffishness and near-starvation in the girl's appearance, was struck by a more subtle quality: a detached stillness and self-command out of keeping with her forlorn state. 'How old are you?' The question was put quite sharply.

The girl flushed and drew a sharp breath as if about to speak, or as if trying to speak. Then she closed her lips and her face became once more as uncommunicative as a mask.

'There was no more life in her,' Bertha told her husband afterwards, 'than in a graven image, although she was old enough to know her own age – and to know plenty more besides if you ask me. There was something about her eyes I didn't like. Something funny. "Well," I said, "if you can't tell your age you can surely tell how you came to be roaming the world all alone among strangers." It's enough to make you shudder.'

Indeed a shudder had been Bertha's reaction to the encounter which had nevertheless distinguished the day from most others, on which nothing half as interesting happened.

'You'll get nothing out of her,' Barney muttered between his teeth. 'She's not all there.'

'I've seen one or two that weren't all there and they weren't like that. There's an oven-bottom cake you can have if you want.'

'I won't say no, Mrs Godwain.' He waited under the fox's head in the porch while she fetched the cake on a piece of newspaper, and presently, their business transaction completed, remounted and took up the reins. 'I'll be off now. Thanks for the cake. It'll likely be September before I'm back.'

The oven-bottom cake was still warm and lavishly buttered. He divided it in two and gave one half to the girl, generously, he felt: he was a vigorous man in his prime and with a healthy appetite. He disposed of his portion in a few hearty gulps and looked round to see how his companion was faring. Hers was a steadier and more thorough demolition. She took bites of an even size and munched unhurriedly. They had covered a quarter of a mile before she wiped her mouth with the back of her hand and settled down once more to her scrutiny of Barney's wares.

Mrs Godwain had turned down his offer of a jelly dish in exchange for the nightshirts and bed cover, preferring one of his enamel picture plates, rather to Barney's regret. The plates were a new line, light in weight and unbreakable. The picture of The Laughing Cavalier was colourful and, as Barney pointed out to his customers, the plates had a variety of uses as teapot-stands, tableware and as ornaments to stand on the mantelpiece. As part of his saleable stock they should fetch ninepence each. It had been a mistake to offer them in exchange for cast-offs. Still, you learn by experience. It wasn't too late to change his strategy. Before leaving the Lodge he had moved the cardboard box containing the eleven remaining plates to the front portion of the cart.

The day's round took them up hill and down dale and encompassed half a dozen hamlets. It was mid-afternoon when Barney stopped at the Halfway Inn on the Hudmorton road and opened the packet of beef sandwiches Mrs Merridon had provided. As usual when pausing for lunch, he read whatever old newspapers had been used as wrappings, on the principle of extracting the maximum profit, intellectual as well as financial, from his trade.

On this occasion he was lucky enough to find a copy of the previous day's *County Advertiser*. Having glanced at the now familiar headlines about the threat of the German navy, he turned to more sensational items of news: a postman mauled by a savage dog, a fight between two farmers over a disputed acre of land, and in Apperfield, a town twenty miles away, the brutal and savage murder of a woman 'of low repute' in a district 'far from salubrious', as the reporter put it. The word was new to Barney, but he divined its meaning and indeed was not without personal experience of such districts. All the same, he had no doubt that people who couldn't keep themselves respectable mostly deserved all they got. Such thoughts had too uncomfortably personal an application, reviving memories he was generally able to suppress. He finished his sandwiches quickly and went into the inn, leaving the girl to eat alone.

She did so with the same deliberation and thoroughness of mastication as before, having also maintained the same unbroken silence. Barney was finding her a depressing companion. The teasing good humour of 'Speak to me, Thora' was getting beyond a joke. Even his tuneful whistling had gradually died away. Her silence was contagious. She was proving a tedious half-crownsworth and no mistake. When he rejoined her ten minutes later he climbed aboard in glum resignation at the prospect of the three or four hours that still lay ahead.

At last fields were left behind and leafy lanes gave way to grimy streets. They entered the town from the south. The Union Workhouse was on its northern fringe. As the cart rattled over the cobbles, some slight animation might have been detected in the nameless stranger, arising perhaps from apprehension at the prospect before her.

'Not long now,' Barney addressed her over his shoulder, 'and then it's straight to where you'll find a clean bed and something to eat.'

They had passed into twilight – not the fragrant dusk of evening but an atmosphere murky with the soot and smoke of the city's forges and household chimneys. From the long rows of narrow houses all colour had long since faded. Stone and brick, doors and sills and window curtains had settled into a uniform drabness relieved only by the yellow donkey-stone on doorsteps gallantly scoured every day. The doors opened directly onto the street where children played or swung on lampposts or waited, listless with hunger, for the buzzer that would signal the closing of workshops and bring their mothers home.

Barney wasted no time on so poverty-stricken an area, but made steadily for his last call at a shop on the corner of the misleadingly named Primrose Lane and Duff Street. Its windows, almost opaque with grime, dimly displayed pork pies and fly-papers, patent medicines and boot polish, soap and jam. He put his head round the door, exchanged a few words with the woman behind the counter and went round to the back yard to collect a crate of bottles.

When he came back a few minutes later the red throne was vacant. The girl had gone.

Barney could scarcely believe his eyes. Was she cowering under the hood at the back of the cart? Only a very short search was needed – she wasn't there. Had she just got down for a minute and wandered away? He paced back and forth, swearing with alarming and futile vigour. Minutes passed. Such light as there still was would soon go: darkness came early to Hudmorton. The narrow alleys and entries were already deeply shadowed.

Suddenly the thick air was pierced by the ear-splitting bray of the works buzzer. In another minute the streets were full of people hurrying home from work, talking, shouting and, unlikely as it might seem, laughing. Several of them called out greetings: he was well known in the district. He answered glumly. Looking for her now would be like looking for a needle in a hay-stack. He didn't even know if she'd gone off on her own or been snatched. Who – and he swore again – would want to snatch a miserable brat like her? And why should he care? Except that he had been paid to deliver her to the Union. Would the rector want his money back? Not likely! He wasn't going to know that he, Barney Trisk, had been made a fool of. Nobody would know. He certainly wasn't going to let on. By the time he turned up at Wood Aston again they would have forgotten all about the lousy little beggar, or would take it for granted that he'd done the job he was paid for – and quite willing to do. Here Barney was on safe ground; it would be much longer than he could know before he appeared at Wood Aston again.

He wiped his brow, now thunderous with exasperation, and climbed aboard, first instinctively casting a professional eye over his goods. Only then, to his unspeakable chagrin, did he realize the depths of treachery to which he had been subjected. Something else was missing besides the girl. With her had vanished his entire stock of Laughing Cavalier plates.

Much was to happen to Barney Trisk in the years immediately ahead. His careless buccaneering days were almost over: he was to be uprooted from his home, shipped overseas, incarcerated in trenches, half drowned in mud, shot at, bombed and gassed. In the space of four years his youth would be spent and his health shattered. He would endure soul-destroying boredom, lose faith, witness hideous slaughter, learn to hate rats, bully beef, sergeant-majors and, to an appreciably lesser extent, the enemy. But his bitterness over the theft of his Laughing Cavalier plates was never to be surpassed. He'd been done. He would never forgive the thieving little bitch. She had slipped through his fingers for the time being, but some day, if he was spared, he'd find her and when he did, she'd better look out.

More than once in his dug-out in a foreign field Barney was to dream of home: of tree-hung English lanes, the scent of clover, the buttery taste of oven-bottom cake. Sometimes, imperceptibly, the remembered scene would change: its soft tints fade to grey, its green boughs dissolve into soot-grimed buildings as he seemed to stand once more on the corner of Primrose Lane in the murk of evening. And he would recall how meanly and silently she had sneaked away like a gutter rat to some far-from-salubrious – yes, that was the word – quarter of the city where she rightly belonged.

CHAPTER 4

It was not until the summer of 1919 that victory celebrations were held in towns and villages throughout
the land. The Armistice, signed in the previous year,
had come too late for rejoicing. The carnage had
been too bloody, long-drawn-out and universal, and
was still too recent to leave the exhausted survivors
in any mood other than relief tempered by a numbed
awareness of the weary aftermath still to be faced.

Nothing would ever be the same again. The old
civilization, already threatened before the slaughter
began, had gone for good with a million men who
might have fathered children to preserve and revitalize
it. But as the months passed and battlefields grew
green again, the sharp edge of grief was dulled by
resignation. A new generation was emerging into adult
life not unaffected by the climate of lost faith, but with
confidence necessary to survive it and a natural taste
for happiness if it could be found.

In that long, hot summer the date chosen by the
Wood Aston Peace Celebration Committee was Saturday 21 June, a day between haymaking and harvest.
A sepia-toned photograph of the entire population
recorded the occasion and was to be seen framed on
pianos and parlour tables for years to come. One or
two prints found their way into folk museums.

Esther had no need of a photograph to remind her
of the day, nor did the day itself, apart from one or two
incidents and a good many Union Jacks, remind her of
the victory. By nightfall she had forgotten both the war
and the fact that it was over, so entirely had her life

43

changed. As unaware of the impending miracle as is a chrysalis of the imago it will become, she stood at the window of her mother's room to watch her father set off on his morning walk, and lingered there, beguiled into idleness by the warm sunshine and the thrilling prospect of the day ahead. What amazing luck that it should be fine on such a day, when a downpour would have ruined everything.

Her father undid the wicket gate and went out on to the field path. How slim and upright he was, how elegant in his country tweeds and soft-brimmed hat, walking-stick in gloved hand. Her pride in his appearance was all the greater because of her growing uneasiness on his behalf, like the discomfort that precedes a toothache. The uneasiness was to do with money. The Aumerys were in trouble. She had always known that they were no longer rich, but in the unthinking days of childhood it hadn't seemed to matter: there were no rich people in Wood Aston, no houses to compare with Lady Green. Life there had merely grown simpler and more unworldly and, as Daniel said, there was no harm in that. But now, with her skirts let down nearly to her ankles and her hair tied up with a stiff black bow as far as it would go without actually being right up, she was old enough to have grasped that the family fortune had dwindled away and to wonder what would happen when the dwindling process was complete.

Five generations of Aumerys had lived in comfort at Lady Green. Their wealth came from the high limestone country to the north-west, an area rich in deposits of lead, where Esther's great-grandfather had owned the mineral rights of one of the liberties. As the nineteenth century progressed, deposits were gradually exhausted. The removal of import duties on Australian lead brought a sharp drop in prices, and the industry waned.

44

Even so, techniques had been learned which could be applied to other branches of industry. When Esther's grandfather, John, wound up the Aumery lead-mining company, it was with the intention of investing his still ample means in the steam and manpower needed by the ironworks and forges at Hudmorton, seven miles from the family estate at Lady Green. But while these projects were still at the exploratory stage, he died suddenly, leaving his son with the capital to carry them out but not, unfortunately, the inclination.

If Edwin Aumery had inherited a modicum of the family energy, he could have consolidated their gains even without becoming the thrusting industrialist whose type he disliked and scorned. The rich farmland of Lady Green, if competently managed, could have yielded well. When farming declined there were still acres of woodland to supply the constant demand for timber. But a gentleman who would rather cultivate his mind than his land, who lived in Italy during his most active years, who returned to England when he was forty and married an extravagant young wife, must sooner or later face the problems created by his own neglect – and aggravated by four years of war, with the resulting rise in the cost of labour and transport.

By temperament, Aumery was averse to facing reality. He had adapted as comfortably as possible to changing circumstances which he regarded as always extraneous and beyond his power to control, a temperament unproductive of effective action but blessed with compensatory good temper and charm of manner.

These disquieting facts had reached Esther through intuition and observation: they had never been explained to her. But now, watching her father's receding figure, she underwent a sudden change of vision and knew that he was a failure. Seen from above, and separated from her by even so short a distance, he seemed – in every sense – smaller, a slight, unforceful man dwarfed by the great green hump of the hill beyond him. She sensed his loneliness and was afraid for him, a mere mortal man walking between the everlasting hills.

Then she saw Godwain coming down the path from Scaur Crag. Her father waited and the two men walked off together towards the wood. All was well. With Godwain her father would be safe. No harm could come to him with Godwain to look after him, no harm could come to him at all, a cultivated gentleman on his own estate in the heart of England – victorious England.

The nagging hint of anxiety was gone. She thought of the celebrations ahead. A pink climbing rose close to her cheek trembled in anticipation. She saw the countryside sparkling with light. The air quivered between emerald grass and sapphire sky.

'What are you doing, Esther? Do close the window.' The voice was plaintive. 'I'm getting up.'

Esther closed the window with the sharp tug needed to secure its ancient latch.

'Need you make such a clatter, dear? It's one of those mornings. The least noise makes my head positively spin.'

Esther took her mother's complaints lightly, sensing that they were made with a similar lightness. Flora Aumery's fractiousness had no sharp edge. Her lips pouted but her eyes smiled. Both lips and eyes were still appealing. Nor had she aged physically. She had, as she put it, kept her skin as well as the rich brown of her hair whose long tresses streamed over the pillow on which she comfortably reclined, her ample curves lost in the lace frilling of her bed jacket. Even Matty had to admit that on such occasions she looked a picture, and if the effect was not entirely that of Venus rising from the foam, it bore some resemblance to advertisements for Vegetine, whose manufacturers promised bright eyes and rosy cheeks in place of headaches and indigestion, the very symptoms that Flora often complained of.

'Take the tray, dear. You don't realize how heavy it is. It would do me good to have a day in bed, but I must make the effort . . .'

Esther poured water from the copper jug into the basin. Washing was one of the few activities Flora enjoyed. Even if her figure had failed her, the skin she had so fortunately kept was fresh and clear. It tingled pleasantly as she soaped and splashed and dried it with a vigour she bestowed on nothing else. Her rounded cheeks glowed. What a shame it was, Esther thought, as she did her mother's hair, that no-one could see her with it let down like this. She brushed slowly, handling the smooth locks with care.

'If you had felt like it,' she said, 'we could have gone for a walk. Godwain won't be bringing the trap round until one o'clock, and it's a lovely day.'

'Well, there it is. One just has to accept the trials of one's constitution.' Country walks with nowhere of the slightest interest to go had always been an abomination to Flora. Esther, of course, must have fresh air and exercise, otherwise she would lose her looks. 'Don't droop, dear. It's so important to hold up your head and not shuffle like one of the lower classes.' And as the dark head was raised obediently to the limits of the slender neck a thrill of satisfaction in her daughter's appearance gave warmth to her voice. 'Give yourself plenty of time to change. You needn't bother with your little tasks this morning.'

She spoke indulgently, as if Esther occupied herself from choice in the pursuits of a young lady with nothing more pressing to do than feed her canary and arrange the flowers. As a rule, by the time Esther had put her own and her parents' room to rights and prepared the vegetables, it was time to sort the linen, dust the downstairs rooms and set the table for lunch.

In so unequal a distribution of labour Esther saw nothing amiss. She had grown adept at making the most of her restricted life, much of it spent in this pretty, old-fashioned room. She liked to turn out the drawers of chests and toilet table and rearrange shawls and fascinators, long unworn, lengths of material never made up, discarded bits of jewellery . . .

'Ah!' Flora would murmur significantly as Esther held up some trinket. 'That pendant!' or 'Real India muslin, but there wasn't enough even for a blouse,' and she would sigh and dream of the dress it might have been if everything had been different.

Sometimes Esther flung open the wardrobe like an impresario presenting a new theatrical production, and they would try on old evening dresses – a form of escape as useless as it was harmless, for the dresses, made in the style of the nineties, were far too big for Esther and quite inaccessible to Flora, however deeply she inhaled, however valiantly Esther dragged hooks towards eyes. Gowns were shaken out, reminisced over and admired, their lace and satin bows smoothed out, their elaborate needlework exclaimed over until the room was awash like an inland sea with faintly scented fabrics, and Flora, grown weary of them all, would stand by the looking-glass, disconsolate in corset and drawers and flinching from her reflection.

'I'm matronly,' she had lamented only the day before. 'It's depressing. Everything changes so quickly.' Then mindful of her daughter, 'That blue could be altered to fit you. It matches your eyes.'

'But where would I wear it?' Esther had caressed the silken folds, hung the dress on the rail with the others and closed the door on them.

'Oh, it's hopeless.' Flora struggled into her brown day dress. 'There's nowhere for you to go.'

No wonder, then, that the Victory Celebration held for Esther all the promise of a royal garden party or a coming-out ball, even if she was to be only an onlooker. Not for her the thrill of representing Faith, Hope or Charity with a silver paper and cardboard cross, anchor or heart – still less Britannia or even a

48

nurse on a Red Cross wagon. But there would be tea in the marquee, and in the evening . . .

'Do you think I could stay to watch the dancing?' The question, long premeditated, was meant to sound casual.

'It won't be real dancing, dear. Not our sort of thing.'

'I've never seen real dancing, so that wouldn't matter.'

The simple words wounded her mother. They revived all her suppressed discontent and irritation with her husband. If they had still had the carriage they could have driven to Wood Aston to watch the rustic revelry from a dignified distance, not to mention the social gatherings in town they would have been able to join. As it was, Esther had not even had the advantage of dancing classes, not that there was anyone she could have danced with, not within miles. Things had come to a pretty pass when her only daughter could hope for no higher diversion than to watch bumpkins and clod-hoppers making an exhibition of themselves on the village green.

'I'm sorry, darling. There would be no-one to be with you and bring you home.'

'If Matty could be there . . . If you could spare her for the evening as well as the afternoon I think she would like it.'

'Well . . .'

Esther recognized the hesitation as the first step towards a concession. Leaving well alone for the time being, she opened the *Hudmorton Chronicle* of the previous day and read out the headlines.

The tedium of this daily exercise was for once relieved by a small item of interest – to Flora, that is – and her tendency to dwell on it aroused Esther's interest too. The annual dinner to commemorate the founding of the Hudmorton and District Company of Ironmasters had been held in the Town Hall. Among others, a toast had been proposed to Major Lincoln on his welcome return to the district after his distinguished service in France.

'Gervase! Home again!' Arrested in'the act of putting on a stocking, Flora sat up, eyes wide. 'What else does it say?'

' " A vote of thanks to their host, the Lord Mayor, brought the occasion to a close." Nothing else about Major Lincoln. You know him?'

'Know him? At one time we were quite – well – how can I put it? Close.' Flora leaned back on the chaise longue with a sad smile. 'Haven't I mentioned him? Our families were neighbours at Risewood.'

It was Hudmorton's most prosperous suburb, but after the deaths of her parents Flora had deliberately lost touch with her friends there. As she told her husband, 'Frankly, I'd be ashamed to have it known how my circumstances have changed. In any case, without a carriage, not to mention a motor, how could I get there?'

But the glamour of Risewood remained and was passed on to Esther in endless anecdotes of balls, garden parties, engagements and marriages.

'I was a mere child, hardly out of the schoolroom when we—' The unfinished sentence suggested much more than was disclosed: small wonder, as the acquaintance had been slight. 'Extremely rich – the Lincolns, I mean. You know – the Lincoln Ironworks at Broom Gate. It might have been . . . but somehow we lost touch.' Flora's eyelids closed as if in remembered heartbreak. 'And then he married, too. A French woman. They spent a good deal of time in France. She died before the war.'

'They had a house in Risewood?'

'No, no. They lived at Barbarrow Hall.'

'Of course . . .'

An empty house: windows shuttered, a sad, desolate place. She and Daniel had come upon it unexpectedly on one of their rambles years ago, had climbed a hill and looked down into the next valley, and there was the house. She had felt the sudden gloom on her spirits of its forlorn silence, and the air of waiting that befalls a house whose owners have gone away. Daniel had been eloquent about the unfair distribution of wealth that made it possible for so fine a place to stand empty when thousands of people were living in slums.

'But who could live here?' Esther had asked. 'What would they do?'

'I don't think you would like Barbarrow,' she told her mother. 'It's much quieter than it is here. That may be why the Lincolns spent so much time abroad.'

'Perhaps. I haven't thought of them for years, not since we came back from Italy that time and someone mentioned that Barbarrow had been closed. You won't remember, you were only two.'

Flora became thoughtful. How strange that she should hear of Gervase again quite by chance and that they were again neighbours! It would be the most natural thing in the world if they were to meet, except that Barbarrow was as remote from Lady Green as darkest Africa, if one lacked the means of getting there. They might as well be Boers.

It would have been such a useful connection for Esther. There must be a family – a son perhaps. Considering the closeness of the friendship she claimed with Gervase Lincoln, Flora's knowledge of his affairs was remarkably vague. She looked appraisingly at her daughter, a slender, graceful girl in her plain skirt and blouse. Even without the advantages she should have had, Esther had a look of breeding. Not for the first time Flora indulged in a rosy dream, not of her own future – it was too late for that – but of Esther's.

For once her mind was attuned to her husband's. For once he, too, was thinking of Esther. He had looked forward to his daily walk with Godwain, who was much more to him than an employee, more to him perhaps than either wife or child. As, one by one, the other workmen had grown old or been dismissed, Aumery relied more heavily on the man he knew to be his superior in efficiency and wisdom, at the same time wondering anxiously how long he would be able to go on paying him.

'Come next winter,' Godwain said as they entered the wood, 'we'd best have some of these trees down. Not that they're worth much. By rights we should have been coppicing over the last twenty years, as I've been telling you for as long as that. And if we'd done that replanting at yon south end . . .'

A plantation of healthy young trees would have been a sound investment. There was no point in harping on the fact that another opportunity had been thrown away: there had been plenty of others.

They halted beside the Aston oak, the greatest and almost the last survivor of what had once been a splendid oakwood, Aumery leaning on his stick of polished elm, Godwain on his stout ash cudgel.

'You're right, Thomas. We'll get that fellow Forster to give us a price for thinning.' Aumery spoke with the false enthusiasm of a man who found the subject boring. 'The trouble about replanting—'

'Ay! The trouble is there'll be the cost of the outlay and no return till you and I are needing no more timber than'll make us a pair of coffins. And there's another thing. This oak's going to be in trouble if something isn't done.'

'What do you mean, man?' Aumery was genuinely surprised. 'You might as well talk about the rock of Gibraltar being in trouble.'

The tree towered above them in full leaf, yet despite its immense height, the great span of branches gave the effect less of tallness than of breadth. To stand in its vast shade was to experience intimations of eternity: minutes, hours, years ceased to have meaning.

'No wonder they used to worship these trees.' Aumery experienced a moment of peace, recognizing the oak with its long past as a link with countless other men with other problems. Like him, they had gathered its acorns as boys, made it their meeting place, kindled fires from its fallen twigs – and before them, long before, others had paid homage and made sacrifices to it. It comforted him to reflect that the trials of those men, as pressing as his own, had passed away and been forgotten.

'Since those rotten birches came down,' Godwain was saying, 'there's a fair amount of shelter gone, too. A gale from the south-west is going to hit this old fellow full blast.'

'Like many a gale before it. It would take a hurricane—'

'I'm not worried about the tree coming down. It's that one branch, the one the lightning struck a good few years back. It could do some damage and likely kill somebody if it broke off.'

They walked halfway round the tree's girth of almost thirty feet to inspect the stricken branch. The thunderbolt had scored a groove running its whole length. Just above it, at some time in the tree's long history, a snag had died back, admitting air and moisture into the heartwood and allowing a wide cavity to form.

'Let's have a look,' Aumery said. 'I could always beat you to the top.' Discarding their hats and jackets, they became boys again, two stiff and awkward boys soon breathless.

'Do you remember the little owl's nest?' Aumery wedged himself safely between branches, his shoulder level with the cavity. 'There's nothing here now.' He thrust in his hand and brought it out, darkened and spattered with a stinking pulp. Moving cautiously, he joined Godwain who sat astride a bough strong enough to bear the weight of half a dozen men. Both were shocked to see how far the damaged branch had died back. Except for a few feet nearest to the trunk it was almost leafless.

'We should have had it off when Forster was clearing that dead stuff away.' Godwain forbore to mention that he had made the suggestion when horses and wagons were at hand and it would have been cheaper to do the job then than to bring woodmen back to take off one branch. Equally Aumery kept from him the unpleasant fact that the hire of men and equipment, even for two more days, would have entailed more expense than he could afford.

They clambered down, brushed dust and bark from their clothes and walked on in amicable silence. Aumery knew that the advice was sound but he had no intention of acting on it. He had enjoyed the climb but he soon forgot the reason for it, finding the whole business tedious. It was hard enough to deal with immediate problems without anticipating others that might never arise. His thoughts had taken a new direction. The cavity half-filled with rotten wood was not the only discovery he had made in the Aston oak. Above the crotch, bark had been scraped away and on the smooth wood, too high for any but a climber to see it, had been cut the outline of a heart enclosing the initials E A and D G. Daniel Godwain and his own Esther?

He should not have been surprised. They had been companions since infancy, like brother and sister, he had supposed, in so far as he had considered the matter at all. It could hardly be otherwise, situated as they were a mile from the village with no other neighbours, not that the village could have supplied suitable friends for Esther. From playmates to child-hood sweethearts was a natural transition, provided it went no further than childhood.

Aumery was indifferent to convention and sufficiently enlightened to be free from snobbery, but he found himself experiencing an unfamiliar discomfort very like guilt. He was fond of Esther, but rarely paid much attention to her apart from moments of aesthetic pleasure in her growing beauty. It would be too much to say that he now thought of her future with any active concern other than the hope that she would never become the kind of young lady her mother wanted her to be. Flora deserved to be thwarted in the absurd pretensions which had helped to ruin him.

It was the narrowness of Esther's life that disturbed him. He in his indifference to money and Flora in her insistence on a carriage, horses, a staff of servants male and female, indoor and out, had brought them all to penury and deprived Esther of opportunities to cultivate her mind by means of books, travel and educated company. Vaguely he understood – his thinking was often vague – that Esther's salvation must lie in a good marriage. Presumably Flora's father had come to a similar conclusion – and with what result? In any case, what was a good marriage? A definition of 'good' interested but eluded him.

They crossed a foot-bridge to the lane which ran along the river bank to Lady Green and came in sight of the house, lying like a grey vessel harboured among trees and green slopes. In the soft brightness of the summer morning it seemed at once untouchable by change, illusory as a dream. The paradox moved him to feel something like love for the old place, his own, yet no longer his own. Remembering the size of the mortgage on it and the impossibility of ever repaying it, he felt a wave of heart-sickness.

'That creeper should have been stripped down last year,' Godwain said as they crossed the gravel sweep to the front door. 'It's going to be all over the roof if it's let be, and the gutters'll be choked up again.'

'We'll have it down in the autumn.' The postponement was instinctive. Thomas was right of course. The creeper, like everything else, had got out of hand. Its next late summer blaze of crimson must be the last for a while. He pulled down one of the stems. It came away without protest. Winding it thread-like round his gloved finger, he thought it a pity that so young and tender a thing should be deprived of growth, its natural impulse forever unfulfilled.

And what of Esther's natural impulses? As her father, he ought to know how to achieve the necessary balance between what was best for her and what she most dearly wanted. How fortunate if the two should prove to be the same! Daniel was a clever lad, high-principled too and his two years in the army had, according to his father, put some stiffening into him. But to marry his daughter to the son of one of his workmen, a lad who ate his tripe and onions with a bone-handled knife and fork at a table spread with oil-cloth!

The scratch of a match as Godwain lit his pipe restored him to the present. Unlike his other worries, the problem of Esther's future could be indefinitely postponed. Having glanced at it, he glanced away. But Esther and Daniel had become united in his mind as inescapably as their initials were united in the symbolic heart. It had created a bond between them which he could not accept, for reasons that he knew to be unworthy.

Pipe clenched between his strong teeth, Godwain enjoyed the pungent aroma of his Heath and Heather Mixture. He, too, had seen the heart and had thought little of it beyond surprise that for all his daft notions Daniel had had the sense to choose little Esther to be sweet on. Very likely he'd grown out of it by this time. The army had certainly sobered him down: he didn't talk quite so much. But his mind was still set on going to college in the autumn, and it would be many a long year before he could think of marrying. Thomas himself had been thirty before he could pop the question and, considering the length of time a man and wife had to live together, thirty was soon enough.

56

'Come to think of it,' he roused himself, 'it nearly slipped my mind. I promised to take Miss Esther and Bertha to see the jollifications this afternoon. There's to be rare rejoicings, from what I've heard.'

'By all means let us rejoice,' Aumery said. 'If we can.'

'That's it then, sir.'

For an instant their eyes met. In Godwain's, humorous and kind, Aumery recognized the sterling loyalty of the one being he truly cared for, recognized, too, the pettiness of his misgivings about Daniel. In mingled affection and self-reproach he said – and his heartiness was no longer assumed – 'Thanks for your advice, Thomas. We'll get to work on that tree in the autumn without fail.' The decision was eminently sensible.

Half a mile away, indifferent in its immense age to the small perplexities of men's lives, the Aston oak spread its branches in the blue air. Did it house, with its myriads of insects and scores of roosting birds, another kind of life? The ancient folk of Wood Aston had been careful to placate the tree with sacrifices, divining in it a power of secret origin growing ever stronger with time, capable of activating events and altering destinies – and best left alone.

Meanwhile Esther's immediate future hung in the balance. She had not mentioned the dancing again, but when, after an early lunch, she dressed for the afternoon and came downstairs to show herself off, Flora's heart melted. The white dress of embroidered voile, with a fall of lace from elbow to wrist, was one of her own. It had been taken in and the Alexandra-style lace neckband had been replaced by a simple flat collar. The result was so becoming, and the white straw hat so charmingly framed her daughter's face, that it was hard to deny her so harmless a plea as to stay and watch the dancing.

The issue was still not settled when, promptly at one o'clock, Thomas and Bertha arrived in the trap.

Esther was all ready and waiting on the steps and Flora came out to see them off.

'About staying in the evening, dear. I'm really not sure—'

'And what's the harm, ma'am,' Bertha said briskly when she had grasped the problem, 'seeing as Thomas and me'll be there – and Daniel if he can be got away from his books? We'll see her safely home. It isn't every day there's a do like this. It'll be like the Coronation, with Union Jacks everywhere. It's not for me to say, but I shouldn't wonder if Ada Matthews might wish she could see the dancing if she's on top of her work.'

'There will be a very good view from Miss Angovil's window and she'll be watching, too.' Esther's apparently guileless remark, the result of crafty calculation, had the desired effect.

'Yes, of course, you could watch from Miss Angovil's.'

Thomas settled the matter by touching his cap and driving off.

Armageddon in Europe had left Wood Aston looking much the same as it had done for centuries, only a little shabbier, but it had not escaped tragedy. Four of the local men had been killed, including Prissie's sweetheart, Jim Burdle, from the forge. Prissie had lost her sparkle. But when the village roused itself to celebrate its country's latest victory as it had celebrated Waterloo and Mafeking, 'Come on, love,' her mother had said. 'It'll have to be you and me as usual, if anything's to be done,' and Prissie had rolled up her sleeves and buckled to with a gallantry to which there would be no memorial.

Esther found the village transformed by bunting, balloons and flags. As she recorded in her diary, simply everybody was there, even – wonder of wonders – Daniel. They had scarcely seen each other during the past two and a half years, and only two or three times since his discharge a month ago. She had called at the Lodge to welcome him home and had been a trifle awed to find him indefinably changed from the boy she had known: as slim, energetic, vital as ever, but more self-contained and authoritative than she remembered. To have seen things she would never see and faced experiences she could barely imagine, made him more . . . impressive?

He had come by the woodland path without bothering to change, and was waiting to help them out of the trap.

'Festivities should be spontaneous,' he informed his mother with a grin when she reproved him for not wearing his best suit. 'Not that I think there's anything to be festive about, but I'm always happy to fraternize with my fellow countrymen, however misguided they may be.'

'We'll have none of that,' his father told him, 'unless you want to finish up in the horse-pond. It isn't the time for that sort of talk, if it ever was.'

There had been a worrying time when Daniel had considered registering as a conscientious objector, and had given sound reasons fluently expressed, for doing so; but when his time came he had gone off like everybody else, without a word of protest, and rather fancied himself in uniform.

They were in time to see the procession of decorated wagons set off on its circular tour of Low Carr and Unnerstone, to return to Wood Aston at tea-time. Meanwhile there were other diversions: competitions for climbing the slippery pole, and log-splitting, egg-and-spoon and potato-picking races, the organization of which somehow fell into Daniel's hands; and it was he who marshalled the motley throng into neat rows for the famous photograph. Even Miss Angovil was lured from her window to join the group, with her self-effacing maid Clairy and Spedding, dour-faced and protesting.

Esther knew most of the people by sight, but there were unfamiliar faces: the gentleman in an alpaca

59

jacket and straw hat who was umpiring the tug-o'-war was a stranger to her.

'Our new Member of Parliament,' Daniel told her. 'The chap from Barbarrow Hall.'

'Major Lincoln. How strange! I'd never heard of him until this morning.'

'*Mr* Lincoln. As you may have heard, the war is over. It's time to discard its ranks along with other titles and meaningless distinctions. Not that there's much hope of progress with such as him in Parliament. He's a deep-dyed Tory. What can you expect from a landowner and ironmaster? The man's a natural enemy of the people.'

Seeing Esther's smile, he smiled too. Both knew how much he relished speech-making, especially to propound a new social order and the abolition of inherited privilege. He regarded his war service not only as a ghastly ordeal but a sinful waste of human effort. He had been under fire at St Quentin little more than a year ago and had escaped physically unscathed, but with an even stronger conviction that such an obscenity must never be allowed to happen again. He was fortunate in that his natural sensitivity was balanced by a certain intellectual detachment which protected him from psychological wounds; but it could not dull his awareness of the tragedy underlying the day's homely festivities for such as Prissie Merridon and Jim Burdle's mother. The two women stood together without a smile as they watched the twenty protagonists in the tug-o'-war heave and grunt with all the force of healthy men left alive.

Esther, standing close by, felt their sadness and sensed a similar lack of joy in the face of Major – or Mr – Lincoln. As the Wood Aston men slid reluctantly to their defeat he held up his hand, declared Unnerstone the winners, and with no more than a word or two walked off – surprisingly – to Priest's House.

'Esther dear.' Miss Iles, the rector's sister, beckoned from the table heaped with prizes. 'Do come and help. I shall get this wrong, I know. If you could look at those labels and hand me the right prize at the right time, that's all I ask; and then I can go home and collapse with an easy mind.'

Half an hour later, the prizes successfully bestowed, Esther made her way through the thinning crowd to Priest's House where Major – or Mr – Lincoln was still drinking tea in Miss Angovil's sitting-room. He got up and acknowledged his introduction to Miss Aumery with a stiff nod.

'From Lady Green,' Miss Angovil told him; but he gave no sign of familiarity with the name either of the house or its owner, and presently took his leave.

'How interesting to meet him!' Released from his intimidating stiffness, Esther took off her hat and burst into speech. 'Only this morning we read in the *Chronicle* that he had come back from France. I didn't know that he was a friend of yours. What a sad-looking man!' It was a nice way of putting it. She privately thought him cold and unfriendly.

'I'm afraid Gervase has suffered a good deal.'

'Oh yes. The war.'

'He was among the very first to enlist. I believe he was glad to get away. The army must have seemed to him then – that was before we realized how dreadful it was going to be – it must have seemed a kind of escape.'

They sat at the table in the window. Clairy brought fresh tea and cake. Miss Angovil had what Esther thought of as an old-fashioned face; not that her own standards could possibly be up-to-date, but there was a dutiful sweetness in the way Miss Angovil drew in the corners of her mouth which, together with a modest downward tilt of the head and the curled fringe on her forehead, brought to mind illustrations in the Princess Alexandra Gift Book. Miss Angovil's entire demeanour suggested a maidenly retreat from all crudity, as if she too were protected by tissue paper

61

like the pictures of rose-leaf-complexioned ladies in the 1860s.

'What was Major Lincoln glad to get away from?'

She had been too blunt, as Miss Angovil made clear by deliberately straightening the tea cosy without reply.

'Mrs Lincoln died, I believe.' Esther moderated her tone to one more suitably infused with respectful regret, a regret to some extent genuine: if Mrs Lincoln had survived, there might at last have been someone on whom she could practise her French.

Miss Angovil acknowledged her friend's demise with a mournful droop of her head. She was clearly disinclined for the cosy kind of chat Esther had learned to expect. Nevertheless she persisted.

'They had children?'

'The Lord giveth and the Lord taketh away,' Miss Angovil allowed herself to say, piously evading a direct answer and placing responsibility where it belonged. 'There was only the one girl.'

'Do you mean that she died? How sad!'

Of a fever probably. That was the sort of thing children usually died of. Esther was on the point of pinning it down to scarlet fever or typhoid when Miss Angovil asked her to ring the bell.

'You'll want to wash your hands and do your hair. Clairy will take up some hot water.'

Banished to a bedroom, Esther spun out the washing and hair-doing for as long as possible, presented herself at each of the three looking-glasses and was left with another hour at least to fill in before the dancing would begin. She was too restless to stay indoors and, without returning to the sitting-room, let herself out quietly. The green was deserted, but judging by the sound of voices that drifted from open windows, cottage parlours were crowded and the Coach and Horses was full to overflowing.

It was still warm, but the sun had sunk behind Long Rake, and the trees cast long shadows.

Since there was nowhere else to go she went into the churchyard. Her mind was still on the Lincolns. She remembered the garden at Barbarrow. While Daniel was filling his pockets with fallen apples, she had wandered along a path between straggling lavender bushes to a sun-dial and an arbour with a narrow wooden seat. There she had sat, imagining herself to be the lady of the house, with a sewing basket or a book, like one of the ladies in Marcus Stone's pictures.

It occurred to her that the dead girl might be buried here at Wood Aston. It would be interesting to know her name. She left the path and peered at the headstones. As they all faced to the east their inscriptions were in shade, but she found familiar names: Merridon, Cotts, Godwain and – in their own plot outside the east window – Aumery; but no Lincolns. Their family graves must be at Risewood or Taybrooke. It would have been pleasant to know the young Lincolns – if there had been any.

She had hoped to find a suitable memorial like the white marble angel above one of the Victorian graves. It was, so to speak, her favourite, and too distinct from the common grey headstones to be passed without an admiring glance. It rose white and smoothly sad behind her to the right, just visible from the corner of her eye and – had it moved? She turned quickly and saw, standing quietly beside the marble figure, the living shape of a young woman.

Across a distance of twenty yards the two faced each other. The stranger didn't move. How long had she been there? The notion that if she were to look round it would be to find that other forms had risen from other graves was as short-lived as it was absurd. All the same, it held her for a moment transfixed. Neither spoke, or expressed any greeting by movement of hand or head. The girl looked at Esther for the space of seconds without embarrassment or constraint. Between them, as if along a tautly held wire, a tremor vibrated.

Then Esther laughed. 'Clairy! I didn't recognize you.' It was the first time she had seen her without her maid's cap. 'I thought you were a ghost.'

'Your thoughts were far away, miss, I could tell. It was hot in the kitchen and the mistress told me to come out for some fresh air.'

She had changed from her black afternoon dress into a light summer frock. Esther waited while she crossed the grass and they walked together to the lychgate. From the green came the sound of a man's voice singing 'Roses of Picardy' to the breathy accompaniment of a concertina. Under the trees it was already dusk. The Chinese lanterns strung from branch to branch had been lit, red and yellow globes shadowed by leaves. Lamplit windows circled the green in a chain of gold.

'How beautiful it is! Will you be dancing, Clairy?'

'Oh no, miss. There's no-one for me to dance with.'

'Then we're the same. There's no-one for me to dance with either. But we can watch.'

'Yes, miss,' Clairy said and went back to Priest's House. In her attic bedroom she tilted the blotched mirror, but could scarcely make out the pale oval of her face, nor did she try. Her vision was of Esther in her soft white dress, her dark hair like a cloud about her delicate features. She had seemed radiant, graceful as the angel in the churchyard, but quivering with life. Clairy sat down on the floor by her window where she could watch what went on below. An observer, they say, sees most of the game, a thoughtful observer most of all.

People were gathering on the green again. Prissie Merridon stuck her head out of the taproom window and called, 'Now then, let's have some help with the piano.'

Half a dozen men manoeuvred the instrument through various doors and out onto the broad flags. A man in a checked waistcoat and white shirt sleeves sat down to play. Men and girls were dragged and pushed into sets for the Lancers. Now that the great moment had come, it was more than could be expected of flesh and blood to go back to Miss Angovil's stuffy sitting-room. By way of compromise, Esther stood well back under the chestnut tree. To her surprise, Thomas and Bertha were among the first to take their places, but that was nothing to her amazement when Matty, severe in shirt blouse and black skirt, was whisked on to the green, unprotesting, by Raymond Grote from Broom Farm.

The mysteries of the dance unfolded: visiting, circle, chain and on to the next set. Absorbed, she watched the transformation of people she had known all her life, marvelling that they knew what to do, as if they drew on some legacy of country lore kept for holidays like their best clothes, and like the lanterns stored in darkness, between one celebration and the next.

All at once Daniel was there beside her. It was as if a gap she had been unaware of had been silently filled. She felt his tall presence with a thrill of something more than satisfaction, but she kept her eyes on the dancing, memorizing the simple steps so that she might almost have been out there with the others instead of just watching.

'I feel conspicuous.' Daniel had been watching her rapt face. 'There are more people dancing than not dancing. We wouldn't want to seem standoffish, would we? Look, they're making up another set and they're one couple short.' He took her hand. She saw that he had changed into his best suit, put on a clean shirt and washed his hair.

'But I don't know how, not exactly. I've only danced with Father.' It had been a means of keeping warm on draughty winter evenings. With Flora at the piano, she had learned to waltz and polka.

'Neither do I, but we can find out, can't we? Keep your eyes open and your wits about you.'

After one or two blunders all was well; all was very much more than well, though their success owed little to Daniel's advice. Dancing, even on rough grass to the thump of an old piano, is no occasion for the sharpening of wits. From the safe edge they had stepped hand in hand into a circle of soft light, rhythmic movement and intimate closeness. Having survived the Lancers, they danced the familiar polka, then a valeta. No-one paid any attention to the fact that they danced together all evening. There was no help for it. Whom else could Esther dance with?

The two had known and cared for each other all their lives, unconscious of their caring. When, years before, Daniel had carved the heart on the Aston oak, he had simply been under the compulsion to try out a new pocket-knife. After carving out his own initials he was temporarily stuck until it came to him as a matter of course to add Esther's. Esther knew nothing about the heart. If she had, at that censorious stage in her life, she would have considered such a display not quite the thing, even if no-one ever saw it.

They had never held hands except in play or when Daniel had helped his smaller companion over a stream or hauled her over a wall. He had never before put his arm round her waist or felt her softness and slightness or noticed the scent of her hair: never been stirred as now in flesh and spirit by what he recognized incredulously as love.

For Esther the whole day had been wonderful, but all her pleasure in it was forgotten in the rapture of dancing with Daniel to the tune of 'If you were the only girl in the world' in lamplit dusk fragrant with summer flowers. She seemed to float, to have no being, only the ecstatic sensation of being with Daniel, already part of him. She had grown up in his shadow but had not been aware of his slim, strong body, his beautiful mouth and dark eyes smiling down at her.

'A garden of Eden Just made for two . . .' someone was singing softly to his partner.

'I was only supposed to watch,' she said, remembering and not caring, unable to believe that from being always alone and on the outside of things, she had become part of the revolving world like everyone else. This was what everyone did.

The music had stopped. They were almost alone. The others were gathering for the bonfire on the other side of the pond. A cheer arose as the twigs crackled into flame. Under the trees at the corner of Church Lane Daniel drew her into the velvet darkness. Each saw the other's face pale with love and saw nothing else. He was astonished at her beauty, touched by her fragility. With a gentleness almost reverent he bent his head and kissed her.

'You're so lovely, Esther. I didn't know . . .'

She had nothing to say, nothing in the wide world to wish for. Her love was as natural as the flow of water in the still stream below, and would be as constant. It had always been there, natural as the beat of her heart and the course of her blood, yet it was also marvellously new and unfamiliar as enchantment. No greater happiness could be expected than now possessed her as she stood enfolded in Daniel's arms, his cheek against hers, the murmur of pure water in her ears and all around her the eternal sheltering hills.

For two such lovers the omens must surely be favourable.

CHAPTER 5

Nothing could be done about it. It was of no use to talk to them. They had no thought of hiding their feelings, even if it had been possible to conceal so rare a blaze of heat and light. Neither of them was by nature inclined to concealment.

'I don't know what's to come of it,' Bertha said yet again in the privacy of her bedroom.

'Ten to one nothing will come of it.' Thomas yawned. After a long day in the open air he was less inclined than his wife to disentangle the mysteries of love. 'Likely it'll soon blow over.' It was said to comfort Bertha. He no longer believed it.

'Somehow they're not like other young folk. There's that about them, the way they look at each other as if there was nothing else in the world to look at. You know our Daniel. Whatever he takes up with he has room in his head for nothing else. It's always been his studies and that's what he should stick to if he's going to make something of himself, as he'll need to do if he wants to marry Miss Esther.'

'Who's talking about marrying? It's another three months before he starts at the college, never mind the time it'll take after that before he can keep a wife. And there'll not be a shilling to come to her.'

'It beats me who he takes after. Nobody on my side. He talks like a book. I shouldn't wonder if he finishes up in Parliament.' Bertha's tone implied that a mother's worst fears are too often confirmed. 'Have they said anything?'

'Not a word to me. The Mester never sees what's

going on under his nose and *she* wouldn't lower herself to say aught.' Thomas put out the candle and was grateful for the dark. His eyes were bothering him. Light could play them tricks, so that the outlines of walls and furniture and, for that matter, trees wavered and grew blurred. He prayed that things would get no worse, and fell asleep.

Bertha lay awake, beset by doubts she could not formulate. She could not know that Flora was also lying awake, victim of anxieties far more acute than hers. For Flora, the worst had already happened. It would be too much to say that she felt herself responsible for this disastrous love. It was all Edwin's fault. If he had managed his affairs successfully, Esther would have made friends of her own kind in Hudmorton or – Flora sighed – Barbarrow Hall. But in allowing her to go with the Godwains to that vulgar junketing on the village green she, Flora, had made a terrible mistake.

She had discovered her error the next morning when Esther drifted into her room, wordless and weightless as thistledown. In the days that followed she seemed scarcely earthbound, needed neither food nor sleep, existed in a dream until evening, when Daniel came home from the school in Unnerstone where he was temporarily employed as an uncertificated teacher at a pittance of £28 a year, a walk of life so unpromising as to fill Flora with despair.

After the evening meal Esther would rise from the table and, well, one could say simply vanish, without being in the least discourteous, so that it was no good protesting. Flora, thinking on these things, actually wept into her pillow. The old companionable days were gone; a new order had come about, one that she could neither accept nor understand. Sometimes, as she watched the flowering of Esther's beauty, she saw in her daughter's face a new delicacy and in her eyes a new light of a spiritual kind; and she trembled

69

at the ethereal quality of this love. At other times she comforted herself with the thought that at such a pitch it could not last.

It would have surprised her to know that some of these impressions were shared by Daniel. The confusion of his own feelings did not blind him to the danger of Esther's absolute faith in him as a being of rare wisdom, knowledge and strength. Like Flora, he felt her to be vulnerable. It bothered him. But if he fell far short of the standard she innocently set for him, at least he could protect and care for her. She became increasingly precious to him. He would rather die, he inwardly vowed, than let any harm come to her.

On a more prosaic level, he took stock of himself, his manners, speech, clothes, found them unworthy of Esther and set about improving them. He bought a secondhand book on etiquette and studied it thoroughly, had his hair regularly trimmed by the Unnerstone barber, and discarded his cap in favour of a soft tweed hat.

One warm afternoon in August they walked over the hill towards Barbarrow. They were fortunate, in view of their different backgrounds, in having the freedom of woods and fields in common, and unfrequented country lanes to wander in. Not that any difference in their social standing would have been apparent to a stranger. Daniel was wearing his new lightweight jacket and Esther a plain blue summer dress.

It was she who wanted to see Barbarrow Hall again. 'Do you remember, we went there once and ate apples. It was empty then.'

She had no idea of the hopes her mother had nurtured for improving their acquaintance with Major Lincoln. The Hall was little more than the object of a walk. It didn't matter where she and Daniel went so long as they were together; and however distant it might seem to Flora, the Hall could be reached by various footpaths in less than an hour.

They chose the rarely used riverside lane going north from Lady Green. Matty, on her way to spend her afternoon off at the Grotes' farm, went with them for the first mile, until the overgrown lane petered out altogether at a roofless and dilapidated barn standing in a patch of nettles and darnel, amid a clutter of fallen timbers and broken roof tiles. There they parted company. Matty squeezed through a stile in the high hedge to the right and set off briskly across the fields to the farm. Esther and Daniel turned left, crossed the stream by stepping-stones and began their leisurely climb of Barrow Hill.

'We must have come this way that other time, but I don't remember it at all. We were so young,' Esther said.

'You're not thinking of calling, I hope.' They had come over the brow of the hill to a low boundary wall.

'Goodness gracious, no. We can prowl about a little and just look.'

Mindful of his most recent branch of study, Daniel preceded her over the stile and offered a helping hand. Elsewhere, according to the book, the lady always took precedence, except when going upstairs when it was permitted (though impossible, he reasoned, on such narrow staircases as the one at Keeper's Lodge) for lady and gentleman to ascend side by side.

The Hall stood on the floor of a valley, as did Lady Green, but the surrounding slopes were less steep. Six chimney stacks rose from above the sheltering foliage of beech and chestnut. The house itself remained hidden. A stable clock struck the half hour.

'How quiet it is!' Instinctively Esther lowered her voice. They had sat down, a grassy bank behind them, the wooded valley at their feet. 'Matty says Mr Lincoln has been advertising for servants, but there doesn't seem to be anyone about. Of course we can only see the upstairs windows from here.'

She got up and went further down the hill, leaving Daniel alone with the wide prospect of hill and sky. Involuntarily his eyes travelled above the highest curve of the horizon to the infinite blue beyond, but they did not rest there as they might once have done. He looked down at the Hall and was aware of a conflict between his approval of its fine blend of grace and dignity and his disapproval of the social order it represented. The man had lived abroad a good deal, he gathered, even before the war. If Barbarrow Hall were his, he'd think twice about leaving it. Not that he would ever own such a place, or any place at all, for that matter. In any case it was immoral to live in luxury and ease, withdrawn from the active and suffering world. Wealth could be put to better use. But how beautiful the place was! A thin finger of grey-blue smoke reached up from chimney-pot to sky. From the courtyard came the whirr of wings as a flight of doves rose, turned and were hidden by the trees.

The sound, the first to break the silence, startled Esther. She had gone farther than she intended, expecting at every step to see the garden, the sun-dial, the arbour. Instead, and at much closer range, she saw their owner with his two Labradors as he came up through the fringe of trees and out into the open. If she had not stopped abruptly and almost turned back, they would have come face to face. The awkwardness of it! Especially as they had been introduced – so that he might think she was actually intending to call – the very last thing she would have thought of doing!

The dogs reached her first and sniffed and wagged, knowing they were in good company. Their master, plodding behind, became aware of her and he, too, stopped some yards away.

'Good afternoon,' Esther murmured. Obviously he saw her unless he was temporarily blind, but she might as well have been invisible. There was no sign of interest in his face, no sign of recognition. If he remembered the young lady he had met at Priest's House, he either failed – or refused – to recognize her in the plainly dressed girl now standing in his way.

'There's no point in your going any further,' he said. 'The situation is filled.' Calling his dogs, he turned and walked back the way he had come.

Esther's lips trembled. Not to remember her at all! It was not only his mistake as to why she was there and his failure to see her as other than a housemaid – or even a scullery maid! Those errors were too flagrant to wound her. But to have made no more impression on him at their first meeting than if she had been a passing shadow! Indignation spurred her flight back to Daniel.

'Shall I kill him,' Daniel asked when she had been caressed and comforted, 'and be hanged for it?'

They laughed and were too happy to care a fig for Mr Lincoln. His behaviour had fallen so far short of the indefinable 'thing' that the younger Esther had set such store by that she quietly removed him from her list of knowable people, banished him to a frosty region beyond the pale, and cherished the forlorn hope that some day she might be able to make him feel as uncomfortable as he had made her.

Barbarrow had lost its charm. The incident was to have more distant reverberations, but its immediate effect was to persuade her that Daniel, as usual, was right to pour scorn on the wealthy and privileged. This was the twentieth century. Marcus Stone's pictures of ladies in high-waisted gowns and young men in tall hats were hopelessly out of date. The embroidery frame vanished with the arbour and the lavender hedge, and was replaced by a basket of darning, symbol of a busy, useful life to be spent in looking after Daniel.

'A schoolhouse can be a very comfortable place,' she remarked, thinking of Mr Horner's snug little Dutch-tiled hearth and long-case clock.

Daniel was slow to see the relevance of the remark, and when he did it was with a slight inward jolt. As yet his plans had reached no further than a two-year course at the Hudmorton Training College. Beyond that, the future had no more definable shape than the luminous clouds piled on the distant horizon but, like them, it would be touched with splendour – a vision he now quickly revised to include crockery and furniture, pounds, shillings and pence.

Esther had slipped her hand into his and was looking at him with shining eyes. 'Some day . . . Oh, Daniel!'

'Some day,' he echoed and forgot everything but his love for her.

Esther's disapproval of Mr Lincoln did not change, even when a possible explanation for his rudeness came to light on that very afternoon and within an hour. They had gone back over the stepping-stones and reached the derelict barn, when Matty called to them and came hurrying across the field to join them.

She had never been as far as the Hall but Mrs Grote, on hearing that the young people were walking that way, had talked a good deal about the major, who was the Grotes' landlord. Matty was not a native of the district and had heard much to interest her.

'In confidence,' she said, putting down her basket and leaning against the remains of some broken-down piece of farm equipment on which Esther was perched. 'When a thing's hushed up the way things were hushed up at Barbarrow Hall, you wonder what there was *to* hush up. Still, it all died down years ago and it's best not to dig it up again.'

'Dig it up?'

Matty's square face, now flushed with exercise, was not unpleasing but it lacked sensitivity, as did her choice of words in telling the tale, in so far as there can be a tale without beginning, middle or end.

'This is all rumour and gossip,' Daniel pointed out,

74

irked by the absence of convincing facts.

Esther, unbound by logic, highly susceptible to melodrama and hopelessly prejudiced, welcomed the rumour and gossip. 'I'd believe anything of that man, – however terrible,' she said with gusto.

'We haven't heard anything to his discredit yet,' Daniel pointed out, 'apart from his politics.'

'A foreign servant,' Matty reminded him, 'and a foreign wife. He was asking for it.'

What he got for the asking was much more than any man deserved, as even Esther acknowledged. In the summer of 1902 the Lincolns had gone abroad, leaving their small daughter in the care of servants and a French nurse.

'She was like one of the family, and she fair worshipped the little girl, Mrs Grote said. A lovely-looking young woman, dark-haired and lady-like. Nobody round about knew her except by sight. With her speaking French they didn't know what to say to her, and she was stand-offish, like the other servants at the Hall. Nobody knew much about them either, or what became of them, seeing as they were all dismissed on the spot when the Lincolns came back.'

They had returned by slow stages so that it was impossible to get in touch with them, and they had arrived at Barbarrow, having had no warning of what had happened two or three days before. It was during haytime, the servants had been helping in the field, the house was empty. An intruder had presumably broken in. There were no signs of a struggle in the nursery or anywhere else in the house and no disorder, but both nurse and child had vanished, leaving no trace.

'Murdered, both of them,' Matty said, 'and buried somewhere thereabouts.' And with a rare flutter, if not a flight of the imagination, she added, 'You could have walked over their bones this very afternoon.' Having delivered herself of the sinister remark, she hurried on

75

ahead to prepare the evening meal.

'It has the makings of a good story, but the various bits don't hang together.' Daniel hoped by this rational approach to reassure Esther, who had turned pale.

'But it must be true about the nurse and the little girl.'

'I'm afraid so; but there are several things I don't quite grasp. Why the secrecy? The police must have been brought in. How could the hunt for a vicious murderer have been kept out of the papers? You know this district. As a rule, if a man changes his bootlaces in his own bedroom with the door locked, the whole neighbourhood knows about it the next day.' He was leaning against the pile of discarded timber stacked against the wall of the barn and absently scraping paint from a piece of wood with a rusted hinge as his tool. 'Remember that murder at Apperfield just before the war? The papers went on about that for weeks.'

Esther did not remember. 'Before the war' suggested a period less remote, but no more interesting than the Dark Ages.

'What was her name, I wonder? The little girl. Somebody must know that, whatever else they don't know. Matty spoke as if all the servants were foreign – French, I suppose – but there must have been local people employed on the estate, and some of them could still be living hereabouts.'

'That's another thing. Is it likely that they'd all be dismissed on the spot and scattered to all points of the compass, never to be heard of again? It doesn't help, in solving a crime, to get rid of every living soul who was somewhere near when it happened. No, I just don't believe that. The Grotes have got it wrong. Naturally the more the thing was hushed up, the more people would concoct versions of their own.'

'Your mother must have heard about it. Hasn't she ever mentioned Barbarrow?'

Daniel reflected. He had learned at an early age to ignore almost everything his mother said, not from lack of regard for her, but from necessity, if he was not to be diverted from his studies by the constant wagging of her tongue. Consequently when it was too cold in his bedroom he could work in the cramped living-room, as oblivious of interruption as in a cloistered cell.

'Not that I know of.'

'I can imagine how the Lincolns felt.' Esther overcame her unwillingness to make excuses, especially for the major. 'About the servants, I mean. They wouldn't want to see any of them again – or the place.'

'You're right about that. It's obvious old Lincoln has tried to blot out the whole tragic business and steer clear of anyone who might bring it all back.'

'And yet he has come back. I wonder why he hasn't sold Barbarrow and gone to live somewhere else.'

'It could be difficult to sell. Country houses are too expensive to keep up these days. They're going at two a penny.' Realizing that this could also apply to Lady Green, Daniel went on quickly, 'The war may have changed his attitude – a whole new history of horrors to set the old ones at a distance and make him feel that it doesn't matter where he lives. When did all this happen, by the way?'

'It must have been while we were in Italy. We were away for three months. I was just about two years old.'

'It's a good thing they took you with them and didn't leave you in the care of a nurse.'

'Daniel!'

They gazed at each other, sharing the terrible possibility of what might have happened, or pretending to, half amused.

'A murderer at large, more than one country house to choose from, whose owners were abroad, in each one a helpless infant . . .' Daniel said casually and applied

77

his improvised tool to another piece of wood, this one with a heavy chain attached.

'When you talk like that it makes me feel involved, as if Fate had made a choice as to who should die, and chose her instead of me – except that I wasn't there to be chosen.' In a creepy sort of way the fantasy rather appealed to her.

'I can understand now why Lincoln treated you as he did.'

' Well, I can't. He barely spoke to me that time at Miss Angovil's and then today—'

'You said yourself that he would hate to be reminded of the tragedy.'

'You're not suggesting that I reminded him of his little girl? She was only a toddler, poor little thing.'

'Not of the toddler. The nurse. You heard what Matty said about her. She was dark-haired and lovely-looking, and so are you, my love. He came face to face with you in that quiet spot where, for all we know, he may often have seen her in the old days. That explains why he thought of you as an employee. It was an unconscious association of ideas.'

'Do you think so?' Concealing her pleasure in the compliment and almost persuaded to accept the theory, Esther left her uncomfortable seat to pick sticky-jacks from her stockings and shake her skirt free of flakes of paint. 'What a mess you're making!'

'The mess was here when we came and has been here for years.'

'And yet I rather like it. We must come again. There'll be plenty of blackberries later on.'

She looked round, intrigued by some quality in the place that defied the sad litter of wood and corrugated iron and had nothing to do with blackberries. It was here that the riverside lane from Lady Green ended, or began, depending on which way one was going: a rough rectangle of sheep-cropped turf fringed by long grasses and nettles. Opposite the barn, its walls warmed by hours of sunshine, a stile in the thick hedge gave access to the Grotes' land; otherwise there was no way out except by the cleft in the river bank leading down between clumps of foxgloves to the stepping-stones.

Yet there lingered in the sheltered spot a sense of human purposes. It seemed a place where people came – had come – and had just left. Their presence would have been intrusive. Their absence was tantalizing.

'But it's time to be going home,' she added regretfully and almost added 'too', so pervasively had others who had come and gone left their invisible imprint on the place.

'If my father saw all these pieces of good elm going to waste,' Daniel threw away the rusty hinge, 'he'd want to make them into something useful.'

'And mine wouldn't even notice them,' Esther said, with the now familiar twinge of anxiety aroused by thoughts of her father. 'What could be made from a heap of old wood anyway?'

'Nothing stylish, I grant you that. But if a man were desperate he could fix himself up with a cart of sorts. There's a wheel here and two more propped inside the barn. This bit with the chain is a tailboard – and you were sitting on one of the side pieces. Just a minute. There's something in your hair.'

He carefully removed a few flakes of yellow paint from the soft waves and tucked in their place a spray of harebells, then took her arm in his, defying etiquette: according to the book this betokened a greater degree of familiarity than when the gentleman offered his arm to the lady.

'I've remembered someone who knows more about Barbarrow than she cares to tell,' Esther said as they sauntered home. 'Miss Angovil. I'll coax it out of her.'

She turned her head to look back. What was it Daniel had said? Some phrase barely noticed, a random combination of words and ideas, teased her mind into almost remembering some other circumstance – some quite different thing – as if a book read long ago had fallen open briefly at a memorable page before being dusted, closed and replaced on its shelf.

CHAPTER 6

Summer passed, and with it the first idyllic phase of their love. Wandering hand in hand by the stream or in the woods could not go on for ever. As the days grew shorter and the evenings cooler they were faced with the problem of where and when to meet, since neither now felt at ease in the other's home.

At the end of September Daniel enrolled at the Hudmorton Training College. He boarded in town with Bertha's younger sister and occasionally came home at weekends, travelling on Friday evenings by train as far as Unnerstone station, a mile and a half from Wood Aston. At first Esther walked halfway to meet him, until the dark winter evenings kept her at home. Inevitably they saw less of each other.

For Esther, too, life was becoming more serious. At Lady Green the arrival of the morning post had become an ordeal. She could only guess at the contents of the letters her father carried off to his study, but she saw his unshared anxieties increase. He had lost his affability and charm and was often morose, short-tempered, irritated sometimes beyond control by Flora's complaints about the draughts, the poor quality of cheap coal, the drudgery of running a big house with only one servant. As her parents drew apart, Esther also withdrew into a private world occupied only by herself and Daniel. In the absence of Daniel himself she made do with thoughts of him: thoughts which in her solitude raised him to such heights as no living man could achieve.

Fortunately there was one place where they had both been welcome, in one capacity or another, all their lives.

Esther's so-called lessons had fizzled out years ago, but she was still a frequent visitor at Priest's House. Miss Angovil had come to regard her as the niece she might have had if Roland had escaped the Boers. Village children, too, had always been welcome at her back door until Spedding put her foot down; but by that time Daniel had graduated from running errands and knocking in nails to borrowing books and lecturing Miss Angovil on their contents. The sitting-room overlooking the green was warmer and cosier, with its clutter of nick-nacks and old-fashioned pictures, than the long, low drawing-room at Lady Green, more comfortable and spacious than the crowded sitting-room at Keeper's Lodge, Miss Angovil more impartial and undemanding than either Flora or Bertha. No assignations were made, but it was surprising how often Esther called and found Daniel making himself useful in the garden or Daniel called and was invited to join the ladies at tea.

Miss Angovil, knitting fleecy bedjackets and babies' bootees as she watched her visitors, was aware of their problems, knew moreover that they were likely to increase; but the knowledge did not disturb her. In her muddled way she saw their inevitable pain, like their happiness, as part of a dimly perceived Divine Plan, enjoyed their company and hoped that nothing would ever happen to make her own life less comfortable.

Certainly she had learned, if nothing else, to be comfortable: a not inconsiderable achievement which had imbued Priest's House with an atmosphere almost too insistently secure. It was expressed in material form by thick Indian carpets overlaid with thicker rugs, by heavily pelmeted curtains at windows and doors, by fires burning bright beneath well-swept chimneys. Esther and Daniel made no bones about enjoying such amenities as, side by side on the sofa, they shared a dish of crumpets while their hostess poured strong tea into Albert china cups.

Meanwhile, in the kitchen, as if to supply a subdued accompaniment to the theme of domestic well-being, Spedding and Clairy enjoyed their share of crumpets and a pot of even stronger tea. They enjoyed, too, an unending, slow-moving current of low-voiced conversation.

'It's such a relief,' Miss Angovil remarked on one occasion, 'that they get on well together. You remember how Spedding treated that other girl. I dreaded it happening again. But she has really taken to Clairy. As she ought to do of course.'

Esther nodded, recognizing the allusion to Clairy's unimpeachable character as testified to by a Baptist minister in Hudmorton. It was generally thought that Miss Angovil had spoilt Spedding, now in her sixties and often ailing.

'I know that she has been given her head,' she admitted. 'Of the two of us Spedding is the stronger character, and I dislike friction of any kind.'

Clairy, it seemed, never put a foot wrong or uttered a word out of place. Naturally the girl must be allowed some time to herself, but she never seemed to want company and had none of the silly ways girls had fallen into these days, such as going to dances and picture palaces. Walks in the country on her own, a quiet hour in her bedroom, an occasional visit to her aunt in Hudmorton, were all she wanted. Nothing was neglected, she was always there when needed. Spedding depended on her far more than she would admit, and even allowed the girl to look after her when she was unwell.

'I overheard them talking the other day. The two voices are so different, Spedding's rather harsh and disagreeable – her liverish attacks make her so difficult – the other so quiet and low. "Leave all that to me," Clairy said. "I'll see to everything." '

There was much more that Miss Angovil did not overhear and would, in any case, have felt it judicious to ignore. Employers well knew of their servants'

83

mysterious propensity for finding things out. News-gathering took the place of other forms of enter-tainment denied to the likes of Spedding and Clairy; and though they themselves were confined to a household where visitors could be counted on one hand, the scope of their interest was wider – was, indeed, unlimited. Spedding had found in her tireless assistant an equally tireless audience. Clairy's entire physique was attentive as, standing or sitting, she listened to Spedding's rambling anecdotes, the angle of her head tilted slightly from the vertical as if always ready to go further and nod agreement, her lips thoughtfully pursed, her eyes – they were the most attentive of all – concentrated on the speaker. The effect was of total submission to what was being said. Small wonder that by the time Clairy had been at Priest's House for a year, and Miss Angovil had raised her wage by a shilling a week, she knew as much of the history of Wood Aston folk and some of those living further afield as Spedding did – and considerably more than Esther.

The tragedy at Barbarrow, for instance. Esther's vow to coax Miss Angovil into revealing all had been largely empty talk. The topic could hardly be described as urgent. Her interest in the story had been roused by the place itself. They had not gone that way again; out of sight, it faded from her mind, until she narrowly missed another meeting with Major Lincoln.

It was a wet morning. She had fled in desperation from the growing tension at Lady Green and trudged through the rain to her only refuge. Her knock was answered immediately. Through the glass panes of the inner door she saw Clairy move swiftly from the direc-tion of the sitting-room, as if she had been hovering in the hall. A moment later, as Esther took off her water-proof in the recess under the stairs, Major Lincoln came out of the sitting-room, picked up his hat from the hall table and left without having seen her. Had Clairy been listening at the sitting-room door? Esther dismissed

84

the uncomfortable thought, remembering the Baptist minister's letter of recommendation in which he had described the girl's conduct in the warmest terms.

'You must have been pleased when Major Lincoln came back to Barbarrow,' she remarked when the conversation showed signs of lapsing. Unpleasant as he was, he was after all Miss Angovil's friend.

'I was surprised. Was it wise, I wonder? But I suppose after such a long time he had given up hope . . .'

'Hope?'

'Er . . . yes.' The comfortable warmth of the fire was making Miss Angovil drowsy. 'It is hope, isn't it, that keeps us going?'

No wonder Daniel despised Miss Angovil's intellect: there were times when she didn't seem to know what she was talking about. She had leaned back, eyes closed. Esther turned the pages of an out-of-date *Ladies' Companion* until the restlessness that had driven her from home brought her to her feet again.

'That little water-colour in the hall,' Miss Angovil murmured. 'Do close the door after you, dear. Clairy left it open when she showed in Major Lincoln. She is usually more careful.'

Esther, who always closed doors, obeyed with exasperated firmness. Old people! The audible closing of the door brought Clairy into the hall with Esther's raincoat which she had taken to the kitchen to dry.

'I'm cross this morning, Clairy.'

'I expect it's the weather, miss.'

She helped Esther into her coat. Being the taller of the two, she could look over Esther's shoulder at the flawless face reflected in the mirror of the hallstand. Esther, pulling on a woollen hat, barely noticed her own face or that of the maid behind her; it was not the sort of face one did notice, though the features were not coarse, the light brown hair under the morning cap was thick and smooth, and the complexion clear. If she had looked into the eyes that watched her as she adjusted her blue shanter, Esther might have found their steady look more searching than was comfortable.

What Esther did see reflected in the mirror was a dim water-colour in a heavy gilt frame on the wall behind her.

'That's what she meant.' She turned. 'I believe it's Barbarrow Hall, and yet it isn't quite . . . No, the Hall is bigger.'

'It is now, miss, but it was like that a long time ago before they built more on to it. Here, on the end.'

'You know it?'

'Spedding told me. She used to work there when she was a girl – and her mother before her. Quite a few of her family have worked there.'

'When Spedding was a girl? That must have been over forty years ago. It would be a different family in those days.'

'Yes, miss. It was the Mowbrays that had the Hall before Major Lincoln's family.'

These simple exchanges made no demand on the intelligence. Perhaps it was her recent escape from Miss Angovil's muzziness that stimulated Esther to feel in Clairy's prompt replies a clarity of mind she had not expected.

'It must have been a pleasant place before the tragedy. Did Spedding tell you about that?'

'Oh yes, miss. She knows all about that.'

'All about it? But nobody can know . . . They never found the murderer.'

'There was no murder. That was only talk. Nobody was murdered – unless they've been murdered since.'

'But Mrs Grote told Matty—'

'People said all sorts of things. What they didn't know they made up, Spedding says.'

'Then what happened to the little girl and the nurse?'

'The nurse took the little girl away, Spedding says.'

'But why?'

'Out of wickedness, miss.'

86

As a purveyor of information Clairy was thoroughly competent. In fact, in passing on these ill tidings she showed an unexpected authority: the kind of power exerted by a quick and clear understanding. There was something eminently reasonable in her reservation – 'unless they've been murdered since' – that reminded Esther of Daniel. It was the sort of thing he would have said. But would Daniel have given so shocking a reason – 'out of spite and wickedness' – in so cool and passionless a tone? The wickedness was indisputable but . . .

'Spite? Why should she feel like that about her employer?'

Esther's vision of the nurse, dark-haired, lovely-looking and lady-like, had so far for personal reasons been sympathetic, but it could not withstand the shock of Clairy's reply.

'Because of what was going on between her and the master.'

'Major Lincoln!' Except that in those days he had been unquestionably Mr.

'Yes, miss.'

Esther had been sufficiently gripped by these revelations to sink down on Miss Angovil's third stair. She got up. Something more than the conventional embargo on gossiping with servants made her feel suddenly ashamed.

'I don't believe we should be talking of such things. I'm surprised at Spedding. She should know better than to spread such a scandalous story.'

In a belated attempt to distance herself from the conversation, she seized her umbrella from the stand. Clairy opened the front door. Her face registered neither embarrassment nor any desire to defend herself or Spedding from the shame of scandal-mongering. As Esther paused on the step to thank her, she caught sight of Clairy's eyes. It was literally so: she had never noticed them before. They were of an unusual colour, neither green, nor blue nor grey, and rather long in shape under eyebrows unexpectedly dark and slanting upwards to the temples in shallow curves like wings. Looking out into the grey of the clouded morning, the eyes had a sudden crystalline brilliance like jewels in a modest setting.

'Clairy. It's an unusual name. I suppose it's Claire really?'

The answering smile and a lift of the eyebrows, the equivalent of a shrug, were momentary and not quite respectful. Why should they be? Plodding home through wet leaves, Esther regretted her own priggishness, especially as she knew very well that she would pass on the scandalous story to Daniel at the earliest opportunity.

'I heard you talking. What was she on about?' Spedding demanded from her rocking-chair by the kitchen fire. With her rheumatic feet swathed in a woollen shawl she looked not unlike a prisoner bound and gagged. 'What did she find to say to you all of a sudden?'

'She was looking at that picture of Barbarrow Hall.'

'The oven's about right for the pie. So – they've got their eye on Major Lincoln, have they? Folks such as them like to stick together.' She rocked herself back from the wave of hot air as Clairy opened the oven door. 'My, the heat!'

'It's the very best thing for your joints.' Clairy wrapped the shawl more tightly and inescapably round the swollen ankles.

'Joints! You'll be putting me in the roasting tin with a bit of dripping one of these days. Where are you off to now?'

'Just going upstairs.'

'It beats me what you do up there for half an hour at a time.'

With her mistress comfortable in the sitting-room and Spedding immovable in the kitchen, Clairy found plenty to do upstairs as she went noiselessly from room to room.

On the following Saturday morning Daniel called for Esther and they walked to Wood Aston to deliver some notepaper which Miss Angovil had asked him to get for her in town. He was full of news of the week's activities: most importantly, he had chosen the subject for his thesis. It was to have as its theme the relative importance of heredity and environment in influencing a child's development.

'Nature – or nurture. I shall begin with a reference to Caliban. In his case heredity won. His mother was a witch: his base nature couldn't be civilized. That's what Prospero said, but was it true?' Esther had no difficulty in looking doubtful. 'The question is how far the nature we are born with can be altered by the way we are brought up. Take identical twins . . .' He took identical twins, separated them at birth ('What a shame!' Esther said), put one in the country, one in a town, caused one to be reared by god-fearing, temperate foster parents, the other by dissolute, irresponsible gambling drunken wretches: then reunited them in maturity with a view to comparing them. 'How much would they still have in common? That would be the hereditary factor.'

'But wouldn't it be difficult to arrange?' Esther asked.

He burst out laughing and hugged her. 'Bless you, it's impossible.' They had come to the Aston oak, and he made as if to batter his head against the trunk in despair. 'Why in heaven's name have I hit on such a hopeless subject? And yet it fascinates me. I've got it into my head and can't give it up. Still, I've almost two years to think about it.'

They lingered at the old meeting place. The weather was mild, the wood a place of soft colours melting into one another, silver and brown and grey above a yellow carpet of leaves.

'They're taking that branch down next week.' Daniel pointed to the bleached bough. 'Father thinks it's unsafe. I wanted them to wait until the Christmas holidays so that I could lend a hand, but your father has made up his mind to get on with it.'

For once Aumery intended to keep his word, but he had baulked at the expense of employing experienced woodmen. Forster's bill for thinning was still unpaid. For the smaller job of taking down a single branch they must manage with the Eddle brothers, Jo and Ben, and Jo's young son Reuben.

'They're hedgers and ditchers over Barbarrow way,' Daniel explained.

It was the opportunity she had been waiting for. Moreover, she was only too willing to evade the subject of her father's problems.

'I've been waiting to tell you. I've found out something more.'

'Go on then. It's your turn.' He put his arm round her as they leaned against the tree, and listened indulgently. 'It's feasible,' he said when she had finished. 'Kidnapping. It would explain the secrecy. Perhaps they didn't even call the police. The nurse may have left a note demanding money for returning the child, and threatening to harm or abandon it if the police were told. In that case the Lincolns would be absolutely at her mercy.'

'And it would explain why Miss Angovil won't say a word about it. She might have got round to talking about a murder but never about a scandal.'

'Murder is thought to be pretty scandalous, I believe.'

'I meant about Mr Lincoln and the nurse. How *could* he?'

'If she was like you, my love, how could he help it?'

'Don't say that. I rather liked being compared with her, but not now that we know what sort of woman she was. She made the Lincolns suffer as much as if the little girl had been murdered, if not more. To have lived all these years not knowing . . .'

The tragedy, a distant affair involving strangers, moved closer. She was safe in the Aumerys' own wood, under the sheltering tree, with Daniel's protective arm around her; and yet she was disturbed by warning signals from an alien world. It was always there, a constant threat to her lightness of heart. There flashed into her mind a memory – the pallid face of a creature in flight from its unimaginable terrors – and her own first awakening to the existence of evil.

'Still, it was an odd business. If there had been a demand for money, Lincoln would have paid it and got the child back. That evidently didn't happen, so either she was done away with or the nurse wanted her and kept her as her own.'

'Kept her? Where? Could she still be alive?'

'Unlikely.' But Daniel's reply was not dismissive. Esther knew from the way he drew in his upper lip and detached himself, leaving a gap between them, that he had grown thoughtful. She hadn't expected the Barbarrow mystery to interest him as it did her.

'But not impossible,' she persisted. 'Just suppose: if she is still alive, suppose she came back. How wonderful! It might make him human again.'

'You're turning it into a fairy tale. Life isn't like that.' He took her arm. 'Come on. You'll catch cold standing here. Besides, if she were found, would she be the daughter he expected? How much would she have been influenced by a different kind of life?'

'Oh, I see. She would be an example to study, like the twins. Perhaps things are better as they are. To wait in suspense all this time and then to be disappointed in her—'

'Why disappointed? The change might be for the better.' His face had lit up. She recognized the symptoms. Caught up in a new train of thought, he walked faster as if with the next step he would take flight. 'There can never be a perfect example of environmental moulding. You'd always be comparing the known with the theoretical. I mean, comparing the person with the person he – or she – might have been. Still, by Jove, it's interesting.'

He would never change. He would soar away into a higher realm beyond her reach. She loved to listen, she told herself. It didn't matter that sometimes she lagged behind. But it mattered very much that he should forget her as he had forgotten her now, though her arm was through his as he hurried her through the damp leaves. Their tender saunter had become a race: she to keep up with him, he in pursuit of ideas that swarmed like bright-winged insects to dazzle and delight him.

It seemed to her that he had taught her everything she knew, though that was little enough. Without him she would have been no better than Caliban, except in appearance of course. It was foolish to feel that they might have spent this precious morning together in talking of simpler things – of each other and their future together; childish to feel that when he was absorbed in his theories he was not entirely her own as she was utterly and completely his. But how wonderfully he talked, and how very much he needed her to talk to! All that separated them for a little while was a mere way of thinking: such a harmless thing. Nothing else in the world could come between them; no other thing; no other person.

At eight o'clock that same morning, Thomas Godwain slung his bag over his shoulder and set off from the Lodge on his morning round, as unremarkable an event as the daily rising of the sun. Why then did Bertha, who was washing up in the scullery, her ears cocked, instantly abandon her dishcloth, dry her hands and hurry to the window of the front room?

It overlooked the field path leading to Scaur Crag, a minute's walk away. At the point where the path began to dip steeply Thomas had stopped. He wasn't doing anything except staring ahead. Although he had his back to her, Bertha was convinced that he was staring and not looking in the way that she was looking at him. The strangeness of their mutual idleness suddenly frightened her. The two of them doing nothing first thing in the morning! It wasn't right. Yet she sensed in the set of his broad shoulders and the back of his neck an unusual tautness, as if he had been brought to a halt and had forgotten where he was going.

Bertha had seen him in this curiously fixed attitude two or three times, at first in the house.

'What's to do, Thomas?' She had found him standing at this very window. 'Is it a fox – or what?'

He had come to himself with a start, shaken his head and walked out of the house. Two days ago she had seen him behaving in the same strange way out of doors. Was it a fit, like Jacob Merridon at the Coach used to have? She had felt the terror known only to working men's wives when faced with the possibility of illness. What would become of them if his health failed? For that matter, if he wasn't careful he'd go tumbling over the Crag and finish up among the boulders at the bottom.

To her relief he came to life and walked on, keeping to the path. The incline took him out of sight, first his gaitered legs, then his jacket, last of all his shoulders and head, as if the land he loved had swallowed him up. In fact, for a while Godwain's mood was cheerful. It was second nature to him, whistling under his breath, to turn his attention outward and lose himself in noting the state of the paths, a new rabbit burrow, a stubborn growth of thistles, a seepage of water from a cracked conduit. From the top of the Crag he had tested his eyes and they had passed the test. He had seen the familiar line of Long Rake, even individual trees on its green slope, and the roof and chimneys of Lady Green; had seen them steady and clear.

At the back of his mind anxiety still lurked. If it had been only his eyes, he would have gone into

93

town months ago and got himself fitted up with spectacles, but the problem went deeper. There were times when he feared that not only his sight was threatened but his mind, too. He knew that there could be tumours in the head. His father's brother, Uncle Robbie, had gone blind from one and practically senseless. Did such things run in families? Which would be worse: to see nothing at all, or to lose your reason and see things that weren't there?

In a good light and in the open his vision was usually clear, though less keen than it had been. After exertion such as hurrying uphill or sawing logs he would see objects waver as if through a cascade of water. But it was in the sparse light under trees that his eyes played tricks on him and he couldn't be sure whether what he saw was really there or only a hallucination.

What had he seen? Godwain paused at the edge of the wood. The path led straight on for about three hundred yards then turned and was lost among trees, bare-branched save for a feathering of leaves which another strong wind or another night of rain would strip away. Even under naked boughs, light had the half-opaque quality peculiar to woodland. The aerial spaces between mossed grey trunks formed no pattern, were infinitely varied in shape and changed at every step.

With open land behind him, he looked into the shade. There was no-one about, no-one for miles. The knowledge brought no satisfaction. It reinforced the suspicion that there hadn't been anyone there at those other times. His senses had misled him when he had looked into the middle distance and seemed to see a movement, when the firm lines of a tree bole had seemed to soften into the suggestion of a ripple. At such times he had walked forward, sure that there was something there, not an animal or a bird, more like a fold of grey cloth that came and went, was there and then not there. Not a twig had snapped nor a leaf rustled, and yet there had grown on him the conviction that he was not alone. Once he had actually called out, 'Is there anybody there?' No-one answered, but the challenge had echoed in his head, a disturbing reminder of how the mind can be deceived. He knew what Bertha would say if he told her.

'Seeing things! It's the sign of a death,' and she would tell for the twentieth time how Madge Ackers had seen her mother walking in the fields when she'd been dead a year, and a week later her father had died. Funnily enough, though he had seen nothing definite, nothing at all, he had carried in his mind the impression that if there had been anything there to see, it would have been a woman. If anyone had answered, it would have been a woman's voice. No living thing nor any supernatural visitation would have frightened him here in his own territory. What he feared was that some disorder could make him conjure up phantoms, like the rats and snakes that torment drunkards in delirium.

The whistle had died on his lips, but he walked steadily in his regular stride and reached his destination, the Aston oak. There was no wind. Nevertheless the dead branch creaked. A few more days and it would be off, and the sooner the better before it killed somebody. It was a pity Dan wouldn't be able to lend a hand, but there'd be four of them plus the mester, not that he'd be a ha'porth of good except to hold on to a rope end and keep it from tangling with another.

The vast boughs were still thinly clad in leaves, some autumnal yellow, some still summer green. Oak leaves are late in falling. He lit his pipe, planning the operation and mentally locating the sling, guide rope and where the cuts should be made and the ladders poised. Two ropes, each secured to the branch, passed over a strong crotch above, brought down and wound twice round the trunk about four feet up with enough slack to pay out as the timber was lowered.

The air was soft, with no hint of winter in it. Later there would be sunshine. A squirrel scaled a neighbouring tree. Godwain watched its upward flow, smooth as water in reverse, and, losing sight of it, transferred his gaze to the path by which he had come. His heart contracted. The woodland ride trembled, grew narrower, broadened again. He screwed his eyes into slits and all was well again, the earth firm beneath his feet. He finished his morning round and went home to join Daniel, just home from Hudmorton, in a second breakfast.

Heavy rain the next day put an end to the mild autumnal weather. By the following Wednesday, the day of the amputation, as Aumery dubbed it, winter had set in and it was bitterly cold. Aumery's grim joke was a sign of nervousness, his assumed jollity quite out of character, like rising devilishly early, huddling into thick clothes and eating his breakfast standing up as if waiting for the signal to go over the top into battle, an experience he had never known, thanks to his age. But having for once made a firm decision, he saw himself as a man of action and assumed a confidence he knew to be bogus. The unsuccessful impersonation increased his nervousness. He loathed the whole business: ladders, ropes, saws, axes, cart-horses, wagons and men he barely knew made him jumpy.

He talked more than usual and strode uneasily back and forth as he and Godwain waited for the Eddles, who were late on account of a horse going lame.

'They're a slow lot at the best of times,' Godwain said, and wished once more that Dan could have been there.

The tree, like the weather, had changed its mood. Its branches, now almost bare, twisted against a sky grey as pewter, in contortions as wild and wicked in shape as those of the fatal lightning.

'They don't like being interfered with, these trees.' Aumery's breath hung in the cold air. He was conscious of babbling. 'They're sacred things, you know. In pagan times it was believed that when a tree was felled its spirit flew out screaming from the cut.'

'We're not felling, thank God. We'd need an army for that.'

'Well, don't be surprised if—' He broke off to listen, hating the compulsive jocularity that had come upon him like an illness.

'Sounds as if they're coming,' Godwain said. They heard the thud of iron-shod hooves beating the soft earth, the rumble of a wagon, twigs snapping against its sides. 'And about time too.'

They talk about it in Wood Aston to this day. At family gatherings, especially funerals, and at the Coach and Horses, there is still speculation as to what went wrong. When tree lopping is mentioned some old inhabitant is sure to hark back to the disaster at the Aston oak as an example of a botched-up job. As to how it should have been done, theories flourished in the absence of a clear eye-witness account of what had actually happened. Of those who were there, none had seen the whole operation. The testimony of the only one who knew what had happened was not available.

The general view was that Aumery was to blame, with his cheese-paring ways. Everything he touched went wrong. He had frittered away a handsome estate, but it was hard to believe that he couldn't raise the money to pay an experienced man such as Forster, who said – and went on saying it for years – that he couldn't understand how it had been bungled, even by the Eddles. If they had no brains at least they had brawn enough, the three of them, to take the church tower down.

The Eddles, who never lent a hand in tree surgery again, swore that it was Godwain's own fault, poor chap. He was the one to give the orders, he was in charge of the guide rope. To start with, he had underestimated the danger from the bough itself. Rot had almost destroyed the heart-wood; the break had come sooner than expected, and he hadn't been concentrating. Something – neither Jo nor Ben nor young Reuben could say what, though they were urged time and again to do so – something had happened to Godwain, a sudden change as if—

'As if what?' they were asked.

'Do you mean he lost his nerve?'

'No, not that.' The one thing the Eddles could be firm about was that Godwain had not lost his nerve. The first section of the great branch had been lowered. At the very moment when the second section was ready to come down, when Jo who was on the ladder felt the saw suddenly go through and shouted to Ben to start paying out the sling ropes, the change in Godwain had occurred. Jo couldn't see it but the other two could. It had come in a flash: a kind of uplifted look. He seemed to forget where he was. He looked happy.

The word was greeted with disbelief. Almost any other, it was felt, would have been more likely. There hadn't been much to be happy about and there was still less now. Godwain alone could have confirmed the aptness of the word, if it could have been done in the few seconds before he ceased to be able to confirm anything. His eyes had troubled him very little that morning and not enough to endanger himself or anyone else. From his position, with Aumery behind him holding the rope, he could see, as clearly as he had ever done, the spray of splinters and powdery dust from the saw, its sharp teeth, and the ripple of muscles in Jo's right arm. It was just before the saw unexpectedly went through, when all his concentration was needed, that a movement between two trees to his left caught his eye. He turned his head and saw a young woman dressed in grey or green, the colour of a tree. She was some distance away but he could see her distinctly. In a flash it came to him that there was nothing wrong with his mind, no tumour, no hallucination. The woman was real. He even recognized her. It was the girl who worked for Miss Angovil at Priest's House making a short cut through the wood. Relief brought a tingling exhilaration.

Almost simultaneously he heard the crack – the shouts – and pushed Aumery to safety. Then a heavy weight fell on him and crushed him to the earth.

CHAPTER 7

Gervase Lincoln, riding along the riverside path to Wood Aston, was startled by a scream of anguish from the neighbouring wood. He dug in his heels, arrived on the scene two or three minutes after the accident, and instantly took charge.

The Eddles had succeeded in lifting the section of the branch from Godwain's unconscious body. Though fearfully injured, he was still breathing. Lincoln administered brandy from his pocket flask and made the others drink too. After a swift assessment of their capabilities he despatched Ben and Reuben to fetch the nearest gate or hurdle to serve as a stretcher, and ordered Jo to cover Godwain with their coats and stay with him until he could be moved. Clearly Aumery had gone to pieces. Apparently the spine-chilling scream had come from him, not Godwain. He had sunk, ashen-grey and trembling, onto the fallen branch, with his head in his hands.

'Pull yourself together, man.' Lincoln thrust the flask between Aumery's chattering teeth. The two men knew each other by sight, but Aumery was no nearer recognizing him than a man dying of thirst in the desert recognizes the nomad who rescues him; and Aumery was lost indeed. Darkness had fallen upon him as crippling to his spirit as if he, too, had been crushed almost to death. He was never to waver in his belief that the fault was his. He should have heeded Thomas's warnings years ago. Then the time would have been favourable, before the world turned against him, as he deserved it should. His neglect and incompetence had set in motion the landslide in his affairs, whose downward rush had become an avalanche carrying away as its chief victim the one human being he loved and needed. Life without Thomas was impossible. He could not speak of it, could not speak at all. A terrible wordlessness held him prisoner within his own mind where he went on hearing, weird as a banshee's screech, the scream he could not recognize as his own. He was possessed, tortured by guilt. No trace of self-pity tempered his recriminations. Having evaded responsibility all his life, he accepted it at last and was destroyed by it.

Lincoln had neither time nor patience to spare for a man whom he diagnosed as crazed by shock. He rode off to Unnerstone to fetch the doctor and telephone the hospital at Hudmorton for an ambulance, calling on his way at the Coach and Horses to see that word was sent to the Lodge and Lady Green.

Bertha was not alone when the wagon arrived with its still unconscious burden. Both Merridons were with her, and Esther had come running up the hill and helped to clear furniture from the sitting-room so that Thomas could be laid on the floor. She and Prissie waited miserably at the gate to watch for the doctor.

'It's his back,' Prissie said, 'and the side of his head and face and goodness knows what else inside of him.'

'But he isn't dead. We must be thankful he's still alive.'

'I'm not so sure. There's worse things than death sometimes.'

'What do you mean?' Esther asked in terror.

'How can he ever be himself again after what's happened? Supposing he is spared, it could be a living death – and him such a fine active man.'

They went indoors to warn Bertha that the doctor's gig had crossed the bridge. She was sitting by the mattress where Thomas lay, and Prince too, head on paws, his mournful eyes never leaving his master's face.

'That dog knows more than many a Christian,' Prissie said.

Her sorrowful predictions were fulfilled. Thomas had not regained consciousness when at last they got him to hospital. For three weeks, except that he breathed, there was no more sign of life in him than in the dead branch that fell on him. He was there all winter. Gradually consciousness returned, the fearful bruises faded, the broken arm and leg mended, he could take food from a spoon. His attempts to speak were so laboured, with such long rests between them, that it was hard to tell whether or not his brain was damaged. He seemed to recognize Bertha and Daniel, who saw him every day – and Aumery, who haunted his bedside, haggard and silent, and was continually held back or beckoned away by nurses acting on Matron's instructions. Mr Aumery upset the patient: his visits were to be discouraged.

Certainly his employer, fleshless as a scarecrow and almost as careless in his dress, affected Thomas as nothing else did. Long before he could speak his eyes signalled some urgent message. Their blue had paled to watery grey pools in his bruised and twisted face. Aumery could not interpret their speechless message, but Thomas's evident need to communicate with him smote his heart. He sat as if rooted to the bedside until ordered away, to go drearily home where he could bear neither his cold study – the whole house was cold – nor the garden, nor the woods. He wore himself out with long walks, pretending that they were necessary now that there was no-one else to oversee the estate. Once, instead of taking the train home as far as Unnerstone, he walked the whole way from town. It began to snow as he left streets behind and struck out into the country. The wilderness of snow and wind awoke in him a response he had not felt for weeks, and in their bitter solitude he found something like peace. But he arrived at Lady Green in such a state of sickness and exhaustion that Flora forgot her own troubles and put him to bed with a tenderness he failed to notice.

Esther was to remember that winter as one of unrelieved misery. An icy chill had fallen on Lady Green. The season was unusually cold, the house low-lying in the shadow of Scaur Crag for most of the winter months. The long rooms and stone floors needed leaping fires to keep them moderately warm. There had always been ample piles of logs and tons of coal to draw upon, but in the year after the war the price of coal had gone up alarmingly, the supplier was unpaid and the sawing and stacking of wood had been one of Thomas's many jobs. The drawing-room, with its three windows and sagging doors, was abandoned; the flagged hall, with its open staircase and wide chimney, was a place to be fled across rather than to be sat in. Esther and her mother spent most of their time in Flora's bedroom, where a small fire burned all day and where they were safe from distressing encounters with her father.

The chill darkness of the house was less depressing than the bloodless apparition of Edwin Aumery, gaunt, silent and unrecognizable as the man whose looks and personality had charmed the younger Flora. Their fading appeal had continued to make an uncongenial life bearable. The alarming change in him stirred even her shallow nature to anxious concern for him: she stopped complaining, urged him to eat and tried to talk to him. But he could not be reached. Meeting his wife or daughter, he would slip away, unable to face them or the piles of unpaid bills on his study table, or the familiar paths he had trodden with Godwain, and wandered aimlessly from room to room until it was time to set off on his daily visit to Hudmorton.

During those unhappy winter months the Aumerys were almost entirely alone, except for occasional visits from Major Lincoln who called to ask for news of Godwain as he would have done in the event of any local disaster. He sat each time for ten minutes in the chilly dining-room, accepted Flora's offer of wine or coffee, chatted tersely but with more amiability than Esther would once have believed possible, and drew his own conclusions as to the state of affairs at Lady Green and the condition of its master.

On his first visit Flora had mentioned their previous acquaintance at Risewood. On hearing her maiden name, he had with an effort recollected her family as neighbours of his own, and that was enough to satisfy Flora who, in her chastened mood, had neither the wish nor the spirit to recall her more prosperous days. Talk was general and superficial.

From the little he saw of Aumery, Major Lincoln suspected the onset of a deep melancholia, a state into which he would probably have fallen in any event. A life without purpose or commitment, isolated and fraught with financial anxieties, could expose a man once past middle age to mental or psychological illness. The wife, a pleasant enough woman, would be out of her depth, having neither the strength nor the pluck to guide the man back to normality. And the daughter . . .

Soft-voiced, quiet in movement, exquisitely polite, Esther poured wine or coffee and set his cup or glass on the table at his side. She then seated herself on an armless chair, her head erect, her back straight as a ramrod, taking no part in the conversation unless drawn into it: the very model of a dutiful and well-bred young lady. A model was what Esther felt herself to be, a lifeless simulacrum of her former self. Moving or at rest, she yearned for Daniel whom she rarely saw. He no longer came home at weekends. So long as his father was in hospital, he must be on hand in town. In any case, the train journey would have been a needless extravagance when every penny must be accounted for. One Sunday he walked home and they had tea at Priest's House in the old way. Miss Angovil withdrew to her dining-room and left them alone, but they were too conscious of the shortness of their time together to make good use of it: they were awkward and dull, had scarcely met, it seemed, when it was time for Daniel to leave.

'You'll come again soon?'

'As soon as I can, but I don't know when—'

'You'll think of me? I think of you all the time.'

'Yes, I will. You know I will,' Daniel promised gloomily, his mind on the long tramp back to Hudmorton, an essay to be finished for the next morning, the memory of his father as he had last seen him, the dread of seeing him again.

'It will be better when they let him come home,' Esther told him. 'That is what Father is living for. It won't be long now. I'm sure it won't.'

They clung to each other and then he was gone.

It was of Daniel that she was thinking as she endured one of the major's visits a few days later. On his first visit he had been aware of having met the girl somewhere and later remembered that it had been at Miss Angovil's. Of the other meeting he had no recollection; he had barely noticed the girl making her way to the Hall, and had had no reason to connect her with the young lady at Priest's House. But as he sat out the awkward minutes of his duty visits to her parents, he had ample opportunity to notice her and to be impressed by the beauty flowering so unseasonably in the sunless house.

But Esther's delicacy of feature and graceful carriage were not all that interested him. Lincoln had seen a number of beautiful women and had known them well, but he felt in the girl a rare inward quality of self-forgetful patience. The hint of sadness in her eyes – large and soft and deep violet-blue in colour – touched him, and he was not easily touched. He wondered what would become of her and hoped she would find – as surely she must – the protective love she deserved and was going to need.

Esther's natural liveliness had been so thoroughly

quenched by recent events that she found nothing either strange or interesting in his presence. Only a few weeks ago she would have seen him as the villain or victim in a melodrama of murder, kidnapping and illicit love. The thrill of uncovering his sensational past was gone. In so far as she remembered it, she regretted its silliness. She had forgotten that the major had treated her rudely and that she had hoped to make him as uncomfortable as he had made her. Her life had taken on a new and drearier pattern, and this man with his clipped blond moustache, keen unsmiling eyes and disciplined manner was part of it. Like other people at that time, he was of little more interest to her than the wallpaper behind him. All the same, one had only to look from Major Lincoln to her father to see which was the stronger. At the sight of her father's constantly twitching lips and hollow eyes – dark blue like her own – her heart ached. He had developed nervous movements of the hands and shoulders. His voice, in contrast to the major's deeper tones, was too high-pitched, as if he misjudged the distance – which was limitless – between himself and other people.

In the depths of Aumery's disorder there flickered still a tiny flame of hope. When Thomas came home things would be better. He would be crippled for life (the flame guttered and almost failed) but with careful nursing he would otherwise become as he had been: would talk, listen, advise. Above all he would be there at Keeper's Lodge where he had always been. Matty and Flora would cook invalid meals, Esther would carry dishes back and forth in a basket. Deaf to reason, blind to probability, he groped in his own darkness for respite from remorse and found rest from his anguish in a picture of Thomas at ease in an armchair in his own home.

The dream became obsessive. It must be as he hoped. Helpless, impractical, ruined, broken in health, he could do one positive thing: he could make sure that

Thomas, having lost so much, would always have a roof over his head, his own roof. Keeper's Lodge was the only unencumbered property left to him. He would give it to Thomas as tangible proof of his remorse and love.

The plan revived him. One day in March he made the now familiar journey to the hospital and found a change. The nurse no longer hovered ready to shoo him away at the end of five minutes. Thomas had been eased from months of lying flat on his back. The upper part of his body was slightly propped on pillows. At the sight of Aumery his mouth fell open in a loose smile.

'He's better?'

'We think he can go home soon,' the nurse said, evading the question.

When he left, Aumery went straight to his solicitor and ordered him to draw up a deed of gift making over the Lodge to Thomas Godwain.

The solicitor was hesitant. 'Can you afford to do this, Mr Aumery?'

Aumery smiled. His plan was so obviously right, so straightforward, responsible and just, that he was not even irritated by the prosaic little man on whom he looked down from the pinnacle of a rare confidence.

'I meant to say,' the man of law pointed out, 'have you given due thought to your wife's interests – and your daughter's?'

Flora? It could make no difference to her whether the Godwains lived at the Lodge rent-free or owned it. And Esther? It had not previously occurred to him, but now, with all the satisfaction of a dutiful parent, he saw that his scheme would benefit her too. She would marry Daniel. Some day the Lodge would be his, to share with Esther until they could find a more suitable home.

'Certainly,' he said, 'I have given the matter careful thought.'

They brought Thomas home in May, a day of soft sunshine. Lambs leapt and gambolled in the field behind the Lodge as they carried him up the path. A blackbird piped him into the little sitting-room, where the lattice stood open to the scent of wallflowers. They hoisted him into a special chair where he half lay, arms and legs dangling, head askew against the high cushions. Prince licked his hand and laid his head on his lap.

'You're home, love,' Bertha said, weeping.

'That's better, isn't it, Dad?' Daniel's throat swelled.

'He knows,' Bertha said, valiantly defying the barrier of his clouded mind.

Perhaps he did know. Sometimes, after long spells when he seemed no more than a hulk of shattered flesh, he muttered words that were recognizable. Bertha learned to interpret them as simple demands like a baby's cry and persuaded herself that he understood when she told him about the poultry, the vegetable patch and what was going on in Wood Aston.

People sent pig's fry, chickens, cakes, soup and meat pies. They lent bed-linen, knitted cardigans, bed-socks and shawls. They visited, sat with Thomas to give Bertha a free hour or two, and went away shaking their heads.

Everyone was kind in sending this and that. Kindest of all was Miss Angovil, who sent Clairy.

CHAPTER 8

'Yes,' Miss Angovil told Esther, 'it will be a sacrifice, but I must not think of my own comfort when the Godwains are in such trouble. I can spare Clairy for two afternoons a week. After all, she is entitled to some free time. Spedding and I will manage. For a while.'

'It's very kind.'

'Well, the idea just came to me. I don't know how ...' She reflected, genuinely puzzled. Was it something Clairy had said? 'She'll be a godsend to the Godwains, and the walk in the fresh air will do her good.'

Clairy in her grey skirt and jacket and felt hat became a familiar figure as she walked back and forth between Priest's House and Keeper's Lodge. On these occasions she did not wear her maid's uniform. It was as a private person that she took off her jacket in the front bedroom at the Lodge, slipped out of her good skirt and covered her old one with an all-enveloping black apron preparatory to setting about the cleaning and dusting. In the sense that the Lodge had never been sprucer, she proved, as Miss Angovil promised, a godsend.

Gradually the range of her activities extended to the sick-room, formerly the sitting-room, where Bertha spent most of her time.

'I'll give Mr Godwain his tea,' she said one day during her second week. 'You can sit in the porch for a while. It's a lovely day.'

It felt strange to sit under the fox's mask, glancing in occasionally through the open door to see Clairy carrying tea things to the invalid and to hear her low murmur as she held a cup to his lips and wiped his chin. Bertha closed her eyes in the warm sunshine and dozed a little.

That same afternoon, as Clairy was about to leave, the doctor called. In the manner of the district he gave a perfunctory knock and walked in. A young woman in a grey skirt and well-cut white blouse was coming down the stairs.

'May I take your hat?' Together with her maid's cap and apron Clairy had discarded the respectful 'sir' and 'ma'am'. Her manner was polite but not submissive.

'You're a visitor? A relative?'

'A friend.' Clairy put his hat on a chair, the only piece of furniture there was room for at the foot of the stairs, wished him good afternoon and walked off down the path.

'I'm glad to see you have a friend to help you.' The doctor watched her departure from the window.

'A friend?' Bertha was momentarily at a loss. 'You mean Clairy. She's the maid at Miss Angovil's.'

'Indeed! And where did Miss Angovil find a young woman like that? My wife complains that there are no servants to be found these days.' He turned to his patient. 'He seems flushed. Has anything disturbed him?'

'It'll likely be the heat,' Bertha suggested.

The doctor's favourable impression of Clairy would have come as a surprise to Bertha if she had been alert enough to feel surprise. The past few months had exhausted her to the point of numbness. Bad feet, swollen legs, interrupted meals, above all the deep sorrow with which she nursed the broken creature who had once been the strong, kind, humorous husband she had been so proud of, would have been too much for most women. She rarely went to bed, but snoozed in a chair by his bed. Consequently there were days when she could scarcely drag herself about. Her response to Clairy had been one of dumb acceptance of an extra pair of hands in whose owner she took no interest, especially as Clairy made no demands on her attention and was indeed the most unobtrusive young woman that Bertha – now that she had been roused to think of her – had ever known.

She didn't talk much, but she would listen without interrupting when Bertha's overcharged feelings found expression in a rambling monologue addressed to no-one but herself; and if she let out things she had kept bottled up and Clairy heard, it didn't matter, Clairy herself being a person that didn't matter. But she didn't mind giving a hand with Thomas, although he disliked being fed or washed by anyone but his own wife. He would shrink back in his chair and look bothered when Clairy went near him, but she paid no attention.

'It's his condition, Mrs Godwain,' she would say. 'He doesn't know what he's doing.'

'I don't know,' Bertha said one afternoon when Clairy was ironing in the kitchen, 'what's to become of us. Sometimes I wonder why the Good Lord in his mercy doesn't take Thomas unto Himself instead of letting him suffer like this.'

'What would you do, Mrs Godwain, if your husband died?' The question was put with the polite interest of an outsider as she took a hot iron from the bar. 'Would you stay here at the Lodge?' She spat on the iron and watched the drops sizzle on the hot metal.

' Well, I don't know.' Bertha sagged in the rocking-chair and peered wearily into the future. 'Likely I'd go to Sadie, my older sister on the other side of Hudmorton. She's a widow and we'd rub along well enough together. It would depend on Daniel. The Lodge'll come to him and he'll be getting married some day . . .'

She yawned and closed her eyes and Clairy went on ironing.

Esther was walking up the road from Wood Aston one afternoon with a heavy basket on her arm when Major Lincoln overtook her in his dog-cart.

'Let me give you a lift.' He took her basket and helped her up. 'This is too heavy for you to carry so far.'

Esther explained that she had been buying a few groceries for Mrs Godwain at the one shop in Wood Aston.

'I'm going to the Lodge too. I'm glad we shall be arriving together. To tell you the truth, I'm a little worried as to whether I've done the right thing.'

He had unearthed from one of his outhouses a stout wheeled invalid chair and had it cleaned and repaired, and was about to deliver it.

'If only he can be got into it,' Esther said. 'I don't know how it can be managed, but it would be wonderful if he could be out of doors and be wheeled about a little. He's spent all his life in the open air.'

'If you could hold the chair steady while Mrs Godwain and I hoist him into it . . .'

As it happened a fourth pair of hands was available, this being one of Clairy's days at the Lodge. Esther's first instinctive wish that it had been otherwise was quite unreasonable. Clairy proved, as usual, to be both useful and efficient, and helped them to move the chair from the dog-cart to the house, where a discussion was held as to the wisdom or otherwise of the plan.

'What harm can it do him?' Bertha asked. 'Things couldn't be much worse for him than they are now, and it'll very likely buck him up a bit.'

Very likely it did. A glimmer of understanding lit his dull eyes. When they had got him into the chair he managed to hold his weakly lolling head more steadily. Bertha ran a comb through his hair and wiped his nose as if he were a child going on a Sunday School outing. The fresh air seemed to revive him. They pushed the chair into the little garden and left it facing west towards Long Rake.

'He's in his element,' Bertha said, 'bless his heart.'

'Oh, it's a success, your plan,' Esther told the major. 'It will make such a difference.'

Lincoln took his leave, looking back over the gate as he closed it. From where he stood Thomas himself could not be fully seen: his unseemliness did not mar the picture of an old-fashioned garden full of flowers, with three women grouped about an invalid. Esther knelt by the chair stroking Thomas's hand and looking into his flabby face for some recognizable sign of her old friend. Bertha, her hand on the chair, had her back to the gate. The other young woman stood a little apart. Who was she? A relation? She alone of the three was not looking at Thomas. She was looking at Esther.

For a full minute Lincoln stayed there, on the point of submitting to a curious impulse to go back – or at least not to go away. There had been times in the past when, in very different circumstances from this and sometimes too late, he had sensed danger: had actually smelt it as a component of the air. He smelt it now, as light but as pervasive as the scent of stocks and lilies in Bertha's flowerbeds. From Lady Green, invisible below Scaur Crag, came the blood-chilling cry of a peacock, in raucous contrast to the quiet hour of sunlit grass and motionless white clouds above Long Rake. Was there a more subtle disharmony, a clash of contrasting elements of a more disturbing kind between the softness of Esther's compassion and the detachment of the other in whose steady observation there was neither softness nor compassion, but a concentration entirely out of place, to be felt but not accounted for?

Without warning, for an instant, with the wonder and pain of resurrection, Lincoln felt a change of heart. Concern – more than that – an impulse close to protective tenderness, reminded him that he had once been capable of love and had loved deeply. At the same time his memory was purged of the suffering love had brought him; distant ghosts faded into forgetfulness. For one heaven-sent moment he could feel again, and

113

with a rush of gratitude, as for rain after drought. It passed. He drove home to face the long twilight alone in Barbarrow's empty rooms.

One of Bertha's many trials was Aumery. As she said, she couldn't get stirred with him cluttering the place. On the other hand she was fully alive to his gener-osity in making over the Lodge to Thomas, even if he couldn't afford to pay him a pension after all he'd done for the family. And Aumery's remorse was so tragically evident in his altered face and manner that she checked her irritation. After all, the mester never tired of wheeling Thomas out in his chair and sitting with him for hours on end.

The road was too rough and steep for an invalid chair. The only comparatively level ground was the stretch of grass across which a path led from the Lodge to the edge of the Scaur, where it turned to the left and went downhill in the lee of a wall. On that gentle slope Aumery wheeled the chair back and forth so many times that the path grew smooth and was doubled in width. Facing westward, Thomas would show signs of interest, though only the most anxiously attentive eyes would recognize them; his expression was less dull and he would try to steady his head, as if to look down on Lady Green and over the wood to the Rake still meant something to him, or so Aumery persuaded himself.

His dream that the old companionship would some day be restored must have persisted against all reason, judging by his reaction when he understood at last that the dream would never be fulfilled. Enlightenment came suddenly and from an unexpected source. It happened late one afternoon when he arrived at the Lodge, just after the doctor had left. By that time Dr Whitman came only when called, not because the Godwains would never be able to pay his bill – to do him justice that would not have weighed with him – but because there was nothing he could do for the patient.

It was some weeks since his last visit. Bertha had been obliged to send for him: for some days Thomas had been restless and uncomfortable in some new way.

It was Clairy who put her finger on the trouble – a development Bertha would never have thought of. 'He's always wanting to look down to Lady Green. You've seen for yourself, Mrs Godwain, how pleased he is when Mr Aumery pushes him along the path to the Scaur. He likes to look at the places he used to see every day.'

It was so obvious that Bertha wondered she hadn't thought of it herself. She and Clairy got into the habit of pushing Thomas out on to the path when Mr Aumery was not about, and leaving him there while they got on with their work.

'Look!' Clairy called Bertha to the window one day. 'He's trying to move the chair himself so that he can see down to Lady Green,' and added, 'You did remember to fix the brake?'

There was no need to reply. Bertha always remembered and went back once or twice to make sure. She had missed the encouraging signs of movement. By the time she got to the window Thomas was sitting in the usual lifeless way, but she was cheered by Clairy's report. 'I do believe he's improving a bit,' she said, but when she went out to make sure that he was comfortable and pat his puffed hand, she was surprised by the determination with which he tried to grasp hers – as if for security. It seemed best to wheel him back to the garden path.

'He's looking flushed again,' she said anxiously. 'I think we'd better have the doctor to him.'

'He can't tell me what he's feeling,' she told Dr Whitman when he was making his examination, 'any more than a baby or a sick dog, but that doesn't mean he can't think. It's not knowing what he's thinking that puts me about. Is he any worse, Doctor?'

'I don't think so. Your husband is a strong man.' But he talked of the slow but inevitable deterioration of the spinal condition and locomotary nerves, prescribed another sedative and left, despondent, passing Aumery at the gate without stopping to talk.

The sitting-room door was open. Seeing that Bertha was attending to Thomas with bucket and sponge, Aumery waited in the lobby. Presently the young woman in the black apron who helped about the house came out of the kitchen, carrying over one arm several folded towels and in the other hand a kettle of hot water. Aumery saw her without interest but some vestige of the courtesy which he had exercised so pleasantly long ago reminded him that he was in the presence of a young female.

' Allow me.' He took the heavy kettle. 'And how is Thomas today? I thought him a little better —'

'No, he's no better. He'll never be better. The doctor has just said so. He'll get slowly worse until he's no better than a vegetable, which is what he is now, more or less.' She laid the towels on the chair. 'I can manage the kettle now.'

Aumery stared at her in horror. This pale-faced woman in her black apron, with a few words spoken without pity or regret, had wrought a change in him that almost sixty years' experience of life had failed to achieve. She had stripped him of his protective dream and delivered him up naked to the hideous truth. There was nothing left to shield him from the pain of knowing that Thomas was doomed to a living death – nor hide him from the truth about himself. He had acknowledged that the fault was his. The year, the month, the day, the fateful moment had been of his choosing. He was not merely the instrument but the cause of his friend's destruction. But that admission had not gone far enough. He had still refused to believe the worst, and had taken refuge from it yet again in self-deception. Every inadequacy in his life, every postponement, every feeble evasion had doomed him to this final confrontation.

This second blow, as cruel as the accident itself, found him already weakened by months of suffering. Who was she, this creature of evil tidings who had stripped his spirit bare and left him no hiding place, no hope? Her eyes seemed to him like no other eyes he had seen: blue-green, brilliant and hard as polished stone under brows like dark wings. To his deranged vision she seemed diabolical – an infernal messenger. Sweat beaded his brow. He looked out on a wilderness of pain. But since there was nothing left – no hope, no light – there need be no hesitation either. For once he knew with certainty what must be done. There rose in him the strength to do it. He went into the sitting-room. Bertha turned in surprise and threw a towel over Thomas's nakedness. Aumery knelt at his side and grasped his hand.

'Goodbye, Thomas,' he said. 'I . . . Goodbye, old friend.'

He went out, carefully avoided flower-heads leaning over the garden path and walked steadily away.

It was still daylight when Clairy left the Lodge to walk home to Priest's House. The afterglow of sunset had faded. The thin arc of a new moon hung in the southern sky above the woods. She chose the field path rather than the road, and went unhurriedly downhill in the shade of the wall. Rabbits crouched in the rough pasture to her right. Below, in its wooded hollow, Lady Green pointed slender chimneys towards a quiet sky. The paths had become familiar. She could have walked them in the dark, and sometimes did, finding her way by natural signposts: the denseness of a pleached hedge, the sound of water, the scent of sweet cicely growing by the footbridge.

Entering the wood, she walked in cool green dusk. Her feet moved soundlessly over deep layers of leaf mould. She was at home here, too, not only on the untrodden paths, but in secret dells and glades where she could be alone. As Miss Angovil said, the silly things that other girls did were of no interest to Clairy. She had her own interests, her own purposes.

These no doubt occupied her without interruption until she came close to the Aston oak and saw in the weird green light a dead man hanging from one of the branches. He dangled like a stoat or a crow hung on a gamekeeper's line, but, unlike the creatures of the wood, he was out of keeping, a grotesque intrusion on the tree's silent dignity. In death, as in life, Edwin Aumery was a misfit.

Clairy felt a wave of nausea, but only for a moment before she went closer to confirm that it was, as she thought, the man whom she had spoken to only an hour or two ago. The change in his appearance might have daunted her; she remained calm. Not only did she neither scream, faint, nor vomit: neither did she run for help. Withdrawing to a little distance, she considered – her opaline eyes as striking in their very different way as those of the dead man. That is, an observer would have been impressed by their gem-like brilliance, as of light reflected from frozen surfaces. Having considered, as if several options had been open to her, she turned back the way she had come and walked quickly, never running, to Lady Green.

CHAPTER 9

From the window of her warm sitting-room, Miss Angovil counted the black umbrellas as they moved in groups of two and three towards the church gate. Rain had been falling steadily all morning. Fallen leaves, yellow and brown, lay thick on the grass and on her flagged path.

'I'm going now, ma'am.'

Clairy had come quietly into the room. She wore a full-length waterproof cape over her black skirt and jacket, and a close-fitting black hat. It suited her rather narrow face, giving it a devotional look except for the unexpected dark, wing-like eyebrows. The gem-like eyes on this solemn occasion were suitably downcast. She looked unassuming and highly respectable, as one would expect: after all she had been recommended – 'sincerely' recommended – by a minister of the Baptist church. It was gratifying, too, that she contrived to dress herself so well, though always plainly, on eight shillings a week.

'Two funerals in just over three months,' Miss Angovil sighed. 'Who would have thought it? And this one so different from the last one.'

'Yes, ma'am,' Clairy said and presently her solitary black umbrella moved across the green to join the others. It concealed her head and shoulders as the cape concealed the rest of her person. Together they deprived her of identity. She could have been almost anybody.

Esther, too, was achingly conscious of the difference between this funeral and the last. Every active adult in Wood Aston, and many from Unnerstone and Low Carr, had come to pay their last respects to Thomas Godwain. There had never been such a drying out and shrinking of funeral blacks as there was to be in the coming week. But as she stood in the rain watching Thomas's coffin being lowered into the grave, it was for her father that Esther's heart ached.

'They're together now,' she thought. 'Two faithful friends.' But she didn't believe it. Thomas had qualified not only for a place in heaven and the just reward of everlasting peace, but also an earthly resting place among his forefathers. She bowed her head and wept – it was an occasion for weeping – but her tears were for the grave in the far corner where the churchyard rambled into unhallowed ground. For her father there had been no solidly massed country mourners, like those behind her and around the open grave.

She was standing as close to Daniel as the umbrellas allowed, close enough to feel his suppressed sob. Her mother was on her left, Daniel on her right side and beyond him Bertha and on Bertha's right, Clairy, between Bertha and her two sisters, like a relation. Bertha herself didn't know how it had happened like that or quite how it was that she had seen so much of Clairy since the accident four days ago. 'Seen' was not the right word. Since Thomas was found at the foot of the Scaur, his poor mutilated body cruelly twisted, his head battered on the boulders, his chair wrecked by the fall – since that first terrible sight of him, Bertha had seen nothing else. She had moved and spoken as if in a dream peopled by shapes she recognized without feeling their reality.

How such a thing could have happened, no-one knew. Since Aumery's death Thomas had become more restless. Whether or not he understood that the master would never come again, he had seemed always to be expecting him. It was pitiful – his struggle to convey to Bertha that he wanted to be pushed out on to the path to look for him. It was Clairy who interpreted his feeble gestures and efforts to speak. She was the only one who understood what he wanted, just as she had been the only one who had noticed his attempts to jerk his chair in the direction of the Scaur and his favourite view.

Once or twice – Bertha would never forgive herself – she had been forced to leave him on the path while she ran back to see to a saucepan or the oven, but never so near the edge as to be in danger. (Had she *always* put on the brake, waiting to hear the final click?) On the afternoon when it happened she had had such a cruel headache that Clairy had persuaded her to lie down on the bed upstairs, with the door shut and the blinds drawn. If she had been up and about, it would never have happened, as Clairy, presumably to comfort her, had said. But it had not comforted her; instead it had made her feel guilty, more so as time went on. To the end of her days she would remember Clairy's urgent voice calling her from her bed, and although everyone said what a blessing it was that Clairy was the one to find him, Bertha couldn't feel the blessedness of it at all. A chair with well-oiled wheels and the wind behind it on a sloping path, they said . . .

Surreptitiously Esther felt for Daniel's hand. It was hot despite the chill rain – and thin. Their touch united them, but by how tenuous a thread, soon broken when Daniel was given a spade and nudged into casting earth into the grave . . . And then all but those most closely connected with the family were moving away. Wreaths of chrysanthemums and lilies, rain-drenched, lay waiting to be heaped on the grave. Esther had time to breathe, 'Whatever shall we do without them both?' before Major Lincoln ushered her and Flora to his motor car. How kind he had been, not only in bringing them to the funeral, but in visiting, and advising them when there was no-one else to turn to. Daniel, for once speechless, took his mother and aunts to the undertaker's coach. There was room for Clairy, too. She would help with the funeral tea at the Lodge, almost, Esther thought with a pang, like a daughter of the house.

Since the night when Clairy had come to Lady Green with the news of its master's death, Esther's attitude to her had changed. Actually she had not previously had an attitude to Clairy. One did not give much thought to other people's servants except to treat them kindly and courteously, as a matter of course. On that terrible night she herself had opened the door to Clairy's knock, had seen her dark against the softer darkness of the summer sky behind her, had heard her cool voice, 'I've come to tell you . . .' It was unjust to feel a revulsion from the bringer of evil tidings. It must have taken courage; most people would shrink from breaking such news. But to Esther, faint and sick with horror, Clairy seemed part of the horror. Her first recoil was instinctive, but even later, when the sickness and panic had left her, and later still, when the first agony of grief had passed, Esther could not detach Clairy from the circumstances of her father's death. If only someone else could have brought the news! If only some other sort of person could have found him!

After the funeral, although Thomas was no longer there to be looked after, Clairy continued to devote her free time to poor Mrs Godwain at the Lodge, with the full approval of Miss Angovil, who would never stand in the way if one of her servants felt compelled to do her duty as a Christian. Even so, Esther was surprised that Clairy could be spared so often and wondered if, like Spedding, she was being spoiled. She was certainly given – or took – a good deal of freedom. Occasionally she went to see her aunt in town or to do shopping for Miss Angovil and possibly for herself as well. She was always well dressed, increasingly so for a woman on so slender a wage, but her clothes were chosen with such quiet taste as to arouse little comment in the village. It was only at close quarters that their quality – that of her new white silk blouse for instance – was apparent. Esther eyed its heavy sheen and mother-of-pearl buttons with a touch of envy.

After her father's death she had never gone to the Lodge without hoping that Clairy wouldn't be there; but it was no time to keep away when Thomas's growing restlessness made it more than ever necessary to give a helping hand. Daniel had been at home for the whole of August and had done his best to comfort her, but he was as much needed by his parents as she was by her remorseful, desolate mother.

'We couldn't have managed without Clairy,' Daniel had once said. 'You know, she's intelligent too. It's a pity she hasn't had more education, but she seems determined to make up for lost time. Have you noticed how her speech has improved? She's picking up your way of speaking. It's amazing how she's got on. As a matter of fact, I've read her some of the notes for my thesis.'

Esther was taken aback to find that Clairy knew more about the famous work than she did. Inevitably there were times when the three of them were thrown together in the garden or in the kitchen at the Lodge. Daniel, of course, dominated the discussion of those vast themes so appealing to the young: the meaning of life, death, religion.

'I know how you're feeling, sweetheart,' he said, 'but it's good for you to talk about such things and try to see your father's death as part of the long history of human suffering.'

That was before his own father's death. Esther had been unable to fix her mind on the long history of human suffering, but she heard in his voice and saw in his eyes how much he loved her – and she was comforted. If only Clairy hadn't been there! With what seemed tactful discretion, she had withdrawn to the far side of the table and was shelling peas – a helpful family friend. Esther marvelled that Miss Angovil's colourless maid had blossomed into a person of such . . . a person who . . . Her thoughts petered out, her head ached. The memory of her mother alone at Lady Green brought her to her feet. When Daniel went out to fetch wood for the fire, she slipped away without saying goodbye. Usually he walked home with her. It would have been hard to explain why she wanted to be alone when she wanted even more to be with him; or why her dislike of leaving him alone with Clairy should be even faintly tinged with fear.

The year drew to a close. Aumery had been dead six months and his estate, if it could be so called, was still to be wound up. It was typical of the family's ill luck that the urgent demand for land immediately after the war had rapidly slumped. If the estate had been offered for sale in the previous year it might have fetched a sum sufficient to pay off the mortgage and leave enough for a small annuity. By 1920 interest in land, especially neglected woodland, had evaporated and the house, low-lying and in sad need of modernization, hung on the market. The future craze for antique furniture lay far ahead: the Aumery four-posters, the Elizabethan court cupboard, the table where six princes were said to have dined, the Hepplewhite chairs and Italian mirrors were sniffed over by grudging dealers, and went for a fraction of the price they would have fetched years later.

Eventually the bank holding the mortgage found a prospective buyer, a successful forge-master, and the sale was being negotiated at a keenly argued price. Esther and Flora waited in suspense, fearing the worst, yet unable to believe that they would be penniless. Mr Greyburn, the solicitor, had assured them that by February the complications would be disentangled, but by the end of April they were still waiting to hear whether anything had been salvaged from the wreck of the Aumery inheritance. To Flora's relief, Matty had given in her notice and gone home to prepare for her wedding to Raymond Grote of Broom Farm. Her departure left them alone in the big house, but it saved Flora the awkwardness of having to dismiss her; and there was a sense of freedom in being able to live like paupers without their poverty-stricken ways being seen and made known.

On a Saturday in May the two of them were in Flora's room, where Esther had spread out the contents of her mother's jewel boxes on the bed.

'They don't amount to much.' Flora picked up a garnet brooch, part of a parure which had belonged to her mother. 'No-one wants this sort of old-fashioned thing. But the pearls are good, and the rings. All the other things are gone. There'll be nothing for you, darling.'

'It doesn't matter.' Esther turned to the window. 'But I hadn't realized that losing Father would make me feel so impoverished. I don't mean because there's no money, but because we seem to have no-one to belong to, except each other.'

'I feel as if I'd been battered and beaten and thrown out into the cold. It serves me right. I didn't value what I had and I deserved to lose it – but not in that terrible way. But you shouldn't feel like that. You have Daniel to love and care for you. You'll make a new life, not what we hoped for you, but you'll be happy in a different way.'

'I believe Father thought of himself as a sacrifice. He offered himself up to atone for what happened to Thomas. He used to tell me about the old rituals in the days when trees like the Aston oak were worshipped.'

'He wasn't himself. Your father wasn't like that – wild and sad and desperate. He was such a civilized man.' Flora brought out the word as she might have handled one of the brooches, feeling that it had lost its value and was perhaps out of date. 'And you will always have a home, you and Daniel. I thought it so strange when your father told me about the Lodge but now – it's the one thing saved from the creditors.'

She wondered if this was the time to urge upon Esther the wisdom of an early marriage. Daniel's training would end in July, he would earn a mere pittance at first, but he could support a wife in a house of their own, and in time he would be promoted. She herself would have to earn a living of some sort. Time and again she had reached the conclusion, more in astonishment than dismay, as she contemplated a way of life so far beyond her wildest imaginings as to be beyond anxiety too. She had no talents, no training, no experience – nothing to offer that other people would pay her for. In the silent hours before falling asleep or on waking in the early light, she strove to see herself as housekeeper to an old gentleman or companion to an invalid lady, but her imagination invariably came to rest upon a vision of herself seated in a station waiting-room in hat, coat and gloves with her luggage at her feet. It would be restful. They used to keep good fires in station waiting-rooms, she recalled. She would sit well back from the swing doors, out of the draught, and watch other people coming and going. She would stay there until . . . She would simply stay there for ever.

'There's the house in Hudmorton,' Esther reminded her.

'A slum – that's all it can be by this time.'

Flora's father had left her, in addition to £5,000, a row of six houses in an unfashionable district of the town. The money had long gone. Five of the houses had been sold, and the sums they fetched had been swallowed up by Lady Green. If the last house were sold, the proceeds would barely keep Flora and Esther for a year. Nevertheless the house existed as a last resort if, as seemed likely, they should find themselves homeless.

'We'll think of something.' Esther's voice had changed. She had seen Daniel coming down from the Scaur and was transported instantly into another world.

'I'll put these things away. You go and enjoy your walk.'

The day was mild as they sauntered along the riverside path. Occasionally Daniel put his arm round her waist and lifted her over a muddy pool as he had done in the old carefree days when they were children. The moist softness of the air and the invisible stirring of the trees into new life were both a reminder and a promise of better days.

'Let's forget all the problems and sad things.' Esther took a deep breath of air filled with the sound and scent of running water. Colour was returning to her cheeks. Sorrow had refined her beauty, her face was thinner, her eyes large and more pensive. 'We've talked them over so many times that I'm sick to death of them.' It was a natural reaction, if not a wise one: an opportunity to talk seriously about their plans for the future was lost.

'Agreed. Let's talk . . .' Of graves, of worms and epitaphs, Daniel had almost said, but he substituted in the nick of time 'of shoes and ships and sealing wax'.

He heard his own voice as if it were someone else's. It must be tiredness. Last night, and for several nights before, he had studied until the small hours. He, too, was sick to death of problems and sad things, and with good reason. The events of the past year had affected him more deeply than the war had done. In the trenches he had been afraid and had schooled himself to recognize fear as a natural reaction; the disease might be incurable, but the symptoms could be controlled. He had kept his head, remained deaf to foul talk, endured mud, filth and vermin, seen comrades blown to bits, stepped over bloated corpses, and had survived without visible scars, though not unchanged; only to suffer, a few months after his homecoming, the heartbreaking deterioration and death of the father who had been his wise and stalwart comrade.

It was his nature to make excessive demands on himself. The self-discipline he valued had so far been sufficient protection against stress, but his nervous state was volatile: he may have been nearer to breaking point than he knew. He had lately been troubled by dreams. Men he knew to be dead had risen, to grope, bleeding and blinded, and fall before he could reach them. He saw his father falling from a great height and was himself rooted to the earth when he tried to save him. He would wake, drenched in sweat and unrefreshed.

His cheekbones now had a constant flush that worried his mother, who accused him of being all skin and bone: small wonder, when he existed on hastily snatched meals and divided his time between visits home and spells of feverishly hard work in the College library or in his unheated, ill-lit room at his Aunt Maud's.

For a few minutes they were content not to talk at all. Both, and at the same time, had been forced to realize the gravity of their responsibilities. To the unthinking closeness of their early years had been added the strange similarity of their more recent experiences: each had lost a father in violent circumstances. Their deaths, separated by so short an interval, had ended a rare attachment as deep and constant as that between their children. In them the bond of first love had been strengthened, as the death of a parent strengthens the bond between brother and sister.

Daniel ought to have known how badly the Aumerys' affairs had gone wrong. Indeed he did know theoretically, but he had grown used to his mother's mournful prophecies concerning the fate of Lady Green, and had listened sympathetically to Esther's diffident half-confidences; but he had not yet fully realized that people of the Aumerys' background could fall into such dire straits. The homeless poor occupied a special place in his thoughts. They existed at a slight distance in time and space, to be approached, dealt with and saved when he would be free to devote his life to them. It did not occur to him that one of them was walking beside him with her hand in his.

'He doesn't know,' Esther was thinking, 'how bad things are. He still doesn't know. How can I tell him that we shall soon have to go away?'

If only he would say right out 'We must get married.' If only he would say it now. There would still be the problem of the mothers. If Bertha went to live with her sister, would Flora live with them at the Lodge – and later, in some cosy little schoolhouse?

Her hand in his was small and soft. Her closeness thrilled and troubled him. For once he was not at ease. The newly languid air – the bird-song, the smell of fresh earth – made him restless. The longing to possess her completely, to love and worship her and find relief in her unfailing tenderness, was becoming a need only less strong than the need to repress it. He couldn't even tell her: she wouldn't understand. She was beyond his reach: they must wait for years. There seemed no end to the waiting, year after year, he thought, in sudden exhaustion of spirit. There was no way except to go on working. Even now he should be working.

They had come to the end of the lane, to the ruined barn, the stile and stepping-stones: a place of meetings and partings, of beginnings and endings, as it had seemed to her on the summer day nearly two years ago when they had waited for Matty. It was just the same, except that the roughly rectangular space seemed wider and lighter between branches still in half-leaf. Winter had thinned the grasses and nettles so that objects hidden in summer now lay open to view.

'There's another wheel,' Daniel said. 'That makes four with the two in the barn.' He looked inside. 'They're still there. It was a four-wheeled cart – and painted yellow – that came to the end of the road, and to the end of its days, here.'

'Daniel!' An unfamiliar urgency in Esther's voice surprised him. 'I know whose cart it was.'

'Well – whose?'

'The man I saw. Oh, ages ago. I must have told you.'

'What man?'

'He frightened me.' She had wakened to the ghostly light of dawn on the looking-glass. 'When we were here the last time you said that if a man were desperate he could make himself a cart.' The idea of a desperate man had almost touched off a memory of white-faced fury – a stumbling horse. 'I remember now. It was the day you found that girl in a blanket.'

'Good Lord! You mean the man who might have dumped her at the school gate. This must have been as far as he got – in the cart, at any rate.'

The incident and its unexpected recall roused a thrill of interest. They exclaimed, wondered, rummaged for more relics.

'I wonder why he came this way. He can't have known that there was no way out for a cart.'

'Did he abandon it, or did it break down, or both?'

'What did he do with the horse?' Esther remembered more. 'Do you know, that was an upsetting sort of day. For me.'

'Why was that?' Daniel's memory was less distinct, less clearly visual, but he remembered how, in the act of raising the girl, he had seen his future life devoted to the rescue of the oppressed and afflicted. What with one thing and another, he thought grimly, not much progress had been made. The glorious career of a latter-day St George had got off to a poor start.

'Oh, I don't know why. I wasn't used to ugliness and nastiness and strange kinds of behaviour.' Esther raised her voice. She had gone down the little gully and was standing by the stepping-stones. 'And there was something odd about it, wasn't there?'

'It can't have been haphazard.' Daniel watched her run across the stepping-stones to turn and face him, smiling, from the last one. She looked, for a disturbing moment, out of reach: a slight, winsome creature separated from him by more than the fast-flowing stream. In the pale sunlight the water glinted like silver, so that she seemed to stand on the luminous stream itself and not on the common earth. He blinked, dazzled, and when he looked again it was at the hill behind her and the path climbing steeply to Barbarrow.

'I've thought of something,' he called. 'By Jove, what an interesting idea!'

She waited as he came down to the water's edge, watching him with as much interest as if she had never seen him before, as if she didn't know every line and hollow of his face and how his eyes kindled as he stood on the brink of one of his wonderful ideas.

'Suppose,' he stepped on the first stone and came slowly across to join her.

'Yes, I'm supposing,' Esther began the return crossing, moving as he moved.

'That girl. How old would she be?'

'I don't know. Older than me, I should think.' Prissie might have known, but the Coach and Horses had changed hands six months ago, and the Merridons had left Wood Aston. 'Why?'

'It's just possible—' They faced each other in midstream. A stone wobbled under his feet.

'It's just possible that we won't fall in.'

'What if the girl wasn't just being dumped in any old village? Suppose she was being returned.'

'Like a parcel?' It was as a lifeless object that Esther had first seen the girl and had continued to think of her until the very last moment when Barney Trisk had turned his horse into Church Lane. 'She never seemed like a real person.' Then, realizing that the word had other implications, 'Returned? Do you mean that she belonged here? But no-one knew anything about her.'

'Suppose she had been kidnapped years before and was being brought back.'

'Daniel!'

'Look out!' He grasped her firmly by the arms. She had almost lost her balance on the unsteady fifth stone. The bright water swirled and dazzled. They stood for a few seconds rigid – in Esther's case rigid with fascinated speculation.

To Clairy, watching from the stile, the two figures precariously poised face to face, formed a single entity. They were united like a piece of sculpture from which no part can be removed without destroying the whole. Their voices had floated up to her as she came across the Grotes' field to the stile and paused on the second rung where she could watch and listen. For how long? Both were rather startled to see her there.

How like her, Esther thought as Daniel led her to safety, to turn up like that and in such an unexpected place. Not without effort she contrived a pleasant greeting.

'You've been to the farm?'

Clairy came down from the stile and explained that she had used the farm path as a short cut from Unnerstone where she had been buying knitting wool for Miss Angovil. Daniel, who wasn't listening, relieved her of the brown carrier bag and was rewarded by one of Clairy's rare smiles, startling and sudden as sunshine on a grey day.

The three set off homeward, but the path was narrow: it was Clairy who fell behind. She did so in a manner that seemed considerate rather than deferential, though it would have been hard to say how the distinction was achieved.

For the rest of the walk Esther was to feel between her shoulder blades that she was there and to hear her soft tread, steady and purposeful, as if, though following, she were going her own way. The sun was still high: there were no shadows, and yet it was as if a shadow walked behind them and would somehow overtake them. Silly to think like that. It was only Clairy. But she had spoiled things by tagging along. And there was always something about her, more than could be seen on the surface. What was she thinking as she walked so steadily behind them?

The few paces that separated her from them made it possible for the other two to talk without needing to include her, not that there was anything intimate in the topic they had hit upon.

'If he was bringing her back,' Esther said, ' why didn't he do it properly instead of leaving her in the village and driving on?'

'I don't know. It certainly didn't make sense to bring a cart this way. But look here, he may have already gone to Barbarrow by the road and found the place empty, locked, bolted and barred. For some reason it was necessary for him to get rid of her, which he did, and then he rushed off at top speed along what seemed a by-road. He didn't know it led nowhere. Suppose he unharnessed and rode off through the fields. Just a theory and far-fetched, I admit. But she would be about the right age, and the chap was a bad lot, from what you said.'

'But she was so disgustingly dirty and stupid. It couldn't have been the Lincoln girl. I'm sure if she'd been at all a nice person I would have felt it. I had quite the opposite feeling about her. If she had come from a good family it would somehow have shown.'

'Wouldn't it depend on what had happened to her after the kidnapping?' It was the cue for Daniel to propound his favourite theory, that environmental influences may be as strong as hereditary factors. 'And another thing – she was very young, wasn't she, when she was taken away? If a child is separated from its mother at an early age there's a real danger that its emotional development will be stunted.'

'Like those twins?'

'Yes, I'm afraid the little dears would suffer, but they would sacrifice themselves willingly in the interests of science. But when the primal bond between mother and child is broken, the child may grow up incapable of normal feeling.'

'You mean – love?'

'Love, sympathy, pity. What's more, it wouldn't understand that other people have such feelings.'

'I should hate to think that the Lincolns' little girl might have turned out like that. You don't really believe—?'

'That she was the one we found? As a matter of fact I don't. And if she was, we're never likely to know it. In any case, it's a waste of time to theorize on the basis of a supposition. Still, whatever happened,' he concluded as they came to Esther's back gate, 'it was rotten bad luck for Lincoln. He's a sounder chap than I took him for. He was good to my father.'

Conscious of the major's many acts of friendship, Esther felt uneasily that they had been making light of a subject that might be painful to him if any hint of it should reach him.

'We oughtn't to mention this to anyone.' She had lowered her voice. 'Do you think she heard?'

Clairy had passed them with a nod, evidently intending to return to the village by way of the Lodge.

'She could have heard.' Daniel was remorseful. 'I'll have a word with her. She isn't the sort to go about blabbing. In fact she strikes me as being pretty good at minding her own business.'

Tomorrow he would be preparing his work for the week and would return to town as usual in the evening. Parting was never easy. Today it was harder than ever to let him go. Their time together had been so short, to be remembered long after as a stolen hour suffused with the gentle radiance of a day in May.

'It's been wonderful.' She waited for his embrace and was amused when he drew back and kissed her hand instead. Oh, she knew why. He had told her: she must not tempt him.

'Some day,' she said. It was a phrase they often used instead of goodbye.

'Some day . . .' Years, he thought. How many years? She caught a different note in his voice, as of yearning without hope, and was instantly downcast, as if they were parting for a long time, for ever, as if they were to be separated by an ocean or a war. The mood passed. What was one short week in a whole lifetime?

She tucked in his buttonhole a spray of lady's-smock she had gathered, and laughed at its limpness.

'I told you it wouldn't last.' He cupped her face in his hands and kissed her brow.

He soon caught up with Clairy, who had been walking slowly. They climbed the hill together.

When Esther went up to her mother's room, Flora was at the window. 'That Clairy person.' Flora looked thoughtful. 'What's her other name?'

'I don't know.' There had never been any need to ask. Mother and daughter peered together through the small leaded panes like lost creatures, Esther had sometimes thought, enmeshed in some kind of net. Daniel had once again taken the bag and with her hands free, Clairy had taken off her hat. She was very much a person who could do as she liked.

'I hate to think of her being the one to find Father.' The feeling burst from her with more force than she had intended.

'Oh, Esther!'

Involuntarily their hands met and were held in speechless misery. Presently Flora said, 'I thought Bertha was still at her sister's.'

'Yes. She's coming back next week.'

The two on the hill path had passed out of sight.

'By the way, I want you to do me another favour.' They had exchanged a few words, chiefly about Bertha. It had not occurred to Daniel that she would come home to an empty larder until Clairy mentioned that she would bring a few provisions and help to settle her in.

'A favour?'

An unfamiliar inflection in her voice and a meaningful stealthiness in Clairy's half-smile made him uncomfortable. He reconsidered his words.

'Not a favour exactly. But – I wonder if you overheard what Esther and I were talking about.'

'I'm afraid I wasn't listening.'

'I was only going to ask you, if you had heard, not to repeat it. We should not have been airing our views like that about another person.'

'I did hear you mention Major Lincoln,' Clairy confessed with an air of frankness. 'Miss Aumery is interested in him, I know. She asked me about him once before.'

Again Daniel felt a prick of distaste, and he was astute enough to see this version of Esther's interest in the Barbarrow tragedy as exactly the kind of distortion he was anxious to prevent.

'Mr Lincoln has had to put up with enough gossip and scandalmongering as it is,' he said. 'I merely wanted to urge you not to repeat anything you may have overheard, and I'm sure your discretion can be relied on.'

In response to this school-masterly speech Clairy smiled again. No contrast could have been greater than that between Daniel's earnest injunction and Clairy's smile. It transformed her face, but not altogether for the better: not quite in the same way as when she had smiled her gratitude and yielded up the carrier bag which now, at the Lodge gate, he handed back to her. She didn't take it, not then.

'I'm coming in,' she said and followed him up the path, past the snarling fox and the innocent conch-shells and into the house. Then she did take the bag and throw it aside. It was she who closed the door behind them.

With the door closed it was almost dark in the hall. At first he was blinded by the abrupt change from wide hills and open sky to this narrow place. Still dazed, he found it unfamiliar, its dimensions and spatial values altered. He turned. She was leaning against the door, her face pale against the dark wood. Grey light from the staircase gave it a faint glimmer, less like the softness of skin than the metallic sheen of scales. Gradually, as his eyes became adjusted to the gloom, he saw the outline of her features, head and neck. The unfamiliarity remained. He had never actually looked at her before. It was as if he had never even seen her until now.

She moved. He saw the brilliance of her eyes. Their glitter revealed no feeling: she seemed scarcely human. But he was suddenly aware that there hung in the air between them a recognition of their situation. It united them in unspoken understanding: neither had said a word. The absence of any sound other than the tick of the wall clock intensified their strange isolation and made it intimate. She had contrived it. Her intention was plain. Her nearness, the half-darkness, a suggestion of furtiveness confused him. His heart thumped. She must hear its beat.

She came nearer. She knew that he would stay, trapped by his own imperative need. He knew it too. It was as if the man he had thought himself to be had died, leaving in his place a demented stranger in a world where everything had changed, except – he heard it as if from an immense distance – the tick of the old clock steadily measuring the seconds as it had measured the minutes, hours and years of his innocent boyhood.

CHAPTER 10

People remarked on the change in Daniel Godwain. The kindlier souls blamed it on over-work and worry. His mother might have been more perceptive, had she been at home, but a few days before she was due to return she had received a letter from Daniel in which he urged her to stay longer, even until his summer holidays began, if she liked. It would save expense as well as fuel, and at weekends he could spend two full days on finishing his thesis.

It surprised Bertha that he should think of saving fuel, as there were enough logs and kindling in the wood-shed to last a year; but she was comfortable with her sister and in no hurry to face housekeeping on her own again. In any case, the Lodge was by rights as much Daniel's as hers, she told herself, with a restful yielding up of responsibility.

Daniel felt sick with shame when he read her reply, as sick as when he had written his own letter: the lies were part, and not the least part, of his degradation. Throughout the fervid dream in which he now passed his days and nights, he was under no illusion as to what was happening: he was ruining himself and couldn't help it. From those first electrifying moments when, by the intimacy of her assured touch, Clairy had set his whole body aflame, he was lost to all decency and self-respect, to everything but desire for her.

Time after time, rising from the abyss into which she drew him, he would glimpse the light – only to plunge into darkness again with a compulsive abandonment that horrified him. All that was left of his power to think was directed towards planning their next meeting: at the Lodge, in an outhouse of the unoccupied Coach and Horses, even – to his terror – in her room at Priest's House, and sometimes in secret woodland places he had not known until she took him there.

He couldn't understand how it had happened, and without warning. Nothing had led up to it. He had always been in command of himself, rational, self-confident – arrogantly so, he now felt. In his moments of sanity he looked back across the gulf that separated him from his former cocksure self with a feeling of homesickness; but no homesickness was ever so acute, no return more impossible. Except that he knew what was happening and could trace every step of his folly, it was more like madness. She was not beautiful, certainly not lovable, nor even likeable. Nor was there in her any of the heat and blaze that burned in him. From the beginning she was purposeful, predatory and strangely unemotional, as if for all the lure of her body there was nothing within. Sometimes when he had made elaborate arrangements to come home, had invented excuses or faked illness in order to avoid lectures and spent money he could ill afford on the extra train fare, he would arrive at the Lodge in a fever of anticipation only to find it empty; wait for her in vain until the last possible minute, and go back to town unable to work or eat or sleep.

Once, having cut a morning's lectures, he was coming out of Unnerstone station as his old schoolmaster was going in.

'Hold on a minute.' Mr Horner seized his arm. Daniel had shown signs of passing with little more than a 'Good morning, sir.' 'I've been wanting a word with you.' Deliberately he scanned his former pupil's face until Daniel's eyes fell. 'I don't like the look of you, Daniel. You look as if you'd been burning the candle at both ends, and it's not doing you a ha'porth of good. You haven't gone off the rails, have you?'

'I don't know what you mean, sir.' The answer was puerile and entirely out of character.

'You've been through a bad time – the war, your father's illness and death . . . If I thought it was a naturally run-down state you were in, I'd advise you to keep going until you've got your Certificate and then have a month's holiday out of doors. But I'm wondering if that's all it is. You haven't been to see me lately. I've missed our talks.' And as Daniel remained unhappily silent, 'I won't ask you what you're doing here when you ought to be in the lecture room: that's your business. But I can tell you, Dan, it'll grieve me to the heart if you fall into loose ways and throw away your chance of a distinction in at least some of your papers. You were the best pupil I ever had or could have hoped for.'

'I'll do my best, sir.' It was Clairy's afternoon off. She should be at the Lodge already. At his quickest pace he could be with her in twenty-five minutes.

'I can see you don't want to talk. Just one more thing. I met your tutor, Tom Giles, at that meeting about day continuation courses. Thought you might be there . . . Well, to be frank, Giles is disappointed in you. He saw you as having brains, maturity and enthusiasm to carry all before you.' He released his hold on Daniel's arm. 'Buck up, my boy. Remember that the next few weeks could affect your whole life.' He hesitated. 'Remember too that any moral irregularity would put paid to your career as surely as if you were to fail in all your subjects.'

'Thank you, sir. Thank you very much.'

They parted and Daniel sped to his rendezvous as if leaping headlong into a fire.

While the madness lasted, by one skilful manoeuvre after another he managed to avoid seeing Esther. Instead he wrote to her from Hudmorton, explaining that he had closed the Lodge for a while: he must stay in town until the examination week was over. Coming home would be a distraction he could not afford.

'I love you. I've always loved you,' he added in a desperate, remorseful postscript.

It was true: the only glint of truth in a concoction of lies. He read the letter once more, scarcely able to believe that he had written it, his sense of alienation so complete as he sealed the envelope that he could not imagine Esther ever opening it. The hand that slid it into the pillar box was not his own.

The worst aspect of his suffering was not that he could not see her in the old way when separation had never really parted them. Even when absent, she had suffused his heart and mind with a steady light that brightened into radiance at each reunion. But now, because he dared not, he could not see her in imagination, could not think of her except as a man at the point of death remembers all that was dearest to him in life. Her form, her look, her voice eluded him. From the nightmare he had submitted to, she was excluded. He could not reach her. With what sanity was left to him he saw the situation clearly. Somehow, despite the failure of will, of principle, of self-respect, his gift of sympathetic insight remained to torture him. He seemed to know to the last merciless pull of the rack how Esther would feel if she knew. The dread of her finding out haunted him.

It was with a similar sense of foreboding that Esther read his letter. Intuition had already warned her that something was amiss. It never occurred to her that he could stop loving her. She accepted the postscript as a matter of course: they had often enough been parted. But she felt his distance as something new. His work, his problems, his interests had come between them more threateningly than ever before, at the very time when she needed him most.

She knew that he could have come to see her if he had wanted to, but she was too weary in spirit to feel resentment. The past weeks had brought worry and grief enough, arising from other causes than his absence. Life at Lady Green was coming to an end. Rooms were dismantled, most of the furniture had gone, the peacocks and poultry had been sold, the dogs had been adopted by Matty, now Mrs Grote of Broom Farm. In another month the Aumerys would be homeless.

Since Daniel had made no offer and was obviously keeping away – no doubt for good reasons – an early marriage was out of the question. There was only one course open to them. The house in Hudmorton was let to a Mrs Capman, of whom they knew nothing except that she had lived there as wife and widow for more than twenty years. For most of that time the rent of £35 a year had been collected by an agency whose services Flora had dispensed with as one of her economies after Edwin's death. Since then Mrs Capman had sent a monthly postal order. When Flora returned the rent book at the end of May she enclosed a letter giving her tenant notice to quit in four weeks' time.

When Bertha went to stay with her sister, Esther had taken charge of Prince. She rarely went out of doors except to exercise him, and usually kept to the riverside path. Woodland walks, especially to the Aston oak, were fraught with painful memories. She also avoided the Lodge for fear of unsettling Prince, and because the closed shutters depressed her.

But one afternoon, on impulse, she climbed the steep path up the Scaur, feeling with every step that it would be a good thing to go away. Wherever she turned there was some reminder of change. Prince had raced ahead to the foot of the Crag where his master had died. Whimpering, he ignored her call. Not until she reached the Lodge did he cease his hopeless search and join her. The gate was unlatched. He pushed it open and in a bound had reached the porch to sniff at the threshold.

'Silly boy.' His anxious whine had broken into an excited bark, like a greeting. 'There's no-one here.'

His only response was another joyous bark, his front paws planted on the step, his body quivering.

'Come away, Prince. Good boy.' She wandered about the little garden, picked a nosegay of forget-me-nots and honeysuckle, and called the dog again. He lay across the threshold, head on paws, in an attitude of faithful waiting that brought tears to her eyes. His stubborn refusal to move suggested so strongly that there was someone within that, half convinced, she looked up at the closed windows as if at any moment the curtains might part and Bertha or Daniel look down. Unwillingly she went up the path and sat in the porch opposite the sea-bleached conch shells where once she had left Daniel's birthday present. His sixteenth birthday! How long ago it seemed. Almost seven years, the fairy-tale period during which strange transformations took place: princess to goose-girl, peasant to prince.

How perversely a shuttered house, the very symbol of desertion and emptiness, conjures up absent forms to people its vacant rooms. It was the time of day when Bertha might be polishing her brasses or doing a bit of dusting as she sang her favourite hymn about the suffering Saviour standing alone on Olive's brow. 'Mount Olive' Daniel had explained when, in youthful ignorance, she had wondered how that could be. Suppose he just happened to come home, now, and found her there; or had already come, was actually in the house, would in the next second open the door. 'Esther!' he would say. 'Sweetheart.'

The silence was like a held breath. She ceased almost to exist except to wait, an unmoving feature of the hushed garden with its lingering scent of honeysuckle, its clumps of feverfew white as the cloud that hung over Long Rake. And slowly the illusion faded. He would not come. Beyond the gate the road was empty. She shivered though the day was warm, no longer remembering the childish thrill of running at daybreak through dew-soaked grass with the gift in her basket, remembering only that he hadn't cared about the torn stocking or the picture on the card: that the Aumery affairs must be settled without reference to Daniel. She and her mother must see to their own future.

'Come here, Prince. At once.' Her voice sounded startlingly loud. She seized him by the scruff of the neck, smacked his rump and dragged him to the gate. Daniel, lying naked with Clairy in his tumbled bed, heard her and felt himself to be in hell. This was damnation, this absence from goodness and light, this letting her go.

'She's gone.' Clairy's cool voice compounded his sense of loss. She was so close that she might have stolen his own words from his own mind. Her body, coiled serpent-like about him, had become part of his own: they were one flesh. Using each other as they had done had bound them to each other, made them alike. He had known from the beginning that it was no more than a physical coupling without sympathy or tenderness. He had not understood that it was a union of lost souls.

In a sudden access of revulsion, he knew at last that he loathed her as much as he loathed himself. Everything about her was hateful to him: her intrusion into his life, her familiarity with his weakness, her strange eyes, her pale limbs. Above all, he hated her knowingness. He knew nothing about her except that whereas he had been ignorant, she had been experienced, a woman plying an ancient trade practised expertly long before she had known him. Why had she not asked for payment? Not yet?

He pushed her from him, sprang up, flung on some clothes and went down to the kitchen. Its homely features greeted him as if he had been away for a long time: the blackened kettle, the red-checked curtains, the clothes-horse with one cracked rail, the brass candlesticks tarnished in his mother's absence, the Laughing Cavalier plate on the mantelpiece. A garish, vulgar thing. His mother prized it. He took it down and with a revival of his old sceptical humour wondered what the chap had found to laugh at: and there came to him like a chink of blue in an overcast sky the conviction that it was over. Some day – it would be a long time, perhaps years before he could be purged of the degradation – but some day he would be free of it.

Clairy, neatly dressed, smooth-haired, came softly down the stairs; came close to him. He drew back. The withdrawal neither escaped nor surprised her. Nothing escaped or surprised her. She made no comment, but he knew that she understood. It was her capacity to hold in reserve a store of secret knowledge that he most hated. It was as if she had never been innocent but born corrupt. Her face, he thought, as he turned away from it, was always mask-like, screening an inward hoard of experience – or inherited taint. Only from time to time did the eyes bring the face to life: as now when, realizing what he held, she took the plate from him, looked at the jovial face, its colours interspersed after seven years with streaks of bare tin. Unaccountably she, too, was amused. She laughed and put the plate back on the mantel-shelf.

The effect was curiously disturbing. He had never heard her laugh before. She had no sense of humour beyond a disposition to mock, and there was mockery in her dismissal, presumably of the cavalier's oafish lack of subtlety. Why else should it amuse her?

'You'd better go,' she said, 'or you'll miss your train.'

'I won't be back for a while.'

She nodded without interest. 'Remember your mother will be coming home a week on Saturday.'

He had forgotten. The reminder cheered him like the promise of a return to normal health – or like an exorcism.

During the next ten days he made valiant efforts to make up for wasted time. He could concentrate again: woke early, was punctual, wrote and talked with the fluency natural to him. It was over. He was free, though not of bitter regret. Every thought of Esther revived the sickening sense of shame and unworthiness. When he

145

was fit to go back to her, he would explain that he had been on the verge of a nervous illness. She need never know the form it had taken: never know about Clairy.

His first exam would be on the following Monday. He went home on the Saturday before, the day of his mother's return, planning to devote the whole of Sunday to revision before going back to town in the evening. At Unnerstone station he ordered the one taxi to meet his mother's train at two o'clock, and walked briskly to the Lodge, suppressing his dread that Clairy might be there.

To his relief, he had the house to himself. Provisions on the kitchen table and in the larder indicated that she had been there – and gone. He ate the sandwiches his Aunt Maud had given him, lit the fire, wound the wall clock and set it right by his father's watch, hunted for the stone hotwater bottle and put it in his mother's bed. Having set out cups and saucers in the parlour, he could think of nothing else to do until it occurred to him to pick some flowers at random, shove them in a vase and put it in the centre of the table.

With a good hour in hand before the taxi could be expected, he stood on the doorstep, sniffing the air with a touch of his old enjoyment in its freshness, then found a towel and went down across fields to the river, to a quiet reach beneath alders half a mile above the mill, a favourite bathing place of village boys. For a few blessed minutes he forgot the world and felt only the benison of cool, clear water, the cleansing, as he swam from the shade of trees and, turning on his back, dared to look up at the sky, his spiritual dwelling place. From this low level the sloping fields were steeper, the hills higher, with a stretch of milky blue far beyond their summits. There would be rain later in the day.

On the bank, his feet on smooth pebbles, he towelled vigorously until his skin glowed. He pulled on shirt and

146

trousers, rubbed his hair. Through wet locks he saw Clairy watching him from under the alders.

'I went to the Lodge. Then I saw you crossing the fields. I wanted to talk to you.'

'What about?' he asked, indifferent, impatient.

'We're expecting a baby,' she said.

CHAPTER 11

Prisoners sentenced for life sometimes beat their fists on the doors of their cells and howl in anguish. Daniel suffered the loss of hope in silence. Words, his natural instrument, failed him as, from the confusion of his mind, there emerged the one inescapable direction he must take, even though speech might have brought relief from the sense of dissolution, a kind of inward weeping that made him physically weak.

He stumbled more than once as they walked across the fields to the Lodge. He was almost unaware of his companion. Having delivered her message, she said no more. Nothing was to be deduced from her smooth face and composure of manner. The hysterical fancy came to him that they would walk through the rest of their lives like this, communicating nothing, never touching. He could never bring himself to touch her – ever again.

But she would be his wife. Nothing could save him from the doom he had brought on himself. By temperament, upbringing, principle, he was helpless to escape his duty. According to the mores of his class and time, an honourable man, having got a girl into trouble, married her. He stole a sidelong look at her. She showed no sign of being in trouble in the emotional sense, presumably because she knew that for her all would be well: he would do his duty.

Not to marry her? The dazzling idea faded instantly. To be known as the father of an illegitimate child would mean the end of his career. The one absolute requirement when an appointment was made under the Board of Education was moral rectitude, immorality the one unquestioned reason for dismissal. Necessity and decency together left him no choice. Nothing could save him – but death.

Death could save him. He saw himself dangling from the Aston oak and with a flash of sympathy thought of Aumery in his extremity. Esther was so much a part of him that in this first phase of wretchedness he could not pity her any more than he pitied himself: they were both beyond pity. As he perished in the shipwreck, she must perish with him. But he was dimly aware that Esther might rather have him dead than married to Clairy. It would be easier to die than to face telling her.

And when he was gone? She would be left to mourn the deaths by suicide of the two men she had loved. Clairy would be left to bear his child, a son perhaps. His sudden jealous resentment gave way to self-reproach. Had he postured and prated about the effect of up-bringing and heredity on a child only to abandon his own to the stigma of illegitimacy and poverty? Not that the child's mother would have difficulty in earning a living. He had little doubt as to how Clairy had earned the clothes she wore with such confidence in their quality.

As for heredity – a lascivious father and loose-living mother! It was a symptom of his recent frenzy that he had committed his whole future to a woman of whose background he knew absolutely nothing.

'What's your name?' he demanded with an abrupt-ness almost savage. 'Clairy What?'

She seemed amused. 'Motte. Godwain will be an improvement, I think.'

'What about your relations?'

Her parents were dead years ago. She had lived with her only aunt, the one she visited in Hudmorton on her days off. 'Until I took to spending them with you.'

A light rain was falling. He made no attempt to hurry, but plodded slowly like an older man. Clairy went quickly ahead. The wall clock was striking two as he came into the kitchen. She had put wood on the fire and set the kettle on the bar.

'Your mother will be here soon. You're not looking very smart.'

He tucked in his shirt and felt vaguely at the neck. He had taken off his stiff collar when he stripped for his swim. The studs were in his waistcoat pocket but . . .

'It's here. You left it on the grass.' She handed him the collar, then poured milk from the brown quart jug into the smaller china one.

When she was his wife, he thought dully, the Lodge would be her home; and eventually, when he died, it would belong to her and their son, not to Esther, and the son would not be Esther's.

'Stay here till Mother comes and tell her I had to go out.'

'I'll tell her you've gone to Lady Green. You'll have to tell Esther, won't you?'

Then she saw his expression. A murderous hatred had seized him. He hated her body, its sensuous smoothness and pallor: he hated her hands and feet, her arms and neck; most of all he hated her imperviousness. Her lack of feeling was a positive offence, dense and suffocating like a thick blanket. He ought to kill her – and their misbegotten child.

He was a tall man. She moved to the other side of the table.

'Kill me,' she said, 'and be hanged for it. How will that help her?'

He turned away and went to the window, remembering how he himself had once used the same words. It was on the hill overlooking Barbarrow Hall. Lincoln had hurt Esther's feelings and she had come to him for comfort. 'Shall I kill him and be hanged for it?' he had said. They had laughed and been happy. He remembered her blue dress, the flight of white doves and all the scents of summer, and how, later on, he had tucked a spray of harebells in her soft dark hair. Remembering

150

the light-hearted sweetness of the day and of all their times together, he forgot the woman he must marry as if she had never come into his life to darken it – as if she had never existed – and thought only of Esther.

From an upstairs window at Lady Green she saw him coming down the Scaur path – at last. There were corded trunks and bulging portmanteaux everywhere, but she scrambled over them and ran downstairs to the front door.

Prince had already heard his master and was at the gate to greet him, to reach up on hind legs and nuzzle at his neck in an ecstatic greeting that brought the first tears to Daniel's eyes, the first inkling that, for all his rottenness, he could still be loved. He forced himself to push the dog away and went to the house.

'Daniel!' Her first impulse had been to run into his arms. She hesitated. The blight that had fallen on him fell instantly on her too. She felt it in her heart. His drawn face, his desperate eyes, his wet untidy hair. No collar! Someone had died? Bertha? 'What's wrong? You're in trouble. My dearest! What is it?'

In the doorway, with the dark panelled hall behind her, she looked small and frail. In the weeks since he had last seen her she had pined. Her face was colourless except for the red of her lips and the shadowed violet of her eyes. His love for her had always been protective. She had never needed his protection more than at this ill-starred moment when he must cast her from him. He had revered her. How could he contaminate her with his squalid story? She would never understand what he had done, how it had happened, why he had done it.

'Please, darling, what's the matter?'

'Don't touch me. You mustn't. Never. Not any more. I'm not fit. You don't know what I'm like – what I've been doing. You won't be able to forgive me. I don't want you to. I just want to tell you, and then go away, and stay away from you.'

He spoke without self-pity or pity for her, without eloquence or any of the pride and vigour she had known in him. She recognized his desperate sincerity. Her features sharpened. Instinctively she moved to lean against the door frame, hands behind her as she gripped it for support.

'Tell me,' she commanded. 'Go on. Now. At once.'

He told her. They stood with the width of the door between them, each gazing at the other's white face.

'You did that? With her? How could you when you love me? It's me you love.'

He tried to explain: he had yielded to a side of his nature she didn't know about, a far worse side than he himself had known. Men were like that sometimes; but it had been worse with him. 'It was as if I went out of my mind.'

'You never did before, not with anyone else?'

'Never. How could I? I was waiting for you.'

'You should have asked me to marry you. *I* was waiting for that. We could have been married and I could have . . . Why did it have to be her?'

'Oh my God, I don't know. I had never looked at her, never thought of her.' (Had she intended it all along?) 'You understand? I shall have to marry her.' He waited, as if somehow even then at the eleventh hour there would be some way of escape he hadn't thought of. 'Esther,' he said, as if she could help – and save him.

'Yes,' she said, 'I understand.'

Behind her yawned rooms empty of furniture, a larder almost empty of food, the dogs gone, the cats already half wild. The ruin of the Aumerys no longer troubled her: it seemed trivial in the face of a disaster so huge that nothing lay beyond it. In their equal wretchedness neither spoke; neither moved, since the only movement must be to part.

At last despair gave her the strength to say, 'You'd better go.' And in a voice small and cold with misery,

'Goodbye.' She held out her hand and stood dry-eyed as he took it and held it, hesitating, then kissed it gently and held it to his cheek and left her.

A drizzle of fine rain half hid the Scaur so that she could not see him clearly as he climbed the hill with Prince at his heels. She waited in an absence of vitality as debilitating as if she had died, unaware that she was watching him, until he became no more than a movement in the grey mist mantling the hillside.

She closed the heavy door. It always had to be slammed because the wood was warped. Though it was far too early she locked, bolted and barred it – clumsily. It took a little time to fix the bars.

Flora, exhausted by anxious days of packing and making decisions, had lain down on her bed and dozed. The slamming of the front door in the early afternoon roused her to get up and look over the banisters.

'Are you there, Esther?'

'Mother!'

At the sight of the girl's upturned face she ran down and folded her in her arms

It was market day in Unnerstone. When Bertha came out of the station she was greeted by Harry Amos, the weekly carrier, who was drinking a mug of tea at the refreshment stall.

'Back home again, Bertha?' He came and took her bags. 'You're in luck. I'll be going your way.'

'Well, I don't know. Our Daniel said he would book the taxi.'

It was waiting, drawn up behind Amos's cart.

'Nay, never mind that. I'll give you a lift and it'll cost you nothing. Hey, Timmy,' he called to the taxi driver. 'You're not short of customers, are you?'

'Not on a Saturday.' Timmy grasped the situation. 'Don't you worry, Mrs Godwain. Two bob's worth saving.'

His good turn was rewarded when, a minute later,

he drove off with another passenger. Consequently Bertha accepted the offer of a free ride with a clear conscience, and enjoyed the opportunity of catching up with local news. She had never before been so long away from home, never before seen familiar things with the fresh vision of a returning traveller. The Lodge, seen from a distance as they breasted the last hill, looked smaller and somehow different from when she was inside, sweeping and scrubbing it. But as the slow plod of Amos's horse took them nearer, she saw that the fluted white barge-board over the gable and the stone roof-tiles yellowed by lichen were just as they had always been. It was a pretty place.

It hadn't really struck home to her, not till now, what a bit of luck it had been when Mr Aumery made it over to Thomas. Not many people in their position had the advantage of owning their own house. She was sorry that she had left it for so long, sorry in a way that she had left it at all. Perched by the roadside on the brow of the hill that went down to Wood Aston, with no other houses in sight, it had a lonely look.

It was raining when they drove up to the gate. The garden would be the better for it. She was later than had been planned, but neither Daniel nor Prince came out to welcome her. Instead it was Clairy who had evidently been watching for her and came quickly to the gate.

'Your tea's ready. Daniel had to go out, but he'll be back soon. Are you going down to the village, Mr Amos? I'll come with you if you don't mind. It won't take me a minute to get my things.'

Amos had barely time to deposit his passenger and her luggage before Clairy came back and mounted to Bertha's place. Naturally she wouldn't want her good clothes to get wet as she hadn't a coat; but Bertha was put out by her being so offhand. Not a word to ask how she was or to welcome her home. Bertha herself could be brusque, but in her unassuming way she had looked forward to being fussed a little on her return by Daniel and Prince and perhaps by Esther who, if she had been there, would have known just what to say in her nice way. She and Esther had always got on together. Whereas she had never, as she admitted later to her sister, to Daniel, to anyone who would listen, got Miss Angovil's maid properly summed up; had never seen what might be called her upshot, or given much heed to it. True, the girl had been useful. But it is equally true that a momentary rebuff can cancel out a debt of gratitude, however well earned.

Weeks of rest and change had not solved the problem of Bertha's bad legs and swollen feet, but they had revived the vitality she had lost in the weary months of nursing Thomas. With all her natural vigour focused on Clairy, she discovered that she didn't like her. She had never liked her. It wouldn't take much – she watched Clairy shake rain from the sleeves of her blouse – to turn the not liking into active dislike. Bertha remembered incidents, times when Clairy had behaved more like a familiar friend than she had any right to, or like a relation, which she definitely was not. Yes, she had been helpful, but she had been about the place too much. Especially when she, Bertha, was away? How often had she been in the house with all Bertha's things lying there to be gone through if she'd a mind to poke and pry? Giving her, his own mother, that message about Daniel being out! As if it had anything to do with her. 'Your tea's ready' indeed!

Standing squarely at her own gate as if to defend it against marauders, Bertha disregarded the rain. Her own clothes – a coat of West of England tweed and a sensible felt hat – had been chosen to last, and would be none the worse for a bit of drizzle. Amos was seeing to his harness and had not yet mounted, so that she had an uninterrupted view of Clairy in the passenger's seat. She had put her hat in her canvas bag to keep it dry and was in the act of tying a scarf under her chin. To Bertha's annoyance – she fairly burned with resentment – it was the dark red scarf Esther had knitted for Daniel. Moreover, the scarf was not the only thing she recognized.

Having arranged everything to her satisfaction, Clairy turned her head and looked down at Bertha. Recent events had altered their relationship. At the Lodge, power was about to change hands. Pleasantness of even the most conventional kind was no longer required. Her unsmiling face was not appealing, certainly not to Bertha. There was something funny about the eyes. She had said so to Thomas once. When? The memory fused with another, of a pale mask-like face swathed in a red scarf: a closed, knowing face looking down from another cart in that very same spot at the Lodge gate. The coolness of it, cadging another lift! Recognition dawned.

'My stars!' Bertha's eyes, round and brown, widened in astonishment quickly followed by condemnation. 'So it's you. You came sneaking back and never said. What for, I wonder. What did you come back for?'

'I'm ready when you are, Mr Amos,' Clairy said, and was driven away.

Bertha wandered uneasily from kitchen to parlour and back again several times. Whether her uneasiness was due entirely to the incident at the gate or whether in her absence her home itself had undergone some redistribution of those vibrations that constitute the atmosphere of a house, she couldn't settle.

Nothing could have been more unexpected than the discovery that she had been harbouring at the Lodge a person who was really somebody else, or at least who was not the person she was thought to be. There was a weirdness in it that she couldn't fathom. She could scarcely wait to tell Daniel. Fortunately she had not been home more than a few minutes, and was in the act of brewing tea when she heard his footsteps on the path. He had been unable to face being alone with Clairy and had sheltered under a hedge until he saw the carrier's van stop at the Lodge and guessed that his mother had arrived.

Bertha turned from the hearth. The news she had been bursting to tell died on her lips. 'What ails you, lad?' Her hand shook. She put down the kettle and gathered her strength to face this new distress, to stare at the unkempt, rain-soaked object barely recognizable as the handsome, confident son she had left. 'You look as if you hadn't had a bite to eat since I went away. How come you've been out in your shirt sleeves – without a collar?' Like Esther, but more severely, she saw the lack of collar as a clear sign of crisis. But it was not so much the outward and visible lapses that frightened her as his look of miserable defeat. Creeping in from the rain like a homeless tramp! 'Come on, let's have it. It's more trouble, I can see that.'

'I've been to see Esther. I had to tell her. We've parted, Mother.'

To speak of it made it real. A mist cleared from his mind. Their very closeness had blinded him to the pain he had inflicted: he had not been able to detach Esther from his own wretchedness. He was visited by the memory of her as he had last seen her, with the dark house behind her. She had seemed too fragile to bear the blow he had inflicted, yet strangely dignified in her anguish. A wave of tenderness deeper than he had ever known brought the realization of all that he had left unsaid in parting from her.

'Tell her you had to part? Why, for pity's sake?'

'I have to marry Clairy.'

Dumbfounded, Bertha lowered her head and stared into the dark depths of the tea-pot. The half-brewed tea wouldn't be fit to drink. She looked round vaguely for the lid, forgot what she was looking for and shakily put the pot down on the fender. That Clairy! Feeling her knees give way under her, she groped for the rocking-chair, sank into it and found her tongue. 'There've been goings-on then between you?'

157

'Yes.' Goings-on, he thought, just about expressed it.

'And she's expecting?'

'Yes.'

Her quick grasp of the situation, her recognition of it as a catastrophe, he was grateful for. He steeled himself to hear the tirade that must follow, and waited.

But he had underestimated the effect of his bleak news. Bertha had no words at her command to express the vastness of her dismay. In an instant, with the sure instinct of love, she had foreseen the ruin of her son. She knew that such a marriage to such a woman, instead of to the girl he idolized, would crush his brightest hopes as surely as the tree had crushed the life out of his father. The very sight of him, a hollow-eyed starveling standing there without a collar, made her sick to the stomach. He looked already – degraded. The word came to her as if spoken by an alien voice from a world she had never known. The threat to his future was hardly less deadly than when he had gone to war. She had wept when she saw him in khaki, but they were tears of pride. Her joy in his safe return, her admiration of his book-learning, his gratifying attachment to the mester's daughter, his determination to raise himself, his faithful support in Thomas's illness – his whole life from infancy to manhood passed before her and brought her back to the present, to the woman who would be her daughter-in-law.

And for all her love of him, despite the comfort of a mother's care which she longed to lavish on him, it was bitterness that inspired the only thing she could find to say. 'Then you'll be marrying that nobody in a dirty blanket that you found under a hedge. It's a pity you didn't leave her to die.'

CHAPTER 12

Daniel entered the wood on the south side. He had come by the longer way down the road, almost as far as the mill, to where the woodland path branched off to the right. The shorter way over the Scaur would have brought him in sight of Lady Green. It was still early, the day would be warm.

He had met no-one, seen nothing of the summer morning. He felt, but did not notice, the extra stillness and the purity of green light as the wood enclosed him, felt, too, the release of tension when a purpose is fulfilled. The urge to seek refuge in the one place where he could be entirely alone had driven him all week from one nerve-racking day to the next, a driving force all the more powerful for having of necessity been held in check and for giving him, in the hopelessness of his condition, one small thing to look forward to without pain.

The examinations towards which he had directed all his will and mental energy, not merely for the past two years but for years before them, were over. They had saved his sanity by forcing him back to the habit of ordered thinking that had become second nature. A weaker vessel might have gone to pieces, but for him there could be no avoidance of the goal to which the whole course of his life had been directed from boyhood. It was absolutely necessary for him to qualify himself for earning a livelihood at a time when thousands were unemployed. He must not lower himself further than he had done already in the eyes of his tutors, his friends, Mr Horner, his mother, Esther. His mind glanced away from her image. The need to avoid thinking of her left numb the tenderest impulse of his being. It was as if he had been viscerated or had his heart torn out.

The Sunday after his mother's return had been a day when his spirit almost failed him, when the mere taste of food made him sick, when the printed page blinded him and made his head spin. In the evening he went back to Hudmorton and to another sleepless night. But the moment he set foot in the College building on the Monday morning, a merciful calmness came upon him. The smell of floor polish, the shining tiles, the bland distempered walls, the portrait of the founder in the entrance hall, the false cheerfulness of the other students, all drew him back into the disciplined routine.

In the examination room, with its rows of desks and piles of virgin paper, his head cleared. He read the questions with a quick grasp of their purport. His mind channelled within their strict limitations, he wrote and calculated and drew sketches, and on the first night and remaining nights of the week, he slept for at least a few hours.

With something like half his mental power, his best faculties in abeyance, he did what he could. When it was over, he thought it probable that he had passed, but without any of the distinction he had counted on. In history and literature where he should have excelled, examples eluded him: his memory, always keen and reliable, let him down. There was a lack of force and amplitude in his answers. Looking over his mathematics paper before handing it in, he spotted inaccuracies and one glaring mistake, too late to alter them. Invariably, after the first hour, he had felt a hungry weakness in his stomach and a general feebleness. More than once his pen had faltered and he had bent forward to avoid fainting.

Those lapses and his poor looks had not escaped notice.

'Godwain's in the soup,' the history lecturer remarked to Daniel's tutor. 'What's come over him? He hasn't been drinking?' The question was idle. Both knew that Godwain could not have afforded drink and had never needed its stimulus.

'He's not the type to make a fool of himself that way. Not a type at all, for that matter. He's the most outstanding man we've had here in my time. He should have gone to the university if his circumstances had been different. It's a pity!' Giles was genuinely concerned. 'Family troubles, I'm afraid. His father's accident was a knock-out blow – and then his death. He's ill, I think, but he hasn't complained and he's sticking it out, I'll say that for him.'

He stuck it out with the help of a sustaining fantasy, a persistent dream. It was of a place he knew where he could be alone, a refuge where he might find the identity he had lost. On the Friday evening he went home and the next morning was up at daylight, drank a cup of water, ate a piece of bread and set out as on a pilgrimage.

Entering the wood, he was received into its silence. It had always been like this: the earth soft underfoot, the scents of leaf-mould and resin. Deep breaths of air purified by green foliage and lush ferns gave him his first sensation of renewal. He saw the sheen of morning light on leaves, green vistas melting as they receded into blue and purple, the occasional glint of silver on brown bark – and ahead of him the vast trunk and wide-spreading branches of the Aston oak.

He went right up to it, under the canopy of boughs now dense with their full summer foliage, stepped over its thick exposed roots, spread his arms as far as they would reach across the trunk and laid his head against the grooved bark. He had reached sanctuary. But it was no Christian shrine. Cast out from Eden, he was not seeking forgiveness for his weakness and sin. This was a hallowed place, but its spirit was pagan. It

161

held the power of life and death: it had destroyed his father, accepted Aumery's penitential sacrifice. His own vision of himself dangling from one of its boughs had lasted for no longer than a few moments of weakness. The escape into death was not for him. He must live and suffer without hope.

The tree would give him quietness and strength. He clung to it, feeling its ancient steadfastness, its immense weight securely held between earth and heaven, its deep roots drawing sustenance from the rich soil. Then he climbed, as he had loved to climb, to the crown of the tree where there would be nothing between him and the sky.

But there was something between him and the impersonal element of air: a forgotten vestige of the past, poignant enough to bring him to a halt, spread-eagled between angular branches halfway up the tree. He had passed the great scar left by the severed branch and was hauling himself up to the next fork when, inches from his eyes, there appeared a patch where the bark had been scraped away and a youthful hand had carved the outline of a heart framing the initials DG and EA.

It seemed to him in his wounded state that the device had been put there by some other agency than his own. It was meant as a merciless reminder of lost happiness, an affirmation that he and Esther were one and should not be parted. With the pain that returning circulation brings to frozen limbs, the numbness left him. He was stricken, ravaged, torn apart by the sharpest grief he had ever known. Leaning forward, his brow against the carved heart, in the heart of the tree where no-one could see or hear him, he wept the bitterest tears of his life.

Then, when it was over, he mounted to his old eyrie and dared to look up into the deepening blue. With an effort of will he tried to assess the circumstances of his life in proportion to the empyrean, apparently limitless yet itself a mere fragment of the cosmos. But his attempt to subdue the littleness of human life to its proper place in the universe was foiled by the persistent interference of human voices. They had the advantage of being much nearer than the music of the spheres.

'It's a pity you didn't leave her to die . . .' 'Why don't you put it down . . . ?' 'I wouldn't let the likes of her over my doorstep . . .'

They had been morally wrong. Besides, she would have survived without him; the help she had needed was supplied by others. He had done nothing – except preach and moralize. In his insistence that the homeless should be housed, he had been right; but what had seemed compassion he now saw as sanctimonious smugness and wished, with heart and mind in conflict, that she had died.

If he had had his way and found her a home, would she have grown into a different person? Since his mother's first staggering pronouncement, he had been hard put to it to identify the woman he was to marry as the foundling of seven years ago. He believed that they were one and the same, but could not realize the connection, could not believe that Clairy had ever been other than the creature who had used him and whom he had used in his frenzy of alternating lust and revulsion. Their loveless exploitation of each other had dragged them down to depths they must share for the rest of their lives. The responsibility was his. She was incapable of it.

'Leave her be,' Bertha had counselled. 'You've no need to ruin yourself for such as her. If it hadn't been you it would have been another. Plenty of others. I saw that in her from the start – and how I never came to recognize her when she sneaked back and crept into this very kitchen, I'll never know. Your father, bless him, couldn't do with her—'

She had stopped abruptly with a strange look of fear, then urged more strongly than before, 'Don't marry her, son. Let her live with her shame.'

163

But she knew that the shame would be his too. There would be his child, her grandchild, who must be brought up decent and respectable, though how that could happen with such a mother, God alone knew. Daniel too – it was his one certainty – was resolved to care for his own child. To abandon him to his mother would be an even worse sin than he had yet committed.

He had not seen her since the previous Saturday. They must talk. The prospect was repugnant, but they must marry as soon as possible, even though it would have been to his advantage to wait until he had secured an appointment to be taken up, with luck, in September.

He looked down between the oak boughs at the broad green ride where, early one morning, he had seen Esther, prim in her summer hat, a basket of books in her gloved hand, the memory of her so clear that all he had striven for – resignation, strength, self-denial – deserted him, leaving only the longing to see her once more. Their parting seemed to him now to have lacked all tenderness. Why had he not taken her in his arms, told her of his gratitude and love, asked about her plans and where she would go?

Was it too late? He slid to the ground, half expecting to find her there, her eyes raised to him in sympathy or admiration, or sparkling with humour. Every inch of the way, as he hurried over the foot-bridge and along the riverside path, was invested with memories: of the kingcups she had gathered, her childish habit of dropping a leaf from the bridge to watch it float downstream, her airing of her sketchy knowledge of French, her love of gossip, her eager questions and respect for his answers . . . her unspoilt freshness, her beauty.

The front gate of Lady Green was padlocked. He rushed round to the door in the wall. That, too, was closed and bolted on the inside. He remembered the trunks and portmanteaux, the gaps where the furniture had been – and turned away.

Halfway up the hill he met the postman on his way to Broom Farm.

'Morning, Dan. Were you wanting to see them at Lady Green? You won't find anyone there. They left on Tuesday. Must have been in a hurry at the last minute. I put a letter through on Wednesday, not knowing. Reckon I did the wrong thing, but I didn't know they'd gone until I heard it at the farm. They've gone abroad, to Italy. That's what Mrs Grote says anyway. They haven't left a forwarding address.' The two men looked down at the house, its chimneys void of smoke, its windows shuttered. 'You can't help feeling sorry, seeing it empty. There wasn't much wrong with the Aumerys except bad luck. Well, that's the last of them gone. There'll be change hereabouts. So long, Dan.'

Daniel climbed the hill slowly to the level stretch leading to the Lodge. He had never before thought of it as a lonely spot. Nothing had happened to account for its look of isolation except that its only neighbours had gone, except that it remained in an otherwise empty world. The last of the Aumerys were homeless. He was more fortunate. His wife and child would have a home. The irony of it! From the wreck of the Aumery fortune, he had come out best and could feel only misery and shame.

PART TWO

ALMA TERRACE

CHAPTER 13

Changes of season passed unnoticed in Alma Terrace.
Spring and summer were less bleak than autumn and
winter: for six months of the year the last surviving lime
tree, in its iron cage at the turning into Duke Street,
bore dusty leaves. Otherwise, solstices and equinoxes
made little difference to the neighbourhood: the solar
system must be taken on trust as a matter of hearsay,
so feebly did the sun penetrate the heavy soot pall
mantling this lower end of the city throughout the
year.

If only it had been true about Italy! 'An excus-
able lie' Flora had called it as she had cradled her
stricken daughter in her arms.

'If I can't die,' Esther had said, white-lipped, 'all I
want is to go right away where nobody will ever find
us or hear of us ever again.'

Flora, having lived unthinkingly for most of her
forty-four years, had in the five minutes after Daniel
left, at last attained maturity; and at the same time,
with the elasticity granted to the human spirit in crisis,
had reverted to the primitive state of a lioness crouched
ready to spring in defence of her threatened cub. Her
first paroxysm of anger and outrage soon passed, she
put it from her. There was no time for that. With
Esther clinging to her as she had not clung since
infancy, she, who had never known what to do about
anything, became miraculously endowed with energy,
foresight and resource. All the existing problems remained; Daniel's defection did not alter them. There
was still only one place where they could go. But

they must be thought to have gone much further, out of reach, out of sight and eventually – it would not take long – out of mind.

The next day she finished the packing. On the Monday morning she walked to Unnerstone and arranged for the trunks to be collected immediately and despatched to the Left Luggage Office at Hudmorton station, and for the few remaining pieces of furniture to be taken to a repository in town. She also ordered the taxi for the following morning. Before boarding the train on Tuesday morning, she posted a letter to Matty enclosing a key and explaining briefly that an opportunity had arisen for them to go at once to Italy.

'You know how my husband and I loved it,' she wrote without a qualm for her new duplicity. 'It will be the very thing. A completely different way of life will do us both a world of good . . .'

A completely different way of life, and much nearer at hand, it was well within the power of Alma Terrace to provide.

'Tell me about the time we did go to Italy,' Esther pleaded as they lay awake in the bed they shared on that first miserable night. Flora, dipping into a past remote as a half-forgotten dream, scooped up memories of those two strangers, Edwin Aumery and his young wife, told of the drowsy heat under southern skies, the sun-baked Tuscan landscape, the huge butterflies in a garden edged with verbena and scented with pink-blossoming oleander, the stone fountain, the painted ceilings in the palazzo, the red wine in the taverns – until Esther, soothed by her drowsy murmurings, drifted into sleep.

Remembering such things, and how the nightingale had sung in the warm evenings and through the starlit nights, Flora rediscovered with them the man who had charmed and indulged her, and she wished that she had understood him then as she understood him now. And so, remembering and regretting, she lay awake in the stuffy room until light crept between the shabby curtains and the clatter of clogs on cobbles heralded another working day for those who had work to go to.

They had spent their first night in Hudmorton at a cheap boarding house recommended, since there was no-one else to ask, by the station taxi-driver whose wife knew the landlady. For all its size – 200,000 inhabitants – Hudmorton had then, and would keep for years to come, a wealth of homely neighbourliness that more than compensated for its poverty in other respects.

The next morning, after a twenty-minute walk through drab streets, they had their first view of Alma Terrace, and stopped on the corner by the dusty lime tree. Their eyes, still unaccustomed to city murk, took in the unswept pavements, the rusted iron railings, the narrow house-fronts of sombre stone. From two ranks of slate roofs, a battery of cowled chimneys were adding their daily output of smoke to an atmosphere already dense enough to reduce the entire scene to a uniform dark grey.

Arm in arm, they went slowly forward, counting the houses, odd numbers on the right, even on the left.

'I think it must be the end house,' Esther said, as a mariner in unknown seas might identify the last in a series of deadly rocks.

In view of their sudden departure from Lady Green, they had not expected the house to be empty. Mrs Capman had not so far acknowledged the notice to quit, which would not expire for another ten days. They were still taking their bearings when the door of Number 11 opened and a dark-suited man carrying a bag came down the three steps and walked briskly off in the opposite direction to a waiting car.

'A respectable-looking man,' Flora judged with some relief. She knocked and when there was no response, rang the bell.

Mrs Capman, at her sewing machine in the front room, didn't hear the knock, which coincided with the delivery of a load of coal to the house next door. The whirr and rattle of the treadle drowned the faint clang of the bell in the nether regions of the house. She was startled when Alice Adams put her red head round the door and bawled, 'There's someone at the door. Can you go? I can't leave him just now,' and vanished again.

Having gazed all morning at lengths of black serge, Mrs Capman had difficulty in focusing her eyes on the two unknown ladies on her doorstep, though they, too, were in black.

'Mrs Capman? My name is Aumery. This is my daughter. May we come in?'

'Well, I never! Mrs Aumery. You certainly can.' In the hall she was at a loss as to where to take them. 'I'm afraid . . . You won't mind? There's only . . .'

The front room, furnished as a sitting-room, was also crammed with the paraphernalia of dressmaking: a cutting-out table, a litter of paper patterns, piles of folded materials and, beside the upright piano, an armless dressmaker's dummy. Since packages covered every chair except the one at the machine, they remained standing.

Mrs Capman was a woman of fifty, with a quantity of fading fair hair puffed up and bundled into a loose roll above a face thinned and sharpened by work and worry and half a lifetime spent in airless rooms.

'You'll have got my letter,' she said nervously. 'You haven't? Oh, dear me. It was the day before yesterday I asked Alice to post it. She's that worried, poor girl. She must have forgotten.'

'I take it, Mrs Capman, that you have been able to make arrangements for moving out.'

'I don't know what to say except, well, no. I've barely closed my eyes since your letter came. I've lain tossing and turning and hoping and praying and wondering what to do.' Her distress was painful to see. 'It would be hard at the best of times to find a place where I could carry on with the dressmaking. It would have to be a decent enough place for customers to come to and somewhere we could afford. But with William in the state he's in . . . I'll tell you straight out, Mrs Aumery, a move would kill him. The doctor's just been, and that's what he said. "Your son survived the trenches, Mrs Capman," he said, "but only just. He won't survive being moved from his bed now. You can tell—"' She stopped. Dr Haggitt had been rude about the unknown landlady who had given them notice after twenty years, without a thought for their circumstances. ' "I take it you have written to her," he said, "telling her that I forbid this. My patient must not be moved."'

Mrs Capman's version of his remarks, though edited, reduced Flora and Esther to dismay.

'I'm at my wits' end, not knowing where to turn. There's this dress to be finished for a funeral tomorrow. I can't leave it. It's for Alice's boss's wife. She's a regular customer and a good payer at any time – and William at death's door with pneumonia. That's what it's come to. He's been in a poor way for weeks with congestion. How could I go hunting for another house? It takes time—'

'I wish I had known sooner.' Flora had braced herself for effective action; she had not been prepared to deal with a dilemma worse than her own. 'You see, we're at our wits' end too. I was obliged to give you notice because we have nowhere else to go.'

'You want the house for yourselves?' Mrs Capman was plainly astonished. 'You've left Lady Green?'

'And with no money to speak of,' said the new, forthright, sensible Flora. 'All we have in the world is this house.'

The impasse defeated them. There being no way forward, they remained where they were: the Aumerys half suffocated by the stale air within the imprisoning lace curtains, Mrs Capman at bay among the tokens of her trade, unconsciously resting a defensive hand on

173

her machine, the silent dummy even more stultified through its inability to move.

It was Esther who broke the unhappy silence. 'I'm very sorry about your son, Mrs Capman.'

The woman's anxious eyes softened. As she told Alice afterwards, those words brought the first ray of light, singling out as they did the thing that mattered most.

'Of course he must not be moved,' Flora said. 'There can be no question of it.' Overcome by a sinking sensation, she glanced round at the encumbered chairs. 'Shall we sit down and talk things over?'

'What's come over me, forgetting my manners?' Mrs Capman moved a length of marocain from the nearest chair, smoothed the seat clear of possible pins and turned the chair from the machine to face the room. Esther perched on the piano stool. So grouped, equal in extremity and oddly united, they talked things over.

Their claims seemed irreconcilable. The house was Flora's, but it was Gertie Capman's home and place of work. She had a roof over her head. The Aumerys had none. No woman owning a house should be homeless especially if also penniless. The Capmans between them had an income, though William's contribution at present was only the fifteen shillings a week unemployment allowance. If Flora took over the house and let some of the rooms furnished as she had planned, she could double the £35 the Capmans were paying her in rent. On the other hand, it would take time to furnish the house and find suitable boarders, and would necessitate dipping into the jealously guarded £150 which was their only safeguard against illness or disaster. Besides, Flora dreaded to find herself saddled with undesirable people in her first-floor rooms. In any case, a young man in danger of dying from pneumonia could not be moved.

Approaching the problems from opposite directions surprisingly enough created no antagonism, rather a sense of sharing, so that sharing the house, too, seemed the natural solution.

'For the time being,' Flora said. 'Until William is better and you have had time to make other arrangements.'

'And you could be quite comfortable in the three rooms upstairs.' Mrs Capman spoke from the depths of a relief so profound that her limbs shook. 'The front room up there was meant as a sitting-room when the houses were built, and the fire draws well. It wouldn't be what you're used to.' She had no idea what they were used to, but you could tell from the look and sound of them that it hadn't been anything like Alma Terrace.

'Nothing is what it used to be.' Involuntarily Flora glanced towards the piano stool and her heart ached afresh as she remembered how Esther used to be. Since the parting from Daniel she had not shed a tear. It was unnatural. Mrs Capman, too, became aware of Esther and feared that there wasn't much to choose between her and William so far as worrying about them went. The girl had a lost look and a yearning sadness in her eyes that showed she'd been through a bad time. She'd likely lost her young man in the war, like thousands of others. She wasn't in full mourning like her mother and wore a white blouse with her black skirt and jacket. Lovely hair, too, done low at the back and coming out of her hat in curling tendrils. Not a bit of swank about her, and so thoughtful, saying that about William.

'I'll show you the house,' she offered. It was the very least she could do, though she couldn't spare a minute from Mrs Skidway's dress. The funeral was tomorrow. She'd just have to stay up all night. Alice would have to come back after work and sit with William.

'They're engaged,' she whispered as they crossed the hall, and explained that as it was an end house they were lucky enough to have a small extra room opening off the kitchen.

175

'William's always slept there. It's warm on account of being near the kitchen range, and that's been a blessing many a time when he's been ill . . .'

On the halfway landing she told them about William. He had come home from the trenches without serious hurt, but with already delicate lungs in a bad state. Before joining up he had just started work as a railway clerk and had hoped to work his way up and make a steady career with the company. But he had been in too junior a position to have it kept for him. After being demobbed he had been able to save his gratuity so long as he was receiving the out-of-work donation for discharged soldiers: twenty-nine shillings a week for twenty-six weeks, then twenty shillings for three weeks. The time had been nearly up when he got a job at Handleys. It was only eighteen shillings a week, but he was over the moon at being at work again – until his health broke down. There had been days when he could hardly drag himself to work, others when the coughing and fever were so bad that he couldn't go at all. The last bout of congestion had lasted for weeks and brought him to his present state.

Mechanically his mother opened doors on rooms into which Flora and Esther glanced only briefly, knowing how pressed she was for time. The houses in Alma Terrace, built in the 1850s at the time of the Crimean War, had been comfortable family homes. The first tenants had been bowler-hatted, upper shop assistants in big stores, partners in small businesses, senior clerks – some of them church-wardens or elders of non-conformist congregations. But after the death of the original owner, a successful builder, the property had been divided, and changed hands several times. The houses, like those sold piecemeal to bolster up the sagging fortunes of Lady Green, were now separately owned by individuals who had chosen to invest their small savings for a safe return in the form of rent, but could not afford to keep the houses in good repair.

Flora had done Number 11 an injustice in prophesying that it would be a slum, but the area was sadly run down: the staid had become sleazy, decent tenants were doing their best to rise above increasingly shabby surroundings and dubious neighbours.

Number 11 was at the upper end in both senses. It stood highest above the river and farthest from the questionable doings at Number 1. It had attics and a cellar into which coal was delivered through a grating under the front window. Besides the first-floor rooms there was a small room above the scullery which Mrs Capman could use as a bedroom.

A call from below interrupted the tour of inspection.

'That'll be Alice going back to work for the afternoon shift.'

'Don't let us keep you,' Flora said.

It was an opportunity to take stock and face the worst. The back room would be their bedroom. It was of a reasonable size, but the old-fashioned dressing-table, washstand, double wardrobe and bed were over poweringly large. The window overlooked a narrow walled yard with a green door leading to a back lane, and two others, one the door to a water-closet, the other to an ash-pit.

'We won't notice,' Esther said, referring to the dreary outlook, 'if we're asleep.'

The front room had a marble fireplace and a bay window facing an identical house over the way.

'Try to think of it without this furniture.'

There would be their own pedestal table, two chairs, armchairs, a cabinet . . . Planning being a constructive exercise, Flora felt less depressed, Esther less listless.

As they went downstairs a red-haired young woman erupted from the kitchen, pulling on her coat. Their first impression of Alice Adams was of a dead-white, tight-mouthed face scowling with resentment towards the two women whom she evidently regarded as flint-hearted intruders.

'You mustn't mind Alice.' Mrs Capman joined them in the hall. 'She can think of nothing but William, and I haven't had a chance yet to tell her how considerate you've been. You'll want to see the kitchen.'

'We won't trouble you now. It would suit us to come at once, today, but it would be best to leave the upset of moving furniture until William is past the crisis.'

A few hastily planned arrangements and they left.

'Real ladies,' Gertie told William as she eased him out of his nightshirt and into a clean one. 'You can always tell breeding. If we can't get on with such as them, we can't get on with anybody.'

'Will they get on with such as us?' William managed to gasp with a hint of his own dry humour that sent his mother back to her treadle daring to hope that he would pull through, that somehow, God willing, they would manage, taking each day at a time and trusting that the morrow would take heed of itself – as was promised.

And somehow they did manage. William battled his way to the crisis and beyond it, though, as Dr Haggitt said yet again, 'only just'. It would be weeks before he recovered, months before he could work again, supposing that work could be found. In any case, by the time the upstairs rooms had been cleared and the Aumerys had manoeuvred themselves into them with the relics from Lady Green, they had neither energy nor spirit left to be other than relieved at having come to port, however uninviting their anchorage. An arrangement made bearable by the knowledge that it was temporary became, as weeks passed, a familiar way of life.

At first the mere overcoming of drawbacks was enough to make the intervals between them tolerable, even agreeable. The shared kitchen, the dank unheated scullery, the water-closet in the yard, since they could not be avoided must be endured, and then came the relief of retreating to their own sitting-room, their own walnut table, their chairs upholstered in maroon velvet, which blended well enough with Mrs Capman's rep curtains.

The room was at its dreariest during the long, twilit summer evenings. As the days shortened they drew the curtains and had tea by firelight to save the gas. The price of coal, which had soared after the war, had slumped to half the cost. Occasionally, when she was neither sewing nor cleaning nor looking after William, Mrs Capman was asked to join them. She always had difficulty afterwards in telling William what they had talked about. Flora had passed on to her daughter the art, when required, of keeping up a flow of conversation without saying anything either personal or controversial.

'What are they keeping dark?' William asked.

'I did wonder . . .' The usual reason for hiding away a young unattached woman had occurred to her and had been dismissed. 'Nothing to be ashamed of, you may be sure. There are things people don't want talked about for other reasons than being ashamed of them.'

'What sort of things?'

'I don't know.' But she knew that concealment and dishonesty were not the same. Moreover Flora had been quite open about wanting to be known as Mrs Green instead of by her real name.

'We have changed our way of life, and I'm particularly anxious to avoid being sought out by anyone who knew us before we came here. A change of name is one way of preventing that, and it can't matter to anyone what we are called.' 'For the time being' she mentally added once more.

Try as she might, she could not believe that she and Esther were doomed for ever to the stone scullery sink, the snail tracks on the floor and the ordeal of the back yard after dark. Meanwhile she wrote to the Society for Distressed Gentlewomen, to which she had contributed in more affluent days, asking their advice in seeking employment. Esther registered at the

Town and Country Employment Agency in City Road and went there every Monday morning, hoping and dreading to find a situation.

Sharing a kitchen and scullery can be a severe test of even the smoothest relationships. Esther and Flora took it in turns to prepare their simple meals, moving quietly past William's door and working as quickly as possible in order to be out of the way before Alice Adams came rushing in on her way to or from work.

Alice was the fly in the ointment. Although Mrs Capman had been at pains to stress the Greens' forbearance in extending the notice to quit and making do with three rooms in their own house, Alice stubbornly refused to believe that they could not have gone elsewhere. Mrs Capman's approval of the intruders, especially Esther, increased her resentment. She was a strong-minded young woman of immense energy directed at full blast towards a single end: to love and care for William and prevent him from dying. An admirable purpose, the Aumerys privately agreed.

Esther's own chief purpose in life at that time was less admirable. It was to be safely upstairs when the front door opened and Alice advanced along the passage as if blown by a strong wind: white face set, thin lips compressed, light brows drawn down, red hair blazing, like a man o'war speeding to the attack. If Esther had the misfortune to be there when Alice blew into the kitchen, she did her best to fade out of sight, relinquishing hob, saucepan or kettle to Alice's more urgent need. If, before fading, she murmured a tentative greeting, it was either ignored or answered with – well, one could only call it a snarl.

Of the three women living at Number 11 only Mrs Capman was in a position to know that every day of Alice's life was a miracle of achievement. Skidways' toffee factory, where she worked, was a small private business, long established and impervious to union rules. The hours of work were elastic, regulated by the state of the order book and rarely less than ten hours a day, with short breaks for lunch and tea. By sheer intelligence and force of personality, Alice had risen to the rank of second in-command. She ordered supplies, supervised packing and distribution, helped with accounts and, if needed, lent a hand at what might be called the sticky side of the business. Throughout William's illness she had looked in at Number 11 every day before going to work, at noon and in the evening. No-one knew when, if ever, she ate and slept. It was a way of life beyond the comprehension of persons used to the leisurely pace of life at Lady Green.

One day not long after their arrival, Esther came downstairs to prepare the mid-day meal and found the kitchen fire almost out. She succeeded in coaxing it back to life and put a dish of yesterday's stew to heat up in the oven. But she had not mastered the peculiarities of the various dampers. An hour later both oven and stew-pot were barely warm. She was alone in the house except for the invalid. It was almost twelve o'clock. In a few minutes the dreaded buzzer would sound and Alice would come storming in. Desperately she scraped the stew from its dish to a saucepan, set it on the gas-ring in the scullery and when the gravy bubbled, transferred it to the kitchen hob to keep hot. Glancing anxiously at her watch, she discovered that Alice was late. Everyone was late.

In her flurry she had forgotten William, whose unseen presence usually pervaded the house, until a fit of coughing in the inner room was followed by a husky voice.

'Alice? Are you there, love?'

'I'm afraid there's only me.' Esther pushed open the door. The room was narrow. William's iron bedstead was against the inner wall. He had wakened to find himself half buried in pillows and was too weak to haul himself up.

'Miss Green?' He was a fair-haired young man in a blue-and-white striped nightshirt, his wrists skeleton thin. He looked up at her with a wry awareness of his disadvantaged state. 'I thought it would be Alice.'

'She's late today and Mrs Capman is shopping. I expect they each thought the other would be back to look after you. Let me prop you up.'

Her confidence returned in response to his need. She put one arm behind his shoulders while with the other she rearranged the pillows. 'Now, a little further up. You'll breathe better like that.' Having smoothed the sheet and straightened the disordered covers, she looked round. 'It's a pleasant little room.'

It was the only one in the house with a south-facing window. A suggestion of pale luminosity that passed for sunshine in Alma Terrace gave it an unexpected cheerfulness. Or did that come, against all probability, from its occupant?

'It is now.' He smiled. Yes, the warmth came from him. The natural friendliness of his expression made her smile too.

'Your broth only needs heating. I know Alice likes to look after you herself, but she wouldn't want you to go without.'

'They've a rush on at the factory. She hadn't time to shave me this morning.' He passed a weak hand over his light brown stubble. 'Old Man Skidway died last week and they're all at sixes and sevens.'

Esther heated the broth and, after he had taken a few sips with difficulty, she fed him with the spoon, then brought warm water and wiped and dried his hands and face.

'I'll stay downstairs until the others come. Call if you need me.'

Flora and Mrs Capman returned together, having met at the street corner. Alice hurried in at ten minutes to one, found William asleep and the broth gone, assumed that his mother had seen to him and hurried off again. But in the evening as she sat at his bedside, 'I had a new nurse today,' he told her.

Without the scowl Alice's face, especially when turned to William, was younger, softer and more pleasing, though her lips were too thin for prettiness, her skin too dead white, her brows too light and too readily drawn down, as they were now when William told her what had happened.

'I missed you, love,' he said, reading the danger signals. 'The sooner I'm up and about the better. It's killing you, this rushing about.'

Involuntarily she sagged and rested her head against the pillows. 'I'd take a lot of killing.'

They remained together for a while, holding hands. Then she kissed him and put on her coat, pausing at the door to threaten, 'I'll not have her meddling, mind. She's not going to patronize either you or me with her ladyfied ways.'

William smiled to himself. The ladyfied ways had suited him very well, but he knew better than to say so.

The state of sixes and sevens at Skidways lasted for several weeks as young Alf Skidway shuffled uneasily into his father's shoes. Without Alice Adams he would have been in a right pickle, as she was the first to point out. She went on to ask for a rise in her weekly wage from a pound to twenty-five shillings.

'Else you'll need to get somebody else to do the books which I was never taken on for,' she reminded him, 'and ten to one it'll be a rogue that'll do you out of more than the five bob I'm asking – and that Mr Skidway promised me when I turned down that office job at Parker's coal depot. I'd have had the rise a month ago if he hadn't been taken, bless him.'

Alf was no more able to refuse the rise than the somewhat shaky roof could have withstood a hurricane; but five shillings a week, useful as they were, did nothing to ease Alice's day into whose twenty-four hours she packed twice as much as they could reasonably hold. Even when William was able to get up and sit in the kitchen, she insisted on coming morning, noon and evening.

Esther watched her comings and goings with awe and continued to melt tactfully away whenever possible. When it was absolutely necessary for them to be in the kitchen together, she schooled herself to remember that this was her mother's house, she had a perfect right to be there, William owed his life to them as well as to Alice . . . in vain. Every sensible reason was routed by the dynamic force of Alice's personality, as her vivid hair, white face and green eyes vanquished the already subdued tints of the room.

'I daren't die,' William said when Esther remarked that he was looking better. 'Alice wouldn't let me.' And Esther could well believe that the grim reaper would turn tail rather than face Alice in one of her belligerent moods.

One Sunday evening she went down to prepare a supper of bread and butter and hot milk, and found the kitchen unexpectedly quiet. William had gone to bed. She was congratulating herself on being alone when she discovered Alice asleep on the horsehair sofa under the window, as uncomfortable a couch as could be found and none too warm at such a distance from the fire. She was deeply asleep, as if pole-axed by fatigue, every overworked muscle relaxed, one arm hanging almost to the floor. Unconscious, defenceless, she appeared as the girl she still was and vulnerable like other girls.

Esther crept about on tiptoe, handling crockery as lightly as eggshells, prepared a second tray – a mug of milk and thinly cut bread and butter – and set it on a chair beside the couch, stealthily unfolded a newly washed blanket from the clothes horse, spread it over the sleeper and went noiselessly upstairs.

*   *   *

It had rained heavily in the night. Esther closed the front door behind her and faced the gloom of a November morning. The rain had stopped, but it had mingled with the layer of coal dust on the pavement to thicken the puddles and rivulets in the gutters and spread a rich black ooze on the flags. Fortunately skirts were being worn a little shorter. Even so, Esther hitched hers up another three inches and trod carefully to avoid splashing her stockings.

Her Monday morning visits to the Town and Country Employment Agency had been, on the whole, unproductive. It should not have been difficult to find a situation: domestic help of any kind was in constant demand. In 1914, a million women had been in domestic service, but the war had drawn them into factories, on to the land, on to buses as clippies, and had widened their horizons beyond the confines of private houses. It had taken a more savage toll of men servants. Consequently the walls of the agency's vestibule were covered with neat white cards giving details of vacancies, and Miss Tinsley's list of would-be employers was as long as her list of applicants.

But Esther Green of Number 11 Alma Terrace was proving difficult to place. Not only was she inexperienced, but her appearance was against her: she looked too delicate, even for the lighter domestic duties she sought and claimed to be used to. A short spell as temporary mother's help had so worn her out that she had been unable to resume her Monday appointment for three weeks. Her air of refinement might have been considered an asset in a companion or nursery maid in a large establishment, but such vacancies were mostly catered for by agencies in the well-to-do suburbs of the city. Miss Tinsley was more used to applications for general servants in smaller households – death-traps, she thought grimly, for such as Esther Green, though it was her business to fill vacancies, not to save lives.

185

Virtue, however, she did feel obliged to save, in certain cases and if possible. There had been Mrs Osman's request for a companion help for her elderly mother who lived with the Osmans.

Esther herself had seen the card on the notice board. 'Would I be suitable? I like looking after people.'

Miss Tinsley, generally regarded as a tough old bird, had hesitated. The girl needed work, the elderly mother needed help – not to mention Mrs Osman.

'It seems the sort of thing I'm looking for.'

It wasn't what she was looking for at all, reflected an unknown and gentler Miss Tinsley. Mindful of certain lost hopes of her own, she recognized in the girl's eyes a haunting need that Mrs Osman's mother, half-crazed and bed-ridden up three flights of stairs, could not be expected to fulfil. Four girls in quick succession had taken the position in the past eight months. Two had left on account of the craziness, the other two on account of Mr Osman. Delivering up Esther Green to Mr Osman would be to deliver a lamb to the slaughter.

'It would be very hard work. An older person . . .' And a much plainer one, Miss Tinsley mentally added. 'I could put you in touch with an agency in the west end of the city,' she added, stretching a point as she had never done before, and wondering what had got into her. 'You're more likely to find a situation in one of the better-off districts such as Copgrove or Risewood.'

The girl's reaction had been unexpected. She had got up abruptly. 'Oh no. I'm afraid—' She actually looked afraid, and with a bare 'Thank you' took her leave.

But if Esther had failed to find a situation, she had made one or two acquaintances. On her first visit another girl had been waiting on the bench in the vestibule, and had moved up to make room for her. She was Mavis Upwood, a stolid girl, slow of speech but friendly enough. They met several times. She was the eldest of five and desperately in need of work. Her father had been killed in the first battle of the Somme in 1916; her mother took in washing, but the family could barely manage without Mavis's few shillings a week. She was experienced, strong and hard-working and had soon found a place, but when Esther arrived on that morning in November, she was just about to tap on Miss Tinsley's door when Mavis reappeared. There was just time to whisper, 'It didn't work out?'

'The missis died. It came on her sudden. It was a good place. I thought I was settled there. I hope to goodness there'll be something soon, with Christmas coming and the boys needing boots.'

'I'll wait until you've been in and we'll talk.'

Miss Tinsley was in an affable mood despite the darkness of the morning. 'I may have good news for you. This letter came in Saturday's post and I want to arrange something quickly. You said that you would take a position in the country?'

'Oh yes.' The answer was fervent.

'It's from a single lady in need of a maid for general duties. There is also a resident housekeeper. She hopes to find a quiet young person used to service in a refined household. She would have her own room, starting at seven shillings a week with all found. Her previous maid left to be married.'

'You said in the country?'

Even if it didn't last, even if she wasn't satisfactory, even if the lady herself and the housekeeper were impossible to live with – to breathe pure air again however briefly, to see fields and trees, to open the window of her own room in the morning, to see moonlight as she lay in bed – even just to go there and be looked over! She had not realized until escape seemed possible, how she had wilted and drooped and peaked and pined in Alma Terrace. She raised her head; her eyes shone; her voice thrilled with energy.

'If you'll give me the lady's name and address, I'll write to her at once.'

'It's a place called Wood Aston. A Miss Angovil.'

187

Miss Tinsley prided herself on the self-command with which she conducted what was at best a difficult and often tiresome line of business, poorly paid at that; but there were times, and this was one of them, when she lost her temper. She had been sympathetic to this girl beyond the call of duty; the position was the best she could hope for; nothing as suitable was likely to turn up for weeks to come. The fact was that Esther Green was unfitted for any kind of service. She had come down in the world without learning to face reality, so that when it came to the point she simply fell to pieces. The girl had no spunk. All the colour had drained from her face. She looked ready to collapse.

'I'm afraid after all . . .' She was actually refusing. Miss Tinsley could bear no more; and if the girl was going to faint, she had better be got rid of and allowed to faint elsewhere.

'Well, that's that.' She slammed the letter down on the desk. 'If a chance like this isn't good enough for you, nothing else is likely to be. This is no place for people with nothing better to do than look pretty and arrange flowers. You've wasted my time. Please don't come here again.'

Esther did not faint. She closed the door carefully behind her and even managed to say as she dragged herself past a startled Mavis (Miss Tinsley had raised her voice), 'She has something that would just suit you – a really good place in the country. Take it if you can get it.'

'You mean you won't be—'

But Esther had gone.

Outside in the City Road the atmosphere had thickened and taken on a brownish tinge. The sky hung just above the roof-tops. Trams rattled and clanged out of the murk and disappeared into it. Only a few lamp-posts ahead, City Road itself was barely visible, so that there seemed no end to it. It was like walking along an interminable, lightless passage. How silly to hitch up her skirt to keep it clean and at the same time to trudge ankle-deep through coal black puddles instead of walking round them! She was ruining her shoes. Head bent, she saw them being ruined as if they were on someone else's feet.

Lamp-posts came nearer one by one and passed her by, and City Road never did come to an end; instead it became Acombe Street. It was as the ruined shoes carried her past the Post Office that she began to cry, not from conscious sadness: she didn't shed the tears, they came of their own accord and there seemed no end to these, either. They flowed unchecked down her face and the front of her jacket, as if washing her whole being away: her brief anger and pride, her feeling of injustice, above all the foolish illusion she had secretly cherished that perhaps the disaster had not happened after all, that somewhere, somehow, by some unimaginable turn of events, at some time however distant, it would all come right. In the firelight of Miss Angovil's sitting-room or in the garden at Lady Green or on the green slope of Long Rake, she and Daniel would meet again and be as they had been.

Instead she had been offered Clairy's place, vacant because Clairy had taken hers. It was in such starkly simple terms that Esther interpreted a situation cruel in its irony. She had known it already, that Daniel would marry Miss Angovil's maid, and felt she had plumbed misery to its depths. But the unalterable reality had not struck home to her until it was confirmed from the indifferent outside world in the voice of Miss Tinsley.

Acombe Street became Thornton Street. Half blinded by tears, she crossed within feet of an oncoming tram and turned into Nightingale Road as the works buzzers sounded their mid-day blast. By the time she reached the corner of Duke Street the pavements were thronged. Some faint returning awareness brought her to a halt beside the forlorn lime tree, to lean against its rusting railings and stay there, head bowed, looking vacantly

189

down at her sodden shoes. She still seemed to be crying, the tears an incurable affliction that had come upon her, and was unaware of curious glances from passers-by or that one of them, a red-haired young woman, had stopped, turned and come back; until she felt an arm round her waist and heard a voice close to her ear.

'Come on home, love, where you can cry in peace.'

CHAPTER 14

Morgan Krantz concluded his lecture on Victorian Reformers, put away the notes he had not needed to consult and, raising his splendid head, looked round at his small audience.

He did it deliberately, bestowing on each individual an equal gaze. He was far too experienced an exponent of the lecturer's art to neglect even the most dull-eyed of his students. The reputation of Ruskin House rested largely on his skill as Warden in not only disseminating wisdom but in uniting, as one flock, a very mixed collection of sheep.

But increasingly during this winter session his compelling gaze was becoming less equal, more particular. He had at last been granted the highest reward a lecturer can hope for: the perfect listener. The seating arrangements at Ruskin House were intentionally informal: oak settles and armchairs arranged in a wide and casual half circle. She always sat directly in front of him. For eight whole hours in as many weeks she had delivered herself up to him with unwavering concentration. This made her irresistible. No matter how fairly he tried to distribute his attention, it veered back to the face upturned to his lectern like a flower turned to the sun.

In making so poetic a comparison, Krantz was not being either fanciful or romantic. He made it with scholarly detachment. It was some time before he noticed, and with less interest, that the face was also pleasing. He felt in its rapt attentiveness the natural turning of a plant to the light: a heliotropic need. It implied the submission of self and an openness to ideas that form the basis of all learning and indeed wisdom, if combined with the sensitive response to experience he himself could once have claimed. In the short break before discussion began he mingled dutifully with the others. By the time they became a group again, she had gone. She never stayed to ask questions or express an opinion. The spell once broken, she slipped away as if urgently needed elsewhere.

Under the portrait of John Ruskin in the gas-lit hall, Esther buttoned her coat and, with a swift backward glance to make sure that she was not being followed, ran down the steps into the dark street. There was no direct tram route from Ruskin House to Alma Terrace and, always supposing she could avoid Vincent Auke, who was becoming rather too persistent, she was glad of the walk, not only for the exercise but because it gave her time to think over the lecture. The most wonderful thing about her renaissance, as she was later to call it, was the discovery that she had a mind and could use it.

It was through exchanging books for William that she had begun to frequent Hudmorton's excellent Free Library, founded by one of the Victorian reformers Krantz had referred to. After some bemused groping among the shelves she found her way to Dickens, Trollope, Mrs Gaskell, Hardy, Arnold Bennet. Deep in their novels she forgot her surroundings, read for hours and was restored to Alma Terrace as if after a long journey. She was not alone, it seemed, in suffering the sadness of lost love; and there was so much more that she hadn't yet read: biography, history, travel . . .

William and Alice had introduced her to Ruskin House. It was one of the early city settlements, a centre for adult education. Its avowed aim was expressed in gilt letters on a panel in the entrance hall: 'Happy is the man that findeth wisdom and that getteth understanding.' It was a social melting pot. Its members came from all walks of life: unemployed working men, ex-servicemen uprooted and dispossessed, housewives, teachers, craftsmen, philanthropists, with a liberal sprinkling of others like herself. Misfits.

'I don't fit in anywhere,' she had declared after her humiliation at the hands of Miss Tinsley. 'You two know who you are and what kind of work you can do—'

'Given the chance,' William reminded her.

'I'm no good at anything. I never even went to school. I was brought up to be rich and useless, and now I'm poor and useless. I'm not a *kind* of person. That makes me a freak.'

'And a good job too,' Alice said. 'You can make your own way. We're stuck.'

'In Skidway's toffee,' William added, 'and you can't get much stickier than that. You've been knocked back on the ropes.' He smiled at the thought of Esther in boxing gloves. 'Get back into the ring and fight.'

'Don't let anything get you down,' Alice said, speaking from experience.

'Commit yourself to life with all your heart and mind,' said William, quoting Morgan Krantz.

'Hearts are breaking all the time. You can practically hear them,' Alice told her. 'But they do mend.'

Between them they had supplied enough good advice to put life into a corpse.

At the end of that same month, November 1921, the Society for Distressed Gentlewomen had put Flora in touch with Mrs Vane, the elderly widow of the late Hubert Vane, founder of a fashionable department store in the centre of Hudmorton. Mrs Vane needed a resident companion, and could scarcely believe her good fortune in having found Mrs Green. Flora's even more profound gratitude at having found Mrs Vane was marred only by the thought that, in escaping to the comfort of the Vane residence in Copgrove Place, she would be abandoning Esther to the rigours of Alma Terrace.

'I shan't mind,' Esther had said.

Flora recognized the ring of truth and was a little startled by the discovery that in the past weeks Esther had changed. The change struck her more forcibly every time they met, which was generally once a week, at Number 11 or in a quiet tea-shop or, if Mrs Vane could not be left, in Flora's pleasant room overlooking the park.

As months passed, it was Esther who took the initiative in varying the nature of their meetings by taking her mother to a museum or to the City Art Gallery where she showed some knowledge of the various artists and pointed out features of their work that would not have occurred to Flora. Esther sometimes kept her waiting in their favourite tea-shop and hurried in late, laden with books, and apologizing for having spent too much time in the library. At the time of the General Election in the following year, Flora was subjected to more than one discourse on the political situation and the threat to the Conservatives of the fast-growing Labour Party: a threat which Esther seemed actually to welcome.

By that time she was working as an orderly at the Abbot Private Nursing Home. Dr Haggitt, visiting his mother-in-law who was a patient there, had learned from the matron that she was temporarily in need of an untrained helper to set trays, make beds and generally fetch and carry. He remembered the girl who occasionally lent a hand in looking after William Capman. In a white coat, presiding over immaculately appointed trays, Esther looked so enchanting that more than one patient, on taking her leave, would gladly have taken Miss Green too, had not the management recognized her as an asset and made her position permanent at seventeen shillings a week.

Consequently mother and daughter had much to tell each other over the blue-and-white tea-cups at the Willow Tea-room in St Peter's Square, a halfway point between downtown Brimlow and prosperous Copgrove Place. Their arrival always had a restorative effect on the weary waitress, who found them interesting, particularly Miss Green. It was not a colourful period in women's fashions: the vogue was for muted colours – navy-blue, fawn, grey and black. The era of cheap, ready-made clothes had barely begun. Even with the wonderful increase in their joint income, the Greens had little to spend on clothes. But as Mrs Capman said, Esther could wear anything and look smart; and she could run her up a dress or a skirt in no time. In return, Esther learned to work buttonholes, put in skirt linings, take up hems, mastered the important art of pressing, and was able to save Mrs Capman hours of time.

When the waitress had fully taken in Miss Green's hairstyle under the black velvet gusseted beret and the floppy black bow at the neck of her blouse, she could give her attention to Mrs Green. Flora was slimmer than in her earlier days; her luxuriant brown hair was still bright, and she dressed plainly, but she was not averse to accepting Mrs Vane's offer of the loan of furs she herself no longer wore. As the two women grew closer and Flora became more like a daughter than a paid companion, she was drawn into the Vane family circle and was sometimes invited to join them for an evening concert or a visit to the theatre. On such occasions, though she never presumed, and saw to it that her position as an employee was clearly understood, it behove her not to look like one, and Mrs Vane's silver fox and Persian lamb suited her very well.

Admitted, if only to the fringe, of a social life she had not hoped to experience again, Flora enjoyed it for its own sake, but her constant thought was for the opportunities it might open up for Esther. Now that the dreadfully unsuitable connection with Keeper's Lodge was finally broken, it was to be hoped that she would meet some young man from at least a professional background. Mrs Vane's solicitor, Henry Ambrose, who was also her nephew, had a younger partner, for instance, and he must have friends . . .

Mr Ambrose was an understanding person of wide experience. She confided in him a good deal, and his wisdom filtered into the Willow Tea-room to compete, though less often to merge, with that of Morgan Krantz, Bernard Shaw and HG Wells. There was indeed much to talk about.

But it wasn't going to be easy to steer Esther into a social life akin to that of Copgrove Place. There were obstacles, the most alarming being that Esther herself was clearly heading in the opposite direction. Her unexpected appetite for mental cultivation was surely commendable, if kept within reasonable bounds, her education having been sadly neglected. But her growing friendship with Alice Adams and William Capman signified, as Flora confided to Henry Ambrose, 'a downward trend'.

'Wider, perhaps.' Henry had grasped and solved her problem with his uncanny skill in putting her mind to rest. 'The old social order no longer exists. Let her learn all she can. They seem good young people. In any case, Esther will find her own level.'

All the same, Flora lost no opportunity of reminding Esther that the present arrangement was only temporary. 'Some day we shall have our own home again,' was her constant theme.

Home? Whenever Flora stressed the word, Esther was reminded of the incident by the lime tree.

'Come home, love,' Alice had said, achieving in three simple words a poignancy the most sublime of poets would have found it hard to surpass. And now, as Esther left Ruskin House and made her way confidently through the network of streets, it was with the sensation of going home.

Morgan Krantz could not know that her capacity for sitting still and taking things in had been fostered by an earlier tutor. Walking home, her head stuffed with information, she could unravel ideas and connect them with doctrine preached to her by Daniel, and so inhabit his world. There was elation in the process, a kind of mental tingling she had not thought herself capable of. Once, during a discussion on the influence of Robert Owen, she was the only person who knew that he had written *A New View of Society*. If only Daniel could have shared the triumphant moment.

He was always with her, in the essence of her being, in the mysterious life of the spirit, in recesses of the mind deeper than memory. When she did actively remember him, she could do so without pain so long as it was in the realm of ideas. As soon as he took physical shape and she recalled his voice, his expression, the light in his eyes, she relived the anguish of losing him. It was part of the natural process of healing that his appearance and the vividness of his personality gradually faded: he remained intangible, like a belief, a point of reference, a space in consciousness for love of an abstract kind.

The night sky blazed from time to time with bursts of light from the forges down by the river. She was aware of the rich variety of life around her in courts and alleys, crescents and terraces. There was no wealth in the Brimlow district of Hudmorton, but many gradations from sober respectability to extreme poverty. An exception – she was coming to it now – was Number 1 Alma Terrace, which was certainly not respectable but which was thought to be financially very successful indeed – unusually so for the mail-order agency it claimed to be. It was commonly known as Olga's Place, and common, according to Alice, was just the word. Esther had first noticed Number 1 as the least shabby of the houses in the terrace. It was well painted and in good repair, and there was a softly welcoming warmth in the pink-shaded lights that shone from its windows before the curtains were drawn.

Enlightened by Alice as to the particular form that welcome took, Esther had been aghast and fascinated. Even now, though she had passed the house scores of times, she could not resist a furtive glance or two, or suppress curious conjectures as to what exactly went on inside.

Lost in thoughts ranging from Victorian reformers to contemporary sinners, she was startled by footsteps behind her and a voice speaking her name.

'Esther!' Vincent Auke sounded breathless. 'You certainly walk fast. It's taken me all this time to catch you up.'

'I'm sorry – and it's too late to talk now.'

They stopped under the street lamp outside Number 11. He was a tall, gaunt young man in a shabby trench coat, and, like most of the Brimlow folk, he was rather pale. There seemed nothing to account for his vaguely artistic look unless it was his hat, slightly wider in the brim than most, and the extra width of his red tie.

'You haven't by any chance changed your mind?' and when she shook her head, 'Well, it was worth another try. Shall I come in and have a word with William?'

'He'll have gone to bed. It's getting late.'

'He's still . . . ?'

'Much the same. He has to be careful.'

The yellow gas-light fell on her face. She, too, was pale except for her lips. Her eyes, no longer blue in the wan light, were dark and lustrous. If only he could catch that look of hers, as if she saw or had seen something expressible in no other way than in their luminous gravity. He put his hand – his real hand, clean but lightly stained with chemicals – under her chin.

'Don't do that.'

'All right. But you know my interest in your face is purely professional.'

It would be impossible, no matter from what angle one pointed the camera, for even the most crass and bungling oaf of a photographer to depict the face in an unflattering light; and, in spite of his rotten fake hand, he was no bungler.

'Yes, I do know. And you know how very much I should dislike being looked at by strangers.'

'If they were strangers it wouldn't matter, would it?'

'It would to me. You can easily find someone else to sit for you. Some people like having their photograph taken. And now I really must go in.'

He held open the gate for her. 'There's still another fortnight if you change your mind.' There was more than a fortnight before the closing date for the competition, but he was still damned slow. It was no good leaving things till the last minute. 'Don't forget,' his smile was rueful, only half joking 'you have it in your power to make a success of me. Oh, I know it's only a small step, but believe me it could be the first step towards my salvation. What does it feel like to have a man's future in the palm of your hand?'

Esther had reached the top step and turned to look down at him. He had asked her half a dozen times to let him enter a photograph of her in the Hudmorton Photographic Society's Competition, the first of its kind. He was working in his uncle's studio and hoped to make photography his career, though as a subaltern he had been just within range of an exploding German shell, escaping the full blast but losing his left hand.

Her refusal to sit for him had been from natural diffidence: she shrank from being a focus of public attention. But now, though he made no protest, she felt his disappointment. Some unique combination of impressions acted upon her to change her mood. Through the darkness came the subdued murmur of distant traffic; she felt the pulse of Brimwood beating harsh and dogged in the night. And in one of the moments of insight that were to illuminate her life, she not only heard Auke's appeal, but understood the courage and despair that inspired it. In the circle of lamplight she saw the young man in the trench coat as the archetype of all the men who had seen their comrades die, and had come back to a world as cruel as the one they had left. For an instant she felt the sadness in the heart of things.

'If I did hold your future in my hands,' she said, 'it would be terrifying – and wonderful. I know you're exaggerating.' All the same, she knew that a mere step, a word, a glance could change a life. 'Would it really help? I've never been useful to anyone in all my life.' She came down the steps again.

'You'll do it?' He was uplifted as if he too had heard the upward rush of wings.

'Yes. I didn't realize . . . It was stupid of me.'

'Esther, you're marvellous. If I can catch you just as you are now, it'll be a knock-out.'

In the event it was her look of grave attentiveness he caught, as if she were listening to the still, sad music of humanity; and the photograph, as he had promised, was a knock-out.

Leaving behind the last of Hudmorton's soot-grimed streets, one came at once into open country. Gervase Lincoln never failed to respond to the sudden transition with a brief lift of the heart: the same sense of liberation he had felt when, as a boy, he had first ridden out from town on his pony. His mood, uncomplicated then by painful memories, had lasted all the way to Barbarrow.

The elation was briefer now. But on a day in March, driving home after lunch at his club, he was for once untouched by the familiar sadness that so often marred his homecoming. The quiet lanes already smelt of new growth. Bare-headed in his open car, he breathed its freshness, caught the first distinct green on haw-thorn twigs and the ardour of fluttering birds, and almost recaptured spring's old deluding promise. But it was not the outward signs of awakening nature, however welcome, that occupied his mind. A small, unforeseen event occurring that morning had given a new direction to his thoughts.

His parliamentary career had been brief. No campaigning had been needed to win the safe seat of Hudmorton North in the coupon election of December 1918, but he had failed to keep it when Bonar Law went to the country in November 1922. He accepted his defeat with relief. He was no politician and had allowed himself to be adopted as Conservative candidate for Hudmorton North from a sense of civic duty. He was an employer. His family's wealth had been made locally, he owned land, and was, moreover, sufficiently free of family and other obligations to have time for public work.

But during his absence on military service he had lost touch with local affairs. Like others of his class, he had feared that the post-war violence in Central Europe and Ireland might be repeated in England, and had been relieved when these fears proved groundless. But he had been slow to realize that, when the Liberal Party was reduced to impotence, as it was at the next election, the largest group in opposition would be the newly flourishing Labour Party.

Lincoln was honest, sincere and compassionate, but he was no good at public speaking. Having made his points tersely, he relied on his position and on old loyalties to do the rest. He was soon to recognize himself as no match for the new breed of fiery idealists dedicated to improving the conditions of working men and women. He made a point of attending some of the Labour meetings, and at one of them had recognized the speaker as young Godwain, son of the keeper who had died tragically some years back. It had been a speech of such burning eloquence that even he, Lincoln, had been moved.

Consequently, after his defeat he was able to step down gracefully and retreat to Barbarrow with a clear conscience, to give his attention to putting the estate in order. Though his visits to Hudmorton became less frequent, he became a magistrate, a member of various governing bodies and patron of a number of organizations in town, including the newly formed Photographic Society.

Its first exhibition, a modest affair, was held in a small gallery above the public library. He had dropped in that morning for a quick look on his way from the bank to his club. It was still early enough in the day to account for the absence of visitors, which might otherwise have been discouraging. There was, in fact, only one other viewer, a young man in a trench coat whose minute examination of the exhibits could be professional rather than merely aesthetic.

The entries were all portraits in black-and-white or sepia, mounted but unframed, and of sitters of all ages and apparently from all walks of life, though there were fewer of the humbler sort than would be the case in later years. Lincoln's interest was a trifle conscientious: he glanced respectfully but briefly at each photograph. Only one held his attention.

He recognized her with a barely suppressed exclamation. Had he actually uttered it? His reaction had evidently been positive enough for the young man to notice.

'You know her?'

Lincoln hesitated. It was years since he had heard anything of the Aumerys. Recalling the unfortunate circumstances surrounding Edwin Aumery's death, he was reluctant to become involved in any discussion of the family, especially with a stranger.

'Sorry. I only asked because that's my entry and I thought you seemed struck by it. Naturally I hoped that was because you like it. Then it occurred to me . . .'

As Auke showed all the readiness of an artist to be discouraged, Lincoln had no hesitation in praising his work and then ignoring him.

The portrait was arresting enough to merit fully the term life-like. He was seeing fulfilled the promise he had recognized in her during that dark winter at Lady Green, in the garden at the Lodge, at her father's funeral, and again at Godwain's. There was something about her that was more than harmony of features. For true beauty there must be an inner quality, and that she had. A visionary look? Was that too high-flown? Perhaps. Nevertheless, whatever quality it was that had moved him during their slight acquaintance had been captured and made permanent in the photograph.

Vincent had brightened with pleasure only to teeter again towards self-doubt.

'The trouble is that, with such an easy subject, the judges may have difficulty in considering it in purely photographic terms. I mean, they'll try so hard to discount Esther's obvious appeal that they may discount the thing altogether. I should have thought of that and chosen a plainer-looking woman. Not difficult.'

'Esther?'

'Esther Green.'

So she was married. He had hoped that she would find someone to care for her as she deserved, and he felt again, more keenly than before, an unusual quality in her, a rareness of spirit. The impression, vague and diffused at that earlier time, was confirmed by another glance at the portrait.

'Your wife?'

'No such luck. A friend. We meet at Ruskin House. I had to plead with her to sit for me. She didn't want to.'

'You've achieved a work of art,' Lincoln said abruptly.

'Oh, I say, sir, that's very good of you.' Vincent was overwhelmed.

'We may meet again. Krantz is an old friend of mine.' He moved nearer to the card giving the photographer's name. 'Auke? I know Auke's studio in Old Church Lane.'

'My uncle.'

'I see you lost a hand.'

'A few inches nearer and it would have been a lot worse.'

'How do you manage?'

Vincent explained that the false hand could be used as a clamp for various gadgets he had devised to overcome its limitations.

'And you've found something well worth doing. Keep at it. You'll make your way.'

At his club Lincoln lunched alone. He was used to solitude. Having suffered from time to time in his relations with others, he valued to the full the personal freedom he now enjoyed. Solitude, he had told himself more than once, is not loneliness. All the same, he was beginning to see himself as an outsider, free from the demands but equally free from the blessings of human ties. He was glad that the little Aumery girl was not to suffer the fate of those thousands of women whom the war had deprived of husbands. Glad? There was little joy in seeing happiness through other people's eyes, or in knowing that in Esther Aumery he had glimpsed a beauty and grace he was unlikely to see again.

He was still thinking of his brief connection with Wood Aston as he drove home in his open car along lanes twisting between deep meadows and leading between copses. It was too soon for daffodils, but under the hedges clumps of primroses had crept into bloom. A picture formed in his mind of Esther Aumery among flowers in an old-fashioned garden, not at Lady Green: it must have been at the Lodge. He had forgotten the circumstances, but he now recalled quite vividly that there had been a whiff of danger: she had been, or was to be, threatened in some way.

The incident had disturbed him, as did the memory of it.

CHAPTER 15

On her next free afternoon, Esther went directly from the Abbot Nursing Home to the Willow Tea-room, where Flora was already waiting. The affair of the photographic competition, of Vincent Auke's pleading, Esther's resistance and ultimate consent, would normally have occupied them for at least a few minutes. But Esther had barely made the preliminary skirmishes when she detected in her mother unmistakable signs of mental flurry. Flora had taken off her gloves and was smoothing the fingers as if dedicated to removing the last crease before bracing herself for an even greater effort.

'Something's happened. You're not listening.' Esther reached over, gave her mother's hand a gentle slap and took charge of the gloves. 'Come along. What is it?'

Flora glanced at the attentive waitress who, to her satisfaction, couldn't help overhearing.

'I don't know how to tell you.' Flora lowered her voice. Their heads almost met across the tea-cups. 'You may not . . . but it's for you too . . . only if you don't . . .' Her lips quivered. 'No-one else in the world matters as much as you, darling, or ever will.'

'That means there is someone else in the world.'

'Henry. He has asked me to marry him. I never expected . . . No, that isn't true. I had begun to think—'

'And you said yes?'

'No. Not yet. Not until I'd talked it over with you. He understands that I can't be happy about it unless you are happy too.'

'Of course I'm happy about it. It's the most wonderful news. You can start all over again.' They were both in tears. The waitress averted her eyes, but for a mere instant. She went regularly to the pictures and knew that tears can express other feelings besides sorrow.

'You realize that we would have our own home again? It seems . . .' Flora drifted, smiling, into the reverie of a happy woman old enough and sufficiently well schooled by experience to appreciate her good fortune. 'You'll like Henry's house – just two or three minutes' across the park from Mrs Vane's—'

'And you'll be almost back in Risewood.'

'I don't mind now. It was foolish ever to mind. Henry knows all about us and why we changed our name. Oh Esther, how I regret being so foolish about not having a carriage and such things as that, as if it mattered. I shall try to be a better wife than I was to your father.' The tears became less happy. Unbidden, the waitress brought another jug of hot water. Sympathy, like tears, takes many forms.

To live in Risewood, albeit on its outermost perimeter? Without any recollection of having been there, Esther had been familiar all her life with its gracious houses, its leafy gardens, its parties and musical evenings, its butlers and footmen (now a vanishing species), its ladies' maids and governesses. Like the perfume that lingered about the evening dresses she had tried on in her mother's room, the glamour of Risewood had haunted her imagination, and, like the perfume, it had gone stale.

'You'll love it,' she said. 'It's where you belong.'

'But you too—'

'No. I don't want to live with you and Henry, dearest. It wouldn't be fair to him. You must be happy together, just the two of you. I'm sure that's what he really wants.'

'But I thought you would . . . Oh, Esther . . .' Flora groped for her handkerchief.

Perceiving the danger signals, the waitress was at a

loss. She had shot her bolt in bringing the hot water, not that the two of them had drunk a drop or eaten a crumb.

'Of course I shall think of it as home, and come as often as you both want me. But I must make my own way now.'

'You can't mean to go on living in Alma Terrace?'

'For a while, yes. It feels like home. Alice and William are the first close friends I've ever had except . . . I have seventeen shillings a week and a roof over my head. That's more than a lot of people have – people who are of more use in the world than I am.'

She'd get over it, Flora thought, this fascination with common life, as she'd got over that dreadful business of Daniel Godwain.

'Let's talk about the wedding,' Esther said. 'And I'm famished.' She removed the cover from the toasted tea-cakes.

'They'll be clay cold, miss.' The waitress moved swiftly and whipped them away. 'Let me bring you some fresh. It won't take a minute.'

'She's very good, isn't she?' Flora said. 'Shall I give her a shilling, do you think?'

'Yes, do.'

They shared a glow of gratitude for having a shilling to give.

The wedding was to be a quiet one, and would have taken place at once if the couple had had only themselves to consider: but there was to be some difficulty in finding a suitable new companion for Mrs Vane. Her distress at having to part with Flora made her hard to please, until eventually a cousin of Henry's first wife stepped into the breach. The marriage took place in August, just over two years after the flight from Lady Green.

Though the distance was not great, their break with Wood Aston had been complete. Country villages at that time, even those nearer to the city, were still isolated. There were few private cars and telephones. Travel was by train. An occasional bus, supplied by the railway company lumbered from station to villages along such roads as were wide enough to take them.

But chinks were to pierce the obscurity into which the Aumerys had disappeared. The announcement of the wedding in *The Hudmorton Chronicle* gave the bride's name as Flora Aumery. By the Vanes and Ambroses and their friends it was accepted that the temporary change of name had been justified by the unfortunate change in her circumstances. Any one of the ladies of the Vane connection, pitched into having to earn a living, might have done the same. What surprised them was that until the wedding day they had seen so little – most of them nothing at all – of Flora's daughter, though someone did remember having seen a photograph of her somewhere.

The wedding breakfast over, the guests moved into the garden at Copgrove Place. To Flora's happiness was added the satisfaction of seeing her hopes for Esther already blossoming. Not only would there be a place for her in the family circle: it was also evident that she would be welcomed for her own sake.

'You must give me your address.' Henry's sister-in-law produced a diary when she and Esther had chatted for a while. 'I shall be having an evening towards the end of September. You must promise to come.'

'How kind of you, Mrs Ambrose. My address is 11 Alma Terrace, Brimlow.'

Where on earth was that? Somewhere down by the river among the forges and steelworks? There had been in the quiet voice an unruffled confidence, as in the girl's manner an enviable poise, qualities which, allied to the elegance of her honey-coloured corded silk dress and matching hat, made her, the youngest person present, the one least able to be overlooked. She must have been to a good finishing school before

208

the Aumerys lost their money. One could always tell. In this case the money had been very well spent. Yet here she was evidently doing social work in rundown Brimlow. It was wonderful what girls did these days.

Mrs Ambrose was somewhat wide of the mark. Esther's apparent poise could more truthfully have been called detachment. In a sense she was not actually there, under the shade of the cedar or in the sunshine on the lawn, among well-dressed strangers. From under the brim of her lacy straw hat she felt herself to be watching them, listening to her own voice using a language she had not needed for a long time. 'How kind', 'It was indeed', 'The theatre? Only very occasionally, I'm afraid' . . .

She was far from unhappy. Her mother's future was assured, the occasion delightful; her dress was a triumph for Mrs Capman. Flora had pleaded with her to go to Miss Shaw, the head dressmaker at Vane's.

'Mrs Capman needs the money more than the Vanes do,' had been Esther's decree. 'But if you would buy the material – something really expensive . . .'

As Mrs Capman said, being chosen instead of the famous Miss Shaw gave her a real lift, and the rumour of her success, starting in Skidway's toffee factory and spreading rapidly, created quite a stir in Brimlow, where the young lady, whose photograph had won a competition, already enjoyed a modest fame. It also brought Mrs Capman as many customers as she could handle in the next twelve months.

The feeling of not belonging, which Esther had seemed to outgrow, threatened her again at the wedding. She was glad when it was time to accompany her mother and Henry to the station. They were to spend a few days in London before leaving on a cruise to Madeira. But having waved them goodbye, she was to find that a morning wedding is inevitably followed by a flat and unprofitable afternoon. She had told the Vanes' chauffeur not to wait: she would make her own way home after perhaps spending an hour in

the Art Gallery. Copgrove Place, as if in revenge for
her failure to appreciate it properly, had made Alma
Terrace seem, just then, uninviting. Restless yet less
than eager to look at pictures, she drifted to a seat
in the concourse, inspected it carefully for cleanliness
and sat down to watch the world go by.

'Miss Esther?' A woman stood close beside her. She
was youngish, pleasant-looking, surely familiar. 'It is
Miss Esther, isn't it?'

'Prissie! It can't be! Oh, how pleased I am to see
you!'

'It's been a long time. At first I wasn't sure. But you
haven't changed, only got to be more grown up.'

'No wonder. I'm twenty-three, you know. Sit down
and tell me all about yourself. What are you doing
here? Do you live in Hudmorton?' It was heartening
to see her so little altered: plumper, perhaps, but with
the same look of hearty competence.

'We've been living in Apperfield. We're going back
on the 2.45. I'm waiting for Barney. He should be here
any minute.'

'Barney? You don't mean—?'

'I do. You wouldn't know. I'm Mrs Trisk now. We've
been married nearly two years. Little Kenneth is six
months old. We left him with his grandma.' There
could be no constraint: they were old friends. An
unexpected meeting after a long parting strengthens
the bond of shared memories. 'I've never been back
to Wood Aston since we left the Coach. It took me
a long time to get over Jim.'

When they left the village, the Merridons had taken
a short lease on a public house on the north side of
Hudmorton, and it was there that Prissie and Barney
had met again.

'He was always come-onish, you know, even when I
was going steady with Jim, but he'd never been one to
settle, even if I'd given him the chance. But the war
toned him down. It put years on him, and he needed

looking after. He has his serious side, has Barney, more than you might think, and he was always good-hearted. So I thought, "Why not?" especially as he was quite willing to have Mother with us.'

He had given up the travelling business, and together they had taken a small hardware shop in Apperfield.

'It's not done too bad but we'd rather be in Hudmorton. That's why we're here now. We saw a place advertised in Duke Street similar to what we've got, but bigger.'

However, the area had not appealed to them and there had been drawbacks.

'So you'll be staying at Apperfield?'

'For a while, till something else turns up. Here's Barney now. Won't he be surprised? Look who's here, Barney. You remember little Miss Esther from Lady Green?'

'Well, I'll be blowed.' His handshake was warm. He did indeed look older than his years, and had lost his swagger but not his pleasant way. 'You were just a little girl the last time I saw you. Now when would that be, Priss?'

'I think I know.' It was Esther who answered; the day had been memorable. 'It was when you took that girl to the workhouse. You remember, Prissie? The girl in the blanket. You gave her a bath and washed her hair.'

'My, you do take me back. Wasn't that a queer going-on? I wonder what happened to her.'

'I can tell you what didn't happen. They never took her in at the workhouse because she never went to the workhouse. Not that day at any rate.' Barney was no longer smiling. His sense of humour had helped him through many a scrape, but it still failed him where that pasty-faced brat was concerned. 'And I'll tell you something else. She pinched all my Laughing Cavalier plates – eleven of them; just one short of the whole damned lot.'

'Language, Barney,' Prissie reminded him. 'But you

had a right to be vexed. Talk about ingratitude after all that was done for her. Here, look at the time. We'll be missing that train – and I haven't asked you what you've been doing, Miss Esther.'

'My mother was married this morning. I've been seeing her off on her honeymoon.'

'There now. It'll be you next, I expect. If ever you're in Apperfield, you'll find our shop just off the Market Place. I wish you could see our little Kenneth.'

Esther went with them to the barrier and watched them board their train.

'Did you think she looked a bit lonely?' Prissie leaned out to wave. 'Daniel Godwain used to be sweet on her, but it can't have come to anything. Well, it couldn't really, could it? Funny we've never been back there. Tell you what, if we do find a place in Hudmorton, we'll take a trip out to Wood Aston one day and see who's still alive.'

Alone again, Esther boarded a tram outside the station and climbed to the upper deck. She had it to herself, and from the front seat could gaze at the gleaming metal lines stretching ahead until her eyelids closed and she was lulled by the swaying movement and the warm air to the edge of sleep, where memory became indistinguishable from dream.

It had also been a warm day then, that time when she had watched Barney's cart as it lurched, clinking and clattering, up the hill towards the Lodge, leaving her alone between earth and sky. She had felt with shivering joy a new awareness of the world around her. It had marked a step from the disconnected responses of childhood towards an adult sense of wholeness. For a few seconds she had seen clouds and corn and scarlet poppies together as never before, and had felt something other than their physical existence, a meaning that united them.

The clank of the tram's bell roused her. The meaning of life? She didn't even remotely know what it was all about. Idly she considered the proposition that, if one sat long enough in a tram and watched the lines stretch hypnotically ahead, one might find out: Daniel had once told her that parallel lines meet in infinity, which was perhaps where all problems were resolved, where all things met, where she and Daniel would meet again at last.

She got down at the next stop, had tea at the Willow Tea-room where the waitress noted every detail of her honey-coloured corded silk dress, and went home to give Mrs Capman and William, and later on Alice, an account of the day's events.

Commonsense and mutual convenience had altered their habits. They now had their evening meal, the high tea customary in Brimlow, in the kitchen together – it had seemed silly for Esther to eat alone from a tray upstairs. If Alice got away from work in time to join them, they would sit on at the table and talk. Those were the times William enjoyed most. He had never gone back to regular work. In the winter he was house-bound, and occupied himself with any light clerical work that came his way: checking the accounts of local tradesmen, addressing envelopes, cyclostyling circulars for societies and charities, including Ruskin House. In summer they sometimes adjourned to Esther's sitting-room to sit at her open window in the warm twilight, and it was there on that same evening that the curtain concealing the old life at Wood Aston was unexpectedly lifted again.

The wedding having been dealt with in detail, Esther went on to tell of her meeting with the Trisks, then by a natural transition to relate the story of the unknown girl who had responded to Barney's kindness by making off with his Laughing Cavalier plates.

'What would they be like?' Mrs Capman asked. 'The plates.'

'It's a famous painting, Mother, by Franz Hals.'

'A man in a plumed hat . . .' With the small pang that nothing, it seemed, would ever cure, Esther remembered the plate on Mrs Godwain's mantelpiece. 'That tawdry rubbish', Daniel had called it, condemning it as an insult to the artist.

'Like that one of your Aunt Maggie's?' Mrs Capman appealed to William. 'When would this be?'

'Oh, ages ago.' Then in response to another random gleam of light, 'It was on July 24th that the girl was found.'

'My, you've got a memory,' William said.

Esther accepted the compliment without confessing that the incident had taken place on a friend's birthday, an historic event in those days.

'Well, if that doesn't beat all!' Mrs Capman compressed her lips and nodded in mysterious triumph. 'As sure as I'm sitting here, I've seen that girl.'

Maggie, her elder sister, lived in Fergus Court off Fergus Road. The little courts were a feature of working-class districts in Hudmorton: respectable artisans' cottages, their front windows facing each other across a flagged square. The front doors were rarely opened and the front rooms never used except for funerals and festivals. The two sisters had been sitting over their tea in the kitchen at the back. The war had just started, so it must have been a day or two after the Bank Holiday at the beginning of August.

'Maggie had the table pushed to the window. It looks into the backyard. And yet we never saw her come . . .' The knock at the back door had so startled them that they had gone together to answer it. 'She was a thin, creeping little thing in a green frock.' Through the mists of time Esther recognized her green merino. 'With some of those very tin plates under her arm. I dare say you'd find a few of them in Fergus Road to this day. Ninepence, she was asking. Your Aunt Maggie was always a bit soft,' she reminded William. 'When the girl had gone I told her, "You'd best keep your back gate locked, Maggie." Seemingly she'd left the bolt drawn because the bread man was coming. "He can always

214

knock at the gate," I told her. "What's to stop the likes of that crafty little piece sneaking in when your back's turned and taking Father's presentation clock?"'

'You and that clock!' William had been calculating. 'Eleven nines are ninety-nine. Eight and threepence if she sold them all. You could buy quite a lot for that before the war.'

'But that's not the end of it.' His mother's nod was even more significant. 'Believe it or not, I saw her again. It would be a bit later on, a few weeks, maybe more. She was dressed different, quite in the fashion with Louis heels on her shoes, her hair done up and flowers round her hat. You'll never guess where, though it didn't surprise me where she'd be likely to finish up. Coming out as bold as brass.' The tilt of her head towards the other end of Alma Terrace conveyed the shameful truth.

'Not Number 1?' Esther gasped.

'Olga's Place. Whether she'd wormed her way in or whether she was inveigled in'll never be known. But that's where I saw her, as I could swear on the Bible.'

There was no denying the fascination of the tale. What a blessing Daniel would never know what had become of the waif he had so much wanted to help! 'We must raise her up,' he had said. How angry he would be with his inveterate enemy, Society, if he knew how low his protégée had sunk! And when was she ever going to root him from her mind? It wasn't fair that every avenue, every by-road should lead her back to him. She leaned her head against the window, forcing herself to think of other things – and saw Alice hurrying to the front door.

When William had gone down to greet her, Mrs Capman and Esther remained upstairs so that the two could have a little time together.

Presently, from her tendency to fidget, it became evident that Mrs Capman had something on her mind.

'Yes,' she said, 'there are bound to be changes.' It seemed no more than one of those meaningless signals across the gap into which a conversation sometimes lapses, but when she added, 'Things can't go on the same for ever,' Esther collected her thoughts.

'Do you mean – now that Mother is married?'

'Well, that's a change, there's no denying. But that wasn't the marriage I had in mind just then.'

'You were thinking of William and Alice. I've often wondered why they don't get married. They've been engaged for so long, and it wouldn't cost them any more—'

'It isn't the money.'

'Some other reason?'

They were interrupted by Alice who came running upstairs to hear about the wedding.

'Esther was asking when the next one's to be.'

'I meant yours. I do wish you and William—'

A faint colour stained Alice's cheeks. She glanced at Mrs Capman, who took the hint and slipped away. 'We'd get married as quick as it takes if it was left to us. It's up to you, Esther.'

'What on earth do you mean?' It was Esther's turn to colour – and in dismay.

'This is your house, and it's for you to say what goes on in it. If we got married, it wouldn't be William leaving but me moving in. We couldn't afford to set up on our own, and he's best here where his mother can keep an eye on him when I'm at work.'

'But why haven't you told me before? I thought perhaps you were waiting until William was really well again. It never occurred to me . . . Alice?'

She had turned her back and stood with her hands flat on the table, fingers outspread, head bowed.

'He'll never be well again, Esther. He hasn't got long.'

The shock and sadness were beyond words. Esther could only offer an encircling arm. The two stared at the table, drawn so close that its shining surface reflected them as one.

'We've known for over a year. One lung's just about gone.'

'You should have told me. In any case, how could you think that I would mind having you here? You've done so much for me. You must be married and be happy for a while. I believe that's all most people can hope for – to be happy for a while.'

Her mother and Henry, Prissie and Barney, Alice and William. They were good marriages, but she knew which of the three came nearest to exemplifying perfect love, and told herself that she was lucky to have come so close to it, even if only as a looker-on.

There were few changes to be made. The kitchen was already the Capmans' living-room. Such of Alice's possessions as could not be crammed into the down-stairs bedroom were stowed in the small room over the front door. They were married in September. There was no reception, but friends and relatives dropped in. William's Aunt Maggie baked and iced a cake, Flora and Henry, still cruising in the Mediterranean, telegraphed an order for the delivery of fruit, flow-ers and wine. Vincent Auke took photographs and wished he was marrying Esther.

Greatly daring, he risked his neck by inviting her to dinner that evening. 'At the Mikado,' he said. 'It's the only place I can afford that isn't actually repellent. No,' when Esther offered to share, 'it's on me. Otherwise I can't boast about it afterwards. Taking you out, I mean. Besides, you've done me a good turn, and I'm grateful.'

Business had picked up at the Auke Studio after the photographic competition. Esther's portrait in their window had been largely responsible, but clients had also come from further afield, and Vincent had been commissioned to photograph other weddings a good deal smarter than the one at Alma Terrace.

'There was a chap at the exhibition one morning,' he told Esther over their mixed grill. 'A military bloke. A bit on the terse side but a decent sort. Incidentally, he rather took to your portrait. Can't think why. I've an idea he may have mentioned me to some of his posh friends.'

By the time they emerged from the sinister, orange-tinted murk of the Mikado it was almost dark. The last of the queue for the second showing of *The Sheikh* had vanished into the deeper darkness of the Victoria cinema.

'It's been a lovely evening,' Esther said. Their trams would take them in opposite directions. 'I was feeling – oh, I don't know.'

'A touch of depression? There's a lot of it about.'

'You too.' It was not a question. A change in his voice had reminded her of how much his usual light mockery must conceal. 'Not so much depression as being unsettled, uncertain.' From the Co-operative Hall further down the street, people were straggling out onto the pavement. 'There must have been a meeting. What about, I wonder.'

'League of Nations. You might have known from the way they're still arguing.'

'Isn't that Morgan Krantz? Ought we to have gone instead of enjoying ourselves in the Mikado?'

'That's a moral problem we must settle some other time. Here comes your tram. I wish you'd let me come with you. No?' He took her arm and saw her to the opposite pavement.

'There's yours, Vincent. Don't miss it. And thank you again.'

He darted back, leapt aboard, and from his seat turned for a last glimpse of her.

A few seconds before the Brimlow tram came to a halt, Esther had glanced again at the supporters – or opponents – of the League of Nations, her interest directed to Morgan Krantz, whose massive shoulders and dark head made him easy enough to pick out. He was still there, but for Esther he suddenly ceased to exist: no-one existed but the last man to leave the hall. He paused on the steps to clap on his hat, then, paying no attention to the others, walked rapidly away.

In one lightning moment as he stood under the lamp, she recognized him and was transformed. Some vital part of her being, for two years dead, thrilled into life again as from a transfusion of blood or an electric charge. Daniel! She did not speak the name: it sounded in her ears, infused with all the old love, all the loneliness and loss that no effort of will, no dutiful commitment to other things had healed. It was more than his name: it held their united history. They were one, more truly so than others who needed marriage to unite them. They were never meant to be parted.

She forgot what it was that had parted them. A fleeting sight of his face, and she forgot the mystical idea of him she had cherished in his absence; he was real as he had always been, more real than anyone else in the world. His face, she thought, was thinner, more worn, older. He had suffered as she had suffered. Irrationally, the thought elated her. They must share their suffering as they had shared so much else. Chance had brought him back. She must not let him go again.

But he had already gone. He would be going to the station for the last train to Unnerstone. She would never catch up with him. There must be short cuts. Keyed up to the highest pitch of thought and feeling, she seemed to see the geography of the city depicted on a vivid mental map, and took to her heels. She skimmed past the knot of bystanders on the pavement, turned from the lamp-lit main street into the narrow walk between the book-shop and the bank, ran down West Street and into Bayes Walk. There were few people to get in her way, long stretches of darkness between gas lamps. The slippery cobbles of the deserted fruit and vegetable market scarcely slowed her down. Once she stopped to take off her shoes, then sped on, no more aware of the pavements under her feet than if she had been flying. It felt like flying, like the mysterious levitation experienced in dreams, a pre-natal memory, they say. She was about to be reborn.

At the station she put on her shoes. In the weird light under the great glass dome she felt the sudden impact of noise: the metallic thud of a locomotive against buffers, the hiss of steam, the rumble of trolleys loaded with mail bags. But the wide concourse was almost empty of travellers. A handful of passengers were waiting at the barrier to the south bay, where the last train for Unnerstone was pulling in. He was not among them. She had got there first.

She couldn't bring herself to sit down, but roamed back and forth – it was like floating – her eyes on the arch he must come through. The ticket collector came and unlocked the gate to admit the small queue.

'Leaves in three minutes, miss,' he warned as Esther passed him for the tenth time.

She moved away and stood where she could see both the entrance and the clock. Across its white face the black finger jerked away the minutes: three, two, one. Her very soul was drawn to the arch where he would hurry in from the street, always late. He would see her and would stop, amazed, delighted, sad. He would rush towards her into the strange glassy light as, many a time, he had come towards her through the green shade of Aston Wood and out into a sunlit clearing. She could not think beyond the moment when she would run into his arms.

Carriage doors were slammed. A whistle blew. The ticket collector locked the gate and went off to the main line platform. It was all at once quiet under the high dome. A ghostly shimmer on the glass far above might have been the moon. She waited. He didn't come. He never came. He would never come.

She had been out of her mind. It wasn't true, all that

about their belonging to each other. He belonged to Clairy. She had deceived herself because she was lonely. Loneliness engulfed her. She could feel nothing but its endless, aching weight on her heart.

All the benches were empty. Everyone had gone home. Having nowhere to go, she sat down. She was very tired, too tired to move or to feel surprise when the wan lights above the waiting-room and the refreshment room became Chinese lanterns hanging from trees; someone was playing a piano, everyone was dancing – even Mattie. Only she, Esther Aumery, was watching from under the chestnut tree. She was only supposed to watch. Joining in hadn't worked . . .

'You'd best be off home, miss.' The ticket collector was also going home. 'There'll be no more trains tonight.'

The street outside was deathly quiet. A prowling cat sniffed at a gutter and stole away. She seemed the only living being in Hudmorton, until the leaning figure of a man detached itself from a lamp-post and came towards her.

'Vincent! You've been waiting all this time?'

'A man has to settle down somewhere. I've taken root here. It hadn't dawned on me what a jolly time one can have simply hanging about at a station for hours on end.'

'I had no idea.'

'You're quite sure you wouldn't like to stay a little longer – say, until morning? You've actually had enough?'

She nodded. He took her arm in his.

'How did you know I was here?' she asked with a dull sense of not herself knowing where she was.

'When people take off and scud through the town at the speed you did, there can be only one reason: a train to catch. You weren't planning to go anywhere, so I reasoned that it was somebody else's train.'

No need to add that he had been fairly keen to find

out whose. He had not enjoyed the past hour and a half. He was no wiser as to whom she had waited for, or who mattered to her so much that his failure to turn up had drained all the life out of her. But he hated the man, whoever he was.

CHAPTER 16

After a long, cold winter the gardens in Copgrove and Risewood were at last showing signs of life. Crocuses followed snowdrops into bloom, trees budded, prams were wheeled into the park. Spring ventured even into Brimlow, where the early morning chirp of sparrows under the eaves of Number 11, Alma Terrace was loud enough to make an alarm clock unnecessary.

In any case, Esther was in the habit of rising at six. It was a twenty-minute walk to the Abbot Nursing Home. She was still glowing from the exercise one morning when Matron found her in the cloakroom as she was putting on her white coat.

'Mrs Bowland is being awkward. Nothing's right for her this morning. It's the great day, remember. The Master cometh.'

The patient in Room 3 was housekeeper to a gentleman whom she always referred to as The Master, so that his promised visit had come to be regarded as a Second Coming, though the staff had privately concluded that the gentleman must be a bit of a Tartar to have inspired so much respect in Mrs Bowland who, once over her operation, was proving herself no weakling.

'But he won't be here until this afternoon. I'm relying on you to calm her down.'

Esther looked in on Mrs Bowland several times during the morning, did her best to exercise a soothing influence, and assured her that she would be made tidy and comfortable *in every way* before her visitor arrived, so that no embarrassment should arise.

She had fulfilled her promise, put on clean pillow-cases, done Mrs Bowland's hair and helped her into her best bed-jacket, when she was called away to a discharged patient who was waiting to say goodbye. Consequently she almost missed meeting Mrs Bowland's visitor. It was agreed afterwards that if she had come upstairs a minute or two later than she actually did, it would have been, to say the least, a pity.

She found the door of Number 3 open, the gentleman on the point of leaving.

'This is Miss Green, sir,' The ordeal over, Mrs Bowland had regained her composure. 'She has been looking after me very nicely.'

'*Miss* Green.'

'Major Lincoln!' She had not thought of him for ages, had almost forgotten him. The years since she had last seen him seemed much longer to her than they did to him. Yet he was unchanged: he had the same spare, upright figure, the same penetrating gaze, though country living had freshened his skin and smoothed away the haggardness of war.

She wondered why, at the moment of recognition, he should have stressed the 'Miss' rather than the 'Green' which should have been more of a surprise to him. How could she know – he himself scarcely knew – that the pleasure of meeting her was all the greater because, whatever she chose to call herself, it was not Mrs. How on earth – he recognized in her all that he had seen when he first knew her: the natural grace, the beauty, the subtler quality that young fellow had got into the photograph – how on earth had she escaped marriage?

'I'm so very glad to see you.' Her voice trembled. Their hands met. She had always thought of him, even in his kindness, as somewhat stiff and stern. She had been wrong, ignorant, childishly unaware of other people. He was smiling down at her, the smile gentle, his hand-clasp warm.

224

'We must talk, Miss Green.'

She remembered that they were not alone. 'How very strange, Mrs Bowland. Major Lincoln and I are old friends.'

'Now isn't that nice?' Such a nice girl too and such a successful visit. The Master was always considerate. And such flowers! With four pillows at her back, she relaxed. Curiosity as to where they had met occupied her mind pleasantly until she drifted off to sleep.

They stood outside in the corridor.

'Where have you been?' His expression was oddly tinged with sadness. 'Where have you been?'

'Oh, there's so much to tell.' It was extraordinary, her instant acceptance of him as a person who would understand. She had known his strength and kindness in the days when she had had no need of a close friend: there had always been Daniel. But now she was drawn to him because he had known her father and her home; he was one of their own kind, yet uninvolved, impartial. He would understand all that she had to tell.

'When can you be free?'

'Tomorrow afternoon?'

He went downstairs. She leaned over the banister as a maid gave him his hat and opened the front door for him: a straight-backed, firm-lipped, authoritative man wondering with the impatience of a boy how best to get through the next twenty-four hours.

At half-past three of the following afternoon the waitress at the Willow Tea-room forgot her aching feet and took on a new lease of life. They hadn't seen as much of Miss Green since her mother got married; only two or three times, and once with one of those arty-looking men with a red tie and a shabby coat. Her arrival in a Bentley with an older, distinguished-looking man raised vibrations that spread rapidly to the kitchen and hastened to record speed the toasting of two teacakes.

The fact that they spoke so low, though disappointing, was a sign that their talk was serious.

'Why didn't you come to me for help?' he asked, and added, 'No. I can see that at such a time and after such a blow you would want to be alone. Other people couldn't help.'

He had not known of her attachment to Godwain's son, nor had he seen much of Daniel in those days; but having heard him speak on the new social order with a fervour and eloquence that held his audience spellbound, he realized that such an attachment must have been less remarkable than it had at first seemed. A pity for a fellow who could have spread his wings and gone far to have fallen into the old trap. A local girl, he gathered.

Esther had not been specific. Not only was she still too loyal to dwell on Daniel's betrayal, she could not bring herself to speak of Clairy at all. Time, far from rendering her image less hateful, had tarnished it beyond repair. Her very name was unspeakable.

No matter how freely confiding a conversation between friends may be, there must be reservations. If Esther slid over details that distressed her, Lincoln, while sympathizing over the outcome of Daniel's folly, was bound to conceal his satisfaction at the way things had turned out.

'Besides,' he went on, 'you didn't need help. You have lived through an unhappy time and made a new life for yourself.'

It only remained, he thought – and was astonished at the speed with which he had reached the decision – to detach her from it and offer another more worthy of her.

He'd enjoyed it, you could tell, the waitress mused. They'd be sure to come again.

Lincoln would not have described the Willow Tearoom as his natural stamping ground. Except as a setting for Esther, he barely saw its oak beams and brass warming-pans. Not since his prep school days had he eaten toasted teacakes and drunk tea from willow-pattern cups, an additional reason, though certainly not the chief one, for feeling years younger as he drove Esther home.

'I won't ask you in,' she said, 'because it's one of Alice's late days, and I promised to see to William's high tea. Mrs Capman is always frightfully busy towards Easter, and then all the local children have new clothes for the Whitsuntide Walks.'

'I should like to meet your friends. Another time perhaps.' They had already arranged to meet on the following Wednesday. 'We may run into each other at Ruskin House. Did I mention that I'm one of the patrons? There's the Annual General Meeting next week.'

For years the AGM notices had found their way, unread, into his wastepaper basket, but he turned up for the next meeting and took to dropping in from time to time. His revived interest in the place was accepted without comment: most things were accepted at Ruskin House. And he and Krantz were pleased to revive a neglected friendship. Many of the local intelligentsia were members, and he enjoyed for the first time in years the lively exchange of ideas he had missed in the army, in the solitude of Barbarrow and even, alas, in the House of Commons.

On his first visit, when the meeting ended, he looked into the coffee room, a monastically bare apartment with a single earthenware jug of flowers to relieve the starkness of its whitewashed walls. Esther was sitting at one of the long tables with Vincent Auke. The sight of them together brought a whiff of envy: they were young and on familiar terms, whereas he was old enough to have a daughter Esther's age. Such pain would once have been for the daughter he had lost, but now it stemmed from the fear that if Esther should have any regard for him, it would be only that of a daughter.

They urged him to join them. Auke fetched him a cup of coffee. Lincoln's self-command was unshaken, but as they talked, he formed a variety of plans for meeting in other places where he could have her to himself. He already knew that he loved her, and with gratitude that his power to feel, long dormant, had not died: far from it, he could feel, for her, passion such as he had never known. To have found the woman who so completely matched his ideal seemed at his age a miracle. But to find was not to possess. He had no idea of her feeling towards him, and doubted his ability to make her love him. Why should she?

It was after one of their meetings at Ruskin House that he drove Esther home and was invited in to meet the Capmans. The three were sitting in the kitchen and made him welcome, but there was some slight constraint and he stayed only a few minutes.

'Alma Terrace is looking up,' William remarked. 'We haven't had many Members of Parliament here lately.'

'There's nothing wrong with Alma Terrace,' Alice rejoined tartly, 'and he's not an MP now.'

'Where did you say he lives?' Mrs Capman asked. 'Barbarrow Hall. That's over Taybrooke way, isn't it? It sounds a big place.' Eyes narrowed, she gave her professional attention to Esther's plain blue belted costume, well enough in its way, and dreamed up a trousseau of well-cut country clothes and evening dresses. Were ladies still wearing tea-gowns? They used to be so pretty, in pale colours with velvet ribbons and plenty of lace. 'One thing I would like if it wasn't so pricey, and that's a copy of *The Tatler*. There was always one lying about when I worked at Madame Frank's and it does give you ideas.'

On one of his visits to town – they had never been more frequent – Lincoln called on the Ambroses and renewed his acquaintance with Flora, whom he found easier to talk to than in the chilly sessions at Lady Green. Restored to a familiar way of life to which she was perfectly suited, chastened by adversity and blessed with a sympathetic husband, Flora interpreted the arrival on the scene of Gervase Lincoln as yet another sign that Providence was acting on her behalf: that is to say, on Esther's.

Bearing in mind Esther's unpredictability these days, she was circumspect; invited Gervase when there were other guests besides Esther, never *en famille,* gave him no other encouragement than as a friend of Henry and herself, and refrained from discussing him with Esther, though not with Henry.

How strange if the plans she had idly made in the old days should materialize after all, and in this roundabout way! She had thought of Barbarrow merely as offering Esther the entry to a wider circle; the possibility of any closer link had not occurred to her. Even now – well, Gervase was her own age, not Esther's. Marriage was unlikely, was out of the question. She put it from her mind and held her breath.

Gervase was even more keenly aware that time was not on his side; he had not a year, a month, a week to lose. There were times when his longing was so intense that the last hour before they met was a delay scarcely to be borne. He knew better than to betray his feelings before she was ready to respond; instead he compensated for his lack of youth by deploying the wisdom of maturity in a campaign he could not bear to lose.

It wasn't easy: she was always so confoundedly busy. He judged correctly that casual meetings at Ruskin House and cups of tea at the Willow Tea-room had advantages over formal dining out, as seeming less significant, more natural. Under the influence of a crank like Morgan Krantz she wasn't likely to be impressed by wealth or by gifts, much as he longed to lavish them upon her.

But as the summer advanced he had the happy idea of taking her to the Botanical Gardens, Hudmorton's pride: a sanctuary of green shade and winding, flower-girt walks where, on long light evenings, they sauntered under the trees or sat in the intimate little rose garden.

'I'd forgotten how much I love the smell of rain on leaves.' They had hurried for shelter to the aviary and the company of crimson and green-plumed macaws and parakeets and brilliant blue humming-birds. She looked at the birds, he looked at her. 'They're beautiful, but do they mind never being free?'

'You mean – always being safe. Why should they mind that? They sound happy enough.' They listened to the soft whistlings and rustlings, to the occasional screech and whirr of rapid flight. 'You see, they have room to fly, enough to eat and drink. What more should they want?'

'There must be something more. It's called divine discontent. That parrot, for instance. No, not that parrot.' She turned to him, smiling, her eyes full of light. The temptation to make love to her was so strong that he moved away. 'I believe you're right. They know how lucky they are to live among trees and flowers. Not that they seem to take much interest in the view.'

Trees encircled the smooth lawns, their leaves shining in the rain. She moved closer to the glass panes, remembering wet days in Aston Wood, the drip of rain on cheeks and hair, the clasp of a beloved hand. He sensed a wistfulness in the droop of her head against the glass. It gave him courage.

'If you could be free one day, I'd like to show you Barbarrow.' He gave no sign of the nervousness he felt. Had the right moment come at last? It was so important that she should like the place. Seen through her eyes, it would seem old-fashioned. The deep seclusion he loved would seem deadly dull to a young person immersed in the vigorous life of Brimlow, with its rich mix of dirt and doggedness, warm neighbourliness and grit of both kinds. 'I believe you'd like it.'

A macaw squawked derisively. He felt depressed, especially as she did indeed hesitate. For her, too, the step would be a significant one. There was danger in it. Twice before she had gone to Barbarrow, each time with Daniel. As children they had scrimped fallen apples in its orchard; as lovers they had looked down on it, admiring and critical, from the hillside.

On the night last September when she had moped in the station and Vincent had rescued her, hunted up a growling taxi driver and taken her home, she had come to her senses. The flight, shoeless, through Hudmorton's dark side-streets had been a single act of lunacy she was unlikely to repeat. Having at last accepted the truth, that she and Daniel had taken separate paths, she could honestly say that she seldom thought of him; not consciously at any rate. Was it wise to risk the revival of regrets she had outgrown?

He misinterpreted her silence. 'I only thought – as the weather is so pleasant – but I dare say it would not be what you would like—'

She had forgotten him and was remorseful. The hesitant phrases were uncharacteristic. She realized – it was a revelation – that he was nervous, that he wanted, yet for some reason feared, to take her to Barbarrow, that his reticence concealed a capacity to suffer. Barbarrow, she remembered, must have tragic associations for him, far more tragic than her own wistful memories of an early romance. She seemed for a moment to see into his heart, to feel her own respond to its vulnerability.

Impulsively she reached out and laid her hand on his. 'I'd love to see Barbarrow.'

It was the first time she had touched him in anything approaching a caress. Taken unawares, he could scarcely conceal his delight.

'That damned bird,' he said as the macaw screeched again.

They laughed, each mistaken as to the other's thoughts, yet drawn closer than ever before.

They drove between hedgerows white with flowering chervil. She had forgotten the scent of meadow grass, the ethereal effect of sunlight on young leaves, the swoop of swallows cleaving a sky of delicate blue. As they drew up in front of the house, white doves rose from their cote, silver-winged in the pure light of a spring morning.

She had not been prepared for the intimate charm of the place, nor for the impression it gave of unprofaned restfulness. The house itself, twin-gabled and stone-tiled, was without grandeur, a rambling manor house typical of the district. Except that it was larger, more lovingly cared for and less shadowed by hills and trees, it was not unlike Lady Green: the same ample porch, the same stone-mullioned and transomed windows, the same lozenge-shaped panes.

But at first she saw only its sunlit façade of weathered stone mantled with the pale green leaves of wistaria, an espaliered pear tree in blossom under an open lattice; and around her the whole domain held in an undisturbed stillness, the deep quiet of the country, with its hoarded past and latent promise.

'Gervase! Listen!' A cuckoo called from the hanging wood. She thrilled to the mystery of its hollow notes. 'I've been away so long, but it's all still here.' Her gesture took in the sky, the wood, meadow and stream. 'It's like coming home.'

With all the resources of language at her disposal she could have said nothing that pleased him more.

Mrs Bowland, now quite recovered, was waiting in the porch, and took her up shallow stairs to a low-beamed bedroom facing south. 'It's a real pleasure to see you, Miss Green. And now it's my turn to look after you.'

They had lunch in a small panelled room, at a table of oak black with age, and he told her how his father had bought the house fifty years ago but had continued to live mainly in town. It was young Gervase who had cared most for Barbarrow.

'I used to ride out here in the holidays and go fishing and exploring. We had a couple living here as caretakers, and Mrs Fairbrother gave me scrambled eggs and fruit pies in the kitchen. They were some of the happiest days of my life.'

She listened, picturing him as the boy whose happiness shone again in his eyes.

'My father knew how I felt about Barbarrow and he left it to me. Some of these old houses have belonged to the same family for generations – like your own home – but to own a house from choice rather than because it belonged to one's ancestors can be a better thing in some ways.'

'Better for the house. It isn't taken for granted. Of course,' Esther added ruefully, 'having the means to care for it makes all the difference.' She found herself telling him about the plight of Lady Green and the fate of the Italian mirrors and the table at which six princes had dined.

'I used to think that they'd all sat there at the same time, a whole gang of princes in velvet doublets and crimson hose like illustrations in a story book. It was quite a long time before—' She broke off, remembering who had rid her of so ridiculous an idea.

'Before?'

'Before I realized that they might have dined there each in his own generation, not all together.' The hesitation had been momentary. She could speak lightly of the early days, and made him laugh over the deficiencies in her education. The conscientious effort of the past two years might have cultivated her mind, but it had left, she confessed, whole areas of ignorance untouched.

He asked her who had bought the table and the mirrors, and groaned inwardly at the mismanagement of the Aumery affairs when she naïvely mentioned the price. But their talk was chiefly about Barbarrow. He told her about the alterations he had made, always with an eye to adapting to modern needs with due reverence for its antiquity. Esther believed that a house was more than the sum of its parts.

'There can be a feeling of something else: a spirit. You must have felt it, especially here. Does it come from the place itself, or from the influence of the people who have lived in it? Both, perhaps. Is it the shape of the rooms, the beautiful things in them, the way the light moves – or is it a lingering kind of essence of all the years people have lived here that makes it so . . . ?'

'Makes it so . . . ?'

She had left the table and gone to the window. It overlooked a lawn where a wagtail ran and rocked, as weightless almost as air. In her pale green dress she seemed to him so slight and slender and young that he could no more hope to hold and keep her there then he could cage a visiting bird.

'So enfolding. Yes, that's the word. You've set your seal on it. I believe if you love a place enough, it loves you back.'

'Do you think it's the same with people?'

Preoccupied with her theory, she didn't answer. As for what she had said, he reminded himself that she was seeing Barbarrow as the home of a friend: she would not have spoken with such warmth had it so much as entered her head that he might ask her to share it. Was it so unthinkable? Was he so hopelessly unsuitable that she had never even thought of him as a lover or husband?

It was almost a relief when she reminded him that he had letters to write and offered to explore the garden while he attended to them. He went to his study and sat at the table, sunk in despair and unable to write a word. He had set such store on her liking the place. She liked it. He was miserable.

Esther strolled along paths between hedges of box and yew, found bluebells growing under a wide-spreading copper beech, rediscovered the flagged way leading to the rustic arbour, and beyond the orchard trees laden with pink and white blossom, a five-barred gate opening on a meadow. Her explorations brought her back to her starting point by way of a vegetable garden – or they would have done if she had not discovered just in time that one of the rooms overlooking the path must be Gervase's study. He was sitting in the window but had not seen her. Elbows on the table, hands clasped to his temples, he looked so dejected that she was shocked. Was it a headache? Had he been suffering all morning and bearing up for her sake?

She went quickly back the way she had come and sat on the stone balustrade at the front of the house to wait for him. For once, his self-command seemed to have failed him. Her thoughts progressed; self-control implied a need for it. She dismissed the headache: he had seemed happy during the drive and lunch. Had some chance remark in their light-hearted conversation touched a hidden spring?

'The spirit of the place?' It was no idle fancy, but distinctly to be felt: an emanation from walls of mellowed stone, the murmur of a stream, laburnum casting golden light on the grass. Her eyes travelled from the garden to the hill and the path climbing to a belt of trees where once she had met Major Lincoln, not Gervase, who was now her friend, her dear friend, but – her smile was touched with shame – the dour-faced enemy of the people who had taken her for a kitchen maid, a deeply unhappy man. Was he unhappy still?

With a pang of self-reproach she remembered Matty's grisly tale of the child and the nursemaid, and her own remark just now about the influence on a house of the people who had lived in it. The spirit of Barbarrow was not wholly benign, interfused as it was with memories of the dead. How cruel that the place he loved best should have been the scene of his deepest suffering! So deep that even now a thoughtless remark could revive a long-buried grief.

So once again they both misread the signals: she in blaming the past for his present depression, he in failing to understand that her open delight in his home was a sign of how much she was at ease with him. Once again, the misunderstanding was to his advantage. When he rejoined her, he found her changed. She looked and spoke with an added gentleness, an awareness of him that, as the afternoon passed, soothed away his fears. They walked through fields and by the river, and came back to tea on the terrace in such companionable ease that he dared to hope again. It gave him inordinate pleasure to see her presiding over the tea-cups as she told him how much she had enjoyed the day.

'You'll come again?'

She did come again, and again, escaping from the smoke-polluted grime of Brimlow to the pure air of the country; and perhaps, as she grew to love it, Barbarrow itself would have been his means of winning her. But there were other factors more persuasive.

Their relationship had changed. Her more protective concern for him released him from the constraint resulting from years of loneliness. Confident of her sympathy, he talked freely, about his estate, the problems of the Lincoln Ironworks, his innumerable committees, and gradually of his boyhood, his experience in the army and – last of all – of the period in between.

Neither of them avoided speaking of his wife. When Esther admired the *gros-point* on a stool, she was told that Anne had loved needlework and had also painted several water-colours. The toilet things placed at Esther's disposal were obviously either Anne's own or had been chosen by her.

'This tree fascinates me.' From a window-seat in the drawing-room, Esther had been watching the constantly changing pattern of light and shade cast by the branches of the copper beech. 'The leaves have changed since I first came, from purple to bronze.'

'I hadn't realized . . .' Gervase had come to look. 'It shades the whole of that space between the path and the wall. Anne liked to sit here. It was a smaller tree in those days.'

'In those days?'

'It's twenty-two years since she died.'

'So long? She must have been quite young.'

'She was twenty-six.'

'Only—' Instinctively she left the thought unspoken. Only two years older than herself. 'You have her photograph?' she said instead.

Rumour had erred in claiming that Anne was French, as it had erred in almost every other respect. Her maternal grandfather had been French, and as a girl she had spent long holidays in Provence. The photograph in Gervase's study was of a faintly smiling young woman, her hair swept up, her brow fringed, her neck swathed in lace.

'She was a gentle person?'

'Too gentle to go on living.'

'After it happened? Are you saying, Gervase, that Anne died of grief?'

'You knew?'

'Only that you lost your little girl.' It was true: the rest had been hearsay. She felt resentful of the gossip, remorseful as to her own part in it. At the same time, she marvelled that in so smooth-running a household, where every object was cherished with care, the most precious thing of all could be lost.

'Lilla,' he said. 'Her real name was Elizabeth.'

In such naturally falling drops of information the story reached her, rather than in any deliberate retelling. He had placed Esther so irrevocably at the centre of his life that he was scarcely aware how much of it was strange to her; but his impulse was to share with her not only his wealth and his home but his thoughts, his feelings, his innermost need. Consequently, when they drove out to Barbarrow one day in June, Esther knew as much as could be known of the tragedy enacted there when she herself was an infant.

It had happened on just such a day in June. Then, as now, hay had been lying in the shorn meadow. Household routine was always relaxed a little at the time of haymaking. The master and mistress being away from home, the maids were free to help in the field. The house was left unguarded, doors unlocked, windows open, all but one of the rooms unoccupied. Those were peaceful days, the Hall as secure amid its sunlit pastures and sheltering trees as at any time in its long history.

After her marriage, Anne Lincoln had kept up her connection with the district in Provence where her grandparents lived. Her friends there included the Lavignes and their daughter Julienne. There had been an interchange of visits, and, when her parents died of typhoid, the Lincolns brought Julie to live with them, ostensibly as nurse to Lilla, but in effect as one of the family. They themselves were young, and she was nineteen when she came to make her home at Barbarrow.

She was pretty, affectionate, kittenishly light and given to innocent flirtations when opportunity arose, which was rarely, but with a fundamental French realism and a devotion to Lilla which was practical as well as loving. Otherwise they would never have left the child in her care, even with the incomparably reliable housekeeper, Mrs Talbot, to keep a watchful eye on them both.

The Lincolns' trip to Provence was a duty, not a holiday. Anne's grandmother was nearing her end and had pleaded for a last visit from her grand-daughter. Even so, they had delayed the journey on account of another outbreak of typhoid: it was for that reason that they left Lilla at home. Provençal standards of sanitation left much to be desired.

Shortly before they were due to return, Mrs Talbot had suffered a slight heart attack. Julie had taken charge and called in the doctor, who prescribed a fortnight's rest. In her anxiety to be well when the Lincolns returned, Mrs Talbot submitted, though unwillingly, and was consequently lying down in her room when it happened – whatever it was that happened. One result of the horrible affair was that it hastened her death. She had the task of breaking the news, blamed herself and never recovered.

The strangest feature of the affair was that no-one knew anything. One maid was having her day off, the other two had Mrs Talbot's permission to help to pike the hay. Cook and the stable boy had carried out the mid-day 'snap' for the workers, and stayed to share it under the elms where Julie and Lilla joined them until it was time for the child's afternoon rest, and Julie took her back to the house. Neither of them was ever seen again.

When all local enquiries had failed to produce even the smallest clue as to what had happened – nothing had been disturbed, nor was there any trace of an intruder – Gervase and Anne dismissed the servants, closed the house and went abroad. For almost two years their life was a restless progress through hotels, pensions and furnished rooms, until Anne showed signs of an early decline. She died at the family home in Provence. For a while Gervase stayed on before returning to Hudmorton and his responsibilities at the ironworks. Then had come the war. He had almost welcomed it.

'We none of us knew what we were in for. Those four years destroyed every vestige of the old world, even the ability to feel its loss. One knew it, yes, but could not feel it or feel anything. Then one day I came back here.'

Esther remembered the words as she leaned on the orchard gate and looked from the shade towards the meadow, stripped by the mowing of all but the sun's amber light. The day was warm, the air scented with clover and cut grass, the scene strangely trance-like as the men slowly turned the hay and the patient horses drowsed in the shade. Closing her eyes, she felt the years fuse into one continuing sequence of summer days; and since perfection cannot last, her thoughts turned again to that other day when the bright scene had darkened without warning. The events of over twenty years ago, which had haunted her with the sadness of an old tale, became as real and immediate as the gate she leaned upon, as startling as the sudden weird cry of a yaffle in the wood. Had they heard it too? They must have come this way, fair-haired Lilla in a frilled apron running ahead between the orchard trees, dark-haired Julie pausing to close the gate.

Nowhere on earth could there be a lovelier spot. No visible flaw marred the serenity of house and garden, stream and hill, all held in the dream-like perfection of an English June. Did the dark undercurrent at Barbarrow heighten one's perception of its beauty? Was it possible to conceive of perfect happiness without having known grief?

'What were you thinking of?' He had come to her across the grass, unheard. They leaned over the gate side by side as she tried to tell him.

'It was brave of you to come back,' she concluded. 'But you don't regret it?'

His motive in returning had been practical: he must either let or sell the place. Sentiment had played no part in his return. Weary of the long-drawn-out bloodshed, he had thought himself indifferent as to where he lived.

'Imagine, Esther. I found it, not as it had been when we left it but as it was when I was a boy – shabby, shuttered, neglected, needing me.' In return it had offered him the freedom and solitude he had enjoyed in the early untroubled days of youth. 'But would I have valued it as I do now without having known the pain of leaving it?'

'That is exactly what I was thinking. To be truly happy one must have been sad.'

It was as if, travelling along different paths, they had reached a destined meeting place. They faced each other in the soft green light under the orchard boughs. She understood his need to love and be loved. There was nothing else she was good at: only loving.

'I could never be happy again, here or anywhere, without you.' His voice broke. 'You have changed the world for me. I don't know if you could ever love me. I'm afraid to ask. But I must tell you how wonderful it has been to be with you . . . hoping . . . I'm so thankful, so deeply grateful.'

Her eyes filled. Their hands met and then their lips. A stranger coming upon them unawares would have seen a young woman in the arms of a much older man and might have felt regret on her behalf, censure of him, not knowing that in their mutual awareness of the other's need, and in their mutual longing to fulfil it, they were equal. His kiss, like hers, was tender and self-forgetting: the pledge of a love unthreatened by rapture and its inevitable fading.

CHAPTER 17

Almost a year had passed since Esther waited at the station, unaware that Daniel no longer lived at Wood Aston and consequently rarely used the rail service to Unnerstone. He was by that time teaching at the school in Aukmarsh and lodging in the village which, being a mere five miles from Hudmorton, he regarded as within comfortable walking distance of town.

When he left the League of Nations meeting – while Esther ran through the lamp-lit streets to the station – he took an opposite direction and called at the Labour Party committee rooms to pick up some pamphlets, before setting off on the familiar tramp back to his lodgings.

He had crossed the river to the shabbier southern outskirts of the town when, in the unlit corner between the old toll-house and the iron railings of the bridge, a movement caught his eye. It was not unexpected.

'Night, Mr Godwain.' The husky greeting was followed by the emergence from the shadows of a small figure, a pinched face upturned.

'Night, Jake,' Daniel came to a halt. 'Ready?'

'Yes, sir.'

'How many inches in a foot?'

'Twelve, sir.'

'What is the name of the king?'

'George, sir. George the fif.'

'Fifth.'

'Fifth, sir.'

'Where is Scotland? North, south, east or west?'

'North, sir.'

'Well done.' Two pennies changed hands. 'Off home now.'

The subtle distinction between Mr Godwain and sir had crept into these exchanges and become part of the game. 'Sir' was a reminder for Jake of the few months when he had been lucky enough to go to school, when he had had a whole jersey, a breakfast every morning and a mother as well as a father. The friendship had begun on a dark and chilly night in the previous winter. Daniel's meditations as he crossed the bridge had been interrupted when he almost stumbled over a small boy crouching by the railings.

'Gi's a penny, mister.'

There was nothing unusual in the plea, apart from the extreme youth of the beggar and his being there alone at that hour.

'You shouldn't be here at this time of night. Go on home.'

'It's only nights when I can come, mister.' The child's teeth chattered from cold.

'Why's that?'

'Billy-on-the-bridge. He said he'd half kill me if I pinched his beat.'

Billy was an institution. He had established himself with his tray of matches long before the war, moving from the south to the north end of the bridge, according to the weather. He was not the man to tolerate a competitor of tender years. Jake had no matches, no socks or boots, no expectations and very little voice beyond a whisper, colds and coughs having played havoc with his vocal cords. But these shortcomings might prove assets in bleeding the public of pence which Billy regarded as rightly his.

'Here.' Daniel had felt in his pocket for a coin, and walked off, seething with anger at the wanton waste of human life, the evils of capitalism, the misapplication of national resources, the scandal of public apathy – and discovered that he was being followed.

'Hi, mister.' They met again in a pool of darkness between widely spaced gas lamps, so that Daniel saw little more than a pair of dark eyes in a pale face and a grimy hand holding out the coin. 'You made a mistake. You give us a two-bob piece. They'll think I pinched it.'

'Who will?'

'Me father and grandma.'

'What's your name?'

'Jake Hildy.'

'Keep the two bob, Jake, and get yourself a pair of boots. Royds may have a pair that'll fit you.' Royd, the pawnbroker and secondhand clothes dealer, had most things.

Since then Jake's grandma had died and his father, an unskilled labourer, was either away from home on spells of casual work or more often unemployed. Daniel knew pretty well the wretchedness of life in such circumstances, and the shame that kept a child from school when other children were at least clean and decently clad. He had given Jake a little book of general knowledge questions and was surprised at his ease in mastering them, and with a speed attributable both to natural intelligence and the urgent need to earn the twopence reward.

On that summer night, the catechism concluded, Jake relaxed.

'You're certainly getting on. I have high hopes of you, Jake. High hopes. Now get off home this minute.'

With the coppers safe in his hand, Jake watched his friend out of sight, then crawled back into the wedge of space between the two walls, squeezed to the farther narrower end, shuffled himself into a sack and fell asleep.

The night was starlit and pleasantly cool. In ten minutes Daniel had left the last straggle of human habitation behind him and swung along the empty road, a tall lean man enjoying the freedom and solitude of the last hours of the day, especially the solitude.

For all the time and energy he necessarily devoted to other people, his inner life was that of a recluse – his compensation for the failure, as he saw it, of his relationship with others, even his mother.

He had been some time in securing a permanent post. His mediocre performance in exams and a whiff of disapproval of his way of life had affected his grading and the tone of his testimonials. He had no choice but to accept a temporary appointment at the school where he had worked when uncertificated, though at a salary increased by a pound a week, until the September of 1922. The appointment to the school in Aukmarsh was certainly welcome, even though the village was further from home and awkward to reach.

'What are they sending you there for, a God-forsaken hole like that?' Bertha had demanded. 'You'll be off at daybreak and back goodness knows when. I can't be by myself all day. I'll be losing the power of speech with nobody to talk to, not even Prince.'

The old dog had died in the previous October, exactly a year after his master. As Bertha said, 'You'd think he knew,' and Daniel, for once as irrational as his mother, privately agreed.

The solution would be to go into lodgings, but he would barely be able to pay for them and at the same time support his mother at the Lodge. As Thomas had worked for a private employer, Bertha did not qualify for a widow's pension. The arrival in Wood Aston of a couple who had sold their farm and needed to rent a house seemed providential. The Lodge was let to them on a one-year lease; Bertha went back to her sister's and Daniel into lodgings at Aukmarsh. Both accepted the situation philosophically. Neither was ever likely to forget how much worse things might have been – and almost were.

On the afternoon of Bertha's homecoming in the previous year, when Clairy had ridden off with Amos in the rain, they had braced themselves to face her return on the following day, and the next, and the next. Day after day Daniel's grim determination to put up the banns was thwarted by her absence and total silence.

'She'll wait until it starts to show, if it's only to disgrace us,' Bertha said when days had become weeks and there was still no sign of her. Daniel saw the embarrassment of a last-minute wedding and decided a dozen times to seek her out at Miss Angovil's where, apart from that one shameful time, he had not set foot since his entanglement with her maid, only to reject the idea: he'd be damned if he'd move an inch to find her. In August a rumour reached the Lodge that Miss Angovil was still looking for a new maid. Not until the end of that month did Clairy reappear. It was afternoon when a taxi stopped at the gate.

'She's here – dressed to kill,' Bertha called from the kitchen window to Daniel in the parlour, and instinctively whipped off her apron.

Clairy tapped at the open door and came into the tiny hall where they all three stood throughout the brief interview. She wore an expensive-looking costume of thin grey worsted, its long jacket piped with black velvet, and a wide black hat. Under its brim her skin was thick and smooth, inanimate as ivory, without any glow of living tissue. In the oval pallor of her face only the strange eyes under their dark, wing-shaped brows were arresting. As always, her clothes seemed not merely put on, but part of her, like the skin of a snake or the shell of an inscrutable sea creature – as Daniel might have thought in a more objective state of mind. He didn't notice what she wore: his impression was less of a woman he knew only too well than of an alien and daemonic force directed against him with a concentration uncomplicated by the weakness or softness of any haphazard quirk of human folly.

'No, I won't sit down,' she said drily.

'You haven't been asked, have you?' Bertha demanded.

'Be quiet, Mother!' Daniel's abhorrence of the vulgar kind of quarrel that seemed to threaten made him brusque. 'Where have you been? We need to discuss things.'

She was more wan than usual, perhaps also less at ease than her calm insolence suggested. Could any woman, however regardless of the feelings of others, be unaffected by the hatred that burned in Daniel's eyes and strangled his voice?

'Where have I been? My whereabouts need not have concerned you. That's what I came to tell you. I won't be marrying you. What I told you wasn't true. I was mistaken.'

'Mistaken? You mean it was a downright lie – or else you've known what to do about it.' At the sight of Daniel's face, Bertha checked her angry outburst. If anything could have added to his wretchedness, it was the possibility that he had begotten a child to a woman callous enough to destroy it: to have recourse to a filthy back-street quack. And when she repeated, 'I was mistaken,' he chose to believe her, though doubt would torment him for the rest of his life. At the same time – relief came tremulously – to be granted the reprieve that conscience had kept him from praying for was like daybreak after the darkest night.

There was oddly little to be said, considering the cataclysmic effect of their disastrous plunge into intimacy. They had never felt the least personal interest in each other. He felt neither curiosity as to how and where she was living nor responsibility for her future.

It was Bertha who asked, 'You'll be finished with Wood Aston then? The Lord must have had some good reason for putting you under that hedge like worse than a pauper in the first place, and He alone knows why you ever bothered to come back.'

'I had *my* reasons too.' The words had stung. Under the black hatbrim her eyes had turned grey as stones.

'And you should be grateful that I've come back to tell you that I won't be marrying your Daniel, and never wanted to. I didn't need to come and put him out of his misery. I could have left him dangling.' She had recovered her poise and with it a cold indifference. 'I'd never have made a poverty-stricken schoolmaster's wife.' With the merest downward glance she seemed to call attention to the sheen of her skirt and the smooth fit of her pearl-grey gloves.

The next moment she was gone. The taxi door slammed. She had passed from them, leaving a vacuum such as nature is said to abhor, a weird suspension of normal life, a warp in time. They listened, speechless, rigid, until the drone of the car engine was lost in the distance. Daniel felt as he had done at St Quentin when a bombardment had ceased but the menace remained: when one waited for a return to normality and normality never came, only the counting of losses and the sense that to survive when others did not was in some way to have died, to have all one's body intact was nevertheless somehow to be maimed.

'You're shut of her, thank God.' Bertha was trembling. 'It's more than you deserve, but you've learned your lesson. It's like the sun coming out, to see the back of her.' But it was sun that gave no warmth or brightness. She couldn't seem to pull herself together. 'I'm only thankful your father didn't have this to go through—' She stopped. Mention of Thomas had revived those strange fears, those unanswerable questions. How had he got so near to the Scaur? She had always been careful to leave his chair near the garden gate. If only she hadn't been persuaded to lie down that afternoon with her curtains drawn. She'd never lain down for a headache before . . . She groped her way to the kitchen and, sinking into the rocking-chair, puzzled her head for answers other than the one she dreaded to acknowledge, until her head ached again as she rocked slowly like an old woman.

Never again from that day on did Bertha feel settled at the Lodge. She had lived there all her married life and had never thought to leave it, but she could find no repose at her kitchen fireside or in the parlour, or even in her bedroom – there least of all, because she could see from its window the green sward stretching to the edge of the Scaur. Sometimes she dreamed of Thomas, sometimes she lay awake missing him from her side, sometimes she looked out and wondered how the chair had got all that way by itself. She knew better than to share such thoughts with Daniel: there was nothing definite enough to share. All the same, when the time came to leave the Lodge she went without a qualm, hoping never to return.

Since then, with all the energy of mind he had so wantonly wasted, Daniel had set himself to amend his life. His natural range of vision stretched to far horizons, but he was also by nature a teacher, his scope at present limited to the enlightenment of country children between the ages of five and fourteen. At first it was a kind of penance, gradually it became a mission. The civilizing of mankind was to be no high-flown affair. It began on the long ladder's lowest rungs, with the wiping of noses and the cleaning of fingernails, mounted to the prohibition of swearing and as far as possible, fighting, thence to the inculcation of reverence and truthfulness, the kindling of imagination and reasoning powers. The steps were slow, the possibilities to a man of his vision, unlimited.

His personal life was ascetic: he ate sparingly, had no indulgences, bought only books and devoted his time to local politics. The self-inflicted scars remained, but as time passed he became aware of an unlooked for source of comfort: he could think of Esther, and with less pain, could remember their early days and their idyllic love. In solitude, she became his unseen companion. He thought of her when he heard the first cuckoo in spring, saw the violets, sheltered from rain

249

under a tree. He shared with her his problems and such poor triumphs as he achieved.

Now as he tramped back to his digs in Aukmarsh, she was with him in his heart and mind, and more persuasively than usual, as if she had come nearer. He was all at once able to remember her voice and actually stopped in the dark road as if she had spoken his name. Where was she now? Were they still in Italy? 'Esther,' he said aloud. 'Esther.'

The air was empty of sound, the trees were motionless. He moved from under their branches and saw above him a sky full of stars. After all, what more could a man want than to walk under the stars, remembering that he had once been loved and hearing the voice of the loved one as if love were timeless? Alone, one cannot wrong another. The power to hurt had gone; the love remained.

Was there anything in this notion of telepathy? Laplanders were said to communicate, mind with mind, across acres of forest and endless wastes of snow. Was he nearer to Esther on this particular night because the letter in his pocket had directed his thoughts towards Wood Aston? Until he was thirty at least he could not hope for a school of his own. Besides, only married men were appointed to headships. But on the morning post had come a letter offering him the post of assistant at Unnerstone, a bigger school at an increased salary and, as it happened, under a headmaster of similar outlook to his own. He would take up the position in October, by which time the lease on the Lodge would have expired. As Bertha would have said, 'It seemed meant.'

Not that she would want to go back to the Lodge. She was content to live where there were shops and a chapel two streets away. He would have the Lodge to himself, with books to read, a garden to dig, a river to swim in, a home to come back to after long days in the classroom, followed by evening meetings. He'd

250

get himself onto the parish council and later, perhaps, put up for the district council.

The following winter was the happiest he had spent for years, and seemed the shortest. The place was his own. He took a pride in making up for years of neglect and enjoyed repairing, painting and reorganizing things to his own needs. In clearing out a shed, he came upon the twisted remains of his father's wheel-chair which some thrifty neighbour had salvaged from the Scaur. It was strongly made and heavy. He had examined it after the accident, so far as was possible in its mangled condition, and had been pretty sure that the brake had not been secured. So tragic an instance of his mother's carelessness had added to his misery at the time. Not that he blamed her: she had been sadly overworked to the point of exhaustion. He had closed the door of the shed and kept the discovery to himself.

Now as he pushed the chair out into the daylight, he experienced a revival of the old uneasiness. At this distance in time he could not regret the death which had ended a broken life. But how had it happened? He had been living in Hudmorton at the time and had never seen his father trying to move the chair himself. When his mother had told him, they had seen it as a sign of recovery, the only one, when in every other way he had seemed to be getting worse. Once in motion with the wind behind it, the brake released . . . on even so slight a slope . . . ?

With an effort, he put the matter from his mind and consigned the chair to removal by the local scrap-dealer. By the time he had filled the shed with unwanted pieces of furniture and decorated the rooms, it was Christmas. He spent two days of boredom, manfully concealed, with his mother and aunt, and returned as soon as was decently possible to his own fireside: to the familiar landscape of Cat Hill and Long Rake, to the pamphlet he was writing on the redirection of funds

251

from expenditure on armaments to social welfare, to a way of life he justly felt to be good.

But when, on his daily walk to Unnerstone, he felt the first hint of spring, when the damp earth felt fresh, and mysterious intimations of change hung in the air, he was less content. As the evenings grew lighter he was lured into spending them at home instead of at meetings in town. Sometimes he took the short cut by Broom Farm. On the stile at the edge of Grotes' pasture he was only a stone's throw from the stepping-stones to the right and the path climbing Barrow Hill, and on his left the ruined barn and the dilapidated cart. Esther had liked the spot. She had thought of it as a place where people had come, had met, had parted. It was there that they had last been happy together. He had not seen her since, except for that one terrible time at Lady Green.

It became his favourite weekend walk, along the river path to the stepping-stones. It meant passing Lady Green, where the newcomers were evidently quiet people. He knew nothing about them except that they had put the place in order without altering it, so that it was much as it had been when he used to call for Esther or leave her at the wicket gate or see her at a window as he came down from the Scaur.

One warm Saturday in July instead of turning back at the stepping-stones he crossed the stream and climbed Barrow Hill from where he could look down on the Hall, then sauntered on to the edge of the sparse woodland on the right, just as Esther had done on that other afternoon while he had stayed in the shade of the wall, admiring the gracious proportions of the Hall. That, too, seemed unaltered. Those country houses certainly stood the test of time. He had overheard someone say – on a bus – or train – that Lincoln was about to marry again. Lucky the bride whom he would bring to such a home!

As he stood by the chestnut fence enclosing the wood, two Labradors came bounding up the hill. Someone was coming from the house: a slender figure in a light dress, a dark-haired young woman moving lightly. She came nearer, near enough to be startled at the sight of a stranger, near enough at last for him to see the light of recognition transform her into the girl she had been when he last saw her there.

'Esther,' he said. 'Esther, love.'

'Daniel! Dearest . . .'

As naturally as if they had never parted, she came into his arms and they clung together as if they would never part again.

Almost at once she drew away. 'We shouldn't. I'd forgotten.' Trees overhung the path. He followed as she moved further into their shade. 'No' – as he came nearer, 'you mustn't.'

There had been no hint of guilt or shame in her reproach, only a reminder that, however easily they had slipped back into the illusion that no-one existed but themselves, they were no longer free to indulge it. They faced each other, their eyes drinking in all that was familiar, discovering changes, as if waking from a dream to find its elusive images made real.

'You've been with me all the time,' he said and saw her eyes fill with tears.

'Even when you . . .' How could she allude to his marriage, how ignore it? She felt the inadequacy of words at such a time. Words made actual what was best left unrealized: the ridiculous banality of asking after his wife and child – or children – when for one heaven-sent moment they had shed the incubus of his marriage and were alone together, probably for the last time! Lost for words, debarred from touch, she submitted to the exquisite, inexpressible pain of loving him.

The miracle of their meeting had overwhelmed him. A random trick of fate had brought her back to him unchanged, except that she was more lovely than ever, the contours of her face refined to a more sculptured

253

beauty now that the girlish roundness was quite gone. At first, having always been free except for a few wretched months some years ago, he had taken her in his arms in the old ecstatic way. It took the sad implication of her rebuke to remind him that she thought of him as a married man. He realized as never before the effect on her of his uncouth behaviour: how ruthlessly he had broken his hateful news, how blindly he had gone away. And all this time she had, naturally, thought of him as married.

But he could not have corrected the mistake. He would not have known where to find her.

'I heard that you had gone to Italy. When did you come back?'

'We never went to Italy. I've been living in Hudmorton, at our house in Alma Terrace.'

His exclamation startled her. He seemed altogether crushed by the news. She had been so near. Why had he made no enquiries? Then he remembered the shame and remorse that would have kept him from her even if he had known where to find her. From the perfect unison of their first embrace he knew that she had forgiven him, but the recollection of his former clumsiness made him cautious. The wonderful news he had now to tell her must be broken gently and without the presumption that she would instantly take him back. He would feel his way, watch her face light up as did his own at the thought.

She saw him unaccountably brighten. 'Esther, sweetheart,' he began. His smile, irrepressible and tender, seemed to come from some secret joy. She was puzzled by his change of mood. He put his arm round her, drew her head to his breast and stroked her hair. She withdrew, more gravely than before.

'Things have changed, Daniel.' Unwillingly, she held up her left hand. He was sufficiently dense at first to see only the diamond, not its significance. 'I'm going to be married – next week.'

The blow was devastating. It would have dawned on him in time, he supposed grimly, that she would be sure to find someone else. He had not paused to wonder why she should be here of all places, a guest sufficiently at home to be taking the dogs for a walk. Vaguely, knowing nothing of women's clothes, he recognized an elegance in what she was wearing, a difference in her manner. She had moved away from him into a different world where she would meet the kind of man who could afford so costly a ring.

Even so, he was dumbfounded when she said, 'I'm going to marry—' and with a tearful glint of mischief, '*Major* Lincoln.' The mischief faded. 'Oh, Daniel.'

'You're not happy?'

'I was happy.'

He had blundered into her life again, having wrecked it once. His years of penance counted for nothing when, by merely turning up again, by being here and at such a time, he threatened her happiness again. He looked down at the Hall and saw its walls, strong as the rock from which their stone was hewn, now softly sunlit, the mild shadows cast by its chimneys on mossed roof tiles; a natural distribution of light and shade that no artist could achieve. He saw a house in perfect affinity with its setting, as impervious to change as the hills that sheltered it; and with a sense of defeat acknowledged its value in the scheme of things, its right to be there. By contrast his objections to all it had once seemed to represent struck him as strident and shrill. He turned again to Esther in hopeless acceptance: she had found her rightful setting and with it the security he could never have given her.

'You love him?'

'Yes. Otherwise how could I think of marrying him? I'm sorry— I didn't mean . . .' She had been tactless. He knew only too well that it was possible to marry without love. 'There are different kinds of love – for different times. Gervase needs me, more than you can

255

need me now, more than you ever did. He's been very lonely. And so have I,' she added and wished it unsaid. It had sounded self-pitying, as if she were a child again appealing to him for comfort.

If loneliness qualified a man for marrying her, he thought, his own claim was as good as Lincoln's. For a brief moment he had dared to hope again and now saw ahead of him years of loneliness beyond cure. But at least he could ensure that she married without any lingering regret on his behalf. Thank God he hadn't told her. Thank God he hadn't blurted out that he was still free if she wanted him.

He took her hand in both of his. 'There can't be any harm in this. Even strangers can shake hands.'

All the same it was a caress. Simply to touch her weakened his resolve and made nonsense of his sacrifice. What were they being noble about? Fate had brought them together in the very nick of time, with the clear intention of putting things right. It was not too late. Engagements could be ended. They were both free, neither of them bound by vows that could not be broken.

Yet he was afraid to speak. What he had to say would alter three lives. He had lost confidence in his ability to do the right thing or to know what the right thing was, whereas Esther in some subtle fashion had gained it. She had submitted to his caress, her expression loving, but with an attentive awareness, a kind of authority he had not seen before.

'Suppose,' he ventured, 'I hadn't married after all. Suppose we had met, both of us free, would you have loved me enough in spite of everything to take me back?'

'Of course. How can you ask?' The simplicity of her answer emphasized their plight, uniting them in its unalterable sadness. 'I saw you once. You came out of a meeting. I thought you were going to the station. I ran all the way, down side-streets in the dark, and waited for you. I sat on a bench and waited. I would have waited for you for ever. I always meant to from the very beginning – all my life.' Her tears flowed. 'But now it's too late. Even if you were free, I'm not. It's all quite settled. He's suffered so much, and he's been so . . . I couldn't leave him now. So what's the use of talking about what might have been?' She blinked her tears away. 'I'm surprised at you, Daniel Godwain. Didn't you tell me not to theorize on the basis of a supposition?'

'I've gone to seed. Completely.' He managed to smile. The temptation had left him. It must be enough, and more than he deserved, to know that she loved him. He put his hands on her shoulders and, stooping, laid his brow against hers.

'Do you remember when you first did that?' She laughed, her lips trembling. 'It was raining—'

'We were too wet – you in your father's oilskins and sou'wester – to get closer.'

And afterwards it had amused them sometimes to stand brow to brow like stags.

'We used to wander about in the rain, not going anywhere, just being together.' She looked round. The dogs had come panting back from their inspection of the wood. 'You didn't bring Prince.' His regretful shake of the head was enough. 'He's dead?'

'I found him lying at the bottom of the Scaur.'

'Prince too.' As if seeing for the first time a terrible sequence in the history they shared, she added wildly, 'It was the tree. Everything went wrong after that. They should have left it alone.'

'Now who's being unreasonable? It wasn't the tree: it was people. It's always people. In this case me. You know very well that the whole wretched business has been my fault. No-one but you would forgive me. And even you will never know what it's done to me. It's called getting one's deserts.'

'But you've made the best of it?' She could scarcely bear to look at him. The impossibility of alluding to

257

or even imagining the circumstances of his life made her for the first time awkward. 'Children must be . . . a help.'

What could he say? It took courage, having gone so far, to complete the deception. 'Children are a help,' he said. It was true: they were a help, all one hundred and twenty of them.

The prevarication served if only in strengthening her reluctance to think of, or to believe in, any life for either of them beyond this tiny fragment of existence which must end in a lifetime spent apart. It had been like a homecoming, but without any hope of staying.

'This is how it was that day when we came,' she said. 'I remember the scent of the pines.'

He nodded, watching the familiar movement of her lips as she spoke. A change in the pattern of leaf shadows stole colour from her face and blurred its clear outline so that for an instant she, too, seemed changed. It was as if in the ruin of their lives she might become less than herself – might fade, might die; and he would be left with nothing more than a memory of her, a dream, a longing. In a sudden urgent need to hold and keep her he took her in his arms and held her close. They stood in the green shade looking out into the sunlight on the hills.

'It was just like this,' she said as if speaking of a death. 'The same perfect weather.' The same thin bell of the stable clock striking four, and after that a deepened silence. 'I must go,' she whispered. 'No, don't kiss me again. It only makes things worse.'

'Nothing could make them worse.'

'It hasn't made them better.' She dragged herself away at last. 'Goodbye. It really is goodbye this time. I won't look back.'

She kept her word. He watched her out of sight and stayed there for a while, incapable of movement like a man weak from starvation and grateful for a crust, even a crumb of comfort. At least he had for once done the right thing, even if her integrity had shamed him into doing it. Their paths need never cross again; and if some day she learned the truth, she would by then be safe from any further pain that he might cause her, safe with Lincoln.

The sun was in the west, leaving the front of the Hall in shade. He turned at last and followed his own shadow back to the Lodge.

He remembered nothing of the walk home other than the dull satisfaction of having met no-one. The same reluctance to take up the threads of life again made him hesitate to go indoors. Leaving the key unturned in the lock, he went to the front gate and even then turned his head away from Wood Aston and other people, and looked towards more distant Unnerstone.

The narrow road was empty in the stillness of evening, its wayside trees held motionless like trees in a picture. Then at the limit of vision came a movement so slight that it might have been a pheasant crossing the road, or a hare. Seconds later it was still there. He went out into the road. The movement became a shape coming nearer and gradually recognizable as the figure of a small boy trudging towards him through the dust: tattered, dazed with exhaustion, over his shoulder a bundle wrapped in a tablecloth.

'Jake!'

The child stumbled up to him. 'Me father's dead. He's been killed, Mr Godwain, sir. There was an explosion at the quarry and he . . . he was crushed under a lot of stones.' His dirty face twisted in misery. 'I don't know what to do, Mr Godwain, sir. There's nobody left to tell me what to do.'

'How did you find me?'

'I asked people.'

Daniel unslung the bundle, put his arms round him, picked him up. He acted instinctively, unprompted

259

by thoughts of social injustice or any such abstraction; nor did it cross his mind as he carried Jake indoors, fed and washed him and put him to bed, that he had once before been involved in a similar situation.

PART THREE
BARBARROW

CHAPTER 18

'Little did we think,' Mrs Capman's tone was reverent, in deference to the mysterious and, in this case, satisfactory working of Providence, 'when I opened the door that day and saw the two of you standing on the step . . .'

Flora sighed and smiled. They had reached the point of agreement at which verbal communication is almost unnecessary.

'Little did we think how things would turn out,' Mrs Capman nevertheless continued. 'Mind you, I had a feeling; there was something about her, and sure enough she's got her reward. And I'll tell you another thing . . .'

Again Flora smiled, this time in anticipation: she had already been told this particular thing several times.

'. . . so has he.'

A haze of morning sunlight softened the imperfections of the upstairs sitting-room at Number 11. It had, after all – Flora looked round, secure in the knowledge that she need never come there again – a certain cosiness. They were drinking coffee from the Aumery bone china cups which, with the pedestal table and the rest of the furniture, were being left for William and Alice. For William? Flora's sigh was of a different kind. But Alice at least would have the comfort of a home at Number 11 for as long as she liked.

It was ostensibly to assure Mrs Capman of the security of her tenancy that she had made this rare visit. A letter would have served as well; but the opportunity to talk over the wedding with the one person who understood all it had meant to her was irresistible.

As for Mrs Capman, 'I don't know myself, sitting here drinking coffee at this time in the morning.'

Except for the constant worry about William, she was content. The house was hers again. What with one thing and another, work had poured in on her. A rumour had got round in Brimlow that she had made Mrs Lincoln's wedding dress. Of course she would have denied it if asked point-blank, but so far she had avoided having to do so.

'Quiet and dignified, that's how she looked, and that means more than excitement and fuss . . .'

Flora, too, approved. Esther's unusual gravity had minimized the difference in age between bride and groom.

'She's the light of his eyes, you could tell.'

Mrs Capman was less inhibited in expression than most of the wedding guests, but she had not been alone in sensing an intensity of feeling that distanced the groom from everyone but his bride. Flora had experienced a thoughtful moment or two. Not that he could ever be disappointed in Esther: she was the easiest person in the world to get on with, she loved him, she had said so and was not a girl who would marry for any other reason. There had been in him, despite his reserve, an exultation and in her a dreamy remoteness that set them apart not only from the confetti, cake, wine and flowers, but from the entire commonplace world of other people; as if each brought to the marriage a rare and delicate quality refined by experience.

One could understand it in him, but in her? Perhaps that early disappointment had given Esther a maturity beyond her years, which in the circumstances was a blessing.

'Well, she's starting a new life. From all I hear Barbarrow is a lovely place. She's promised me some photographs. Speaking of which, there's *The Tatler* to look forward to. It should be here by now, and William's *Daily Herald* hasn't come either. It's a new boy and he doesn't know his round yet.'

The newspaper boy had already been. Finding the letter-box too narrow to admit the magazine, he had left it on the door-step where Mrs Capman found it as she saw her visitor out. She turned the pages at her cutting-out table. In the wedding section, pride of place had been given to the Lincoln wedding, with a central photograph of bride and groom and two of the reception.

'Not bad.' William had joined her. 'But there'll never be a better photograph of Esther than the one Vincent took.'

'Well, I never!' His mother had flicked to the last page. 'I thought it felt thick. He's left two. This is mine. They've put the number on the front.'

'Who else in the Terrace takes *The Tatler*? My, you're in good company.' He pointed to the figure pencilled on the cover of the second copy and grinned at his mother's consternation.

'Number 1! Her!'

'It's a free country, Mother.'

'I'll find somebody to run down with it.'

They went to the door. At that hour there was not a child in sight.

'Give it to me,' William said, and as she held it away from him, 'you can trust me. I'm a happily married man. I won't set foot over her doorstep, however strong the temptation.'

'Don't be silly. It isn't that, although you never know what people might think if they saw you there.' The visitor, the coffee-drinking from china cups and the wasted hour had evidently stirred in Gertie a spirit of adventure. 'I'll pop down with it myself. Oh, I won't go in, but I've always wanted to have a look inside. They say she has carpet on every inch of the floor and a bead curtain at the bottom of the stairs.'

265

'If you're not back in half an hour, I'll come for you. Remember, you're past the age for that sort of thing.'

'Go on with you.'

There issued from Number 1 a kind of atmosphere, starting with the brass knocker and white painted door opening on a hall dimly recognizable as similar to Gertie's own, but lit even in daytime by rose-shaded lights and – yes, thickly carpeted with roses right into the front room and up the stairs, mysteriously half-revealed between looped-back bead curtains. Disappointingly – what sort of person had she expected? – the hand on the door belonged to a smallish, middle-aged woman in a plain black dress and holding a pair of spectacles in her other hand. Gertie explained her errand.

'Thank you. You're Mrs Capman, aren't you? How is your son?'

You could have knocked Gertie down with a feather as she told William and Alice. Like an ordinary neighbour! Her – Olga – for Olga it was! Not that she said so, but you could tell she was the boss. She was a bit like Miss Foxley in the accounts department at Vane's, business-like, you couldn't say otherwise, which made you wonder if it wasn't just a mail-order business after all.

Having responded to the kind enquiry about William, Gertie could not resist mentioning with proprietary pride her special reason for having ordered *The Tatler*, and then as Olga flicked over the pages to the wedding section, wished she hadn't. It didn't seem suitable and yet . . .

'Not even made up,' she told Alice. 'Powder, I grant you, and a marcel-wave, but you'd never pick her out for what she is.'

'I suppose it's mainly the others,' Alice said.

Was it one of the others who was waiting in the room, half living-room, half office, to which Olga returned? She was a younger woman, stylishly dressed. Her cloche-shaped hat framed a pale face, unremarkable except for the upward-sweeping dark eyebrows and the brilliant eyes, neither definitely blue nor distinctly grey.

'I'll finish this letter.' Olga sat down at her desk. 'You can be looking at the happy brides.'

The magazine was still open at the wedding page. The visitor glanced at it, then turned her back and went to the window for a closer look.

'So,' Olga sealed an envelope, 'you're on your own again.'

'I'm always on my own.'

'That's true.' Olga eyed her thoughtfully. 'No matter who it is you're . . .' She hesitated. 'Whoever you're with, you're on your own: out for yourself and bad luck to anybody that gets in your way.'

'Nobody does.'

'Well, you keep on turning up. I don't know what you've come for this time, but I may as well tell you straight out, you're not getting your foot in my door again. I took you in to save you from the gutter, and for Lena's sake, not your own. There was nothing about you then to make me like you and there's nothing now.'

She spoke without anger, rather with aversion, though the other's behaviour seemed too negative to provoke hostility. It could even be said that she graced the plain room, almost like a lady, as she had seemed to the little maid who had admitted her twenty minutes before.

'If it's money you're needing—'

'I don't need money.' It was said with amusement, as if needing money were a foolish state to be in.

'No, it isn't money you need. It's something else that drives you. I'm never likely to know just what it is. Don't want to either.' She licked a stamp. 'You can have a bit of lunch, but you'll have to have it on your own. I'm busy.'

'No, thank you. I have things to do.'

'You didn't care for Paris then, any more than London?'

'They had their advantages.'

'Then why come back to one-horse Hudmorton?'

'A person must have somewhere to come back to.'

'Or somebody? Why do I ask? There's no-one in the world you'd move an inch for.'

'You're right – Auntie.'

'That's enough.' Olga looked annoyed, as she was meant to. 'Lena was like a sister to me in the old days, but she wasn't my sister, poor God-forsaken little bitch. Nor was she your mother, as well you know. There wasn't much harm in her apart from the company she kept; and she didn't deserve what she got. Who would?' Olga's confidence faltered; her eyes registered a memory of horror. 'I don't suppose you've heard anything of him?' A shake of the head sufficed. 'Well, he got away with it. Lucky he didn't finish you off too.'

'He wanted to. You can be sure of that. But when he saw what he'd done, he was terrified, too sick to do it again. He couldn't bear the sight of me, much less have me on his conscience too; but he didn't dare leave me either.'

'He couldn't have picked a better time to disappear. There must have been plenty like him that were glad to join up and shake off everybody that knew them. The war finished off all those good men. Let's hope it took plenty of the other kind too, him among them.'

Her visitor shrugged as if the topic, reverted to from time to time since it had first brought them together, had grown stale. She returned the magazine to the desk, adjusted her hat at the mirror over the mantel and picked up her handbag.

'You look smart.'

It was true, but more impressive than the fashionable clothes was the suggestion of an inward confidence expressed in a bearing unusually controlled. She could go anywhere, Olga thought, unwillingly impressed as she recalled the forlorn little wretch she had taken in – how many years ago? Even then there had been nothing to be got out of her except what had happened to Lena.

She looked again at the magazine, at the well-dressed wedding guests from Copgrove, Risewood and further afield.

'You should have your photograph taken.' The remark, a sardonic comment on her companion's upward progress, was dismissive too. She took up her pen.

'Just one more thing. Until I have an address in Hudmorton, I'll have my letters sent here.'

'You will, will you? Not "Do you mind?"'

'Whether you mind or not.' The tone was, for an instant, icy. 'You've done well here. It would be a pity if anything spoiled your success – at your time of life. If anything leaked out, I mean.'

In response to a change in her manner the atmosphere in the room changed. On Olga the effect was instant.

'So that's how you do it. That's how you can afford to live like you do and dress like nobody else I know can dress. It's so easy – if you don't mind how low you stoop. It's so easy, threatening to tell unless you're paid to keep quiet.' For a moment anger rescued her from an instinctive dread of the woman. 'No wonder this place was too small for you. You'll have done a lot better on your own. It wouldn't have taken me long to find out you were playing a double game and ruining us all. Clients don't expect to pay twice – once for their comfort – and again, a lot more, to keep from being found out. And now you're trying it on me. It won't work. I'll never lift a finger to help you again, whatever you care to tell . . .' She felt herself to be blustering, knew that she was helpless.

'As I said,' her visitor continued smoothly, 'it would be a pity if anything leaked out. I've often thought there can't be many people who know more about this place than I do.' She went quietly to the door. 'I shan't need to call for the letters. I'll let you have an address and you can send them on.'

269

It was a relief to be rid of her. For the time being. Relief quickly gave way to anxiety and resentment mounting to hatred of an intensity alarming to Olga, who was of an equable disposition. It was of no comfort to know that she was not the only one: there must have been plenty of others that she had made use of in ways of her own, the treacherous two-faced bitch. No-one was safe. Not even . . .

There had been that bit in the local paper a few weeks ago about the death of a Baptist minister. It had been brought in as suicide. She had recognized the name. It had reminded her of an incident years ago when she had seen it as the signature to a letter.

'You'll need a reference,' she had been saying, 'if you want to go into service, and who's going to—' The letter thrust into her hand was sufficient answer. 'My, how did you get hold of him?'

Olga found it in her heart to pity the man as she sat idle at her desk, facing the prospect of her own ruin.

Heads were turned in Duke Street for a second glance at the woman, too well dressed for Brimlow, and perhaps a foreigner, who walked smoothly, holding her own course on the pavement and paying no attention to others until she came to the taxi rank in City Road.

A studio portrait? One never knew when it might prove useful. If other people had photographs taken, why shouldn't she? 'Other people' meant Esther Aumery. When, with the magazine in her hand, she had gone to the window, it was in order to be alone with her sudden exposure to an influence she had both striven against and used. Given a modicum of imagination or conscience in the viewer, the face of the bride might have stirred reproach. Instead it goaded her to envy as it had done when she first saw it from the straw pallet on the wash-house floor at the Coach and Horses; and years later across the graves in Wood Aston churchyard. From her window at Priest's House she had looked down through wavering lamplight on the dancers on the green, and had seen only Esther in her white dress. Prey to a fascination that angered her, she had still been mastered by it even when the two met almost daily at the Lodge, until the last time when she had seen Esther poised on the stepping-stones, her face irradiated by more than light from sun and stream: by some inward brightness incomprehensible to the observer on the stile. Most constantly recurring among such memories, most bitterly resented of all was that of the voice, gentle and hesitant: 'Would you like to have this dress? I think it might fit you.'

From the beginning she had sensed in Esther a quality she could not emulate, only seek to destroy. The despoliation had not been complete. Having no knowledge of love, she could not know the agony she had inflicted in her seduction of Daniel. Her purpose had been to separate the lovers, prevent their marriage and gain for herself the security that should have been Esther's; until she realized her own power to venture into a wider sphere than that of Keeper's Lodge. Her manoeuvre had been more successful than she knew, but it seemed to her, limited as she was to values other than those of love, that in becoming the mistress of Barbarrow, Esther had got the better of her again. The revival of envy roused impulses stronger than rational thought, urges in her sterile nature which answered a need left unsatisfied by her inability to feel.

The taxi took her to the boarding house where she had taken a room. Half an hour later she emerged, wearing a plain green skirt and jacket, a soft pull-on hat and walking shoes, a style of dress that attracted no attention as she boarded the afternoon train to Unnerstone. Avoiding the town, she took a by-road and made her way through twisting lanes to the familiar path skirting one of

Grotes' fields, and so to the stepping-stones and the path climbing Barrow Hill.

From the brow she looked down on the Hall. Faint sounds rose from the kitchen, voices, the clatter of tools in a garden shed. A maid appeared and shooed away hens from a flowerbed. If she had looked up the hill, she would have seen nothing that moved in the green leaf-shade.

Was the unseen observer aware of the mellow beauty of the house; or its air of quiet submission in the summer stillness to the passing of another season in its long history? She noted the lay-out of the gardens, such out-houses as could be seen from her vantage point, the orchard, the gate to the meadow – and stayed there for a long time, until a car came purring along the private road and drew up at the front door. The driver got out, opened the door for his passenger and put his arm round her as they went indoors. She knew them both. Not until a gong sounded softly in the depths of the house did she turn away and walk quickly back to the stream, along the lane past Lady Green and into the wood. Unhesitatingly, not along known paths, but following a way of her own, she reached her destination – a hollow fringed with ferns and carpeted with moss, remote even in that unfrequented part of the wood. She stepped down into it, fell to her knees and bent lower, lay face down and breathed the long sigh of a wayfarer come home at last.

But not to rest. Isolated, safe from intrusion, as regardless of physical comfort as if she had no outward form, she directed the whole force of her energy inward in yet one more effort – to remember experiences which time and outraged nature had together erased from her mind. The need to remember had become more urgent than ever before, and for reasons so compelling that she could not accept failure. Her inability to penetrate the forgotten era of her earliest years seemed a paralysis of mind to which she would not submit. She

lay rigid, fists clenched in fierce and unbroken concentration, until the sheer intensity of effort exhausted
her and with a long sigh of frustration she relaxed.
She should have known by this time that the strength
of her will, so effective in every other circumstance,
was powerless to unravel the infinite complexities of
the mind. Memories came only of their own accord,
unbidden, never when sought.

Turning on her back, she eased her shoulders on her
pillow of moss and let her arms lie limp, her fingers
grow soft. She became inert, depersonalized, she who
was also rootless, of nameless origin, and homeless
except for this hidden hollow which, since her first days
at Wood Aston, had been her refuge. Minutes passed;
the detritus of the day slipped from her mind, leaving it
empty of recent human contacts. It was in such a state
that she had sometimes begun to remember words
from the past: distant voices had reached her, bringing
no comfort, to be welcomed only because they were
necessary, like the first unwholesome drops from a long
disused tap before the steady rush of water comes.

'She never seemed like a real person . . .'

'I wouldn't let the likes of her over my doorstep . . .'

'There must be something wrong with her, else she'd
never have been cast away like a poisoned cat . . .'

They merged, to become a chorus of negatives denying her an identity and confirming her own sense
of unreality, as if she hovered like a phantom on
the threshold of human society and would never be
allowed in.

Under the trees it was almost dark. She had not eaten
since breakfast, but she was unconscious of hunger,
aware only of the rank scent of ferns and the first stars
between the branches. Closing her eyes, she felt the
blackness under their lids as a dense curtain between
her and the past that she had tried again and again to
recall, with all her faculties keyed to their highest pitch,
almost always in vain, sometimes with small successes,

so that as well as voices there were fragmentary scenes to be pieced together like patchwork and with a similar lack of a distinct pattern.

There were also, of course, the things so indelibly imprinted on her mind that she had never forgotten them; they would always be there, things that no-one could forget. They included other voices still more distant, one of them a man's. 'Just you keep your mouth shut or you know what you'll get . . .'

For a vivid instant he was there again, struggling into his clothes and fumbling with buttons; and there was Lena lying on the bed, her head upside down, her eyes standing out, the pale stain of vomit on the quilt. Afterwards there had been the dark alley, the smell of the horse and the reeking bundles in the cart, the bottle thrust into her mouth, its rim rattling against her teeth as she gulped.

But before that? The room was Lena's. It was Lena who scratched together the meals they ate, Lena who bundled her out on to the landing when the men came, who licked a cloth to wipe her face and sent her to the shop. And further back still? Had there been someone else? The impression of hands bathing her feet and brushing her hair didn't fit into her life with Lena. Had there been some event, indescribable, unremembered, to be felt only as a sudden blotting out, from which she had emerged as from total blankness to find Lena buttoning her boots?

It had never happened again, the having her boots buttoned by Lena. She had slip-slopped with them gaping open until she learned to button them herself.

'Do it yourself,' Lena had said of that and other things. 'I'm not your mother, God knows. I've too much sense to be anybody's mother.'

A mother there must have been, and a father. Who? Where? Cradled in the earth (had she ever lain in a real cradle?) she yielded her whole being to a single thought: Who am I?

274

With Lena, there had been no conversation, no idly revealing chatter, certainly no confidences. Except for that last highly memorable view of her, she had forgotten what Lena looked like; but she remembered her muttered remarks as she hauled herself, spiritless, out of bed and drifted, unwashed, into another disheartening day.

'Where's the comb? A hole in your stocking! My, My! Think yourself lucky you've got stockings.' And, 'How can you live decent in a place like this?' she would demand as she hammered a slab of wood over a rat-gnawed floorboard or scraped congealed grease from plates into the stinking bin on the landing.

The implication that Lena had known decency or had at least known places where decency was possible seeped into the frowsy room already charged with unanswered questions and the necessity of keeping one's mouth shut; except, of course, when lies were called for, as in the case of the rent man or the School Attendance Officer, silence or lies being above all necessary on the subject of the other men who came, the strangers.

Breathing an atmosphere so fraught with threats and evasions, even the least astute of children might grasp their import, though without understanding the ungraspable adult world they stemmed from. The child in question was more than ordinarily astute and soon developed the sharpening of faculties and thickness of skin necessary for survival. But with the loss of innocence came a crippling of the imagination. Curiosity was dulled. Dodging blows, trying to keep warm, rubbing her itching chilblains and scratching her flea-bites, gobbling more than her share of bread and treacle and slab-cake from the fly-blown shop, she had paid too little attention to other things, had missed the vital clues she now so desperately needed. Questions had been nipped in the bud and had not seemed worth repeating.

'They called me a bastard.'

'Take no notice. Find something to call them. There's plenty you could say about them . . .'

From this distance she realized that it had all been said without anger on Lena's part, without real peevishness and, more surprisingly, without despair. Taking a small tentative step towards enlightenment, she became belatedly aware of Lena's good nature. Lena had been soft, was Clairy's way of acknowledging the discovery. And there was something Lena had said, more than once and in different ways – if only she could remember more clearly – that had to do with Lena's own awareness of a fatal softness, something on the lines of, 'I must have been out of my mind', or 'It would happen to me, wouldn't it?'

'What was it, anyway?' Clairy had once asked.

'Oh, never you mind.'

'Well, it wasn't my fault, was it?'

Doomed to her foetid dungeon, Lena must have kept, at the back of her disorderly mind, a dream of escape. 'I could get away if I wanted to. I could go to Olga's in Hudmorton. That's a bigger place than this. They needn't think—' 'They' were the nameless hostile forces responsible for her plight, for the rats and debts and drunkenness and personal humiliation. 'They needn't think I'm short of friends. Olga would take me in. Any time.'

That one thing at least Clairy had remembered: that Olga at Hudmorton took people in. Later, alone on the city streets, she had quickly selected the right sort of person to direct her to Olga's place.

In the soft dusk, under faint stars, in the sweet, uncontaminated woodland air, she found that Lena, who had been all-pervading as life itself, had shrunk to recognizable dimensions: she had become the poor little bitch that Olga had called her. Not that Clairy saw her as a woman of flesh and blood, warmly and wretchedly alive, rather as a human shape in continual unreasoning movement, like a puppet activated by unseen hands. She felt no gratitude to Lena, no sadness on her behalf. In so far as she felt anything it was the soothing, non-human quality of her present surroundings: the moist smell of earth and foliage and the ancient stillness of the wood. This was her natural element. It was satisfying to think that trees had been here for hundreds of years, outlasting the people who had gone to and fro beneath them. They diminished the importance of human time so that life in an Appperfield slum had lasted no more than a moment: the span of years between then and now had dwindled to a mere breathing space. And yet, reaching across so narrow a gap with all the intensity of her will, she could not remember . . .

She had not belonged there. Stirred by that one certainty, she raised herself. At some earlier time, right at the beginning, she had belonged elsewhere. Was it to some green and wooded country? If not, why did she feel at home in such a place as this? Had she been conditioned in infancy to respond to country sights and sounds, and with such strength as to challenge her later conditioning? Again she faced the insoluble problem of her parentage. She didn't even know where or when she was born. Lacking so much, she even lacked a birthday. Lena could at least have told her who her parents were. If there had been time, she would eventually have got it out of Lena, who, feckless in death as in life, had not lasted long enough to tell.

Reluctantly she turned her thoughts to the third member of the triangle. Had he known her history? Nature, in helping her to recover, had for a long time banished him from her mind. For years she had been able to avoid thinking of him. But gradually he had slunk back, forcing her to remember him: pale-faced, vicious, often drunk. His name was Rodd. The sombre monosyllable served as both first name and surname and was rarely used, scarcely needed.

They would hear the front door slam, slow footsteps on the stairs, the creak of the landing.

'That'll be him. You'll have to go,' and Lena would give her a blanket and something on a plate and hustle her out.

In winter, when he was there, she slept on the landing. Once the woman upstairs had come down and offered to take her in. She had not replied but turned her face to the damp-mottled wall, and the offer was not repeated. In summer she had sometimes slept under Rodd's cart – it was there that she had seen his name on the label of a sack of skins from Pegg's slaughter-yard – until she had been 'interfered with' by the stableman from the public house. She had left the marks of her teeth on his ravishing hands and he had not bothered her again; but after that she slept on the landing whatever the season. She had long known that on the other side of the door a similar interfering was taking place, but with Lena's complicity.

In the morning she was admitted to breakfast on bread and tea. When Rodd was about she went to school to be out of the way. On such mornings he might still be in bed, his black trousers sprawling lecherously over the chair. Lena would be fractious and dull-eyed as she trailed her feet from cupboard to gas-ring or drooped over the wash-bowl, her irritable remarks directed impartially at her two burdensome companions. As the butt of her irritation they were conjoined in a way that Clairy resented, but she had learned to shut her ears as well as her lips and simply did not hear. This she now regretted.

On the fatal night she and Lena had been alone. He had not been there for two or three weeks and was not expected. They had stayed up during the long twilight, half stupefied by the airlessness of the room after a hot day, until it was quite dark and the whole house was quiet, its numberless occupants having at last gone to bed, as Lena had done, to luxuriate in

278

being there alone. Presently Clairy would creep in beside her. She was crouching on the floor by the empty grate, stroking the black cat that prowled the landing. Downstairs the outer door slammed; footsteps sounded heavily on the stairs.

'My God, it's him,' Lena said and in a moment he was there in the doorway. With a startled mew the cat raised its tail, arched its back, picked its way to the door and escaped. It was too late for Clairy to follow. Hidden by the bed, she sank lower, cautiously stretched her limbs and eventually slept on the hard floorboards – so that she never knew what it was that led to the crisis.

Violent movements of fury and panic in the bed woke her. A candle was burning. The familiar voices sounded unfamiliar, Lena's strangely distorted. Looking up, she saw Lena's left hand appear from under the bed clothes. It gripped the edge of the mattress like a frenzied claw. Then the bed heaved again under his frantic lunge and Lena's desperate recoil. Gradually the hand released its grip and hung limp, almost touching her face. She stood up. He was still leaning towards the pillows, all his weight on his arms, his hands still on Lena's throat.

She waited. The silence he had imposed on Lena had struck dumb the two of them left alive. They were united, inescapably. There came to her across the candle-lit bed a sense of his absolute ruin. The fury had gone out of him. The unexpected appearance of a witness could add no more than the brush of a feather to the weight that already crushed him. Slowly he stood upright, looked at his hands and flexed the fingers, then looked up at the ceiling as a man might gaze at the sky and send a howl of despair into the wilderness. He moved his head vaguely from side to side in the ghost of a denial; his mouth drooped and quivered.

She waited, as motionless as Lena until it came, the inevitable warning.

'You! Damn you!' He spoke with brooding savagery. He saw dully what she was seeing clearly, that she was a problem, an intruder, unwanted to a degree not yet reached in all her unwanted existence – and disposable. 'Keep out of this, or else. One word from you and I'll do the same to you as what I've done to her.'

She knew (she would always be quick to spot another's weakness) that it was an empty threat, even though a word or two from her could hang him. His act had isolated him, breaking all links with the shabby world he had known. He had become an outcast and knew it with the loneliness of the damned. In his desolation there was no-one left who mattered enough to strangle. Something of this she perceived. She had seen his horror-stricken reaction from what was left of Lena. From his expression as he brought himself to look at her, she sensed in him an aversion that was not murderous but sickening: he could hardly bring himself to touch her. And so, as there was nothing she could do and nothing she could say, she waited while he fumbled with his clothes, until, dressed at last, he reached for a blanket discarded on a chair because of the heat; draped it over his head and shoulders, picked up his boots and, holding them and the ends of the blanket in one hand, with the other yanked her round the bed, seized her like an empty sack and crept downstairs.

Then later, waking in daylight, she had heard Esther's description of him: 'Very pale, in a terrible hurry, as if . . .' The diffident voice had faltered. Clairy had sunk again into a snoring stupor and by the time she woke fully in the Merridons' wash-house it was to the realization that she was free of him. Pale and in a terrible hurry, he was gone – a man reduced to a description. She could forget him. Justifiably in the circumstances, she did so and faced instead the immediate compulsions of her plight, remembering to keep her mouth shut and for a time her eyes but not her ears.

Had she, by suppressing one memory, lost access to others? It was now necessary to think of him. Cool calculation, her most formidable asset, told her how useful he could have been. Could be? Could he be still alive? If he had not been killed in the war he could be skulking under an invented name and in another country. She saw him more clearly as a deserter and escaped murderer than as a fallen hero. Someone, somewhere must have known him: Rodd, dealer in skins and hides. Few people were as devoid of friends and relatives as she was; someone might still be in touch with him. It was possible, even likely that he had known her history. If by any chance he was alive and could be traced . . .

She smiled. There was no-one there to interpret the baleful twist of her lips, not a living soul to know in how many ways he could be made to pay for what he had done to Lena – and to her. Chiefly to her. She writhed at the memory of the humiliation he had exposed her to: the crowd of whispering children, the shame of her near-nakedness under the stained blanket, the hateful patronage of the soft-eyed pitying girl and her shy offer, 'Would you like to have this dress? I think it will fit you.' Esther's reluctant sympathy rankled more deeply than all the rest, including Daniel's efforts to help, which she had barely noticed and quickly forgot.

And it was Esther who had lightly dismissed her as not quite real, on the last occasion when the three of them had been together, on the riverside path leading to Lady Green. She had walked behind, her eyes on their clasped hands, and missed not a word of their conversation. If there had been, and might still be, more repercussions unfavourable to Esther, hadn't she invited them? Wasn't it only fair . . . ?

A night breeze rustling the leaves brought no answer. Clairy shivered, came to herself, looked at her watch and returned to the world she had learned to exploit but not to understand.

CHAPTER 19

Esther's quietness in the early days of their marriage was seen by Gervase as reassuring. Youthful outbursts, however natural and delightful, might have made him feel older and more staid. Instead it was he who tingled with the life and energy of renewed youth. He had known that his passion for her could have no equal in her feeling for him: her loving submission moved him to gratitude for the happiness she brought him, as did her obvious pleasure in their home. He had no reason to suspect in her apparent contentment an undercurrent of despair.

The calm of resignation may not be distinguishable, by the unsuspecting, from true serenity. Esther suffered, but not from indecision. The meeting with Daniel, brief, anguished and final, had not shaken her conviction that it was right to marry Gervase. She could perhaps have faced the alternative: to live alone in futile regret for what might have been. What she could not have faced – the absolutely impossible thing – would be to disappoint Gervase. He had already suffered enough. To break the engagement on the very brink of marriage would be to break his heart.

The final wedding preparations had been over-shadowed by memories of Daniel. Night after sleepless night she had relived their reunion, heard his voice, felt his kiss and she knew that in their renewed close-ness there had nevertheless been something she had missed. Had there been a lack of complete openness in his manner, a faintly sensed restraint, signs disre-garded at the time? Recalled, they puzzled her. On the whole he had said very little, as if his natural flow of words had failed him.

Of course his marriage must have altered and subdued him. (At this point she dissolved into black misery.) He must all the time have been uneasily aware of all that could not be talked about, and fearful of what she might ask. There had been a moment when his face had lit up as if he were about to propound one of his wonderful ideas. She had interrupted by showing him her ring. What had he been going to say?

No bride could have felt more deeply the solemnity of her marriage vows and their uncompromising finality, but she was denied the solace of their simplicity. No-one guessed, as she stood pale and still at the altar, how keenly she suffered the duality of her situation; how the sincerity of her nature recoiled from her inability to think solely of Gervase; how the promises she made to him and pledged herself to keep were each in turn reminders that she could never make them to Daniel. These had been her feelings until, when they were pronounced man and wife, Gervase turned to her with such unconcealed love for her and such trust in hers for him, that the tranquillity she had prayed for came to her at last.

She had guessed that he felt no urge to go abroad again and pleaded, though there was no need, that they should spend their honeymoon at home. Their love of Barbarrow was to be an additional bond between them. To her it brought consolation and healing. Waking in the quiet of the country was like waking as a child at Lady Green. The years at Brimlow receded. Halfdreaming, she heard from her frilled pillow the rustle of birds beyond the open lattice, and presently she would hear Gervase returning from his early morning ride. For a while it was warm enough to breakfast on the terrace or in the small dining-room with all the windows open. She filled bowls and vases with asters, dahlias and late roses. Creeper reddened on the stable walls; pears were gathered. On the hillside, bracken turned from green to bronze.

When autumn mists shrouded the hills and the evenings grew cool, there were fires of apple logs. Day after day, from her favourite window-seat, she saw the copper beech shed its leaves until the slender boughs stretched naked against November sunsets – and remembered how, as a girl, she had loved to watch daylight yield to the slow-moving clouds of night, and then light the lamps and draw the curtains.

The illusion of returning to an untroubled early life was an escape from the sharpness of regret and the loss of freedom to grieve. With everything in the world a woman could want except for the one thing it was useless to want, how could she fail to be content, and, as months passed, to be more nearly happy than had at first seemed possible?

Gervase's friends in business and politics, and neighbours from Taybrooke and surrounding country houses, called on the new Mrs Lincoln, and hospitality was exchanged; but Gervase had no wish to become involved in the conventional life of country gentry. In Esther he had all he wanted, and she could invite anyone she pleased. Few of her friends were free to make the journey to Barbarrow, but the Ambroses were frequent visitors.

While Henry and Gervase walked the dogs or shot – or failed to shoot – partridges and pheasants, Flora and Esther resumed a companionship so like the one at Lady Green that, as Flora said, it was as if time stood still. She made the remark one cold day in February, as they inspected the contents of Esther's wardrobe.

'You remember those old dresses we used to try on? And my shabby old room?'

She adjusted the cushion at her back and stretched out her feet to the hearth. Mrs Bowland had sent up a tray, and the silver and china glittered in reflected firelight. The bed was piled with garments. Esther held them up, one by one.

'Most of them you'll be able to go on wearing for a while. Come and sit down. Annie can put them away. You mustn't tire yourself.'

'You're as bad as Gervase.' Esther joined her at the fireside. 'Millions of women go on working until the very day they give birth, and then get up and start working again as if nothing had happened.'

'I know. Toiling in paddy fields and turning mangles. And I do understand how you feel. One can so easily get used to being pampered and revelling in luxury.' She glanced appreciatively round the warm room, almost helped herself to another biscuit glistening with sugar, and refrained. 'That should never happen to us. The revelling, I mean. Otherwise we would have learned nothing from our ups and downs. As a matter of fact . . .'

It was better not to say it, not to mention her persistent feeling as she recalled the old four-poster strewn with faded dresses, that this repetition in so altered a form had somehow been contrived by Someone or Something as a Test. One must accept good fortune cautiously. It would be unwise to *gloat*. Her fingers found the mahogany frame of the comfortably padded chair and tapped it noiselessly.

Esther appeared not to notice the unfinished sentence. She was often rather remote these days. One could call it the raptness of approaching motherhood, only it wasn't just that, if it was that at all.

'You're still feeling perfectly well?'

'Perfectly.' Her smile was one of amusement at her mother's fussing rather than of confidence in her own well-being. They were silent for a while. 'There's just one thing—' and after another pause, 'If only one could know which it will be!'

'But surely it doesn't matter. You'll love it whichever—'

285

'Of course. But I do so hope for Gervase's sake that it's a boy. It's wrong, I know, but I actually pray for a boy.'

'Naturally a man likes to have a son to carry on the business, and inherit the estate—'

'It isn't that. I hope we'll have other children. But it would be best for the first one not to be another girl.'

'Oh, I see. You mean he would be reminded . . .'

Flora's prick of anxiety was not for Gervase – that was nonsense – but for Esther. She was so much in earnest. Her eyes had darkened, as they always did when she was under stress. She was leaning forward, hands gripping the edge of her chair, as if possessed by a single thought: the necessity of not having a daughter.

Unwillingly Flora was reminded of another time when Esther's singleness of mind had worried her; when she had seemed to lose touch with the ground under her feet, to need neither food nor sleep, her whole being suffused by one emotion. That had been the bliss of first love, but it was a tendency she had evidently not outgrown.

'You're working yourself up into one of your states. Do try to keep a sense of proportion. It's possible that if Gervase has another daughter he'll be reminded of little Lilla. But it isn't such a rare thing to lose a child.' That was the wrong thing to have said. 'I mean, parents grieve, naturally, but they have other children and love them all the more for having suffered a loss. You're forgetting how new and special and different every baby is, how absolutely itself, how it alters everything. In fact, having another daughter might be the very best thing for Gervase.'

'I expect you're right. I'm being silly. It's just that the circumstances were so dreadful. Worse in a way than if Lilla had died of an illness. Death is final and must be accepted. But when a thing is left unfinished . . . That's probably why it haunts me as it must haunt Gervase.'

'Has he said so?'

286

'He doesn't need to. I know how he feels.'

'You don't know anything of the kind. Women don't know what goes on in their husbands' minds, especially women who've been married for less than a year. And they don't know what goes on in ours, thank goodness, unless we're rash enough to tell them. Still, it's a relief to know that you're just like everybody else.' Flora spoke with more confidence than she felt. 'Yes, it's quite normal for pregnant women to have weird fancies, and this is one of them. It will pass. You'll forget it.'

'Did you—'

'Of course. I got it into my head before you were born that the beam in our bedroom ceiling was getting lower every day. Remember how it sagged? Obviously it would come crashing down and crush us to death.'

'And obviously it didn't.'

They laughed and wandered off into other reminiscences, thence to layettes, the need to sit with one's feet up, the importance of light, nourishing meals and finally to the recollection that Henry disliked driving after dark.

The house seemed very quiet after they left. The absence of noise, especially at dusk, created a void into which crept other sensations: of presences almost taking shape, feelings increasing in strength until they threatened to become the people who roused them. At such times the cool chime of the mantel clock was both a dismissal of unwelcome visitations and a summons to more purposeful activity. She had not enough to do, and Gervase was often out all day or in his study.

Her mother's advice had been helpful, so far as it went. But no appeal to reason can control the imagination. Barbarrow itself was to be reckoned with. The accumulated impressions she had tried to define on her first visit as the spirit of the place were proving too persuasive to be dispelled by common sense. It was unreasonable when there was so much to delight the eye, to be increasingly aware of the unseen, as if one's attention were drawn with each movement of light to the cavity of shade it left.

Mindful of her health, she took solitary walks, glad to escape from ancient walls and low ceilings into the open air, to trees and hills and rocks. But the feelings they roused were not always soothing. The idea that natural objects embody a coherent living force was not new to her: as a child she had felt it in the Aston oak, and she had later come upon the idea in books. Alone at Barbarrow, with time on her hands, she could persuade herself that there was meaning in the upward thrust of branches; the ceaseless prattle of the stream seemed purposeful. In certain moods she was by no means sure that the meaning and purpose were benign, especially when the bough of a tree suggested a human shape, or when a boulder looked like a head. Once she was startled by a movement some little distance ahead between trees. Was someone there? She stopped, waited; nothing moved. It must have been no more than winter sunlight glancing off green bark.

She could not have said when it was that she began to be troubled by images more distinct and peculiar to Barbarrow: of a young wife only a little older than herself, a girl dark-haired like herself, a lost child. Like the child she was carrying? They were not yet an obsession, merely a preoccupation and harmless, but as the months of her pregnancy dragged by, she found herself dwelling on the Lincoln tragedy. It was perhaps inevitable that living in its shadow, she should, with a leap of imagination, predict its recurrence. What if history should repeat itself in the form of a new tragedy involving, like the old one, the loss of a child?

Gervase found her less talkative, the lilt of laughter in her voice more rare; but her triumph on finding that she was pregnant had been so heartfelt, her rapturous 'Gervase, you'll never guess' had so convinced him of her delight that he accepted this latest change of mood as purely physical in origin. Any anxiety he felt was for her health: she was not robust. The spiritual look he loved seemed to him to have intensified, increasing both his love and his protective care.

Undoubtedly he pampered her too much; she teased him about it. The harmony of their companionship was as near perfection as human companionship can be. On every issue concerning the baby they were in agreement. He or she should be brought up to value simple things. There were to be few toys, so that each could be cherished. The old nursery would be turned into the night nursery, the small adjoining room would be the nurse's room; a bedroom with windows facing east and south would be the new nursery, bright, airy and plain. The choice of a name was to be postponed until its owner arrived.

And the nurse? Here was a problem fraught with so many reservations on Esther's part that she might have been treading on ice. She could not say outright 'No-one in the least like Julie', nor must it be anyone likely to become an intimate member of the household, nor, worse still, a stranger. Consequently the qualifications to be looked for were so unspecified and vague as to culminate in the desperate demand,

'Do we need a nurse, Gervase? Why have a nurse at all?' She looked up at him from her low chair, her features sharpened, her brow puckered in an anxious frown. He knew that all this fuss was on his account – he was not to be reminded of the past, hence the new nursery and the uneasiness about the nurse.

'Just what I was thinking,' he said. 'There are four adults in this household besides ourselves, as well as two gardeners and a groom. Between us we should be capable of looking after one infant. Of course there'll have to be somebody to deal with the extra work. We don't want the rest of them to leave in a body. Some homely, motherly soul. But that can be settled when the time comes. In the meantime I've been hatching a plan . . .'

They had already considered the possibility of bringing William to Barbarrow for a change of air. When the Hall was modernized, Gervase had converted and extended the coach-house to make living quarters for staff if they should be needed.

'He'd be comfortable there without having to exert himself to be sociable. He could join us or be alone. Alice could come at week-ends. We could collect her on Saturdays.'

'Gervase! You are simply the most wonderful man.'

'I've often thought so. It's gratifying to know that I was right.'

'Not only about William. But to have him here! You must have read my mind.'

He cradled her face in his hands and kissed her. 'If there's anything there that I haven't read, anything interesting, I wish you'd tell me. Any worries, for instance.'

'How could there be?' She clung to his hand as he released her. 'And the same applies to you. I want to share your problems too. Promise you'd let me if anything troubled you.'

'I promise.' The pledge, lightly given, was to prove less easy to keep.

In overhauling the coach-house and equipping it with everything William might need, Esther revived. The one possible hitch, that Alice wouldn't let him come, did not materialize. She and Mrs Capman seized on the opportunity of William's absence to have Number 11 redecorated, not before time. Without brusqueness, rather with a politeness learned in recent years, Alice declined Gervase's offer to fetch her in his car: there were trains from Hudmorton to Taybrooke. It would be kind of him, if not inconvenient, to meet her at the station there, as that would give her more time with William; otherwise the walk would do her no harm.

She came on the first Saturday evening in June and left by the last train on Sunday. Her white face, thin enough to shock Esther, who had not seen her for several months, was to seem whiter and thinner each time she said goodbye to William.

'We planned this for William.' Esther was waiting on the terrace when Gervase came back from Taybrooke. 'We didn't think of Alice. All that commotion at Number 11, work at the factory, rushing out here at week-ends. Suppose her health breaks down.'

'I'll insist on fetching her and taking her back to town. You must write and tell her that I'll pick her up at Number 11 on Saturday evening. If I'm there she can't turn me away. And why shouldn't she stay here on Sunday nights too? I could take her direct to Skidways on Monday mornings. It would suit me very well. An early start would give me an extra hour free in the evenings.'

Alice was too tired to protest. Long idle Sundays at Barbarrow must have done her good, but they were so far removed from the life she knew that she could scarcely settle to enjoy them. It seemed to her, a town-dweller born and bred, that there was nothing to do in the country. Her visits were too short to acclimatize her.

For William it was different. He got up late and went early to bed, sometimes to spend wakeful nights when his cough disturbed him or his temperature was high. But to feel on his face the soft air from his open window, to hear the screech of an owl, feel in the night the eerie stirring of the earth as it turned towards daybreak and then to listen for cock-crow, were experiences new to him and strangely soothing, like signals from the invisible world whose mysteries he would soon have to face.

On warm days he lay among the cushions in a wicker chair on a willow-shaded lawn at the side of the house, where he need not be disturbed by callers. He could look at clouds above Barrow Hill, or close at hand, at steps leading down to an artificial grotto where water spilled from a hidden spout into a stone basin with a sound as soothing as the drone of bees in foxgloves by the wall. Sometimes, waking from a doze, he would find that Esther had slipped into the hammock and was obediently lying with her feet up.

His company was all that she could have wished for in the languor of waiting. It was an immense satisfaction to see that he had tempting meals and cooling drinks, make him put on his hat or muffler, move him into or out of the shade. Gervase liked to hear their voices from his study: a burst of laughter or brief remarks lapsing into silence. To the end of her life Esther would remember the peaceful days on William's lawn: the play of sunlight on narrow leaves, the retreat of small concerns, the imminence of new life and of death.

Morgan Krantz was a frequent visitor. He and Gervase had been friends at school, but Esther was given the credit for having brought them together again after a long separation. Two or three times a month he would appear in the lane, his head and shoulders over-topping the hedges – and would arrive booming a greeting and breathing intellectual fire. His largeness was more than that of impressive physique. His disciples, who included in their number William and Esther, would have claimed for him more than a touch of greatness. Certainly he had the capacity to rise above the humdrum trivialities, as he saw them, of earthly existence and to take a chosen few of those disciples with him.

But he, too, could be influenced. Settled on the stoutest wooden seat Barbarrow could offer, he gave himself up to the sheltered quiet of the garden, lowered the pitch of his voice and limited his range of topics in deference to the delicate condition of his companions. But he had worked on them too successfully in the past. There was to be no respite. William and Esther, facing the enigma of life from opposite directions, spent a good deal of time in trying to solve it.

'It's come home to me,' William said one afternoon of drowsy heat during the last week of his stay, 'why people think of Paradise as a garden.'

'Elysium. The garden of the gods where they feast on nectar and ambrosia.' Morgan accepted his fourth cup of tea. 'For ever and ever.'

'The whole thing started in a garden,' Esther reminded them. 'In the Garden of Eden.'

'All myths,' William said. 'But always a garden.' He closed his eyes. Talking was sometimes an effort, increasingly so, as Esther noted with a sinking of the heart. 'If the next life is like this, on a day like this, only better, for ever and ever, who would want to leave it and come back to start life all over again? That idea of reincarnation. What would be the point of it?'

Morgan Krantz was silent. The theory of Karma was not one he chose to propound in William's company and at such a time.

'Come back as someone else,' William laboured on. 'That book you once lent me. It seems we can never call our soul our own, because it might have been somebody else's.'

'I don't like that idea,' Esther said, 'and I don't believe it.' She remembered the book in question. Elbows on the kitchen table at Number 11, she and Alice and William had argued over its contents and had on the whole dismissed its scholarly researches with unscholarly confidence. Smiling, she thought of Alice's declaration: 'One thing's for sure. Nobody'll get me back into the toffee business, not Skidways nor anybody else's.' Her smile faded as she remembered what had prompted the remark – a theory that the soul, released by death, especially by an untimely death, might return to the environment it had left, to inhabit the body of a newborn child. 'I don't believe it.' She sat up, slurping tea on to the tray. 'It simply isn't possible.'

Morgan came to the rescue with his suitably large handkerchief and took the opportunity of having his cup refilled. He had heard the change in her voice. 'This is no time to grow heated over ill-digested theories. We were talking about mythological gardens. We are not gods and cannot hope for Elysium. It's too late to go back to the Garden of Eden. Let us be thankful that destiny has placed us here and provided us with tea and cucumber sandwiches in the shade of a green willow.' Regretfully, he took the last sandwich. 'Looked down on from above, we must seem members of a chosen race.'

'From above?' Esther noted the empty plate and cut into the cake. 'By God?'

'Possibly. But I was thinking of that woman.'

'What woman?'

'Up there on the hill by those trees. Don't get up.' Esther, screened by willow boughs, had made a move. 'She's gone.'

'What was she doing?'

'Nothing. Just being there, like us. We aren't doing anything either apart from being here – and how delightful it is!' He munched a generous slice of cherry cake and presently went for a walk. Despite the heat, he chose to climb Barrow Hill. They saw him as he came level with the belt of trees. He turned to wave before disappearing over the brow.

Esther eased herself out of her chair and went slowly indoors. It was too far-fetched for words, the idea that the soul of Lilla might return, so that her baby would not only remind Gervase of Lilla, but would in essence actually be Lilla. Feeling sick and tired to death, as if her swollen body were no more than a medium for the continuation of a tragedy in which she herself had no part, she lay on her bed, overwhelmed by a sense of defeat. She would never have another child, would never read another book. She would stop thinking altogether, would never utter another word.

294

She would tell Alice about it and Alice would say . . . Remembering Alice's determination to steer her soul away from the toffee business, she giggled, relaxed, pulled the pins from her hair, wondered if she would dare to have it cut short, yawned. Into her mind on the cloudy verge of sleep came the memory of words spoken as from a great distance, their message stark but reassuring. Whoever had said it had been speaking of Barbarrow. 'No-one was murdered.' That meant that somehow, somewhere, Lilla must still be alive, her soul was her own.

There was nothing to be afraid of. She felt the baby move in her womb: in her own body, part of her yet completely new, different, absolutely itself. Himself. It would be a boy. Together, they drifted into sleep.

All went smoothly. William went home claiming to be a new man. For the remaining weeks Esther enjoyed excellent health. Mysterious chemical processes operating within dispelled such discomforts as headaches and indigestion, as well as the bogies and demons which she could now dismiss as figments of the imagination and forget. Apart from the obvious awkwardness of her increased size, she had never felt better.

Gervase planned every aspect of the event with military precision. Thanks to Alice, he found exactly the kind of help needed in the nursery. Alf Skidway's cousin Ada had trained as a nurse before she married; she was now forty-five and a widow. Her two children were grown up, she had lived all her life in Brimlow. That circumstance alone would have endeared her to Esther. It was understood that she would come for a trial period of three months. She moved into her quarters in the middle of August. Flora came a week later and, eventually, the midwife.

When it was over and Esther lay drained, weary and sublimely content, she was aware of Gervase at her side; and afterwards she was glad that her dearest and most abiding memory was not only of her own exquisite joy, but of its reflection in his face as he bent over the bed.

'All that I hoped for . . . and she has your eyes, my darling.' He touched the tiny hand. 'Let's call her Viola.'

CHAPTER 20

Winter came early. October was a month of rain and wind that stripped trees bare before their time. There followed a spell of hard frost, with an occasional powdering of snow on the hills. The house, with its thick walls and ample fireplaces, came into its own. It was a time neither for going out nor for receiving visitors.

Esther's attention was focused entirely on life indoors, as snug and safe a life for her as for Viola, asleep in her warm nursery under Ada's watchful eye. Ada and Gervase had between them undermined Esther's intention to do without a nurse. She knew that she had been outmanoeuvred and was profoundly thankful. Ada's eye, though watchful, was placid: she had brought up two of her own in circumstances that made Barbarrow seem to her, as she told Esther, like heaven with the gates closed. The trial period of three months was never mentioned. Clearly Ada was staying.

For Gervase, the harsh weather provided an excuse for spending more time at home. It was an opportunity to deal with arrears of paper work as well as to enjoy the company of his wife and daughter in the home he loved. He had lavished on the old house all that taste and wealth could achieve; it had lacked only the very thing it had been created for: a family. For him, the barren years had ended. As he and Esther sat at meals or by the fire, or when they played with Viola, he talked more freely than he had ever done, was more at ease and happier than ever before. Consequently, when the time came, Esther was quick to notice the change in him.

It came on a cold, windless day early in the new year. Gervase had set off in mid-morning to walk to Taybrooke, intending to call on Emson, a local builder, to discuss repairs to one of his cottages. Esther expected him home for lunch, but she had finished her own meal, an informal one, when he returned, much later than planned. She was interested in the cottage and remained at the table to ply him with questions as he ate. He did not join her, but with only a smile of greeting went to the fire and stood with his back to her.

'You must be chilled to the bone.'

He ignored her offer of hot soup, and rather to her surprise – he was an abstemious man – went to the sideboard, poured out a stiff measure of whisky and swallowed it at a gulp.

'You're not feeling ill?'

'No, no. Just cold.' He lingered by the fire, and when he did sit down, ate little.

Esther left him in his favourite wing chair. It was unusual for him to seem so tired. He leaned back, eyes closed, unaware of her. Even more surprising, he was still there an hour later. Coming into the room, she looked at once at his face against the high back of the chair. His expression belied the restful attitude. The frown between his brows seemed one of concentration. Was it some worry about business? With a pang she remembered her father, prematurely aged by worries about his property. But Gervase was a very different kind of man; she had immense faith in his ability to deal with problems of that kind – of any kind. Besides, he had been quite himself when he left for Taybrooke, and putting a cottage to rights was a trifling matter to the managing director of the Lincoln Ironworks.

She wasted no time on irritating questions and instead produced an infallible cure in the shape of Viola, who kicked and gurgled on her blanket on the hearth rug and waved her arms about as if putting on a performance to divert her father. It was successful: the cloud lifted. He took her on his knee, submitted to her fascinated exploration of his right ear and encouraged her to find its counterpart on the other side of his head. Presently he put her down again. When Esther looked up from her embroidery he was dangling a blue woollen monkey just out of Viola's reach and gazing into space in an absence of mind that her wail of frustration failed to penetrate.

'Daddy is going to have a cup of tea in peace.'

At the door she turned, and with a slight shock saw Gervase's eyes fixed on the child with such unconcealed love as seemed quite at variance from his usual reserve: a love troubled by anxiety and doubt, which were altogether new.

That night it snowed, and throughout the next day. For most of the week they remained housebound. Gervase telephoned his office each day, but took his enforced absence without complaint, apparently content to stay indoors. But for her anxiety about him, Esther would have enjoyed what seemed a winter holiday of the most exclusive kind; but she was not mistaken: there was something wrong. More than once when the thaw released him, he came home untalkative and unsmiling. One evening when he switched on the reading lamp by his chair, she saw in the sudden light on his face that he had lost weight. A firmness had gone from his cheeks. He didn't immediately go on reading: certainly no page was turned.

'You are feeling quite well, Gervase? I've wondered a little—'

As she had expected her tentative enquiry received short shrift.

'Yes, yes. Quite well.' With an effort, she thought, he gave his mind to his book.

Her fear was confirmed one morning during the following week. She was on her way to speak to Mrs Bowland – it was their day for going over the weekly accounts – when, in the short passage leading to the housekeeper's room, she heard a man's voice, that of Cordman the gardener. It was Mrs Bowland's habit to leave her door half open as proof of her constant vigilance. Esther could be vigilant too. Sensing a confidential quality in the low-pitched conversation, and quickly identifying the 'he' and 'she' as herself and Gervase, she made no bones about eavesdropping. There could be no disloyalty on their part: both were trustworthy, their regard for Gervase unquestioned.

'. . . stood there like a statue, not hearing a word I said about taking out some of the rhododendrons, come a mild spell. It was him that wanted it done in the first place, but you'd have thought he'd never heard tell of a rhododendron.'

'. . . something on his mind. Do you think it's his health and he doesn't want her to know? What a shame if it's something serious and her with a young baby! Do you know of anything in the family? They were before my time.'

'So far as I know old Mr Lincoln was taken with a heart attack, but that would be in Hudmorton. I never knew him . . .'

Esther retreated, to fidget with newspapers on the hall table and try to compose herself. She had not imagined it: Cordman and Mrs Bowland had known Gervase for years, they must be right. He was not himself. She ought to have insisted on knowing what was wrong and made him see a doctor.

It was only half past nine in the morning. The day seemed endless. He was late. She was on the point of ordering dinner to be put back when he arrived. After a long cold day one could expect him to be tired and disinclined to talk, but she was taken aback by his haggardness. As he stooped to kiss her, their eyes met and she saw in his a pained bewilderment: a driven look that almost brought tears to her own.

She poured out his drink, installed him by the fire, and brought down his house-shoes and jacket. He accepted the small services wearily, tacitly acknowledging his need of them. A threshold had been crossed, a turning-point reached, or, she thought with dread, a breaking-point.

They ate at a small table by the fire. Food and wine brought colour to his cheeks. When the meal was over and they were alone, she went and knelt beside his chair, on her lips the question she must ask.

But he was the first to speak. 'Esther, there's something I must tell you. I've been wanting to, but I kept on hoping that it wouldn't be necessary. No, I'm not ill. It's a problem I can't deal with. You must help me, Esther. You must tell me what to do.'

She sat at his feet to listen.

It was on a grey still morning that Gervase had set off for Taybrooke, where he had arranged to meet the builder to discuss renovations to the cottage. His mind occupied with problems of drainage and crumbling stone work, he paid little attention to his surroundings. Every step of the way was familiar, most of it by field paths on his own land. Grass was white with frost, the ground iron-hard. He congratulated himself as he avoided puddles frozen to the smoothness of glass that he had not put his mare at risk. The silence of the countryside at that dead time of the year held for him no hint of warning, no premonition that he was about to meet a crisis in his life. It merely occurred to him that he had been unlucky to fix on a day when he – and Emson too no doubt – could have been more usefully employed at his desk: a day when sensible people, given the choice, would elect to stay indoors.

He was all the more surprised, therefore, to meet someone who had chosen otherwise. He had reached the spot, a quarter of a mile from home, where the field path joined a farm lane leading between elms to a gate. By the last of the elms, about twenty yards ahead, stood a woman. She had presumably come through the gate and, seeing him, had hesitated.

But hesitation implies uncertainty, and as he drew nearer his impression was of a different kind. Unmoving under the bare tree in her long grey coat with its deep collar and cuffs of fur, she appeared too strongly – even startlingly – defined to be capable of embarrassment or awkwardness. She simply stood close to the gate, facing him as he approached.

It was he who felt very slightly at a disadvantage, which accounted for his brusque comment,

'You probably know that you are on private land.'

His breath hung in a cloud on the frosty air. She was perhaps ten feet away from him: a young woman, or youngish, he would have said, unconsciously comparing her, as he did all women, with Esther, whose youthful outward-going vitality had no parallel in the stranger's face. It was inexpressive and composed.

'I know that. I'm trespassing. But I would have done no harm.'

He was mollified. She had not been apologetic, but neither had she been defiant. Her tone was reasonable: it implied an intention other than the negative one of doing no harm.

'You have some reason for being here?'

'A personal one.'

There was something vaguely familiar about her, though he could not recall having seen her before. She was not a local woman. Refined? He was not entirely sure. She had the poise of sophistication. Could she be a friend of Esther? Oddly enough, one or two inflections in her voice reminded him of Esther; at the same time he couldn't quite see her as Esther's friend. Quite strongly, even in those few minutes before his pulse quickened, he didn't want her to be.

'You have some connection with the Hall?'

'I don't know. That is precisely my difficulty – that I don't know.'

The answer was unexpected. It roused him to full alertness. 'Would you care to explain yourself?' Junior officers would have recognized the tone and quailed.

'That might take a long time, longer than one would choose to spend out of doors in this weather.'

'Then why are you here?'

She had come closer. The brim of her grey hat was lined with blue velvet. The eyes beneath were of a paler, colder blue. They explored his face in a scrutiny more searching than he could understand – or tolerate. He stepped back.

'I beg your pardon, Major Lincoln. You dislike it, naturally. But my interest in you may be natural too. Yes, in the fullest sense. That is why I'm here, not from choice. I couldn't help coming. I couldn't help it.'

It could have been interpreted as a cry of distress, but there was no weakness of appeal in her manner. She spoke as if some force other than reason had brought her there and, by virtue of its mysterious strength, justified her presence.

To have put the obvious question 'Why here?' would have been a normal reaction. By this time Gervase's mood was not entirely normal. Her few remarks could hardly have been simpler, yet combined with her deliberate – and unwelcome – examination of his features, their effect had been disturbing. She had used the words 'natural . . . and in the fullest sense.' Was it instinct that stirred in him some vestigial memory, of a being long lost, once part of himself and bound to him by the closest of natural ties? The sudden recall of an event distanced by half a lifetime, yet fused with the very fibre of his own being, demanded a change of focus too abrupt, as if a chasm might open at his feet to reveal a darkness he could not penetrate without pain.

Moreover, he was annoyed that an encounter of no importance whatsoever had somehow developed significance. He hesitated. The one sure thing was that he must be rid of her, at least for the time being. He must be alone to think and to deal with an uneasiness difficult to suppress. Yet he felt the strongest reluctance to leave her free to go on as far as the Hall. To walk with her and see her off the premises was equally out of the question, especially as she too would probably be going as far as Taybrooke.

It was she who resolved the dilemma by moving to the gate as if aware that there could be no conventional response to what she had said. By indicating that she expected no other kind of response, she increased his feeling that in this little episode it was she who had kept her head. He opened the gate for her and remained on the inside.

'Goodbye, Major Lincoln.' She turned to go, then paused. 'My name is Motte. Miss Clarice Motte. I'm sorry to have intruded. I'm staying in Taybrooke and I'm not familiar with the district. Not so far as I know. And yet—' A curious expression crossed her face. She seemed to forget him as she looked around her at the grey-green hollows between bare boughs. Raising her head, she breathed in the cold air as if to savour it, 'It's almost as if . . . I don't know.' She gave a little bow of farewell and walked away.

What did she mean? One knows or does not know a district. 'That is precisely my difficulty, that I don't know . . .' Doubt infected him too, distorting both mind and vision so that the well-known scene was strange to him. The stones of the boundary wall, the dead grass and hoary bracken were not as they had been.

He was too punctilious to ignore his appointment with Emson, yet determined at all costs not to over-take the woman on the Taybrooke road, and stood irresolute until he remembered the old pack-horse way, long disused and overgrown, by which he could reach Taybrooke without using the road. In forcing his way through hazel, elder and thorn, he tore his coat and stockings but regained his equilibrium. The impact of the woman in grey wore off. Her eccentricity in being there at such a time had led him to misinterpret her remarks and relate them to an experience whose wounds would never be healed.

Emson was waiting at the cottage when he arrived, dishevelled, and explained that he had wanted to see if the pack-horse way was still accessible. They became absorbed in problems of decaying woodwork and rising damp. Afterwards Emson walked back to the Hall with him to pick up some plans. There had been no time to dwell on the incident earlier in the day.

But his mood was troubled: he felt out of sorts and more tired than the exertions of the morning warranted. Esther, more than ever thoughtful of his comfort, the restfulness of their home, the welcoming fire – all failed to cheer him. His amusement at Viola's antics faded into vague anxiety for her future – and Esther's. He slept badly. As a rule he could lie at peace in wakeful hours, aware of Esther asleep at his side, knowing himself to be blessed with all a man could want; but on that night her quiet breathing stirred in him nameless fears that in some way their life might change: that it must change as all things change. He slept at last and woke to an unusual lightness in the room. From the window he saw a white world. It was still snowing heavily.

He was wonderfully relieved. Not that he had planned any action; but the weather had intervened to prevent any action he might have decided to take. There was nothing to be done, no need to do anything; but there hovered in his mind the thought that he could, if he wished, seek the woman out, demand an explanation of her cryptic remarks and then forget them. They were probably meaningless. She had seemed the kind of woman, he thought, remembering her ominous stillness under the elms, who saw herself as some sort of clairvoyant. It was a pose. Mysterious utterances were an affectation calculated to impress a naïve listener. In earlier times, such a woman would have given charms and potions to village girls and, earlier still, would have been hustled to the horse pond as a suspected witch. He derived a little grim amusement from these vengeful fantasies, absurd in every respect except as an indication of dislike. Nevertheless it was his duty as a landlord at least to make enquiries about any possibly undesirable trespasser on his land; not to mention the duty far more profound which he must force himself to face.

And when he saw her again it was no longer possible to dismiss her as neurotic or affected; even dislike, if not dispelled, was without reasonable foundation. By the time the thaw came, he had accepted the necessity of seeking her out. Assuming that blocked roads and railways would have kept her at Taybrooke, he called on one of the women whom he knew to have rooms to let and asked for Miss Motte. She was not there, but the woman directed him to Ivy Villa where the young lady was staying, and wondered what Major Lincoln could want with Miss Motte. For that matter, she and her friend Mrs Overton at the Villa had wondered what Miss Motte was doing here anyway, and always on her own. There wasn't much for the likes of her in Taybrooke, which was probably why she spent so much time in town, coming and going like a shuttle, and often away for a week at a time.

At Ivy Villa he was ushered into Miss Motte's sitting-room. She rose from her chair, a book in her hand. 'I wondered if we would meet again.' She relieved him of his hat and gloves and sat down again, with a gesture inviting him to take the chair on the opposite side of the hearth.

'I have thought over certain things you said when we last met. I found them puzzling. Was I right in taking them literally, that you have some particular interest in the Hall and in me?'

'An interest, yes. I'm not sure whether it is a particular interest. A person in my position – but then I know of no-one else in such a position, and can speak only for myself.'

'What is your position?' He was aware that the question had been invited; nevertheless she paused, apparently bracing herself to make a difficult pronouncement.

As before, her speech was slow and careful, as if from the need to convey the exact truth.

'I'm in the position of not knowing who I am.'

He heard the hiss of a flaring coal and the ticking of a clock; he heard and felt the thud of his heart's irregular beat and bent his head to combat a sudden dizziness.

'Can you imagine what it is like, not to know who you are? Of course you can't. You know your place in the world. You know where you belong.' Again she paused. 'You know who your parents were.'

With an effort he controlled his physical distress. She had been looking into the fire so that he had seen her face in profile. Now, as she turned, he forced himself to look her in the face. But he could find nothing in the pale oval that was distinctive, and therefore nothing to recognize: nose, mouth, chin were well shaped enough, eyes bluish like his own – or more nearly grey? They were badly served by the thinly plucked eyebrows which deprived the whole face of definition. It was a face without expression or light or appeal. She talked to him but made no contact with him. He felt an absence . . . Of what? Of identity? Was that what happened when a child lost its parents? Or was lost to them?

'Are you new to this part of the world?'

'To Taybrooke, yes. I've known Hudmorton since I was a girl.'

'You were born there?'

'I don't know where I was born.'

'But you know your name.'

307

'It's a name. Everyone must have a name, even the most *déracinée* of individuals. I don't know how I came by it.'

'You speak French?' The name, too, could be French.

'A little. I spent some time in Paris recently and found it easy to pick up a smattering of the language. It seemed to come quite naturally.' She indicated the book she had been reading. It was a French novel.

'What makes you think Motte is not your family name?'

She took time to consider her answer. 'How far into the past can memory reach? Some things come back clearly, like patches of light surrounded by darkness. A child reared in squalor may know without actually remembering, that there was once another kind of life. I lived in a town, in the gutter you could say, until I was a grown girl; then when I first came into the country it was familiar to me, as if I'd always known it. I felt at home, especially among trees . . . It's the same with my name. I know it isn't my name but I can't remember how I know.' Her testimony, having no factual basis, could not be put to the test, but it had the ring of truth. 'It must have been the memory of that other kind of life – no, not the memory: I don't remember it. I should say, the knowing that there was such a life made me want to rise above the dirt and misery. And when I did escape them, I soon found that to hold your own in the world you need to use your brains and be educated.'

'Undoubtedly,' he murmured. Clearly she had intelligence and had put it to good use. There was certainly no trace of the gutter in her appearance or speech, or in her smooth conduct of this extraordinary interview.

'Perhaps I should make it clear that I'm not in need of help. I have suffered humiliation and hardship, and have overcome them by my own efforts. No-one can help me as well as I can help myself. Except for the one thing I most want: to know who I am.' Her voice changed. 'Look at me, Major Lincoln. I am a foundling.

I was literally found, wrapped in a blanket under a hedge.'

He felt his whole body relax. He sagged with relief. So she had been abandoned as a baby. It was not, alas, so very unusual; he was sorry, but her history was certainly not his affair. As soon as decent politeness allowed he was free to leave. He took a few deep breaths and was himself again, his relief so intense that only then did he realize fully how great had been the strain.

There was time, too, before either of them spoke again to ask himself why he had been afraid. Ought he not to have been overjoyed at the prospect of finding in her the child so deeply mourned and for so long? Ought he not to be bitterly disappointed at not having been granted the one thing he had most wanted?

Any more than she had been granted what she most wanted. With the short-lived pity a released prisoner feels for those he leaves behind, he pitied her, though she in no way invited pity.

'It isn't much,' she resumed, 'but that is one of the very few facts I can give you.'

'There is no need to give me any facts.' He was affable in his relief. 'Why should you?'

'There was no need for you to come here. Why did you?'

'My reason doesn't matter now.' He got up. 'I sympathize with you in your need to know your background. Try to think of your parents without bitterness. Remember – people must be under very great stress to abandon a helpless baby.' He took up his hat and gloves, and was all at once aware of inconsistencies: the things she had said about memory, for instance. How could she have . . . ?

She had also risen. Her expression made him uncomfortable. So far he had been unaware of any expression on a face as blank as if there were nothing within for it to express. There had risen as it were to its surface an intention, in response to which the lips curved in a smile devoid of amusement.

'You have misunderstood,' she told him. 'I said that I was found wrapped in a blanket under a hedge. That was twelve years ago,' and as the colour drained from his face, 'just over the hill from Barbarrow Hall.'

CHAPTER 21

The fire had burned low. Esther heaped on more logs. It was very late, but neither of them would sleep.

'It's possible, isn't it?' he had asked again and again. 'Her age. She wasn't sure, of course, but she thought she was about fifteen when she was found.'

'But small for her age.'

She had looked half-starved. Esther did not enlarge on her own recollections of the girl. At the age of thirteen she had been strangely disturbed by the discovery of the bundle under the hedge, an incident in sharp contradiction of accepted rules of behaviour. The staggering news that the girl had come back, and in so very different a guise, revived a similar sense of abnormality. With such a person anything was possible.

Such thoughts would be of no comfort to Gervase, nor would the reports of her activities gleaned from Barney and Mrs Capman; and she longed above all else to comfort him. Since his appeal for help, wrung from a torment of doubt, she had realized as never before how truly and absolutely she was his wife. She had borne their child, shared with him the triumph of her first smile and plans for her future, but it was in his distress that she felt most nearly at one with him and recognized his need of her.

'Why has it made me feel like this? Why should I be afraid? To find Lilla after all these years ought to be the miracle Anne and I prayed for. It must be. And yet I can't feel it like that. It's as if I didn't want her back.'

'It's the uncertainty. We don't know that she is Lilla.'

She couldn't be. She mustn't be. The stolen plates could

be forgotten: she had probably been taught to steal. On the other hand, a person who had never been taught to be honest could cheat and lie as a matter of course and could well be an impostor. As for Olga's Place . . . She hesitated. If the person was Lilla, to blacken her character at the outset would make it more difficult for Gervase to accept her, as presumably he must. 'It's the not knowing that upsets you, and the shock. You had lived through the grief, not forgetting Lilla but thinking of her as if she had died. It would be quite natural to be afraid if a person came back from the dead. The person wouldn't be – as you remembered her.'

What was it Daniel had said when in those light-hearted days they had speculated on the Lincoln tragedy? 'If she came back she wouldn't be the daughter he expected. Why shouldn't she be better?' Something like that. Impossible to think of the incident at the school gate without thinking of Daniel, so that in this crisis which involved her so deeply, he too was involved.

'Does the name Motte mean anything to you?' Gervase had begun. And when she shook her head, 'Did you ever hear of a girl being found under a hedge?' And instantly she had thought of Daniel, even remembering his rapt expression as he picked up the girl and held her in his arms.

'Yes, of course. I was there,' she said, and listened with mounting concern to what he had to tell.

He had not left Ivy Villa as he had intended, but had sat down again. Now that necessity demanded it, he took charge and experienced, as he plied Miss Motte with a steady stream of questions, a revival of his confidence in dealing with facts. She had answered willingly, hesitating only where uncertainty was justified.

The childhood home she remembered was a dilapidated back-street dwelling in the town of Apperfield. She believed, though she had no means of knowing if she was right, that she might have suffered some serious illness in her earliest years; meningitis or severe scarlet fever. That was how she accounted for a hiatus in her memory: a blotting out of earlier events. More precisely, for a long time she had believed that it must have been an illness, but later came to wonder if some kind of shock had resulted in amnesia. She remembered a sensation like that of coming out of a dark place and finding herself in the filthy room where she was to live for, she thought, just over ten years.

The house was over-crowded: there were other children, slatternly women, men who came and went. The woman she lived with was not her mother, she had told her so. On her last night in Apperfield her foster mother had quarrelled violently with a man who was often there. She wondered if the quarrel had been in some way connected with herself. He had told her that he was taking her to a better place and had given her something to drink. She must have been drugged.

'If he had intended to return her to us,' Gervase said, 'and came by the south road, he would find the place empty. It's feasible that he found her a burden on his hands and simply left her where she was sure to be found. I'm speaking of it as if it had happened to strangers. I cannot think of that waif as Lilla, our beautiful little girl. I cannot make the mental connection. Nor can I think of that woman as Lilla grown up.' He reverted to the chief cause of his distress. 'She may be my daughter. I loved Lilla just as I love Viola. But this woman I cannot love.'

It was not her fault, he went on. There was much to admire in her determination to rise above the squalor in which she had grown up: she was intelligent, she had talked of innate tendencies and inherited characteristics . . .

Esther heard the familiar phrases with sadness. One might think Miss Motte had sat at Daniel's feet and absorbed his ideas as she herself had done. 'Your instinct may be telling you that she is not your daughter.' It would have been much more like him to be kind to an unknown woman whose life had been so difficult – whoever she was. The phrase was to recur again and again. 'You feel intuitively that she is not genuine?'

'I might have felt that, if she had made some claim on me; but she wants nothing from me, only to know who she is.'

'Did she tell you anything about her life after she was found?' Respect for his feelings inhibited Esther from mentioning that the girl had been carted off to the workhouse. Not that she had arrived there.

'There was someone in Hudmorton, a connection of her foster mother who took her in until she could make her own way. She came into a little money. She didn't say how.'

'It was just that, well, I wonder how she found her way to Barbarrow. I mean – what happened here was very little talked of, even in the district. How had she heard of it?'

'Servants' gossip. She was quite frank about having been in service. And something she overheard quite by chance put the idea into her head. No, that's not right. It suggests a deliberate intention.' Gervase had recovered sufficiently to review his experience at Ivy Villa with more detachment than would have been possible an hour ago. 'There was so much to grapple with that I didn't notice it at the time, but she never mentioned Lilla or the Hall, or why she had come to Taybrooke. She didn't make any attempt to treat me as her father.' What exactly had she done, he wondered in bewilderment. 'She has done nothing except answer my questions.'

Nothing, Esther thought, except to be there. She had simply stood by the gate, silent until he addressed her, yet the monstrous significance of it had changed their lives.

'You do understand, Esther? My obligation. How can I ignore the possibility – the fact very likely – that she is my daughter and has the same claim on me as Viola?'

'There isn't any proof—'

'There never can be. The doubt, and the duty, will be with me for the rest of my life. We blamed ourselves when Lilla was lost. We should never have left her. I've lived with the guilt, knowing that if she died it was my fault. If she is alive, if she is here at Taybrooke, whatever has happened to her since she was lost, whatever influences have shaped her, I'm responsible for those too. She was as defenceless and innocent as Viola.'

If he knew what influences had shaped her, at Number 1, Alma Terrace, for instance, he would feel even more culpable. In an attempt to avoid the subject, Esther seized rather desperately on another. 'What happened to Julie?'

There could be no answer. The name reverberated in a void and died into silence, as when a pebble falls into a well so deep that not a sound registers its fall.

'She's gone. God knows where or how or why. We shall never know.' He put his hand over his eyes. 'What ought I to do, Esther?'

His helplessness wrung her heart. He had always been so competent, so protective and strong, equal to any circumstance, except this one. The woman at Taybrooke, whoever she was, had found his weakest point. By merely standing in his way she had destroyed the peace it had taken him more than twenty years to achieve. If it was not done in innocence or by chance, how clever the woman must be. How frighteningly clever! One could only pray that whoever she was, she was not Lilla. Please, Esther silently urged, don't let her be Lilla.

'What do you think Anne would have wanted to do?'

'We must think about that tomorrow. It's very late.'

The curtains were rimmed with grey daylight. She put up the fireguard and helped him out of his chair as she would an invalid. Hands clasped, they went upstairs.

What would Anne have wanted? If, instead of herself, it was Anne who sat in the nursery, morning sunlight on her fair hair . . . With Viola bouncing vigorously on her lap, Esther found it simpler to consider what she herself would do if, after years of being presumed dead, Viola came back in the form of a strange woman, strange in more senses than one. What, in so preposterous a situation, could anyone do?

Was it necessary to do anything at all? The woman had made no claim: life at Barbarrow could go on as if the incident had never occurred. On the other hand, Gervase could seek her out again, make more enquiries and if it could not be proved that she was not his daughter, assume that she was. Or, an alternative infinitely preferable, if it could not be proved that she was his daughter, assume that she was not.

She put Viola down and watched her reach out purposefully for the yellow cushion she loved. If that woman was Gervase's daughter, he must treat her as such. Where would she live? It took Esther a little while to realize the long-term implications. For the moment it was more than enough to envisage the arrival in their family circle of a fourth member, the stealer of Barney's plates and habituée of Number 1, Alma Terrace. Esther gritted her teeth and took a longer view. Viola would have a half-sister, an older half-sister. Instinctively she picked up her own child again. The elder sister would have as strong, if not a stronger, claim on her father than the younger. Gervase must provide for her in his will.

He might soften towards her. It was to be hoped so. To live with a daughter he disliked would be an affliction: it would make him ill. If he were to die . . . Imagination is a tyranny and can be selective. Bypassing the grief she would feel, she saw herself at Barbarrow without Gervase but with Miss Motte and Viola: an uncomfortable ménage to say the least.

From her window she saw Gervase setting out for a walk with the dogs as she had seen her father at Lady Green. She had been anxious on his account too. Time had distanced those fears and brought others more complex. She knew that Gervase, walking slowly, head bent, was more fully aware than she was of the difficulties ahead. Her role was to ease them, to rise above prejudice, to humanize a situation she had so far treated as a puzzle to be solved. She must meet the woman. Had they met by chance, they would not have recognized each other. The girl in the blanket had barely opened her eyes, and that was twelve years ago when she herself had been too young to be fully observant. She would suggest to Gervase . . .

'Wave to Daddy.' She knocked on the window. Viola gesticulated gladly at her own reflection in the window pane. She was a happy child with an enthusiasm for life, as Gervase put it. They tried hard not to be silly about her, not to dote; but to her mother, pale and drawn after a sleepless night, she seemed all at once infinitely precious, and she knew how Anne would have felt, and how she herself would have felt if it had been Viola instead of Lilla at Ivy Villa. How strange that she had fancied Lilla might return in spirit to possess the newborn child! It was happening, but in a different way. She was returning as a separate person and in the flesh. But was it a return, and was the flesh Lilla's?

At this point Annie appeared, bringing a telegram. It was from Alice, her news not unexpected. She had promised to let them know of any serious change in William's condition. 'Come now while there is still time' conveyed all that was needed. For the time being the problem of Miss Motte must be shelved.

'Let's try to forget her,' Esther said as they got into the car.

'Let's try,' Gervase echoed sardonically, and she was not mentioned again.

317

They were in time. The next day would have been too late. The house was quiet. There was no fuss or outward display of grief.

'We know he has to go,' Gertie said, dry-eyed and desolate.

Alice had gone with him as far as is permitted, to the last frontier between life and death, and looked as frail as if she meant to go all the way with him.

'I told him you would be coming,' The door of the little room next to the kitchen was open. 'It's Esther, love.'

'William.'

'Esther.' His lips barely moved. His voice was almost gone. 'We've talked a lot about—'

'About everything.' She took his hand. 'It's been wonderful. You and Alice. You saved me.'

'You'll stick to Alice?' She saw in his eyes the last glimmer of their favourite joke.

'I'll stick,' she said. 'I'll never let her go.'

He closed his eyes and did not open them as he murmured, 'That garden.'

She kissed his brow and crept away to sit on the stairs and weep for him, knowing that a steady brightness was passing from her life. When they went again the next day, it was over: he had died in the early hours.

'There'll never be another like him,' she told Alice. 'You should be proud to be the wife he deserved.'

'You can't be proud when half of you's gone, as if an axe had split you in two.' She went into the little room and closed the door.

Gervase, too was grieved, and bitter. 'One of the forgotten men,' he said. 'He was as much a casualty of war as if he'd died in battle. There must be thousands of them. They struggle on for a few years. By the time they die of damaged hearts, rotted lungs, pneumonia or consumption, people have forgotten what they died for. Patriotism is out of date. It's all the League of Nations now. A good thing if it works.'

318

William's death affected Esther deeply. In his simple goodness there had been a depth of sympathetic understanding she could only now appreciate. True sympathy, she thought, was not just an impulse to give comfort: it could be a positive act of the imagination, a sensitive insight into another person's condition, circumstances, need; Miss Motte for instance, to take the most immediate example of her own failure of sympathy.

Her mood was further influenced by a conversation with another friend. Each day until the funeral Gervase took her to Brimlow on his way to the works and called for her in the evening. It was hard to be separated from Viola, but there were ways in which she could be useful to the Capmans and they were glad of her company. Friends and relatives called, among them Morgan Krantz, who came to offer help and to tell them that a memorial service for William was to be held at Ruskin House. When he was leaving, Esther went with him to the door.

'That was a good day,' he said. 'William and you and I in the garden.'

'I believe he remembered it right to the end. He tried to say something about a garden.'

'We talked of Paradise on earth.'

'Like members of a chosen race, you said.' The three had sat in the shade, remote from earthly cares. Picturing the scene, she remembered why she had turned her heavy body to look beyond the screening willows. 'You saw someone looking down on us. A woman.'

'So I did.' He was putting on his muffler, and with a dramatic gesture gave it a final fling over his shoulder. 'Paradise on earth is a contradiction in terms. Adam and Eve had only the one serpent. We have one each, all to ourselves.'

With this gnomic utterance he took his leave and strode down Alma Terrace in a manner which Esther recognized with amusement as rather sublime.

He had not forgotten the woman on Barrow Hill. He had been aware of her for a good half hour as he partook of cucumber sandwiches and five cups of tea. Her gaze, so far as he could tell, never left the Hall; her interest in it had been devouring. Some serpents do devour, he reflected, or at least swallow things whole; others coil and twist and squeeze out life. When he had climbed the hill, a steep one for a man of his weight, she had gone.

It was not the first time he had seen her. Walking from Taybrooke station, he had seen her several times in the vicinity of the Hall, standing, sauntering, walking away, always well dressed, always alone. She had seemed out of place, a feature of the landscape both incongruous and intrusive. Why was she there? It amused him to try to fit her into a prevailing pattern as all phenomena must be brought into relationship in the eternal quest for truth.

It must have been her, Esther was thinking ungrammatically, and on a somewhat lower level; and that was in June, eight months ago. The weary search for her identity must be a fixation with the poor creature. To have no rightful name, no certainty as to one's place or time of birth, no memory of father or mother, was to spend one's life as an outsider always looking in, as through a misted window into a lighted room. She needed help, whoever she was.

The funeral took place the next morning. Esther took a tearful leave of Alice and Gertie in the afternoon. They would be in close touch, she would come again soon, they must both come to Barbarrow, it would soon be spring.

Already in the country the earth was stirring into new life. Snowdrops pierced the soil on either side of the gates. With a revival of energy she leapt out of the car and flew upstairs for an emotional reunion with the infant she had not seen since morning. Mrs Bowland met her on the landing.

'You'll find everything in the nursery as it should be, madam – Mrs Lincoln.' Esther had expressed a strong objection to being addressed as madam. 'I don't know whether you were expecting visitors. You didn't say. But a lady called this morning, a Miss Motte. She asked for the master and when Annie said he was not at home, she asked for Mrs Lincoln.'

'Did she say that she would call again?'

'To tell you the truth, ma-Mrs Lincoln, I can't say.'

She explained that Annie had closed the door on the caller, who had evidently gone no more than a step or two when she met Ada bringing Viola back from an airing in the garden. As Ada had her hands full, Miss Motte had obligingly opened the door for her. Ada happened to catch her heel on the step and stumbled. Oh no, she hadn't fallen, nothing like that; but the baby had been so lively that the big shawl Ada had been careful to wrap her in had slipped to the ground. 'Let me help,' the lady had said and she picked up the shawl and followed Ada upstairs.

'Where was Annie?' Esther demanded.

'Annie was in the store cupboard. There hadn't been another knock for her to hear but she heard voices, and seeing the lady on the stairs, she went up after her. She's a sensible girl, Annie, not that there was anything to be sensible about. I wouldn't have mentioned it except that you asked if Miss Motte would be calling again; and what with Annie telling me about her going upstairs, I omitted to ask her if she had left a message. Shall I send Annie to you now?'

'Yes please, Mrs Bowland.'

'I don't recall ever having seen a Miss Motte, but it can't have been the first time she was here. I've been trying to think . . . I've been here since December 1918 when the master came home from the war. That was nearly eight years ago and I don't remember her coming, not in my time.'

'What makes you think she has been here before?'

'A remark she made to Ada as she went into the nursery. "There's been a change," she said. "Surely the nursery door was at the end of the passage." She seemed bemused, Annie said, like a sleep-walker.'

'Thank you, Mrs Bowland. There's no need to send Annie.'

No need to ask if Miss Motte intended to call again. She would be sure to come back. There was no longer any doubt as to who she was. She had found her way home at last.

The fact must be accepted, and with as little regret as was humanly possible. To welcome home Gervase's long-lost daughter was clearly the right thing to do. Ada had gone so far as to describe life at Barbarrow as heaven with the gates closed. The gates must be opened wide enough to admit the person who had as much right to be there as she had. She lost no time in passing on Mrs Bowland's account of the morning's incident.

Gervase was plainly troubled by this new development and was almost convinced, though as he pointed out, anyone could see – and even smell – that the nursery wing had recently been altered and redecorated. If the door of the old nursery at the end of the passage was open, Miss Motte could have seen the bars on the window and would naturally assume that it had once been the day nursery.

'I hadn't thought of that.' Esther would gladly have been convinced. She refrained from reminding him that his sensible explanation didn't quite tally with the phrasing of Miss Motte's remark, or with its effect on Ada and Annie.

Nor was Gervase convinced by his own argument. If he was convinced of anything it was of Miss Motte's competence in handling any situation in which she was involved. To gain her own ends? The suspicion was unjust; but she could quite reasonably be described as having an end in sight.

'You still think I should acknowledge her as my daughter?'

Esther agreed that Miss Motte's remark about the nursery door would seem too flimsy a basis for such a step, but, taken in conjunction with other factors, it did suggest that she had known the house as a child and in once familiar surroundings a memory had revived: a conclusion reached with so much reluctance that she could scarcely bring herself to ask, 'Do you think you could, Gervase?'

'You know that it would mean much more than to call her by her rightful name.' He was scoring the paper on his desk with troubled strokes of his pen.

'I have thought about it a good deal. Perhaps it would help if you stopped trying to think of her as little Lilla and accepted her as your daughter, Elizabeth Lincoln.'

'What difference would that make?'

'If you could get to know her in her own right, as she is now, talk to her as you would to someone you had met in a normal way about things that interested you both . . .' It sounded hopelessly theoretical. How could the entire past be obliterated by conversations on topics of mutual interest, assuming that mutual interests could be found? 'Do you see what I mean?'

'I see that you are doing your best to help me, my love, and yes, you may be right. As a matter of fact, once she was satisfied as to her identity she would probably go her own way and lead her own life. She might find our kind of existence dull.' He smiled in the old way and lowered his voice in the manner of a conspirator. 'We could try hard to be too dull for her. It would be easy for me. You would find it harder. In fact you'd make a fearful hash of it.'

Two young women of much the same age? What would be the effect of Esther on Elizabeth? He tried out the name. Would she be happy to be outshone by the beauty that delighted him every time he set eyes on his wife? Hers were now large in her earnestness, violet blue in a delicately tinted face, lips parted to rebuke him for his teasing: features lovely in themselves, and unshadowed by guile or impurity of mind. And what would Esther see in the other's face?

'We have no reason to think that she would want to live with us,' he said. 'Some parents see very little of their grown-up children except at weddings and funerals.'

'And she may marry.'

'An ideal solution that would make everyone happy.'

They considered the next step to be taken. Should they both go to Ivy Villa or should Gervase go alone? Or should Elizabeth be formally invited to the Hall? No decision was reached that day – or the next. A week passed, and another. The luxury of postponement was all the pleasanter for the knowledge that it could not last. Something must be done, but not yet. No sign came from Ivy Villa. A shadow hung over them but life resumed its normal course.

Then, on a Saturday afternoon in March, Annie opened the door to the lady who had called once before.

Neither Major Lincoln nor Mrs Lincoln was at home, Annie told her, but the master was in the grounds and would be back presently. Mrs Bowland herself took Miss Motte into the sitting-room overlooking the front garden, and then hovered unobtrusively in the passage outside just in case. You never knew these days. Ada was upstairs with the baby. Mrs Lincoln was in town.

As Gervase passed the window he caught a glimpse of someone on the sofa, assumed that Esther had come home earlier than she had planned and was taken aback to find Miss Motte – Elizabeth. Unprepared, he felt at a disadvantage in the very place where he should have felt most confident. Afterwards, when he had recovered a little from its disastrous end, he acknowledged to himself that the meeting had been presided over by his visitor, also that she had done it very well. No fault could be found in what she said or in her manner of saying it.

'The past few weeks have been anxious for me,' she began at once. 'I felt that it was absolutely necessary for us to meet again, but this situation is so unusual that I have not been able to decide how to deal with it.'

'You are describing my own position and my wife's. We too have wondered what to do.'

It must be her extraordinary self-command that made her seem older than her years. In the candid light of the spring afternoon her face was a trifle haggard. There were lines about the eyes and a fixed droop to the shape of her mouth: she was experienced, and the experience had been harsh. She was charmingly dressed in a dark blue skirt and jacket, the revers of pale blue, like her hat. As she spoke, the faint feeling of familiarity came and went. Had he seen her before, a long time ago? Or was it that, despite the absence of any likeness or any gentleness of expression, she reminded him in some way of Anne? The thought had a softening effect.

'I decided that the best thing to do was to speak plainly. It's always best to be straightforward.' As there could be only one response to such a remark Gervase made none. 'We both know that I may be your daughter. If only we could be sure it would put both our minds at rest. We can't be sure. I came to tell you that you have nothing to fear from me. I have no wish to intrude. You have others to consider. I have no-one. I don't know what it feels like to be protected and cared for. It won't make any difference to me to go on with the life I lead . . .'

Once again he felt at a disadvantage, wretchedly so. It was she who had achieved a mature view of their problem: he who was helpless under the weight of an obligation all the heavier because he didn't know how to discharge it. He wanted to act from a magnanimity similar to hers. At the same time he felt more strongly than ever the need for caution.

As before, she seemed devoid of feeling. She had spoken, as it were, into empty space and not to him directly. Her speech lacked warmth and spontaneity; it could have been rehearsed. But if she had prepared it, was not that a sensible thing to do, the occasion being so awkward? And was not her coldness a direct result of the deprivation she had described? If she lacked the ability to feel, it was not her fault but his. His was the guilt of a father who had failed his child. It was frail consolation that through some gift of nature, some inherited refinement, she had risen above experiences that might have doomed her to a life of vice.

'I was wrong to say that it would make no difference.' She got up and went slowly, as though drawn, to the window. 'There will be the comfort of knowing that I may have been born in a place like this, that my father may have been a man like you, that in my origins at least I may have nothing to be ashamed of.'

Emotion tightened his throat. 'A place like this.' She already cared for Barbarrow. Already? Or still? Had it cast its spell upon her as a child and so remained in her unconscious mind to be revived on her return as Esther had suggested?

'I appreciate your coming. You were right to speak plainly. For the time being we can only feel our way and perhaps as we come to know each other better . . .' What was he saying? What future could he promise? He was loath to commit himself, yet ashamed of so grudging a commitment.

She had been gazing out into the garden where golden aconites starred the shade under the trees. With reluctance, it seemed, she turned. 'I must go.'

'We must keep in touch. Let me have your address if you move elsewhere. If ever you are in need of help of any kind . . .' He remembered that she had come into a little money and wondered how much and from whom.

He saw her to the front door. On the top step of the shallow flight she held out her hand. He felt the uncanny significance of their shaking hands, as if in a farewell belated by twenty-four years. Yet the hand-shake also confirmed a partnership, as if the precarious balance of doubt and belief united them as allies. As relations?

Instinctively it was in some such way that Esther saw it as she got out of the taxi, a reaction not unusual in a housewife returning to find that her husband has entertained a visitor in her absence. She came nearer.

To his consternation Gervase saw her face blanch, her eyes darken to blackness, her figure grow rigid as she realized who it was that looked down on her from the house while she, its mistress, stood outside. In the flash of horrified recognition it seemed to her that she was being supplanted a second time by the woman she had hoped never to see again, whose name she could scarcely bring herself to utter. Daniel's wife! And Gervase's daughter? Miss Angovil's maid! The dead-seeming creature in the reeking blanket?

How had it happened? Where had she come from? There flashed into her bewilderment the memory of another meeting when they had faced each other across the churchyard. She had appeared startlingly as if risen from a grave. The dead Lilla? Who was she – really?

Shocked, outraged, unbelieving, Esther was sure of only one thing – that the woman was dangerous and false. Wherever she went she inflicted pain. Whoever she was, her motive in coming to Barbarrow was not the straightforward one she claimed. She had ruined Daniel and would ruin Gervase. She herself could not exist for an instant under the same roof, could not set foot in her own home. She bowed her head in distress like a

327

victim waiting for a final blow. It was soon to come.

None of the three moved. Gervase, thinking only of Esther, paid no attention to his companion. He would have learned nothing from her expression. Of the three, she alone had been prepared for such a moment: for how long and to what degree of preparedness she alone knew. She must have expected the question Esther put to her when she could bring herself to speak; she could not have foreseen the transformation in the once gentle face.

'Why have you come here calling yourself Miss Motte? It isn't your name, is it, Mrs Godwain?'

The question was infused with such contempt that the answer, though too swift and smooth, seemed calmly reasonable. 'Because in so far as I have a name, it is still Motte. We didn't marry after all, you know. It wouldn't have been a success.'

'Esther!' Gervase came quickly down to her. The wild look she turned on him deterred him from touching her. Crushed by the sheer cruelty of the blow, she had seemed to shrink as from a withering of spirit. Contempt and hatred left her, swept away by a flood of misery so intense that she felt herself actually disintegrate as in a violent death. It was more than she could bear. The world had gone wrong. She could no longer live in it. The packages she had been holding slipped from her hands. She turned her back and walked slowly away, her limbs shaking.

'Esther!'

She didn't hear him. That last day up there on the hill, Daniel had been free. He had been on the point of telling her when she interrupted and showed him her ring. He had deceived her because he loved her. There was no other love to compare with his love for her or hers for him. It was as natural as the trees and streams of the countryside where they had grown up, their native place. It had been an act against nature to marry anyone but Daniel. It had been possible

328

all the time until two years ago, and now it was of all things the most impossible.

She had come as far as the great stone urn on its pedestal above the grotto and paused to lean against it. Sadness possessed her. In its desperate calm she saw the complexities of life as movements on the surface of an underlying simplicity: the inescapable agony of living. It was their own fault, Daniel's and hers. If Clairy had been the medium through whom disaster had spread from Lady Green and the Lodge to Barbarrow, she herself and Daniel had been to blame. They were responsible for their own lives and had been weak: Daniel in sinking to Clairy's level, she in not boldly insisting that they should marry after their fathers' deaths. Instead they had waited like good children until it was too late.

Too late. Time in its passage brought not only a weary succession of hours, days, years, but the inexorable fading of all happiness. She felt as aching a nostalgia for the old innocent days at Wood Aston as if she too were old, and leaned against the urn, drooping and weak like an old woman.

From the terrace Gervase watched and waited. In his heart-sickness he, too, was visited by a vision from the past. It was of Lilla. She had learned to haul herself up by the balustrade, climb up to the urn and clutch its rim in triumph. More than once she had been scolded and led indoors, weeping. Had she been a wayward child? Did she remember? He had forgotten her. She was still at the door. He forgot her again in his concern for Esther.

'Come indoors, dearest. We'll talk this over together. You mustn't—' The few yards that separated them seemed much more; a wasteland. He crossed it. 'Where are you going?'

She shook off his protective arm and went blindly to the gate that opened on the path to Barrow Hill.

CHAPTER 22

Gervase let her go. He stood irresolute, watching her toil up the path she would normally have skimmed like a bird. Soothing words, all that he had to offer, would be hopelessly out of tune. Besides, soothing words would be hard to find.

He felt the danger of taking a false step. The revelation that the two knew each other was entirely unexpected. He had been startled by Esther's question. She had been devastated by the reply, the softness gone from her voice, her face contorted as if her very nature had altered. He was left to deduce that Clarice Motte was the girl with whom Daniel Godwain had been involved. At the back of his mind and ready to advance, bringing no comfort – no comfort at all – hovered the thought that Godwain, unless married to someone else, was a factor to be reckoned with. In her distress it was to him that Esther was turning, not to her husband.

Unwillingly he went back to the house. To his intense relief the visitor had gone. She must have walked quickly and was already beyond the curve in the lane. He never wanted to see her again; and yet, standing unhappily at his front door, he acknowledged that their situation was unaltered, his obligation to her remained. Nothing could release him, short of definite proof that she was not his daughter.

The fact that she had never claimed to be exonerated her from the charge of imposture. In her entire behaviour there had seemed no hint of falsehood, nothing to be seized on as a sign that she was motivated by anything but the natural desire to know her parentage.

Racked by indecision, unable to see a clear course of action, he remembered how, on the day of his return from the war, he had opened shutters, unlocked doors, explored rooms unused for years. In one of the lumber rooms cobwebs hung so thick that in crossing to the window he had become entangled in myriads of viscous threads and had struggled in brief panic to be free. They had clung to his hands and face and mouth as now a score of unanswerable questions entangled and threatened to stifle him.

It was necessary for a minute or two to do nothing, to stand there at the heart of his domain and to feel himself enfolded by it. The word was Esther's. Deliberately, as he had taught himself to do in many a crisis, he relaxed and turned his attention outward: to slim buds on the pear tree, the blue and russet plumage of a chaffinch, yellow-headed daffodils on a green bank. Barbarrow would absorb into its long history another day of mortal heartache, its own tranquillity undisturbed. Seen by the eternal eye, how transitory the recent episode, how amenable its wounds to the healing processes of time.

The self-administered treatment brought little relief. His picture of the episode was incomplete. He had seen Esther recoil with loathing from someone she had known too well. How had the other reacted? Had she known that Esther Aumery was his wife? She had never mentioned his wife at all. In the circumstances, was not her failure to allude to her possible stepmother strange: a sign that she knew, rather than that she did not know, who Mrs Lincoln was? And if she did know . . .

When Esther had confided in him over the tea-cups at the Willow Tea-room, she had not named the woman whom Godwain had supposedly married: a neighbour's maid who occasionally helped out at the Lodge. For the first time it occurred to him that he might have seen her there: one of the three women grouped about the wheel-chair he had given the Godwains.

There had been Mrs Godwain, Esther and a third. Details of the scene had faded from his mind, but he remembered that while Esther and Mrs Godwain had been occupied with Thomas, the other woman had stood upright, her eyes intent on Esther. Suppose his fleeting sense of danger had been more than mere fancy: a premonition now being fulfilled.

It was not an idea to be taken seriously. All the same . . . What if the so-called Miss Motte had even then intended some mischief, directed towards Esther? She had succeeded in parting Esther from Daniel, and was threatening his own marriage. It was tempting to postulate at least an absence of innocence if not the presence of actual ill-will.

But if that were true, she could still be his daughter, his lost four-year-old grown corrupt, unscrupulous, jealous: tendencies made more dangerous by an outward refinement. He went to his study and from a drawer in his desk took a leather folder. It contained three photographs of Lilla: as an infant prone on a rug, as a two-year-old with Anne, mother and daughter cheek to cheek, as a three-year-old in frills and holding a basket of flowers. The face was clearly outlined: blue candid eyes of childhood, cheeks rounded but not plump, a stately little neck, symmetrically curved, unsmiling lips. He and Esther had pored over these details, Esther from interest, he in search of a resemblance.

On first meeting Clarice Motte at Taybrooke he had experienced a faint sense of familiarity. It had disposed him to wonder if she might indeed be Lilla. He knew now that it was no more than an imperfect memory of an actual meeting, more than one, at Wood Aston. He also remembered his first instinctive distrust of the woman under the elms. Uncertainty tortured him. In the ebb and flow of doubt and belief, only his responsibility as a parent remained constant. In withdrawing it from Clarice Motte, he might once again be failing the little girl who was his daughter.

There could be no solution to the dilemma, no end. Esther had tried to share it, but she was no longer there to help him; he longed for her, knowing that she, too, was suffering and that her conflict was all the more bitter because she was young.

But it was not to him that she had turned for comfort. She had gone instinctively to Godwain. He knew better than to follow her. He must wait until the storm had subsided; but he felt in his heart that he had lost her.

On his visits to the Hall to photograph the baby, Vincent Auke had discovered the charm of its surroundings and had got into the habit, on an occasional free afternoon, of taking a train to Taybrooke and exploring the countryside on foot. Rustic scenes provided a welcome change from thumb-sucking infants and more inhibited adults dolled up in their best clothes. He never called at the Hall except professionally, but his rambling did sometimes take him into Lincoln territory, as happened one Saturday afternoon in March.

He had closed a gate behind him and entered a rutted lane with a row of elms on his left; on his right a vista of green fields and blue sky framed by curving boughs made a promising picture. He became absorbed in the calculation of distance, perspective and values of light and shade, decided that the result would lack definition, and turned to see a woman walking towards him from the direction of the Hall.

Recognition was mutual, an encounter unavoidable.

'Good afternoon, Mr Auke.'

'Miss Motte. I didn't expect to see you here.' The surprise was justified. He had not expected to see anyone there, least of all one of his clients. Moreover she was too stylishly dressed for a country ramble, and it was a good half mile along the road to Taybrooke.

'Such a nice day.' She barely paused. He opened the gate for her, she nodded and went on and that was all.

But Vincent, viewing her with a professional eye, had seen something to interest him. She had come to the studio one day in July of the year before last. He had found her, as a sitter, uninspiring. Taken full length she could have been impressive, but she had wanted a portrait of head and shoulders. Hers was a boring face except for the eyebrows. They were distinctive. He had seized on them, so to speak, as the feature on which to concentrate. As a matter of fact he had thought them satanic and in at least one of the poses that was how they appeared.

She had given him an address which he recognized and asked him to post the proofs; but happening to be in Old Church Lane one day she had called instead. She had looked at them all carefully for some time, especially the satanic one, which she rejected. He remembered it clearly: the downward tilt of the head, the upward sideways look from under the dark, wing-like brows. He had managed it well, perhaps too well. Be that as it may, he had made an unpromising face remarkable.

Why on earth had she mercilessly plucked – or shaved – the eyebrows right out of existence? And without improving her looks, especially as the thinly pencilled half hoops were slightly at variance with the marginal bone of the eye cavity. Why should she ruthlessly destroy her one distinctive feature? Her face could now be anybody's face. Well, that was going too far: the eyes, given their natural setting, might have redeemed it. But if she should happen to be lying dead on a mortuary slab, eyes closed, there would be nothing outward to identify her by. Just how such macabre imaginings could have obtruded on his pleasant afternoon, Vincent could not have explained. If forced, he would have admitted merely to a lack of respect for her. Not that he had anything against Olga's girls, and Olga herself was a decent sort. The fact remained that Miss Motte struck him as the kind of woman who might finish up on a mortuary slab if she wasn't careful, having positively encouraged some poor devil to do her in.

What had she been doing at the Hall? She couldn't possibly have any connection with Esther, even when they lived at opposite ends of Alma Terrace, nor with the Major, not now, if ever, and not in the precincts of the Hall. He was pretty sure about that. He rambled on, his thoughts wandering too, to Esther, now further than ever beyond his reach. It had always been hopeless; but he knew that she cared for him as a friend in what she had once described as 'a special kind of way'. That would have to do; and he was genuinely glad that she had found the happiness she deserved.

As a student of faces, he was bothered by those eyebrows.

Esther came to the Lodge without knowing how she had got there. As she passed Lady Green and climbed the Scaur, there had grown on her a dreamlike sensation of returning childhood. The illusion persisted as she pushed open the familiar gate, so that she was not surprised to see that the porch was occupied, as it had so often been, by a boy. Through the mist that seemed to be affecting her eyes, she saw that he was kneeling. The seat opposite to the fox's head was strewn with screws and bits of metal.

At the unexpected sight of a lady standing mid-way along the garden path, he got up. She was not an ordinary person. She was beautiful and sad. They gazed at each other, speechless.

Emerging from her dream, Esther thought confusedly that this must be the child: Daniel's son, dark-eyed and alert like Daniel.

'Are you— Who are you?'

'Jake Hildy.'

Of course he was too old – eight or nine years old, perhaps. She wondered vaguely about the child who had parted her from Daniel.

335

'Mr Godwain's out, but he'll be back soon.'

'I'll wait.' Still mist-bound, she found her way to the porch, carefully removed the conch shells and sat down.

'It's my clock,' he said as she glanced vacantly at the clutter on the opposite seat. 'I brought it with me. It never used to go. I took it to pieces and now I'm putting it together again. Trying to, me and Mr Godwain. We did it once, but there were a lot of parts left over and it wouldn't go.'

'Do you come here often?'

'I live here.' He had lowered his voice as if in awe. Delight wavered. She saw anxiety in his eyes. 'For the time being.' It was evidently a quotation. He became, sternly, a clock-maker again. His hand trembled as he tried unsuccessfully to tighten a small screw. 'That's the wrong one.'

'There are so many.'

'It'll take years I expect. Mr Godwain says if you start a thing you should keep at it.' He eyed her, bit his lip, hesitated and risked a confidence. 'He has high hopes of me, Mr Godwain has.'

'You'll do it in the end; but I hope you have some fun in between,' she roused herself to say.

'Fun?' He chuckled. 'We have fun all right, Mr Godwain and me.'

'Where is he now?'

'Gone to see Mr Horner.' He began to arrange the baffling components of the clock in neat rows in a cardboard box. 'We've got boiled ham for tea.'

She felt herself to be in motion and drifted out into the lane. As he crossed the bridge by the mill Daniel saw her sitting on the low wall. She looked ill and vaguely bedraggled. A few breathless moments and she was in his arms, weeping. Caught unawares, astonished, shaken, he caressed her as if she were still his own, then lifted her over the wall and led her into the privacy of the wood.

'I should have told you,' he said when he had heard her story and told her his, when they had pieced together things known to one and not to the other. 'I tried to put things right by not telling you, and it's only made things worse.'

'I didn't know. How could I know?' Repeated several times it became a lament like the chorus of a mournful ballad. 'How could I know that Clairy was that girl . . . or that Miss Motte would turn out to be Clairy? I can't think of her as real, like other people. I never did, from the day she was found. She's like something from another world.'

They walked slowly, he adapting his step to hers, she tightly held within his arm, so that they moved in unison like a single being. Their talk was disjointed, their mutual understanding so quick that the words each spoke were words the other had almost said. So that, when they came in sight of the Aston oak, both paused at the same moment and for the same reason.

'Not there,' she said. They turned back, then turned again, walking back and forth on the soft woodland path in heaven-sent isolation, regardless of time, conscious only of the need to avoid the oak; until, from being out of bounds, it became the pivot of their loitering and at last a resting place.

'This is where we used to sit.'

'No, here, facing west.'

Under its boughs, though bare as yet, light fell more softly on their faces. In their hunger to redress the adverse balance of years it was as if they saw each other with the freshness of a first time and the sadness of the last. He saw in her the love he had wantonly cast away and the trust he had betrayed. His face, lean and mobile, was as familiar to her as her own. He was the first person after her parents whose physical self she had known. She remembered the bones of his hands and, as he kissed her, the smell of his skin; the primitive sensations of childhood matured and

337

intensified in a love both knew to be lifelong and destined never to be fulfilled.

'What shall I do?' He had so often told her what she should do. This time she knew what the answer must be and asked simply for the luxury of confirmation.

'You have no choice. I'm probably the only person who knows what Lincoln is feeling. I know what it feels like to lose you. He's just finding out. Do you want to make him wretched too?'

'And Viola.' She drew away from him. 'I've been out of my mind.'

'Your hair's coming down. You've got mud on your shoes. Tidy yourself up, my love, and go home.'

'I came just as I was – to be with you again.'

'I know. He shouldn't grudge us this one last time.'

'I meant what shall I do about *her*?'

'There's nothing you can do, nothing drastic or positive. No-one knows or ever can know whether she is Elizabeth Lincoln, including her. She's sown the seed of doubt in his mind, poor chap. It will always be there.'

'And she will always be there between us.'

'No, not between. You are his wife and you'll have to face it together. You can't let her spoil your life and his and the baby's. Oh, I know I have no room to speak. But you must be stronger than she is. You have no choice now but to—'

'I know. If you start a thing you should keep at it. Jake told me that. Where did you find him?' And when he had told her, 'It's what you always wanted to do, to save a lost child and give it a second chance.'

'He came at the right time to save me and give me another chance; and this time there's first-rate material to work on. I have high hopes for him.'

'So he told me. You will keep him with you? Tell him so. You're all the world to him.'

They went back by way of the footbridge and parted where the lane ended at the old barn.

'What do you think happened to him, Daniel? The man.'

'We'll never know that either. You were the only one who saw him. Perhaps you were dreaming.'

'I didn't dream the cart.'

Pieces of timber still patched with yellow lay on the turf and under the hedge. The past hour had brought so strong a sense of continuity that to say goodbye seemed no more than an incident in the love no parting could alter; but their last desperate kiss ended in a desolation as deep as the love.

'No, don't come any further.'

She went carefully over the stepping-stones, leaving him at the stream's edge to watch the ever-changing waters keep their unchanging course, the pattern of brown and silver and white foam constantly renewed. Long after she had gone he stayed there. Solitude had become emptiness. Beyond the busy rush of the stream there was nothing to be heard, no help on earth or in the sky: only a terrible silence.

Jake had laid the table and put out the ham, loaf, butter and milk but he was in a dilemma about the kettle. He was allowed to fill it and put it on the fire, but not to lift it off when it boiled. To keep it singing without boiling involved him in a constant lifting off and putting on. Trips back and forth to look down the lane grew wearisome. Two long hours passed. At length he heard the swing of the gate and footsteps, unexpectedly slow, on the path.

'The tea's ready, Mr Godwain. The kettle's nearly boiling.'

They sat down to eat in silence. The triumphant announcement had fallen flat. Jake was hungry but he did not enjoy the meal.

'There's been a lady here.' he ventured. 'A real lady with rings on her fingers.'

'I know.'

Jake crept back into his shell. He had known it wouldn't last. It couldn't have. It had been too good to last. Mr Godwain had gone out the same as always and had come back different.

'Gervase.'

He was sitting at his desk, head in hands, as she had seen him once before, less than two years ago. He looked up. His face expressed neither welcome nor reproach. With a rush of affection and remorse she saw how deeply she had hurt him.

He got up slowly. In its cloud of dark hair her face was pinched and anxious. Her forlorn look touched his heart.

'I'm sorry, Gervase. Please – forgive me.'

He put out his arms, then let them fall, no longer confident. Instead he kissed her cheek and drew her to a chair. 'I understand. It's as if we married under false pretences, isn't it, except that neither of us deceived the other. You told me about him. I knew that he was your first love and now . . . You still love him?'

'Yes. It all happened long before I knew you. My earliest memories are of him. Then when we fell in love it seemed as though it was meant to happen, that we were bound together. But we both know that we must live apart.' She felt his sense of rejection. 'And I'm bound to you too, Gervase, even more, and I love you too. No-one was ever so good and unselfishly loving as you have been. We've been very happy. It was the shock of finding out who she was and that they weren't married after all that made me behave as I did. It will never happen again. And you'll forgive me?'

'I've been trying to face the prospect of losing you. Can you face staying with me? It can't be the same for either of us, I know that, but to have you back on any terms will give me something to live for. Without you, there would be nothing.'

Later, when they had talked and schooled themselves back to normal behaviour so that there was no disturbance in the household routine, they went to the nursery where Viola, bathed, fed, drowsily content, smiled at them from her cot.

'She'll soon be crawling,' Ada said. 'I was just saying to Annie, you've a beautiful daughter and she's as good as gold.'

'Somehow,' she told Mrs Bowland later, 'when I said that they both seemed – what shall I say?'

'Pleased, I expect.'

'Solemn. It seemed to strike both of them as if I'd said something special. If it had been anyone else but him I'd have sworn there were tears in his eyes.'

'Well, he's human, isn't he?'

'She put her arm through his and they went downstairs. A lovely couple. Search the highways and by-ways and you won't find two people better suited to each other. I've said it before and I'll say it again. This place is like heaven with the gates closed.'

CHAPTER 23

Ada's notion of divine bliss did not allow for the addition to a marriage of two other people. Nothing was heard of Clarice Motte; Gervase made no attempt to see her. She had promised not to intrude, but she had already cast a constant shadow on the Lincoln household, and the shadow cast by Daniel, though of a different kind, was no less persistent. For a while neither was mentioned. It might have been wiser to talk freely: the unspoken taboo on the subject of the intruders set them apart, on the one hand as sinister and on the other – more dangerously – as sacred.

Esther pined inwardly, but she was by nature un-assertive and had been drilled early in the discipline of adapting to circumstances. Gervase, used to action and responsibility, was frustrated by constant indecision, and was soon to be faced with conflict of a more serious kind.

In May, labour unrest came to a head in the General Strike. The long neglect of the mines by all political parties had embittered the men who worked in them. Crisis was reached when the Government, under Baldwin, decided to discontinue the coal subsidy; the miners, faced with the prospect of lower pay or unemployment, refused to accept the findings of the Samuel Report. Breaking point came when printers refused to print the *Daily Mail* because of its criticism of the unions' proposal to take direct action. As a result, on 3 May the Cabinet decided to break off negotiations with the union leaders, and a General Strike was called with almost the whole of industry supporting the miners.

For eight days the Lincoln Ironworks closed down together with mines, forges, steelworks, public transport and most newspapers. A few of them published a single sheet: *The Times* consisted of a typescript page, the Government issued a bulletin, *The British Gazette* edited by Winston Churchill. Otherwise the general public had no means of knowing what was going on. The black-out of news and the closure of his works reduced Gervase to enforced idleness, which left him free to brood over his personal problems and drove him at last to seek help, if only by unburdening himself to someone who would listen: someone discreet, thoughtful, detached . . .

It was strangely quiet in the streets surrounding Ruskin House. Without the clank and rumble of trams and drays there were spells of unnatural silence, not the soothing quietness to be found in the countryside but rather the awful stillness of the desert, or of a region depopulated by plague; until the pause was ended by the unquenchable flow of voices, the sound of a private car, the clop of hooves and the coming and going of Saturday morning shoppers.

In his tiny book-lined study overlooking the street, Morgan Krantz loomed disproportionately large. It was as if, channelled within the smallest possible physical space, his energy must of necessity be directed upwards to soar into realms of pure thought: a region too rarefied, Gervase told himself, for the topic he hesitated to introduce. Half regretting that he had come, he resorted for the time being to another.

'Things can't go on like this.' He was not referring to the uncushioned narrowness of his chair but to the national emergency. 'What does Baldwin think he's doing?'

'Baldwin, as you know, is better at doing nothing than any man alive. On the rare occasions when he takes the initiative, he raises new problems.' There could be little doubt as to where Morgan's sympathies lay. 'You heard his broadcast last night? He and John Simon between them have turned a thoroughly bad situation into a dangerous one.'

It was Saturday, 8 May, the day on which it became known that on the previous Thursday Sir John Simon, Liberal leader and eminent lawyer, had declared the strike to be illegal. This changed the climate of the dispute and increased tension, leaving the rank and file of strikers dismayed, their leaders embittered and those who regarded them as lawless scoundrels more firmly entrenched in their opposition.

'There've been blunders on both sides,' Gervase said gloomily. 'I see what you mean about this ultimatum of Baldwin's.'

In his broadcast on the previous evening the Prime Minister had affirmed that until the strike was called off, negotiations would not be resumed. Though their attitudes were not identical, both Gervase and Morgan saw the strike as the most serious threat to national stability in recent history – since the Civil War, according to Morgan who, as usual, took a long view. Gervase, though naturally concerned about the abrupt decline in trade and the damaging effect on his works of a protracted shut-down, agreed that intransigence on the part of the Government could force the strike leaders to adopt more extreme measures. Neither side could want a long-drawn-out struggle in which those already suffering most would suffer more. Both sides were drifting dangerously into false positions.

'This insistence on unconditional surrender is bound to harden attitudes,' Morgan said. 'Simon has already classed the strikers as rebels and criminals. If they stay out after Baldwin's speech, there's only one option left to the Government – and that frightens me.'

'To arrest the union leaders. My God! What would that lead to?'

'Violence in the streets. Bloodshed.'

The word brought reasonable discussion to an end.

It coincided with a period of quiet in the street below, in which Gervase underwent a mental adjustment. Against the wider spectrum of national conflict, the problem of what to do about Clarice Motte seemed less pressing. Then in the distance a greengrocer on his cart called: 'Er-ripe bananas! Er-lovely oranges.' Children's voices rose from the pavement; the demands of normal life once more prevailed.

Yet it was with difficulty that he said, 'I rather wanted to talk to you about something else . . .'

'. . . You want to get at the truth?' Morgan had certainly listened and with unflagging attention. 'To resolve conflicting possibilities? No, I'm not trying to fob you off with philosophical abstractions. The fact is, that indecision is disharmony, disharmony is a source of evil, evil a factor of daily life to be controlled, if not overcome, by the exercise of reason.' His rich voice vied with and outdid the voices of the unreasoning urchins engaged in inharmonious play below.

'God! How he talks,' Gervase thought, but he submitted and the sensation was restful.

'In this case can we put our fingers on the source or sources of your difficulty? Esther's former experience of the woman, the nature of the woman herself, her rootlessness and dubious background, your own sense of guilt. An unwholesome brew! Let us deal with your conscience. You went to Provence to give comfort to a dying woman, Anne's grandmother. You left Lilla at home to avoid the risk of typhoid. She was far more safely provided for in your absence than most children are at any time in their lives. Listen!' He edged his way round the table and opened the window. On the sunnier side of the grimy street children were playing on the pavement at marbles, hopscotch or at knocking each other about. 'Look at them: ill-clad, badly fed, flea-ridden, prone to infection, to rickets and consumption; not a responsible adult in sight. Their parents can't afford to feel guilty. You acted for the best. If, in spite of

345

every precaution, things went wrong, it wasn't through neglect on your part. Stop feeling guilty.'

'But now, what about my responsibility to this woman?'

Morgan did not reply immediately, and his question when it came was unexpected. 'Would you describe your first wife as a clever woman?'

'I don't know . . . Anne was quiet and home-loving. Intelligent, of course, but . . . no, not actively intellectual or a keen thinker, I suppose. Not like—'

'Is there anything of Anne's bearing or appearance in this woman?'

'Nothing. But it's been so long. I can't remember. And clothes, style and circumstances are so different now. Clarice Motte is remarkably intelligent, assured, articulate . . .' More so, he discovered, marvelling, than either Anne or Esther.

'Do you know what interests me most?' Morgan had remained standing, but not with the intention of bringing their talk to an end. 'The actual disappearance, twenty-four years ago. Who was at the bottom of it? If some villain kidnapped Lilla, why did he also take Julie? Even stranger – if he wanted Julie, why take Lilla? Why no demand for a ransom? For what conceivable purpose would anyone abduct a young woman and a four-year-old if not for money? We are forced into trying to envisage some combination of circumstances so far from the normal as to defy conjecture, or . . .' He paused before saying slowly, 'or to believe that the person involved was in some way – extraordinary.'

The word was disturbing. With an effort Gervase evaded its chilling implications and gave his mind to the questions that preceded it. 'The police had a theory that Julie had stolen Lilla. We tried to convince them that it would have been entirely out of character and very difficult for her to vanish without trace. A person of her appearance and speech, with a child, would have been noticed.' He explained

346

wearily that questioning had continued for months at farms, railway stations, taxi-ranks, hotels and boarding houses both in Britain and France.

'It's highly unlikely that she would deliberately take the child away and take nothing else: not a warm coat or an extra pair of shoes, or any of her own things. Women are concerned with possessions even in the worst crisis or when acting on impulse.' Morgan lapsed into thought.

They had talked for over an hour. Though appreciative of Morgan's genuine interest and unexpectedly brisk grasp of practical detail, Gervase was confirmed in the belief that his problem was insoluble. It would have been unreasonable to expect a solution – or anything more than the lightening of a burden that comes from sharing it.

'It cannot be proved that Clarice Motte is your daughter,' Morgan said suddenly. 'But it might be possible to prove that she is not. If it could be established that she is someone else's daughter . . . If another father, the actual one, could be found . . . What about her birth certificate? Have you mentioned the subject? No? Well, I don't suppose there'd be much point in asking her if she has one. If she really is Lilla she will say, truthfully, that she has never seen her birth certificate or known where it might be. But if she is not Lilla, she could make exactly the same reply. You don't believe that Motte is her real name, do you? Even if her name is not Lincoln. In that case, no enquiries can be made as to the registration of her birth. Besides, not all births are registered, I imagine. Find out more about the Apperfield connection. You'll feel better with something definite to do. And see that Esther has plenty to do. She was happy looking after William Capman. I can think of other ways of putting that coach-house of yours to good use. You've only to say the word.'

They were interrupted by another caller. As Gervase was leaving, Morgan put a hand on his shoulder.

347

'Think first of Esther. The other can look after herself.'

There was no time to elaborate, nor would he have been willing to do so, but he had seen and heard enough of the woman to convince him of the need for caution in admitting her into a family circle.

For Gervase the visit had after all been worthwhile. He was determined to take Morgan's advice and try to trace Clarice Motte's history in reverse, beginning with her first appearance in Wood Aston and working backwards. The next day being Sunday, he could do nothing. On the Monday he went to Apperfield.

'That's a fine Blue Hen you have there.' Gervase had been watching pigeons on the let board of a ramshackle loft when their owner emerged from an equally ramshackle back door: a short, sallow man less well fed perhaps than his birds. 'Not too big, a good firm back and no dip.'

'And she handles well.' The man lifted the bird and held her on the flat of his hand. 'See that?'

'The steady tail? Not a flicker.'

'You keep pigeons?'

'A few. Mostly Pouters and Tumblers.' He didn't mention the Fantails and the rare pure white Cumulets.

'You don't race?' There was condescension in the tone.

'Haven't time, I'm afraid.'

The companionable moment was the pleasantest so far in an unrewarding morning; the iridescent blues and pearl greys of the birds gave a touch of grace to the surrounding drabness. As if to detach themselves from its squalor, two of them took wing and rose into a sky high and blue enough to make Gervase wish himself back at Barbarrow.

He could have enlisted official help in his enquiries but he had been reluctant to attract public attention to a search so delicate and unformulated, preferring to act on his own, at least for the time being. He had tackled Apperfield systematically, studied a street map and a directory, eliminated the more prosperous upper part of the town and made his way to the district known locally as Old Apper, a slum area by the river. It consisted of a warren of half a dozen streets with interconnecting courts and alleys. Dilapidated houses with broken windows overlooked a clutter of hen-coops topped with corrugated iron, bits of broken furniture, abandoned wash-tubs and bicycles. With nothing else to recommend it, Old Apper had remained a close-knit, inbred community. Neighbours knew each other's business, relationships were intricate.

'You've come from the council?'

'No, nothing like that. Someone I know had connections with this part of Apperfield a good many years ago. Thought I'd take a look round. There must have been changes.'

'It's changed a bit.' The man came out into the back lane, sucking from his teeth the remnants of a late breakfast or an early lunch. He was unshaven, his braces hung loose down the back of his legs, his bootlaces dangled untied. 'If there's anything you want to know about Old Apper, you've come to the right one. Anybody'll tell you. They all know me, Kit Salter. Even the new ones.'

'People still move here then?'

'A few. As soon as there's a house empty. This chap you know. Did he live here?'

'I'm not sure. It would be before the war.'

They sauntered to the end of Kit Salter's row and faced across a cobbled square to a group of older buildings and between them the entrance to a narrow alley.

'Yon's the Snick.'

Judging the visitor to be a man of eccentric tastes, Kit led him into the alley. It opened on an inner court with three-storied dwellings on two sides and

349

disconcertingly close to the reeking slaughter-yard of a butcher's shop at the farther end. Doors stood open, toddlers staggered on the broken and slimy cobbles. Gervase tried not to think about the drainage system, if there was one. All the houses seemed to be occupied, except the third on the right where all the windows were boarded up.

'Is that house to let?'

'Yon? Nobody lives there. Hasn't done for years. Hey, Hettie!' Kit addressed a woman who was pegging clothes on to a line. 'This gent's asking if Tappers is to let.'

She was a woman in her forties and looked much older. She smiled grimly but without answering.

'There was a murder done there.' Kit lowered his voice. Depraved Old Apper might be, but murder was beyond the pale, and in those days rare. 'There would be twenty folk or more living in that house, but they scattered like rats after it happened and none of them came back. That'd be in the war.'

'You're wrong, Kit.' The woman took a peg from her mouth. 'The war hadn't started. It didn't start till a few days after. The police was still poking about here the next week after it happened, and it was one of them that told us war had broken out. What with that and what was done at Tappers, the place changed all of a sudden.' She shook out a grey sheet and draped it on the line.

'A terrible thing to happen,' Gervase remarked, 'and on your very doorstep.'

'Next door, not that I hardly ever saw her, considering the way she went on.'

'It was a woman?'

'Lena Dane they called her. Horrible, when they found her, from what I heard.'

'They found the murderer?'

'Never. They never did.'

'No-one was suspected?'

The woman's tightly closed lips suggested an answer she would not give. She turned her back and pegged out a blue-and-white striped shirt.

'There was a lot of coming and going. Men in and out all the time.' Kit was confidential. 'She lived low, Lena Dane did. You understand me? They ask for it – and she got it all right. Strangled. Like a maniac he must have been.'

'Had the woman any family? Children?'

'They didn't stay children very long at Tappers. They grew up fast.' The woman had come to the end of her line. 'They were like rabbits in there, all sorts, except husbands. There was a girl that lived with Lena Dane and used to run messages for her. She was a sly little thing that never said a word.'

'I suppose the police would question her.'

'They likely would've if she had been there. So far as I know she sneaked off for good before they had the chance – and good riddance. But it makes you wonder why she took off like that. It certainly makes you wonder.'

It certainly did. One wondered, for instance, who the sly little thing was and where she sneaked off to. It would have been hasty to assume that she was the girl he hoped to trace; among the twenty or so inhabitants of Tappers there must have been other children who ran messages, children whose slyness was as natural an outcome of their circumstances as are the furtive movements of young animals in the wild. And yet it was hard not to connect the sneaking off of the sly little thing who lived with Lena Dane with the otherwise inexplicable appearance of the girl in the blanket at Wood Aston on the morning of 24 July, possibly only hours after the murder. Esther had been precise about the date. Moreover, Hettie's direful manner raised in Gervase darker thoughts than would otherwise have occurred to him. He tried to put them from him. It wasn't possible: she had been little more than a child. Strangling, he

351

told himself, needed a strength and ferocity she would not have been capable of. Not then.

Perhaps now? He remembered his first sight of Clarice Motte as she stood in the frozen lane under the leafless elms, as perfectly still as if she, too, were icebound. But his first impression had been of an extraordinary power, a curious, controlled energy, both power and control so strong as to be . . . Abnormal? And dangerous? The first impression had faded in later encounters, but from this most recent and more distant standpoint he recognized her as a woman capable of anything. Had it always been so with her? Lacking physical strength, one could kill by cunning. Even a child could do it, certainly a girl forced too early into womanhood.

He was suddenly and cruelly visited by a memory of Lilla's childish prattle as she helped Julie to gather cowslips: an instant's vision of pink bows and white muslin, of flowers and blue-eyed innocence left him harrowed and exhausted. This latest turn of the screw was more than he could bear. He reminded himself that it was mere conjecture to identify Lena Dane's young companion as Clarice Motte, and hence his own Lilla. With an effort of will he pulled himself together.

'Some of the folk living here are decent working people, though you might not think it.' Hettie had picked up her basket. 'And we're a bit particular even if we've got nothing to be particular about. It isn't our fault if nothing's been done to this place since the war, barring a few slates put back and a new water pipe when the whole of the ground from here to Pegg's yard was flooded.'

'I believe you,' Gervase said. 'I know the problems and how hard life can be when landlords neglect their property. By the way, who is the landlord?'

The original Tapper, it appeared, had died years ago. The present owner was of the absentee kind. Neither Kit nor Hettie knew his name. Rents were collected by the agency which managed most of the property in Old Apper: Durrells in Market Street.

'There's just one more thing, if you don't mind.' Gervase raised his hat as she moved away. 'It's asking you to cast your mind back a long way, about twenty-four years. Do you remember ever seeing a foreign young lady here? A French lady?'

'French? No, sir.' The raised hat had been appreciated. 'Not that I can think of. I'd have remembered that. The only foreigners is tinkers and gypsies every year for the Feast.'

The dread sound of a despairing beast being led to the slaughter encouraged a swift departure. Gervase, already framing a letter to the Borough Health Department, was inattentive to Kit's remarks until, 'It seems them next door heard someone come in late. They say there was a man she might have had a row with. He was there a lot. He was in the hide-and-bone trade. That'd be why he came here in the first place, on account of Pegg's slaughter-yard. A chap with a yellow cart and a brown-and-white horse. He never came again after that night. No-one's ever seen hide or hair of him, you might say. Never no more.'

Gervase gave no sign of his immense relief. It was as if circulation and breathing were restored after a heart attack. He had actually forgotten about the man with the cart whom Esther had seen in flight, surely the man who had killed Lena Dane. His mere existence, not to mention his desperate need to get away, put an end to the absurdity of thinking that a young girl could have committed such a crime. The girl and the man had fled together. Temporarily he ceased to think of her as Lilla while continuing to see her as a younger version of Miss Motte, whose enigmatic personality still suggested a very wide range of possibilities. At any rate here at last was circumstantial evidence: the yellowness of the cart and the skewbaldness of the horse proved

353

beyond reasonable doubt that Miss Motte and the girl who lived with Lena Dane were the same.

'Have you had any bother with worms?'

The change of subject, though justified by their return to the pigeon loft, was sufficiently abrupt to leave Gervase momentarily at a loss. 'Worms? No. Fungus one year. We had to destroy a few birds, but it didn't show up again.'

'I gave mine some stuff they use for worms in hens and it killed six birds. It's a disgrace. They ought to be took to court.'

With a hasty – and hopeless – reference to the need for cleanliness especially in water, Gervase succeeded in getting away.

It had been a mistake to refer to Julie as a lady. If by evil chance she had come or been brought to Old Apper, she would already have lost the outward marks of refinement. He forced himself not to think of her and thought instead of Old Apper at the later time of 1914, of a woman lying strangled, a man driving away – only Esther could testify to having seen him. To the child she was then, he had seemed desperate 'as if the devil were after him.'

In such a plight, at the risk of being caught and hanged, would he have wasted time on returning a girl abducted twelve years earlier? There could have been other reasons for Clairy's being put in the cart and for being got out of it. In the crowded house someone must surely have heard or even seen the murder, one person, perhaps, who must be removed to stop her from telling; it would be dangerous to leave her behind. The headlong drive, the early summer dawn, a loss of direction, a tired and flagging horse, the prospect of having to continue his escape on foot – it was easy to see that the girl would seem a burden to be jettisoned. And it was one small factor to the man's credit that he had left her where she could soon be found. After all, he could have finished her off too.

How could he be sure that she would never tell? Since he had taken that risk it was charitable to assume some lingering trace of humanity in a brutish nature, more tempting still to imagine that he had spared her because of some kinship – a close relationship? A man might be driven to commit murder and yet retain some sense of responsibility for his own child.

It was weakness to indulge in wishful thinking. If the man was her father, must she not have known? If so she was an impostor, as well as being an accessory to the crime, if not an accomplice. Yet amid all the uncertainty of his dealings with her, in one respect she had been entirely convincing: in her desire to know who she was. She was apparently as ignorant about her parentage as he was, and if she was Lilla, should he not be ashamed of imagining, hoping, wishing that she could have been the daughter of the brute who murdered Lena Dane? She had conducted her search with dignity, and once again he marvelled at her success in having overcome so many disadvantages, not least the ordeal she had undergone on the night of 23–24 July 1914.

Lost in thought, he made his way back to the centre of the town. Durrells' Property Agency declared its existence in white letters on a first-floor window of one of the buildings between the Bank and the Conservative Club. Business was slack, as it was everywhere on the last day but one of the strike, but Gervase's impression as he breathed the stale air of the General Office was that business had been slack there for a long time. The room was barely furnished with a writing table, two or three chairs, a small iron safe and shelves accommodating a few folders and box files.

The only occupant was a man of about his own age with lavishly oiled dark hair parted in the middle and a toothbrush moustache. He wore a stiff white collar, a navy-blue suit and brown shoes, his whole attire visible at a glance as he lolled in a round-backed chair with his feet on the table.

355

'Yes,' he said without looking up from the green sporting paper he held in his nicotine-stained hands. That the paper was a week old owing to the present printers' strike was a further sign of the lack of urgent business.

'I'd like a word with Mr Durrell.' Gervase's tone and the appearance of his card thrust between the reader's eyes and the sporting news caused him to sit up. A glance at his visitor and at the card induced him to remove his feet from the table.

'I'm Durrell,' he said. 'Take a seat.'

'I believe you handle some of the property in Old Apperfield.'

'That's right.' Durrell's manner combined calculation with caution increasing to wariness when Gervase added, 'A property known as Tappers?'

Durrell looked again at the card. Major Lincoln. Barbarrow Hall. Not from the council: he knew all their chaps anyway. More likely his visit had some connection with another recent visit. Why the sudden interest in Tappers of all places? 'You're in the development line?' It was a forlorn hope but you could never tell.

'As a landlord myself I'm always interested in property, but my reason for calling is not to do with business. I was hoping you could help me with information about previous tenants. It's all right, I have no connection with the police. It's an entirely private matter.'

'How far back?'

'Rather a long way, I'm afraid. May I ask how long you've been in charge of the letting?'

He'd been at it, man and boy, for most of his life, he told Gervase wearily. The business had been his father's.

'The people I would like to trace would be living there in 1914, and for some time before that. If it would involve you in some inconvenience to go so far back in your files, I would of course be willing to pay you for your time and trouble.'

He fully expected to hear that the records of tenancies dating so far back had been destroyed, but to his surprise Durrell got up and took from the shelf nearest at hand a red-spined box-file, separate from the others as if it were being kept readily available – or had been consulted recently. The film of dust to which Durrell applied his handkerchief was relatively thin.

'It's been a dead loss, Tappers, for the last twelve years at least. A few of the rooms were let on and off during the war to Irish workmen and such like. None of them stayed long, and for the last five or six years it's been boarded up as unsafe.'

'The house has a reputation, I understand.'

'The information you're after? Has it anything to do with Lena Dane?'

In the natural course of events Lena would surely have remained unknown to fame. Her pathetic life in a drab underworld whose inhabitants would be the last to draw attention to themselves, or to each other, could have been expected to end in obscurity. But in death her fate had been reversed. By being murdered she had secured for herself a degree of permanence. Her name had been entered in the annals of Apperfield and had become part of its history. Of all the dubious tenants who had paid or had not paid their rent to Durrells, she alone was sure of being remembered. For that very reason, Gervase thought, there was no need to keep the record of her tenancy so readily at hand, especially as Durrell had apparently no need to refresh his memory. He had opened the file, but neither then nor later did he look at its contents.

'More to do with the people who lived with her – or in the same house. Have you any information about them?'

Durrell shook his head. 'She was the tenant. There

was only the one room, and it was her name on the rent book. She was always in arrears. At one time she took to pestering us to let her take another room as well. There was one empty on the same landing. Reckoned she was going to be married and one room wasn't enough for three people.'

'Three?'

'There was a child. A little girl.'

'When would that be?'

'I can't be sure. We haven't any record because we didn't let her have the room. It wasn't right to have a child in with a married couple, I grant you, but we didn't believe her story. Who would want to marry her?'

'You said a *little* girl.'

'The chap who collected the rent in those days was old Matt Hobroyd. It was Matt that told us she was bothering him about the other room. I never saw the woman myself. It was definitely the lower end of the business that poor old Matt got landed with. I heard him telling my dad that there was a girl there old enough to be going to school.'

At last a glimmer of light? Matt Hobroyd had actually seen the child. Impossible to calculate how many years ago, but there was just the faintest chance that he might remember her; he might even recall some detail, some remark concerning the child, particularly as police enquiries at the time of the murder would have obliged him to search his memory for any information he could give them about Lena Dane's mode of life. This seemed his nearest approach so far to . . . To whom? Clairy? Lilla? Or the two in one?

'Could I get in touch with him?'

'Matt died a while back. Heart trouble. I remember him having his first attack at the Coronation tea party in his street. After that he never came back to work.'

Gervase's own heart resumed its normal beat. The link had in any case been a fragile one; he had not dared to hope. Indeed hope and dread were so closely

358

intermingled in his search that fear of what he might find out was proving stronger than disappointment at having reached another dead end. Yet there was no respite: each setback gave rise to new questions.

Coronation? That would be in 1911. How long before that had Hobroyd told Durrell Senior about the girl, and when and how regularly did she go to school? Without his testimony there was no way of calculating her age. By 1911 Lilla would have been thirteen. Despair tinged with the relief he was ashamed of had almost brought him to his feet when Durrell spoke.

'As a matter of fact there was someone here a few weeks ago asking about Lena Dane.'

The lady had been making enquiries on behalf of an elderly servant who had for years been worried about her lack of news of a younger sister. She had kept the worry to herself until recently when she was taken ill and seemed likely to die. Only then had she confided in her mistress. The younger sister had gone away to service before the war and had written occasionally to her parents but she had never gone back home and after a year or so the letters had stopped. She had last been heard of in the Apperfield district. The family had kept quiet about her absence because they were afraid she might have got herself into trouble and would bring disgrace on them. The parents had long been dead but the elder sister was remorseful, now that her own days were numbered, on account of having made no effort to find her: Helena shortened to Lena.

The lady's visit to Durrells' was purely compassionate. She had already made exhaustive enquiries. Having, with horror, identified her quarry as the murdered woman, she had confessed to feeling unequal to the task of breaking the dreadful news to the ailing sister. She supposed there had been a man in Lena's life. Had Mr Durrell any idea what had become of him? She was shocked to hear that there had been more than one man, and wondered if Lena Dane had had any friends who might be able to give her details which could be passed on to the sister.

'Strange that we should both be enquiring about the same set of people.' Gervase had found much to interest him in Durrell's account of the lady. 'I wonder if she was anyone I know. Do you mind telling me her name?'

She had not given her name. She was a smartly dressed lady, politely spoken, youngish, with lightish hair. Durrell broke off, looking puzzled.

'It's a funny thing. She was the sort you'd turn to look at: sort of stylish, and yet I'm blowed if I can tell you anything about her face. There was nothing you could pick out to remember.' He tried and evidently failed. 'Not a thing. But out of the ordinary all the same.'

Inventive too, Gervase reflected as he took his leave. It was highly unlikely that Durrell's visitor could have been anyone other than Miss Motte, who had effortlessly acquired a husband and an elderly servant at death's door, and who was so sensitive about breaking bad news. Who else, at this particular time, would want information about Lena Dane's associates? Miss Motte was an accomplished liar, a fact to be taken into account in assessing her honesty in other directions; and yet, pondering on the implications of her visit to Apperfield, he was forced to conclude that she had, as usual, been acting reasonably. Precisely as he was doing, she was trying to trace her origins; trying at least to find out how she got to Tappers in the first place, since Lena Dane was not her mother. One had to admit that in doing her best to discover the truth, she was playing fair.

But how successfully she had presented herself to Durrell as someone other than the person she was! How convincing she could be! How competently she could interweave truth with fiction!

He had cranked the engine of his car when the sight of the basket on the passenger seat reminded him that Esther had asked him to call on the Trisks. The ironmongery shop in a side street off the Market Place was empty. He saw at a glance that the absence of customers was not solely due to the strike. The deathlike inactivity to be felt during the first week had inevitably given way to more normal life in the streets. But even those lucky enough to have money to spend were not in the habit of spending it at Trisks, judging by the dust and rust and the poverty of the stock.

Prissie, who came from a room at the back a full minute after the bell clanged, was not the girl he remembered seeing at the Coach and Horses, but she was genuinely pleased to see him, apart from wishing he hadn't caught her in an old pinafore.

'What a surprise to see you in Apperfield, sir! Come in and tell us how things are over your way. Mother's seeing to a friend that's been taken with bronchitis, and Barney had to go out, but he'll be back shortly.'

The pinafore rapidly removed, the major seated, Esther's jars of honey and preserves presented on the one hand and Kenneth, now an active three-year-old, presented on the other and then firmly impounded behind the sofa – they exchanged news.

'I'll tell you plainly, we're up against it here. There just isn't the money, and there's the Co-op and Rocket's Cut Price Stores both selling ironmongery. We'd have done better in a little general shop in one of the back streets in Hudmorton. A poor man's pantry. You know what I mean – the bell going all the time. How long do you think this strike's going to last?'

'Not much longer, I hope, not the total shut-down. The unions won't be able to hold out much longer. But I don't know what the miners will do.'

What could the poor chaps do? The owners wanted longer hours for lower pay, a downward spiral the union was sure to resist. 'Business is bound to suffer for a while, I'm afraid. Will you be able to hold on until things improve?'

'Mother helps me a bit. I worry about Barney. He used to be so cheerful, but this last year or two he's been depressed and awkward. To tell you the truth, he isn't easy to live with these days. Still—' she made an effort, 'we never died in a winter yet. Have you time for a cup of tea? It won't take above a minute.'

Gervase took the opportunity of releasing Kenneth and showing him the picture book on whose fly-leaf Esther had inscribed: 'To Kenneth from Viola with best wishes', and the date.

'There now. Isn't that just like her?' Prissie handed him his cup. 'She doesn't forget her old friends. And here's Barney now.' The door into the shop was open. 'We've got a visitor, Barney,' and when he appeared, 'It's Major Lincoln.'

The two men met for the first time and Gervase promised himself that it would also be the last. No wonder Prissie found the man hard to live with. Not a word or smile of welcome passed his lips, even when Prissie prompted, 'Miss Esther's husband, Barney, from Barbarrow Hall.' If anything the surliness of his broad face darkened. He nodded curtly in the visitor's direction without looking at him.

They were rescued from an uncomfortable situation when the shop bell rang again. Barney left them, as if to attend to a customer. Instead he walked straight through the shop and out into the street, leaving Prissie on the verge of tears.

'You see what I mean. It isn't normal, sir, is it?'

'No, it isn't. Is he drinking?'

'Not so as you'd call it drinking. That's never been his weakness; and nor he's never been a worrier when money's been short.'

'There may be some physical cause. I suppose he won't see a doctor?'

'He wouldn't hear of it. He gets quite wild if I ask him what's wrong. He frightens me sometimes.'

There was no time for more: the customer must be served. Kenneth, sniffing agitation in the air, set up a deafening wail and stamped ungratefully on his glossy new picture book. It was definitely time to leave.

CHAPTER 24

The strike ended on 12 May without having achieved its
aim. The miners were to hold out for another twenty-six
weeks until hunger drove them back to work, for longer
hours and lower pay. Owing to the closure of unproductive pits, as many as 200,000 of them remained
unemployed, many of them for the rest of their lives.

Gervase could feel no satisfaction in the government's triumph, but he welcomed the resumption of a
normal routine in which personal difficulties could for
hours at a time be forgotten. In their mutual longing
to restore life at Barbarrow to its former harmony, the
Lincolns were not entirely unsuccessful; but even by
the utmost effort of imagination neither could quite
unravel the complexity of the other's inward conflict.
Esther knew that Gervase had confided in Morgan and
had made enquiries in Apperfield. He had given her
the bare facts of his visit which had brought him no
nearer to solving the mystery of Lilla's disappearance
or to identifying Clairy as Lilla. His sordid picture of
vice and murder at Old Apper revived in her something
of the instinctive dread she had felt as a child when the
unknown girl had brought with her intimations of a
darker world than she had then been able to accept
as real.

She also knew that Gervase could never feel as bitterly
towards Clairy as she did, and that he had seen her
again on one of her walks and had spoken to her.
Clairy had assured him that she would not trespass
on his land again, a gesture that goaded him into
offering her the freedom of Barbarrow. If she had

availed herself of the offer, she had done so discreetly and had not been seen near the Hall.

Esther's valiant efforts to seem happier than she was exhausted her spirit. She thought and dreamed of Daniel, and learned the bitter lesson that trying to stifle regret merely made it stronger, to yield to it made it no less. It was incurable. As Morgan diagnosed, she suffered from not having enough to do and became obsessed with Viola, could barely let her out of her sight, and developed unreasonable fears for her safety, remembering what had happened to Lilla. Thinking of Lilla meant thinking of Clairy who had come into her life to take from her what she most loved. Viola must be kept safe from Clairy.

'No matter who calls,' she told Ada, 'they're not to see her unless I'm there. You understand?'

'Yes,' said Ada who also understood that Mrs Lincoln was getting nervy these days and needed to go out more. 'How's Alice making out, I wonder? It's near enough to four months since William passed on. The first year's always the worst to get over.'

Conscience-pricked, remembering her promise to William, Esther went to town the next day, a Saturday, and had lunch with her mother and Henry. Some restraint was needed as she and Gervase had decided that with the exception of Morgan they would keep the problem of Clairy to themselves. At the same time it was good to talk of other things, and she left for Brimlow satisfied that her mother suspected nothing.

'She's not happy,' Flora said as the front door closed. 'There's something wrong. What in the world can it be?' And for once Henry could find no reassuring answer.

The two Mrs Capmans saw Esther from the upstairs window where they were sitting in unnatural idleness. For the time being life had lost meaning for them, like a clock still ticking but failing to chime the hours. The red of Alice's hair was less strident,

her voice subdued. Esther felt an undemanding stillness in the room and was grateful. They were all
three blessedly at ease together.

'Alma Terrace doesn't change,' she remarked.

'Well, I don't know about that.' Gertie handed her
the Lady Green teacups from the china cabinet. 'If
you'd come the other way you'd have seen a house
to let. Number 1.'

'You don't mean . . . ? Olga's Place?'

'Not now it isn't. Olga's gone. Where? Nobody
knows.'

'She's given up the mail order business,' Alice said
drily.

'They say somebody threatened to report her. But
I'm not sure. There's been too much gossip.' Gertie
had not forgotten Olga's kind enquiry about William.
'Her doings may have been very much exaggerated.
She struck me as being no different from anyone
else – and nicer than some.'

'We're thinking of having a bead curtain at the
bottom of the stairs,' Alice said, 'and a carpet with
roses on it all the way up.'

Esther took to dropping in at Number 11 on Saturdays when Alice was most likely to be at home.
Unfortunately Saturday was also the day when Gervase
was at home so that for weeks on end they spent only
evenings and Sundays together.

For obvious reasons she had lost touch with another
old friend. The flight from Lady Green had cut her off
from Wood Aston; the new life at Barbarrow had been
so absorbing as to leave no time for outside interests. A
visit to Miss Angovil would revive painful memories and
– perhaps the most cogent reason of all – Priest's House
could not be reached without passing the Lodge.

But now there was neither reason nor excuse for
postponing the visit. Gervase had bought a second
car chiefly for her use, with Stevens the handyman as
chauffeur, but there was nothing now to deter her from

walking past the Lodge. Avoidance of painful meetings seemed merely small-minded in a situation of total disaster. Nothing worse could happen. Nothing mattered now that everything had gone wrong. In such a state of mind she experienced a dreary sense of freedom.

All the same, having arranged for Stevens to come and drive her home, she chose to visit Miss Angovil on a weekday when the Lodge would be empty, and reached it in the wild hope that it would not be. But house and garden, fields and distant hills lay as still and empty of human life as if she trod the earth alone. On impulse she went up the path and sat for a few minutes in the porch under the scrutiny of the tirelessly snarling fox. The walk had tired her more than it would once have done. The last stretch, which had always seemed level compared with the steep climb up to the Scaur, was a distinct slope nevertheless. She could still shudder at the thought of Thomas, helpless in his wheel-chair as it gathered momentum; and she wondered once again that he had had the strength to set it in motion by those rocking movements Clairy had described.

The thought of Clairy drove her from the Lodge. Ten minutes later she knocked at the door of Priest's House, and was admitted by someone she had almost forgotten.

'Mavis! You came! And you've been here ever since?'

'It was all due to you.' Mavis had got her breath back. 'I've never had a chance to tell you. Fancy seeing you again. I can't get over it! Do you know Miss Angovil?' And then when Esther murmured an affirmative, 'It's a wonder you didn't want this place yourself. Most girls would have jumped at it.'

It seemed a lifetime since they had last met at the Town and Country Employment Agency, but the sting of humiliation was still sharp enough to make Esther change the subject.

'You look well. I'm so glad you're happy here.'

'It suits me down to the ground.'

'How is Miss Angovil?'

'I'll tell her you're here.' Mavis nodded towards the sitting-room. 'She's mostly well enough. Shall I say "Miss Green"?'

'Oh, I'm Mrs Lincoln, now but just say "Miss Esther".'

The years had aged Miss Angovil, as they had every right to do. The armchair she had comfortably filled now seemed too big, her mauve marocain dress too wide. At first she responded to her visitor with a slightly vacant stare, until Esther kissed her and sat down in her own accustomed chair and was recognized with a smile, not so much of surprised recognition as of acceptance, as if she had been there yesterday and would come again tomorrow as usual. Gradually as she chatted about the weather, the walk, the garden, disconnected memories clicked into place and all was well.

'Of course I understood,' Miss Angovil said when Esther had broached the subject of her long absence. 'You were abroad for such a long time, and then married soon after you came back. I had the card and the wedding cake. I was delighted that you and Gervase . . .' She turned her eyes doubtfully to the sofa. '. . . You and . . . But so much more suitable. And your parents?'

'Father died, you remember, and Mother has married again.'

They fell into something like the old gossiping relationship. Esther stayed for an early lunch, prepared and served by Mavis, who appeared to be managing the household single-handed; so that when Esther asked, 'What happened to Spedding?' it was on the assumption that she had been pensioned off or had died. But Spedding was still there, though she now never left the kitchen except to be helped upstairs to bed. Her rheumatism was worse but her temper less tetchy, as Esther found when she sat with her for a few minutes after lunch while Miss Angovil 'dropped off'.

'She's a good girl, Mavis is,' Spedding actually brought herself to say. 'No trouble, not from the start. For one thing she doesn't tie me to this chair like the last one did, to keep my joints warm, so she said. "You'll be putting me in the roasting tin next," I told her, "speaking of joints." And Mavis doesn't pester me with questions about other places where I once worked – how much they paid, how many in the family, what did they wear, what did they talk about, how many rooms, likewise all the places where my mother had worked and all my kin. "Anyone would think you were writing a book," I told her, which I dare say she could have done, she was clever enough and good at her work; but she got above herself and left all of a sudden to get married. The mistress gave her ten pounds. Yes, ten, I tell you no lie; and we've never seen or heard of her since. It just goes to show . . .'

The topic was not one that Esther would have chosen, and she was glad to go back to the sitting-room. Refreshed by her nap, Miss Angovil talked more coherently. Obviously she would be stimulated by company; being alone too much, she had been living in the past. Even now she referred continually to her younger brother, the beloved Roland, well known to Esther as a paragon of virtue. On this occasion, however, she was to see him in a somewhat different light.

'I dare say he was a trifle spoiled, being the youngest, but he was such an endearing little boy and he grew up to be a kind, generous brother, always giving presents when he couldn't really afford them. That was the reason, I'm sure . . . the only reason why he . . . It should have been taken into account when his career was decided upon – his generosity, I mean. One can see now that a bank . . . such a temptation. I wouldn't speak of it to anyone but you, Esther. It was so very little when one remembers that he gave his life for England.'

Such anxious references to Roland's unnamed misdemeanours gave way to talk of other things only to return and reach a climax in the plaintive outburst, 'I treasured his letters. They were all I had left of him, the last of my family. But I should have burned them long ago. It doesn't do to keep such things, Esther.'

'But why should you burn them? They are mementoes of Roland and very precious to you.'

Miss Angovil sank back in her too commodious chair in a sudden yielding to defeat. 'There were certain things in them that I wouldn't want anyone to see. Things that might be misconstrued. They might make Roland appear to have been – well, dishonest. I always kept them in a little drawer in my bureau upstairs, their special place.'

'Do you mean that they aren't there?'

'They're gone. I can't find them. I've searched everywhere, over and over again.'

Esther's experience at the Abbot Nursing Home had taught her that confused elderly people were forever losing their possessions, purses and wallets in particular. Moreover Priest's House was crammed with objects hoarded by several generations of Angovils. Searching for a few misplaced letters could entail endless rummaging. It was even possible that Miss Angovil had already destroyed them and had forgotten the fact.

'You may have moved them to a safer place and gone on picturing them in the drawer. They'll probably turn up unexpectedly when you're looking for something else.'

'You think so? I'll look again.'

She appeared so anxious to start another search that Esther felt herself to be in the way.

'Miss Angovil seems restless,' she told Mavis in the hall.

'Has she told you about them letters? They're on her mind all the time.'

'I'm afraid it's a sign of old age. And she was always so . . .' Comfortable was the word. So very comfortable. 'When did this trouble begin?'

'It must be a few years ago. She came downstairs one day all flushed and worried and she's been worried ever since.'

'I must come more often. Promise to let me know if ever Miss Angovil is ill or in real trouble. You could send someone over to Barbarrow with a note. That would be quicker than the post.'

With almost an hour to spare before Stevens could be expected, she crossed the green to the church, pausing with her hand on the lych-gate to look back at the white railings and brass knocker, the roses and hollyhocks of Priest's House. It troubled her that even Miss Angovil, that harmless elderly bird snug in her nest, should have her share of unhappiness, self-imposed as it surely was. She wondered where Roland's letters might be. Though she had entertained the idea, she couldn't really believe that Miss Angovil would have destroyed them. The next time she called she would offer to help to look for them; after all she was no stranger. She had, in a sense, known Roland for years, or rather had known Miss Angovil's version of him. When they did come to light she might tactfully suggest that if there was anything in them to cast the slightest doubt on Roland's honesty it would be best to burn them, with due reverence to the writer.

How comfortable they had been in the old days, how very comfortable as they sat at the round table in the window, eyes occasionally on their books, more often on the green and the comings and goings of the village folk! Of the so-called lessons she remembered little: they had served chiefly to dignify the placid mornings with an aura of seriousness, as now the memory of them; added a melancholy touch to more potent reminders that life could never be as comfortable again.

In those early days before ever they fell in love, Daniel had been there, scarcely noticed. He had always been near, at Priest's House, at Lady Green, at the Lodge, in the wood, by the stream. She had been as unaware of him as she was of herself; their closeness had been unrealized, yet so strong that it had shaped and bound their inward selves for ever. Its sudden eruption into the ecstasy of love had been a natural flowering from that early seed-time. There had been no fulfilment. Instead, as sudden and savage as dismemberment, had come the parting. A wave of regret overwhelmed her, deeper, more devastating and more lasting than the sharper pangs of misery she had known. Their lives – her own and Daniel's and Gervase's – had changed irrevocably, not through natural growth but violently through the impact of evil emanating from the region she had known nothing of until her first glimpse of the man with the cart. For a fearful instant she had felt the horror that had seemed to possess him. It was as though even then she had foreseen their quiet life at Wood Aston threatened by such a man in such a plight, as though the disorder of his world might spill over into theirs.

A confused vision of ungodly and unnatural acts made her turn her back on the church. In such a mood she could not face the unconsecrated grave beyond the farther churchyard wall. Mercifully, the clamour of playtime in the school yard reminded her that she had intended to call on Mr Horner. His old-fashioned sitting-room, with its blue-and-white tiled fireplace and long-case clock, was unchanged, but more than one pupil teacher had come and gone since Daniel's time, and Prissie's place had been taken by an older woman.

Mr Horner was interested to hear that Gervase had seen the Trisks. Esther mentioned that Barney's health was causing concern.

'My husband thinks he may be suffering from nervous exhaustion as a result of the war . . .'

But there was time for only a brief exchange of news. A sudden silence signalled the end of playtime. The bay window overlooked the yard where the children stood in two lines before marching into school. Jake looked up and saw the lady, the real lady with rings on her fingers. She was smiling at him.

'It's Jake. What do you think of him, Mr Horner? Is he doing well at his lessons?'

'Very well. I wish you could have seen him when he first came. The change in him has been a small miracle, thanks to Daniel. He learns easily, has imagination and he's growing more like Daniel every day in his speech and manner. Boys like Jake have a better chance in life now that there are scholarships to the grammar school in Hudmorton. He should go far.' His voice changed. 'That's what I expected of Daniel – that he would go far. Is there still time, I wonder, for him to find his way?'

'Is Jake a cheerful little boy?' Esther spoke at random, forcing back tears. 'He looked rather downcast just then.'

'He hasn't been quite as bright as usual lately. It happens. A new stage of growth, no doubt.'

To Esther it seemed more likely that Jake, faithfully reflecting Daniel's speech, manner and ideas, was also reflecting Daniel's present mood. The discovery brought one of those changes of direction that prove momentous. She closed the school gate and stood in the shadow of the hedge where the complex drama of their interwoven lives had begun. She and Daniel and Clairy had been brought together entirely by chance – she could not think of the ill-starred moment as pre-ordained – and nothing now could disentangle them. Nothing that had happened could be undone, the situation was irreversible. She saw the unhappiness it had brought as a contagion which could spread to other lives: from Daniel to Jake, from herself to Gervase and so inevitably to Viola. There was no knowing how wide the spread of the disease might be, or how many others had already fallen victim.

There was nothing now under the hawthorns but a tangle of wayside weeds and the faded petals of fallen may blossom. Outwardly all was as it had been before Clairy came. And after all, Clairy had herself been a victim of the contagion, not its source. They now knew that she had been exposed to evil in its vilest form: she had almost certainly seen murder done. Was it possible to survive such an experience, to be made sick by it and yet to return to health? Standing at her window at Lady Green, she herself had merely seen the murderer, a sudden intruder on the innocence of the morning. She had felt him to be a creature set apart, had learned in a flash that people could be diabolical, and had shivered in her nightdress, still unaware that *only* people can be diabolical. But it had not been her misfortune to see his face or his hands as he gripped Lena Dane's throat and squeezed her life out; or to see her one protectress, feckless, corrupt, harsh though she might have been, all at once cease to exist. As for the man, he too had been infected. There was no point in trying to trace evil to its source. It existed and was eternally passed on. The chain of misery it caused was endless.

No, that wouldn't do. Her soul rose in protest. Life wasn't meant to be like that. Misery could be passed on to others, but it could also be transmuted into something else: understanding, tenderness, love. Evil could only contaminate through the weakness and apathy of those it threatened. Sorrow must come, but woe unto him – or her – through whom it came. In so far as it had come through her, she must put a stop to it. She had been ignorant, weak and cowardly – and passive when she should have been active. How to turn the tide? She had no idea. The answer would come like the tingling sense of revival that thrilled her blood. It was time to take things in hand and deal with them. What was it Morgan had once said? (What had Morgan not said?) Something about circumstances being less important than one's reaction to them. She had allowed herself to become the prey of circumstances instead of creating them and directing their course.

Overlooking the vastness and vagueness of the scheme, forgetting that she had asked Stevens to fetch her (he was soon to be rousing the village in search of her), she took the woodland path and walked slowly home, too deep in thought to be aware of familiar landmarks, even the Aston oak in all its summer splendour of sunlit leaves and vast shade, where she and Daniel had lain in agony and bliss. Her pace quickened as she crossed the footbridge, skimmed past Lady Green with the merest glance at her old window, sped along the lane, disregarding the ruined barn and rotting timbers of the yellow cart, ran across the stepping-stones and scarcely paused to draw breath before tackling the hill.

'Gervase!' He had just come home and gone directly to his study. 'Gervase!' She stood in the doorway, breathless, her eyes a blue blaze. 'Isn't it wonderful? I've come to life. I'm going to put things right.' She threw her arms round his neck. 'I don't know how. You must help me.'

How had it happened? A return to physical health: a flowering of sensitive insight, the reaction of a sane mind from a surfeit of distress? Morgan Krantz might so have analysed Esther's experience of resurrection, but he would also have understood that their sudden swift concurrence seemed to her – and was – a heaven-sent soaring of the spirit.

No miracle ensued. She would have been the first to admit the limitations of her scope and capabilities: that she wasn't really good at anything. The mammoth task of changing the world order, as Gervase pointed out, would take time; they must begin in a relatively small way. It was illogical to take as their starting point the one individual who was, beyond doubt, happy.

'Viola must see more people. Do you realize that she has never seen another baby?'

'We must arrange to have some sent in. It shouldn't be difficult. There are a lot of them about.'

'I don't want her to grow up as I did, cut off from other children. It came to me when I saw the children in the school yard, that I had never played like that, in that pushing and shoving sort of way. That's what's wrong with me.'

'There's nothing wrong with you, my love. Nothing that pushing and shoving would improve.'

From such conversations emerged Esther's proposal to have Mr Horner's entire flock at Barbarrow for a day. She remembered having heard that there had been an annual School Treat at Lady Green in her grandfather's time.

'It's further of course.' She saw them swarming gladly over the hill, Viola crowing a welcome.

'A charabanc,' Gervase said, 'and a marquee. It may rain.'

'And let's ask Vincent to take photographs.'

To throw open Barbarrow to fifty-three children for a day was no more than a minor skirmish. There were far more difficult adjustments to be made. One morning, without thinking too much about it for fear of losing her nerve, she had Stevens drive her to Ivy Villa. It was cowardly to skulk in the car, and send him to knock, silly to hope that Miss Motte was not at home; but when Stevens came back and opened the car door, her courage returned.

It was needed. For the first time in their chequered relationship Clairy was on her own ground. The over-furnished little sitting-room was for the time being hers. She stood, immaculate as ever, by the fireless grate. On the table lay coins and notes from an emptied purse. She said nothing, did nothing, but waited. The frigid silence was discouraging, but it was not the worst feature of the ordeal. To Esther, unused to so small a room, the woman she faced seemed larger than life. She had not foreseen the effect on her of Clairy's actual physical presence now that she was close enough to touch. She was taken aback by an acute awareness of the smooth pallid skin, the lips slightly parted, the redness within, and of the shape of the body under the blue dress. With cruel vividness she saw it naked in Daniel's arms and loathed what she saw. Her prepared speech had no bearing on the hateful reality of the situation. It occurred to her that she could leave at once without a word. The preposterous nature of their relationship absolved her from even the slightest of social decencies. All the same—

'I must talk to you,' she heard herself saying. 'We have never been alone together to talk. I behaved foolishly that day at the Hall. You see, when my husband spoke of you I hadn't realized who you were and—'

'Who am I?' The question was stark, the manner bleak.

'That is the whole problem, isn't it? What I want to say is – I don't want to go on running away from it. Can we somehow make the best of a terrible difficulty and not let it make us all unhappy?'

'What do you suggest?'

'That we behave as if we were acquaintances in a normal way. It should be possible to meet occasionally and talk about other things. If meeting leads to friendship, that will be a good thing.' Except that it's impossible, Esther thought, daunted in spite of herself by the other's impervious manner and by her own unconquerable resentment. 'If there is no pleasure in it for any of us, we can cease to meet. In the meantime my husband will do all he can to find out the true position and naturally you'll do the same.'

Was there the faintest indication of a thaw? No steady drip of icicles from eaves, merely the slightest possible quiver in the unresponsive face?

'You'll want to think about it. Would you like to come to tea one afternoon when we are both at home? The day after tomorrow?'

'Thank you.'

'Stevens will come for you at half-past three.'

'Thank you.'

One could probably get used to anything, Esther reflected when safely back in the car, even leaping into an Arctic sea. The first petrifying plunge would be the worst – and that was over.

CHAPTER 25

Civilized social intercourse need not preclude – indeed demands – certain precautions. Revitalized and competent Esther might feel herself to be, all the same she bade Ada keep her precious lamb safe in the nursery while the she-wolf took tea in the sheep-fold. Sheer superstitious nonsense, but she couldn't help it. Gervase's defensive action took the form of inviting Morgan to spend the day with them.

They had tea on William's lawn and talked of the prolonged miners' strike, soup kitchens, the forthcoming School Treat, the amount of lemonade a normal child could safely consume in the space of six or seven hours, plans to use the coach-house for needy convalescents and the next season of lectures at Ruskin House.

Considering how faintly the conversation reflected the feelings of the quartet, its smoothness was remarkable. Clairy said little, observed much. While the others talked, she looked about her: at the grey walls mantled with stonecrop, at the stone urn brimming with flowers, at the steps leading down to the cool green grotto, whence came the endless quiet gush of water from a spout shaped like a satyr's head. She looked, Esther imagined, with no mere casual interest; she was thoughtful, rather, as with a mental seeing and listening – at least it might have been so in any other person. On the whole the lady in blue (since she had taken to wearing blue her eyes were more blue than grey) remained withdrawn. The hands holding her saucer and raising her cup were slim and white. She had learned the delicate art of partaking of food without seeming to eat.

When she consulted her watch and left them, declaring that there was no need to trouble Stevens and, 'Yes, thank you' she would be pleased to look in on the School Treat, it was not until the curve in the lane took her out of sight that Esther realized how successful her plan had been: not once in the past hour had she thought of the foundling abandoned under the hedge, or of her reappearance at Number 1 Alma Terrace. But whose success had it been?

'A clever woman,' Morgan mused, lingering over his final cup of tea when the others had gone indoors, and pondering over Gervase's account of his visit to Old Apper. Miss Motte's progress from her unhelpful early environment (to put it mildly) had been a remarkable feat of evolution. Almost as remarkable was his own failure to approve its outcome. Was not self-improvement the cornerstone of his teaching? Ah yes, but it must start from within in response to an impulse of the spirit as well as of the mind. Miss Motte's spiritual state, under so impenetrable an outer gloss, it was impossible to assess. With distaste he saw her as the embodiment of doubt and ambiguity, those inveterate enemies of his thinking. Was she or was she not what she seemed to be? Were seeming and reality necessarily opposed? How could one define *what* she seemed to be, when her appearance of well-mannered gentility and refinement and her blameless search for her identity must always be coloured by one's knowledge of her history, if one could apply the word to a ragbag of unauthenticated items salvaged from her largely unknown past. His reflections as he sipped were interspersed with impulses of sympathy for Gervase: despite all his blessings a man to be pitied.

How could one know? Seated at the writing table in his study with the door closed, Gervase succumbed to the weariness to which months of uncertainty had reduced him. How could one ever know? Yet never to know would mean that as long as he lived he must suffer mental torture of this peculiar kind, unknown to any Inquisition, fiendishly devised for him alone.

She could be his daughter. There was nothing in her appearance, manner or dress to rule out the possibility. If Lilla had been spared to grow up at the Hall, she would in all likelihood have dressed and moved in much the same way. A caller ignorant of the situation, coming upon them in the garden just now, would have seen them as a family group and assumed that the light-haired young woman and the man of similar colouring were father and daughter.

Reluctantly he took the photographs from the drawer and stared at them for the twentieth time; then with a magnifying glass studied the brows, cheeks and features of Anne and her infant daughter. They gave no clue as to Lilla's possible appearance more than twenty years later, any more than Clarice Motte's unremarkable face gave any indication of what she had looked like at the age of four.

Dear Anne! As a living personality she had quite gone from him. Memory could no longer breathe life into the face nor bring back speech to the faintly smiling lips. But he remembered her quietness as a positive quality, and not the mere absence of vivacity. Had Clarice Motte's quietness this afternoon been of a similar kind? Anne's had been the serene repose of a woman confident of her situation in life and of her ability to maintain it without assertiveness. It stemmed from the very factors lacking in the life of Clarice Motte, whose reserve could be compared to the surface stillness of deep water concealing much that would not bear the light of day. He put away the photographs, the only visible and tangible evidence in a situation of maddening conjecture, yet useless except to confirm that no comparison was possible. Clarice Motte was unique, solitary: an emanation from no source, having no future he could bear to think of.

He must go to Esther. His frown gave way to a smile of mournful tenderness. He must tell her that she had been right to try the experiment. He had been touched by her naïve determination to put things right. 'Things', he knew, included much more than the problem of Clarice Motte. He had never doubted Esther's love for him nor her fidelity. It was simply that she loved Godwain more. No-one was to blame, except Godwain perhaps. He had made a hash of things by getting himself entangled with Clarice Motte when he was too young and ignorant to steer clear of her. She was not easy to steer clear of. He wished to God she had never been born. His own daughter? The reminder startled him. He had been tempted once again to forget who she was (who was she?) and to think of her as a sort of Nemesis. But what was he being punished for? It was not his fault that Godwain had been first in the field, or that he himself had arrived on the scene too late: a misfortune that neither Esther nor anyone else could rectify. Unless . . . A late entry might be followed by an early departure, one of the final kind. That would leave her safely in the hands – and arms – of Godwain. And at the mercy of Clarice Motte? No departure could be thought of until the matter of Clarice Motte was settled.

He tried to give his mind to more immediate aspects of his quandary. He must find Esther; but not quite yet. He leaned back in his chair, wondering what to do.

Clairy had taken leave of the Lincolns, having thanked them with precisely the degree of restrained warmth required – a point midway between graciousness and the smooth conventionality of a person used to many such leave-takings after many such visits. Her pace, as she walked down the drive, was so regulated as to suggest an intelligent interest in her surroundings combined with the intention of fulfilling another and more important engagement.

Once she was out of sight, her pace slackened and became a leisurely and thoughtful saunter. The lane stretched ahead between thick hedgerows and over-hanging trees, their stillness luminous in the golden light of late afternoon. She was indistinctly aware of her surroundings, having much to occupy her mind; but an unconscious response to their charm may have influenced her revision of the social intercourse she had just, and for the first time, shared.

She was able to compare it with other encounters and to recognize it as different in quality from even the least unsavoury of her contacts in London, Paris and Hudmorton; and to see in them a gloss of world-liness which – she was astute enough to realize – Krantz and Lincoln would have despised. With the same quickness she had been aware, under the willow tree, of a self-forgetfulness in the other three as they put aside personal preoccupations in the interests of what they felt to be the demands of the occasion – and did so with the ease of habit. She was quite struck by the discovery. It surprised her, though with-out warming her towards them.

She had watched Esther Lincoln presiding over the silver tea-pot as one born to the life she was leading; at Lady Green she had led a similar life, however poverty-stricken. Her distinction of manner came not from her environment alone, but also from innate tendencies passed on to her by generations of people who had led similar lives. As for her looks, with her slim wrists and ankles, the poise of her head, her symmetry of bone and grace of movement, she *looked* well bred.

Clairy stopped in the yellow dust and looked down at her own ankles, then stretched her right wrist free of its cuff: a needless reminder that her bones were as slender as Esther Lincoln's. She herself had certainly not been gently bred, but for a long time – since Daniel Godwain had shown her his thesis and lectured her remorselessly on the formative influences of heredity and environment – she had believed herself to be of gentle birth. Her revulsion from the sordid life at Old Apper, and the speed with which she had acquired education and fastidious habits (to be sacrificed with cold calculation when necessary), were surely proof of an inborn refinement that Old Apper had not been able to counteract. But she had never until that afternoon experienced the life of leisure and privilege from the inside. The sheltered garden, the warm shade and the murmur of low-pitched voices had stirred in her some hitherto unquickened faculty. As in responding to beauty one casts a backward glance to a Golden Age, forgotten, instinctively known, Clairy felt the new sensation as one of recognition, but recognition of a more specific kind.

'This is my world. This is the life from which I was banished and remain exiled. All this has been withheld from me.'

Such was her state of mind, whether or not she would so have expressed it. As recently as two years ago she would have thought of such a life in general terms without particular reference to Barbarrow. Since then she had come to know it well, though never as intimately as in the past two hours. The experience left her with an unfamiliar sense of well-being. She walked more lightly, without the impression she usually gave of steady purpose; and it was entirely without purpose that she paused at a gap in the pink curtain of wild roses draping the hedge and looked into a meadow deep in grass and fragrant with flowers she could not have named. It was alive with butterflies. A sort of lightening in her inmost being was somehow connected with their bodiless flight, their soft weightlessness and absence of flesh, and with the openness of flower-heads, blue and mauve and yellow, to receive them. Being unused to such a feeling, she did not recognize it as happiness, not then. To recognize happiness before it begins to fade is a blessing rarely granted.

Nevertheless it was then, with that first tentative look outward from the narrow and enclosed lane, through the parted curtain of roses, and into the meadow that she underwent a more fundamental change of view. Until that very instant she had been playing a part, deliberately acting out of spite and envy. There was nothing genuine in her heartless masquerade, nothing sincere in her entire life except her constant desire to know her parentage. She was no nearer knowing it. The attempt to find Rodd had so far failed: even he might not have known. She was still, as always, haunted by an impression that if only she had paid more heed to Lena's muttered remarks, she would have picked up at least a clue; but her memory, brilliant and retentive in other respects, failed her in that one immensely important direction.

She would never, without prompting, have connected her own history with that of the missing Lincoln girl. She had seen no connection at all. Ironically the prompting had come from Esther. It was Esther's interest in the Lincoln tragedy that first turned her attention to Barbarrow. With no particular aim, purely from a magpie turn of mind, she had gathered such information as was available about the Hall and its inhabitants. Walking behind Esther and Daniel along the river path, she had overheard their idle suggestion, idly dismissed, that the foundling in the blanket could have been the lost child. She had paid less attention to so far-fetched a possibility than to Esther's ill-judged remark: 'She was so disgustingly dirty and stupid. If she had come from a good family it would somehow have shown.'

That it did show had been amply proved. It showed in her speech, her manner, her clothes and in the slenderness of her ankles. Clairy's smile was both triumphant and bitter. Inevitably, if by devious means, she had achieved entry into the enviable world to which by nature she belonged. But so far Barbarrow had featured merely as an example of it. Through coincidence and by means of her intervention between Daniel and Esther resulting in Esther's marriage, a situation had arisen, had fallen into her hands and had been used. As well as a strong tide of resentment and malice, the enterprise had needed skill and restraint. She had been careful to avoid argument and persuasion, to make no claim and to leave the others to fit together details and reach their own conclusions or, more uncomfortably for them, fail to reach a conclusion. Apart from their approximate ages – and she didn't even know her own age – her story and that of the Lincoln girl were alike only in their shortage of facts. She had turned their very absence to her advantage. The enterprise had been successful so far.

She had not bargained for its complete and dazzling success about to culminate in a development undreamed of and unforeseen. As she gazed – unseeing now – at the butterflies, their seemingly random flutterings governed by a force they could neither control nor resist, she realized how convincingly events had fallen into place, how feasible it must all seem – how more than feasible, considering that the whole case rested on the direction Rodd had chosen to take. He could have dumped her anywhere. Why had he come this way? She had asked herself that question before, needless to say, but only to be ready with an acceptable answer should the question ever be raised by others: that he must have meant to return her to Barbarrow and had come as near to it as he dared; to reach the Hall would have involved an awkward detour and the delay would have endangered his escape.

It was a reasonable answer, the only one likely to convince. In a flash of comprehension that set her pulse racing, she understood why. *Because it was the right answer.* The explanation she had fabricated was the true explanation. He actually had intended to bring her back. Once that fact was accepted, the entire mystery of her past was resolved and the course of her future altered. The scheme had certainly been successful: it had convinced the least credulous of the people involved – herself.

So tremendous a mental adjustment took her breath away. A thrill of nervous fear shook her whole body to the very fingertips. Who wouldn't be afraid if the figures on a canvas slipped a little, moved of their own accord and took on life? She had nothing of the artist's creativity. The distinction between real and unreal had never concerned her: factual reality and the distortion of facts were all she knew. She had been so intent on presenting a false case that she had not even entertained the idea that it might be true.

And it was true. In seconds she passed like a redeemed sinner from unbelief to faith, as if born again. What had seemed at best improbable had been all along, quite simply, true: she had been born at Barbarrow, in the dark period of childhood when memory was blotted out, she had been taken away. Rodd knew her history and was bringing her back.

The events of the day had opened her mind to new experiences, and now time and place together wrought another change: the slow strange dawn of imagination. Perhaps the scene itself, the mild sky, the roses and the butterflies, played their part. There came to her a faint perception that in human affairs there might be another unsuspected dimension that so far she had missed. Briefly she seemed to take a view less dark and disillusioned. Briefly she sensed how, in certain circumstances, other people might have felt. Rodd for instance. She dismissed the possibility that he had been her abductor: so daring a crime would have been beyond him. He would never have ventured so far from his own squalid haunts, not of his own accord. But that he had been implicated, she had now no doubt. He knew the place, or knew of it, knew of the crime and who had done it; someone had passed her on to Rodd and he had passed her on to Lena . . .

When he saw Lena dead he had been transformed. He had been beside himself. Lacking the gift of sympathy, she had no conception of remorse, but she saw a befuddled kind of logic in his behaviour. That he might in his brutish way have loved Lena did not occur to her, but she did understand the impulse to strike a bargain. Having done murder, had he hoped somehow to make amends? She had witnessed not only the crime, but his terror of damnation. Some people believed in that sort of thing. He could not restore Lena to life and be forgiven, but he could restore Lena's unwanted protégée to her rightful home and so stand a better chance of saving his soul. He might have thought like that: he was never very bright at the best of times. In any case, he had to take her somewhere, and what other place could there be? It was obvious. He would never even have known of this quiet spot if he had not known about the crime. Of course he had failed in his intention to bring her home as he had failed in everything else in his life, but he had done his best. The rest she had accomplished herself, and here she was – at last – where she belonged.

For a while she could not move. The revelation, vivid as lightning, had drained her of energy and the power to act until, as she became aware once more of the earth beneath her feet, the tall hedgerows and the scent of meadow grass, there stole into her mind the thought that somewhere in the world there might at some future time be, even for her, intervals of peace and pleasantness: the daily use of delicate china and silver, the soothing sounds of quiet conversation against a background of softly flowing water and the murmuring of bees. She almost believed that there could be sweetness in life. She put out her hand to touch rose petals and, feeling their softness, smiled and thought: That is the hand of Elizabeth Lincoln.

And so, having already assumed more than one role, she slipped smoothly into another; but this one was different. It involved no pretence; no mutation was required. It happened with the ease of a natural process. She simply resumed, after twenty-four years, her own interrupted identity and, walking slowly, came out from the shade of the narrow lane into full sunlight.

She came, Esther thought, and nothing happened, no harm had come of it. Nothing could disturb the serenity of Barbarrow in June. The windows stood open to the scent of roses: wistaria had unfolded its mauve flowers on the front wall. The orchard grass was barred with slender tree-shadows. Hens picked among fallen petals. She went to the gate at the far end and looked over it into the meadow. From its rich growth of clover and moon-daisies and flowering grasses, butterflies rose, and settled and rose again. There was no other movement. It would soon be haytime, but as yet the pastoral scene was deserted: no heavy-breathing horses, no voices, no little girl in a frilled white pinafore running ahead of her nurse, running into oblivion.

Esther rubbed her hands: they were ice-cold. No earthly beauty could drive out fear. Neither reason nor common sense could save her from its onslaught. Thoughts of the past, fears for the future, a mingling of memory and foreboding chilled her. Barbarrow at its loveliest in a June like this had not been proof against evil. What madness it had been to open its gates deliberately and let in a stranger: a bringer of ill-tidings, an interloper from the dark, disordered world of crime and vice, where normal rules of behaviour could not be counted on.

A stranger? Or Lilla come home?

Perplexed and nervous, she fled back to the nursery as with protective wings outspread. From the window she saw that the marquee had come. Workmen were erecting it in the home field.

389

CHAPTER 26

Barbarrow Hall, standing firm on its deep foundations, withstood the onslaught of fifty-three schoolchildren and remained apparently unchanged. The cataclysmic change in the lives of its inhabitants had nothing to do with the invasion except that it happened on the same day.

Afterwards, some time after, that is, when they could give their minds to such trivialities, the Lincolns congratulated themselves on having planned an early start to the Treat and consequently an early end. The weather was mercifully warm and dry. The charabanc arrived shortly after ten o'clock and returned at four, which gave time for an early lunch of meat pies and ice-cream, rambles by the river, games in the field and finally a tea of buns and cakes served in individual bags and eaten on the grass.

A blue sky, gardens full of flowers, maids in caps and aprons, all the girls in white dresses, fifty-three heads of hair washed the night before and no lessons, made it for the children a day to be remembered – and recorded in a photograph which, for many of them, was their first.

'Come early,' Esther had instructed Vincent, 'while they're all still fit to be seen.'

He came out on a morning train, and the photographs were taken before lunch.

Memorable the occasion might prove to be for the children. For the adults at Barbarrow it was to slip so rapidly from the mind as to be recalled only as a pleasant blur, clearing here and there to bring into focus an incident or two of special interest, one of them to be seen long afterwards – and not only by the adults – as the beginning of a new chapter in the family history.

Viola's initiation into the astonishing existence of other children was administered in small doses. An adoring circle of schoolgirls round her pram was not what Esther had had in mind, though Viola didn't mind at all, and protested when wheeled away, until diverted by the novelty of being pushed by the eldest girl; and then, a rota having been rapidly drawn up, 'minded' by the next in age. Later, when Esther had released them to find the arbour she herself had enjoyed at their age, some of the boys crossed the courtyard on their way back from the river, among them one she knew.

'Jake!' He recognized her shyly and paused. 'Come and see my little girl.'

He advanced cautiously. Viola, sitting up nicely against snowy pillows in white lawn and pink ribbons and waving her rattle imperiously, was a sight to see.

'She's very – clean,' he mumbled and was ashamed. It wasn't the right word, not what he had meant. Mr Godwain said you should always use the right word, and there were plenty to choose from.

What Viola saw of Jake – a face with dark eyes at a much lower level than her mother's and turned fully in her direction – there was no knowing. But to Esther's delight, she smiled at it, bounced towards it and held out her rattle.

'It's for you, Jake. She likes you. You've found a friend.'

He flushed to his ears. Fortunately the other boys had gone. He took the rattle, shook it, returned it and backed away from an incident he would never forget.

The sun declined to the west; flowers were cut for the girls to take home to their mothers. The eldest boy, oppressed all day by the prospect of having to say Thank you, said it at last and began to enjoy himself. Gervase, mindful of sing-songs with the troops and the need to put an end to them somehow, called for three cheers and hoped he would never again be called on to demonstrate the mechanism of the internal combustion engine. The charabanc rumbled away.

It was over; house and gardens were quiet again, lapped in the deeper silence of hills and woods.

'It was wonderful,' Esther said.

'Wonderful.' They stood on the terrace, hand in hand.

'She came.'

'Yes. What did you talk about?'

'We didn't. I thought she must be with you.'

'No. Has she gone?'

'I don't know.'

Into the air stole the now familiar unease. Each felt the other's fingers tighten. Both started at the sound of a footstep behind them, then relaxed. It was Vincent.

'We're planning a quiet cup of tea,' Esther said, 'now that they've all gone.'

'Except Miss Motte.'

'Where is she?'

'Sitting in the arbour.'

Gervase released Esther's hand and arranged chairs round the table. Catching her eye, he indicated their number: three. She nodded.

'Three cups, Annie.' The maid had been hovering.

'I didn't realize that you knew her.' Gervase felt the usual wearisome uncertainty as to how to refer to her, by what name.

'She was a client a couple of years ago.'

Gervase had placed the chairs so that both he and Esther faced the flagged walk leading between clipped yew hedges to the arbour. Between honeysuckle and clematis on its white lattice could be seen glimpses of a blue dress.

Clairy had come to Barbarrow as the children were being rounded up for tea. With so much going on she had not bothered to find her hosts. It was a rare opportunity to wander alone in the garden as freely as if it were her own: as if its paved paths and parterres, like orchard, paddock and meadow, were hers by right. So it might have appeared if there had been anyone there to see her pause in her unhurried walk to read the shadow of the gnomon on the dial, as other ladies – daughters, sisters, wives – had done long before there were Lincolns at the Hall. She was not pretending: she was too cynical for self-deception, and had never known the childlike delight of pretending to be somebody else. She could scheme, pervert the truth to suit her own purpose and mislead others, could act without regard for morality or kindness; but she could not pretend to herself that things were other than they were.

True, there had been times when she had seemed to know how it would feel if Barbarrow belonged to her by right instead of to Esther, but within the space of the last three days that phase had been outgrown. The position was entirely altered. The ownership of the Hall was not an issue. Barbarrow did not yet belong to her. What mattered was that she belonged to Barbarrow.

On her way back to Taybrooke three days ago she had faced the fact that the fairy tale was true, not that she knew much about fairy tales. She had, so to speak, missed out on them; they were not her line. It was more a case of realizing that her manipulations and evasions had been a partial representation of what was actually true: that she was Gervase Lincoln's daughter. Within her, interpenetrating her mind and body, there had come into being another self. The two remained separate yet coexistent. As possibility grew into probability and so into belief, they merged and became her total self. By the time she came to Barbarrow again she had become Elizabeth Lincoln.

It was to her credit that she rose to the discovery with dignity. She felt no urge to confront the Lincolns with the truth. How could she? There was no proof beyond her own certainty. She remained sufficiently vindictive to speculate on how much worse it would be for them to go on unhappily wondering, than to know. She would not tell them or make any public claim until she judged the time to be right, however far ahead that time might be. Besides, there was no need to tell them; to be acknowledged had not been her aim, but to disturb and distress and make them suffer, especially Esther. What she had most wanted from life was to know who she was, and now she knew.

She knew with certainty because she recognized in herself, especially in this mood of serene confidence, the behaviour of a well-bred woman; because she was of the right age, because she had been brought – in all the length and breadth of England – to within walking distance of the place from which she had been stolen, because of the gap in memory resulting from the shock of her abduction. But most of all, most deeply and surely of all, she knew it because the place itself, without her help and of its own accord, had claimed her. For once she was influenced less by thought than by instinct, in which reason had no part.

It didn't matter that Esther Lincoln was for the time being mistress of the Hall. What mattered was the feeling, unlike any other within her range of feeling, narrow as that was, that Barbarrow had accepted her and had made her part of itself. Left to herself as she was now, she could indulge the sensation of being where she belonged. It was not to be shared. Its inviolate secrecy heightened a mood which was the nearest she had ever come to tranquillity.

The confidence was new, but the place had cast its spell on her almost from the beginning and had strengthened its hold with insidious persuasiveness. When, more than a year ago, she had explored the outer reaches of the estate, her eyes had rested on a stile, a shaded path, a view of the Hall between trees as the eyes of a wanderer might select a pleasing picture with a sense of its rightness. Seen again, the place is recognized, known, familiar, as forgotten scenes from childhood rise to the surface of the mind. In her case they were like signals from the early blank period of which she had no other knowledge.

The spell worked fitfully. And then in March when she first called at the Hall, climbed its stairs, waited in a sitting-room, looked out of a window, she felt as never before at one with her surroundings. There seemed an appropriateness in her being there, a satisfaction untarnished by greed or self-interest. It came like a flicker of light where there had been no light at all. She remained coldly detached from the Lincolns: her affinity was with the place. Consequently, when all the other reasons clicked into position, they merely reinforced what inwardly she already knew.

No-one would have suspected the immense change she had undergone three days ago. She gave no outward sign of it as she strolled between yew hedges and saw ahead of her at the end of the flagged path, half-hidden by trailing honeysuckle and clematis, a white-latticed arbour. It was enclosed on three sides and on the fourth open to the garden: a retreat well suited to her own withdrawn and secretive nature.

She stepped inside and sat down on the bench, hearing the distant voices of those others in whom she had no interest, from whom she was distinct and separate. Screened by the white criss-crossing bars and the wide purple flowers of clematis, she could forget other people. She had only to wait until it came, warm and deep, the sensation of having come home: warmer and deeper than if she had never known the comfortless years before. It would steal upon her and she would yield to it, at rest, drawn close to the very heart of Barbarrow. She who had been unwelcome wherever she went, was welcome here.

It came, and with an intensity she had not known or expected. Belief had become conviction, the one certainty in a world where nothing else could be relied on, no-one trusted. From birth her senses had been conditioned to respond to the sights and sounds of Barbarrow. As an infant she had breathed the air she now breathed again. The first shapes she had recognized were those she now saw. How else could so intimate a closeness be accounted for? Who could say that she was wrong?

For the first time in her life she wanted nothing, needed nothing. That she was Lilla Lincoln, daughter of Gervase, meant little. The Lincolns were people, that was all. All that mattered was that she knew where her life had begun. The mysterious rootedness that others took for granted was hers too. She was their equal. There was no longer any need to envy or emulate or outdo them. She was herself. The harsh years of scheming and contriving seemed as distant as the voices borne on the warm, lavender-scented air. She could see the grey walls of the house, a power unto itself, indifferent as to whose feet, other than hers, trod its paths and to whose hand, if not hers, locked its doors. It existed for its own sake as she did, regardless of other people.

She leaned back and closed her eyes in a languor untroubled by thought. The purple flowers lay open to the westering sun, existing for no other purpose than to be as nature had intended; and so, for that blessed space of time, did she.

'So you know her too,' Vincent said.

'She is staying at Taybrooke,' Esther said.

Vincent had seen the fleeting glance she had exchanged with Lincoln and understood that their acquaintance with Miss Motte was none of his business. But a person who sat in the arbour and was not offered tea, raised interesting questions, especially as he had already spotted an ambiguous quality in Miss Motte.

'She came to the studio about two years ago. She's altered her appearance a little since then,' he began, and had their immediate attention. But only for a second. Almost simultaneously the dogs barked and Gervase asked,

'Were you expecting someone? Two people?'

'Oh dear, who can it be?'

The iron gates were open, giving a view of the lane. The two people, evidently a man and a woman, were too far away as yet to be recognized; but even in the distance their progress could be seen as slow and halting. More than once they stopped. The woman, who appeared the stronger, took the man's arm as if to coax or support him. They reached the open gates and stopped again, this time to talk; at least the woman talked. The man shook his head, backed away from her and leaned heavily against one of the stone gate-posts.

The three on the terrace had watched with little more than murmurs of surprise. Suddenly Esther got up.

'It's the Trisks. Prissie and Barney! They're in trouble, Gervase. He's ill.'

She ran down the steps and out into the drive. Gervase and Vincent followed. Coming close, they were shocked by Barney's sickly look, and even more by the wildness of his expression.

'Oh, Miss Esther. Major Lincoln. Thank God I've got him here. I thought we'd never do it.' Prissie, stretched beyond her strength, relapsed into tears.

It occurred to both Esther and Gervase that the Trisks were at their lowest ebb and had come unwillingly to ask for financial help. But it was no time to talk.

'Keep going, man,' Gervase took his arm, 'until we get you into the house.'

Their desertion of the terrace had alerted the staff. Stevens appeared and the three men took charge of Barney. Esther sat Prissie down at the table on the terrace and gave her tea laced with brandy.

'We had to come. He didn't want to. I'm worn out with trying to persuade him. There've been times when I thought he might do away with hisself—'

'Drink your tea, and when you've washed and had a rest you can tell me what's wrong. You did right to come. No, don't talk yet.'

She slipped away to talk to Mrs Bowland and returned a few minutes later to find Prissie more composed; but her theme was unchanged.

'If you knew what it's taken to get him here! But it was the only way. It couldn't go on. The worry's killing him. He doesn't sleep; no more do I. Coming here today – it's our last hope. Things might take a better turn only I'm so ashamed—'

'There are times when everyone needs help, and you've always been the first to give it, Prissie.' To the elegant Miss Motte in the arbour, for one, Esther thought, remembering the steaming wash-house, the red chair, the bowl of bread and milk and the hearty confidence of Prissie in her bloom. She was sitting slumped over the table, her face bloated with heat and tears.

'My husband will be able to advise and help, I'm sure.' Her reference to Gervase, intended to comfort, only revived Prissie's distress.

'Barney'll have to . . .' She looked anxiously at the windows. 'It's for Barney to talk to him, not me. I made him come and that was the best I could do.'

They must be in debt, the ever-threatening nightmare for such people as the Merridons; she would not have expected Barney to mind it so much. His life must always have had its ups and downs. So far as she could remember, he had seemed to enjoy them. As a little girl she had thrilled to the clatter of his cart with its mysterious cargo, and had waved to him as he raised his whip in cheerful salute and rattled off to unknown places, singing the latest popular song. The war was to blame for this sad change in him. He had survived it and yet was being destroyed by it, as William had been.

Mrs Bowland appeared and was waiting in her firmest manner. She had had a heavy day.

'Everything is ready for the lady upstairs, madam, if you would like me to take her up.'

Barney had been taken to the drawing-room so that he could lie down on a sofa. When Esther went in, he was sitting up again, his collar undone, his feet on the floor. Vincent and Stevens had gone.

'You're feeling better?'

He nodded, then burst out, 'I won't feel right till I get it off my chest, what I've come for. Not that I'll be right then if I'm ever right again.'

'Out with it then. It can't be as bad as that.' Gervase drew up a chair for Esther and he, too, sat down. 'Fire away. We're listening.'

It was not the right approach. The prospect of unburdening himself to two well-disposed and attentive listeners proved too much for Barney. He looked in desperation from one to the other, then buried his face in his hands.

'Just give me a minute . . .'

'I believe I know what it is,' Esther began and was momentarily halted by the upward jerk of his head and his stare of consternation. 'It's about money, isn't it? You need help with money?'

'Money! I wish to God it was only money. It isn't money that's been driving me out of my mind until for two pins I'd have cut my throat, if it hadn't been for Prissie and Kenneth. I'll tell you what it is – and then I can still cut my throat if I want to – and maybe make a better job of that than I've made of anything else.' His forehead was beaded with sweat. His voice broke. 'It's about your little girl.'

'Viola!' A tongue of fire seared Esther from head to foot.

'No. The other little girl.' He turned to Gervase. 'The one that was lost.'

'Go on,' Gervase brought himself to say as the terrible pause lengthened. 'What about her?'

'I know where she is.'

CHAPTER 27

There could have been no quieter grave. It was in a hidden grove sheltered by silver birch and larch trees on the far southern side, out of sight of the house and well away from the path by the stream. After almost a quarter of a century Barney had no difficulty in finding the place, though not the exact spot. A rowan leaning over the stream marked the point where he and Julie had turned to the right and gone into the wood. He had scraped away layers of leaves and larch needles and felt about with the spade for a place where the earth was soft and unhampered by roots. The rowan had thickened and leaned further over the water. All the trees were taller, their shade more dense. Since the object had been to conceal it, there was nothing to mark the grave.

'She's here.' He looked down on a brown carpet of dead leaves. 'Somewhere about here.'

The words broke a fearful silence. They had followed, speechless, stunned by the terrible disclosure; and now, dazzled by long beams of sunlight between branches, they looked down, convinced yet unbelieving, so that all three stood there for a few moments, heads bowed. It could have been Viola, Esther thought. If it had been Viola . . . But any child's death diminishes those left alive – as Barney had felt at the time and felt still.

'We did no harm, sir. Not to her. There was no harm done to her by anyone. The harm was in not telling and as God knows, I'm sorry. It's preyed on me and eaten my heart out. I wish it was me lying there. But it

400

was because *she* cared so much that she couldn't bring herself to face you and tell you . . .'

When Julie had found Lilla lying at the bottom of the steps into the grotto with her neck broken, she had gone mad: literally out of her mind. She did not shriek or foam at the mouth; nevertheless shock and grief and shame and dread of having to tell the Lincolns, knowing that she had failed them, turned her from a sweet, light-hearted loving girl into a staring frenzied lunatic, her entire crazed mind bent on escape.

'I knew it was wrong, but I couldn't deal with her. She could always twist me round her little finger . . .'

He had been a hawker's lad when she won his heart, and was learning his father's business, a profitable one which he later inherited. In those days the van plied regularly twice a week between Unnerstone and Wood Aston; Barney used to take a handcart or basket to places more difficult of access, such as Lady Green and Broom Farm.

It was from the stile by the stepping-stones that he had first seen Julie and the little girl sailing boats of birch bark. To an inexperienced and impressionable lad, Julie had seemed an entrancing creature from a more glamorous world. She must have found him good-looking, not backward, and the only young man on whom she could practise her innocent wiles. While the Lincolns were abroad he had gone twice over the hill to Barbarrow, invented excuses for returning late and been stormed at by his father.

'If only I'd left it at that and never come again!'

The third time would have to be – and was – the last. It was a harmless flirtation, but they had dallied too long in the grotto. With the housekeeper in bed, Lilla having her afternoon rest and everyone else in the hayfield, they had been in no hurry to part. The child had evidently wakened, come downstairs and run out of the house.

'She must have climbed on that big urn and fallen. There were flowers in her hand . . .'

Barney, too, had been terrified as well as grieved and awestruck at the sight of the dead child, and the feel of her body in his arms. He knew his duty, but could not bring himself to act on it, nor could he reason with the maniac Julie had become. His instinct, like hers, was to run away from a situation far beyond his scope. They could not bring themselves to abandon the child, nor to leave her unburied. To hide her away would postpone the reckoning that must come, as come it had at last. The horror and panic of sneaking to the toolshed for a spade before the others came back, and of finding a burial place, had haunted him ever since, but he had been able to live with their memory until his own child was born.

'I've many a time looked at our Kenneth and thought of her, barely cold when I buried her just as she was, without even a coffin to cover her . . .'

But it was when he heard that Miss Esther had come to Barbarrow and that she, too, had a little girl, that the memories he had buried rose again, and the guilt he had suppressed began to torment him beyond bearing.

'It's been on my mind, day and night.'

In such a state, it seemed in no way extraordinary when he deliberately knelt down.

'Forgive me, sir, if you can. I won't blame you if you can't. You can do what you like with me. I can face the police – prison – the lot, now that I've faced you. There can't be anything worse than what I've been through.'

'You think I don't know what it's been like.' Gervase's throat and lips had stiffened so that he could scarcely voice the words, his first since they had left the house. 'Do you think I haven't felt guilty too? Being sorry doesn't end it. There's no end to it. We have to live with it. Get up, man. It's not for me to forgive.' And as

Barney shifted awkwardly to one knee. 'You were young and ignorant, and under pressure. She—'

'Julie!' Esther said. 'You haven't told us about Julie.'

She had sworn, over and over again, that she would never go back to the house. Barney, if only he could be rid of her, never wanted to see her again. He gave her the few shillings he had been paid at the farm. Some of the coins had fallen from her aimless hands. He had picked them up and folded her cold fingers over them as she threw her head from side to side, whimpering. He last saw her running over the fields towards Long Rake, in her summer dress and light shoes, her hair loose, her clothes and face soiled with the earth in which she had scrabbled and delved with her bare hands.

Barney got heavily to his feet. Shaken as he was, there was just perceptible in him the spectre of the swashbuckling pirate he had once been – and fainter still, the wraith of a good-looking lad who had so disastrously fallen in love.

'He'll get over it,' Esther thought as he stumbled to the bank of the stream and scooped up water to bathe his face. It was to be hoped that he would, for Prissie's sake.

'But what happened to Julie?' she asked, knowing there could be no answer.

With the sun behind it, Long Rake was dark-edged. Beyond the two or three farms on its lower slopes there was no sign of life, only an occasional solitary tree looking small and lost in a wide desolation. Those were quiet days. In 1902 the countryside had been quieter still.

'If she found her way to one of the farms,' Gervase said, 'they'd be more likely to turn her away than to take her in. The life they lead doesn't make them soft-hearted, not towards strangers. Beyond Crow's Look there's nothing, not even a barn. She wouldn't last long up there, even in summer. If she'd been seen, we would have heard.'

Lost, demented, without food, she could have wandered until her strength gave out and then lain down to die. If, long after, a shepherd had found bones and tattered clothing, he would have no reason to connect them with the Hall which, from 1902, had been unoccupied for seventeen years. If a ghost walked on those lonely hills, Esther thought, it would be Julie's ghost.

To Esther, who had never known her, she could be little more than a ghost, a name: one of those unknown people whose presence she had imagined at the meeting-place by the ruined barn, people who had met, lingered and gone their separate ways by stepping-stones or field paths. To the pictures she had already formed of nurse and child, she could add another: of young faces reflected in clear water, and frail boats of birch bark floating downstream. From the last picture of all, in the sunless grotto, she looked away.

If Barney's confession had left her sick at heart, what had it done to Gervase? The iron habit of self-control held him stiff-shouldered and grim-faced. She knew that he was suffering intensely and was bearing the grief as he bore everything, alone and reliant on his own quiet strength. This latest distress, added to the unhappiness she had already caused him, was an affliction heavier than he deserved. He was the kindest of men. It was from sheer kindness that he had helped and advised at the time of her father's death; they had had no claim on him and scarcely knew him. In her numbed and bewildered state she must have seemed to take his unobtrusive neighbourliness for granted. In almost two years of marriage his love for her had never faltered. He had not uttered a word of reproach when, in her misery, she had separated herself from him; it was she who had drawn away. She had never fully entered into the tragedy of his first marriage or the wretched uncertainty as to what had happened to Lilla – never until now. Barney had done more than confess: he had brought home to her a new understanding and sharpened her awareness of suffering, his own, Julie's, and nearest of all . . .

'Gervase.' She went to him, put her hands on the lapels of his coat and looked up into his face. It remained stern and withdrawn. As he looked down at her she saw in his eyes, in their very depths, an infinite loneliness. 'Gervase.' The look changed to one common to all humanity regardless of age or character or experience. She recognized it as an appeal for help, as if the lost child looked out from her father's eyes. She reached up and laid her cheek against his. 'You must let me help you. It's my turn to help you. Remember—' she glanced down through tears at the concealing earth, at what might be the place. 'Remember you still have me. I want – so very much – to be with you and comfort you.'

She felt a strength of love she had never felt before: a different, deeper kind of love encompassing all the interweaving strands a woman can ply in marriage. She loved him as a mother loves her child, as a wife cherishes a grieving husband, as a comrade and partner; and for him, it seemed, there was something more . . .

'I haven't forgotten.' He smiled. 'You know, you're the light of my eyes. If Lilla had lived—' he cleared his throat, 'I hope she would have been like you, just as you are now. You don't know how the thought of that comforts me.'

He put his arms round her, and for a whole minute they stood together in a sympathy closer than they had ever known.

By the stream Barney was wiping his face on his sleeve. He stood shamefaced as Esther went to him. Would he believe her? Would he understand if she told him how wonderfully and lastingly he had helped her?

'Thank you, Barney. It was brave of you to come.' She hesitated. 'You've made things better, much better.'

He didn't understand, but the warmth in her voice soothed his bruised heart as he trudged back to Prissie.

405

'What shall we do, Gervase?'

'Do? Nothing. Think what it would mean to let this be known. No-one need know. We'll send the Trisks to Apperfield in the car. Mrs Bowland and the others will think as we did, that they came for help of some sort. This concerns no-one but ourselves and the Trisks.' He came out of the shade of the trees and into the late sunlight. 'Let her rest in peace.'

He was too weary to talk. She took his arm. Together they looked back into the green twilight under the sheltering boughs, at the shroud of fallen leaves and larch needles covering all that was left of her. It was soft and deep.

'She's become part of Barbarrow,' Esther said.

It was too long ago, too late to mourn with as piercing a grief as if she had died yesterday: rather a time to grieve that she had died so soon, to add a sorrow deeper than personal grief to the universal mourning for dead children.

It was not until the Trisks had been driven away that Esther remembered. 'There is someone else who will have to know.'

'Yes. She will have to be told,' and with a sudden yielding to the strain of the past hour, 'I can't face her, Esther. Not now, if ever. I ought to, but I can't. I suppose . . . you couldn't . . .'

'I'll do it. I'll tell her.'

From a stillness close to sleep, Clairy was roused by the sound of the charabanc, but she did not stir from the arbour until a small commotion forced itself on her attention. Unnoticed, she witnessed the arrival of the Trisks whom she would not have recognized if she had not overheard their names. She registered the fact that they were married, but without interest, and having no wish to meet either of them, she took the opportunity of making a leisurely exploration of the more sheltered parts of the garden.

More than an hour later she returned to the arbour where she had left her gloves, but was foiled in her intention of slipping away.

'I was hoping you hadn't gone.'

Esther was nervous, but the recent discovery had been so momentous as to reduce this mission on Gervase's behalf to a few minutes of mere unpleasantness, or so she thought. But the convolutions of their relationship were so intricate, and the emotions roused in her by this woman so deep and painful, that it was hard to begin. It didn't help to be visited by the memory of a former time when they had faced each other with a similar purpose, their roles reversed: Clairy had told her, coming quickly and coolly to the point, what she had found hanging from the Aston oak. Now it was her turn to act as messenger. The blow she had to deliver – if it was a blow – was of an altogether lesser kind. And yet . . .

She hesitated. Standing in the arbour in her soft summer dress and straw hat, one white hand holding her gloves, Clairy did not seem out of place. She could be – Esther was reminded of her own childish daydream – one of Marcus Stone's ladies brought discreetly up to date. Between background and figure there was no discord: the picture was just right. It was almost as though – she had to remind herself that the news she brought made it impossible – but if she had seen Clairy in this setting an hour or two ago, she would have been almost convinced that the woman she faced was here by right of birth: that she lived here at Barbarrow. It was disconcerting. Moreover, her own arrival had caught Clairy unprepared. Her slight start made her seem more vulnerable.

'I have something to tell you. My husband is too much upset to tell you himself. We didn't know until just now. It concerns you, too. Very much.'

It was not so much a blow that she delivered as a gradual administering, drop by hesitant drop, of a near-fatal draught. With concern, she saw the strange eyes lose their brilliance and become grey rims round dilated pupils. The mouth drooped, the face and shoulders sagged, the hands grew nerveless; and in the silence, when she had finished, she knew how it felt to inflict mortal pain and to watch the victim suffer.

She remembered, too, as the blood drained from Clairy's lips, how it felt to be told that the most precious thing in life was yours no longer: how she had stood in the doorway of Lady Green, sick at heart, while Daniel told her that they must part, how he had gone away in the rain, leaving her desolate. She seemed to see the same desolation reflected in Clairy's face and recognized in her a disappointment so devastating that she herself was shaken. With a flash of perception she understood.

'You wanted it to be true. You believed it? You actually believed that you were Lilla? I hadn't realized. I didn't think—'

'You're surprised.' She brought herself to speak calmly, leaning a little against the lattice. 'Naturally you thought I was trying to cheat you. No wonder. I always have. And I've never believed in anything—'

'Except that. That you were Lilla. You really believed that.'

The sting of incredulity had a reviving effect. 'Not at first. I meant to make trouble in so very comfortable a hen-roost. But it could have been true, couldn't it? And it wasn't my idea in the first place. It was you and Daniel . . . An interesting idea, he called it. Suppose the girl in the blanket was being returned to Barbarrow . . . She couldn't be the Lincoln girl, you said. She was too disgustingly dirty and stupid to have come from a good family—'

'I'm sorry. How could I have known that you were the girl? It was a silly thing to say, in any case.'

'And you've gone on thinking of me in that way, even though you can see how I've changed since then.'

'I'm sorry.'

'I didn't believe it any more than you did. Not then. But I didn't forget it either. And was it so preposterous an idea?' She was speaking slowly, as if uncertain of her voice. 'There were things that made it seem possible, weren't there? It grew more and more likely. And the place itself. It was as if I knew it. It's as if I've become part of it, not for the first time, but again. It had to be true.' Waking fully to the knowledge that it wasn't true, she woke also to the harsh reality of all that she had seemed to escape. 'But it isn't true. I might have known. It doesn't matter.' With immense effort she regained something of her usual poise. 'You wouldn't know – but I've seen murder done. After that, nothing else matters much.'

She smoothed back a strand of hair, adjusted her hat and pulled on a glove. Esther saw the face under the hat brim become mask-like, as empty of feeling as it had been when, hoisted on the red throne, the unknown girl had been driven off to Hudmorton, driver and passenger each with a grim secret. They had narrowly missed meeting again little more than an hour ago. She had the strangest feeling that in spite of all that had happened, nothing had changed. She felt just as she had felt at the beginning by the school gate: a mixture of pity and fear of a world beyond her experience, from which the unknown girl had come. She was still unknown. She was unknowable. That gave her a kind of power – the not knowing what she would do, or where she would go, or whether she would . . . come back?

'So Lilla's dead.' Clairy stepped down on to the path. 'She was the lucky one, to leave early and yet to stay. Never to have to go away. To stay here always.'

The words lingered after she had gone, leaving Esther with the uneasy impression that it was not only Lilla who had died.

She sank down on the seat Clairy had left unoccupied. To be free of her brought relief, naturally, but also remorse for her own ignorance and immaturity.

How could she even in those heedless days have made such shallow remarks? To have passed judgement in that way on a homeless waif! There was no denying that she had shrunk from her with a sense of some nameless deviation from normality. Had it been a forewarning? Of what? A sequence of disasters which she herself, perhaps by that very shrinking, had helped to set in motion. Good family! What could she possibly have meant, she who at that time had known no family but her own and Daniel's? If personal qualities were to be compared, Clairy was cleverer than she was, stronger, had more courage . . . In spite of herself she could go no further. The catalogue of Clairy's virtues ended there. She was sorry for her. Very sorry. All the same . . .

She stepped out of the arbour. Would she ever sit there again without wondering who Clairy was? Would she ever sit there again?

Had the lane grown longer? It was taking her a long time to be quit of the place, as if Barbarrow held her and would not let her go, no matter how quickly she walked. Once or twice she stumbled, a white-faced woman in a light dress strangely conveying an impression of darkness. Beyond the rose-hung hedge, butterflies still hovered above the clover. Bronze and white and clouded yellow, they dipped and clung to the purple-pink petals and rose up again in a wavering, airy cloud. She didn't stop to look at them; didn't see or think of them. Stripped of the mad notion that there might be sweetness in the world, she was back where she had started, on her own, in a colder, harsher loneliness than before. With no outward resting place for her thoughts, she was forced back within the confines of her own self, not the person she had been lured into believing herself to be, but the same rootless, nameless, hungry creature she had always been and must always be. And from somewhere within that creature's skull came a voice – her own – demanding once again, 'Who am I? If not Lilla, then who?'

She had learned at last to suffer, and to know that she was suffering. Chance had in store for her a further blow more cruel still, but to the first bitter pangs of disappointment, her reaction was curiously like Esther's: a conviction that nothing had changed. She might as well be back in the filthy blanket under the thorn hedge by the school gate, being pitied by Esther Aumery, as suffer the more mature and clearly shown pity of Esther Lincoln. Pity degraded her more than the most sordid of her adventures. Soon the mere memory of Esther's concern for her would revive the implacable malice she had briefly put aside; but for a while she succumbed, hating her own weakness, to pity for herself.

She had tried to raise herself up only to be dragged down again, so low that she could almost feel once more the hard neck of the bottle against her teeth and smell the reeking timbers of Rodd's cart. More vividly than ever, as if having nowhere else to go, she had actually gone back to it, she recalled the dismal room and saw again Lena's lank hair and broken fingernails as she held out two thick white cups of dark brown tea, one in each hand. What was she saying, with her self-mocking disillusioned smile? 'I must have been out of my mind . . . '?

For some reason the two white cups troubled her. They had risen from the darkened past to force themselves on her attention, as she stumbled along in the soft green shade of the lane. She saw them, thick, white and steaming, one in each of Lena's grimy hands. A trembling came upon her as she thought of them: an immense reluctance to acknowledge why she was afraid. Was it because of what Lena had been saying as she offered the cups? Two cups. Yet should she not have welcomed the memory? She had so often tried to dredge up some of the things Lena had said, clues that she might have missed.

411

She came out at last from between the screening hedgerows to where elms bordered the lane on her right, behind them a grassy slope overgrown with gorse and bramble. In less than a minute she would come to the gate marking the limit of the Lincolns' land. She would go through it, close it behind her and all would be over. She stopped, instinctively postponing the final moment, and was all at once exhausted, beaten, the brief surge of hope, the treacherous glimmer of light quite gone. And it was in that rare moment of defeat that some perverse trick of memory, as if to test her newly acquired ability to suffer, once more forced upon her vision the two white cups, this time with the words that went with them.

'Here you are, you two. Don't say I don't look after you. My God, I must have been out of my mind to take you on, the pair of you.'

There were two of them. They were a pair – connected – the child and the man, herself and Rodd. Lena had taken them on, a twofold burden, together. They had arrived there together and had left together. But not for Barbarrow. He must have been making for Hudmorton, intending to palm her off on Olga. First Lena, then Olga. Father and daughter? No, she pleaded. Not that. There had been a connection of some sort, but not necessarily a sharing of blood. Not with him. They would have told her. Even if they told her nothing else, they would have told her that. And yet, in their feckless, untender lives, in his erratic comings and goings, what space had there been for more than the wordless relationship of savages?

The stab of pain was savage, too, as from an actual physical wound. Rodd! Anger and disgust sickened her and brought her close to fainting. It was no remedy to look back towards the Hall, now out of sight, to close her eyes and try to see it still, mellow in sunshine, secure amid its trees, flower-scented and forbidden. Mockery distorted her vision. Gently born? Better not

412

to have been born at all than to have been fathered by that filthy drunken murderer. It wasn't true. It could be true, but it was not true.

She left the path and clambered unheeding through vicious spikes of gorse to a space between bushes. Tearing off her hat she sank to the ground, drew up her knees and clasped them, head bowed, wishing she had died in the womb of the unknown woman who had conceived her, or could be buried and lying at peace under trees like the child she had never been: safely dead, like Lilla.

Or like Lena? To be found, eyes starting from her head and hustled into an untended grave? He had strangled the life out of Lena. Why had he stopped there? Why hadn't he done the same to her? He had let her live because she was his daughter, bone of his bone, flesh of his flesh. He had forced life upon her. Something had restrained him from ending it. She thought of it as a primitive taboo or animal instinct, not as a yielding to compassion.

She was his daughter. It was the only reasonable conclusion. Suppose more than reason were involved. Suppose she were to find confirmation of their relationship in her own self, in her physical being, her disposition and thinking, in her reaction to every circumstance. She had thought herself free; there was no such thing as freedom. No tyranny could equal the tyranny of inherited tendencies. One didn't choose to be born. One couldn't choose one's parents. Parents imposed life on their children, and by transmitting to them their own natures, determined the course that life would take. No matter where she went, there was no escaping her sinister legacy. Rodd had abandoned her, but she could never be free of him. Dead or alive, he existed within her. She was inextricably bound to him.

It did not occur to her that she had also inherited the ability to think in such a way, with a detachment that could have saved her. She thought only of all that was

413

detestable in the man. Was she like him in appearance? She looked at her right hand and tried to remember his, reaching for the cup. She groped in her handbag for the mirror and stared at her face. It stared back at her, its steadiness devoid of personality. It told her nothing. It could be anybody's face.

It didn't matter. Nothing mattered now that she knew who she was. The search for her identity, the chief purpose of her life, was at an end. There was nothing now to live for, nowhere to go. The sustaining power of will drained from her. She collapsed on her side, still clutching her knees, making herself small, clinging to the earth as it spun. There was nothing else to cling to.

Vincent caught sight of a blue shape lying limp and apparently lifeless among undergrowth a short distance from the lane. At the sound of the car perhaps, it moved as if shrinking further from sight. All the same he told Stevens to stop.

'There's someone I want to speak to. Wait for me in the road. I won't be more than a few minutes.'

He opened the gate and when the car had gone through, turned back. 'Miss Motte?' He went nearer. She had sat up and was resting awkwardly on one arm. 'You don't look well. Is there anything I can do?'

'No. I was just resting.'

She must have been there for some time, long enough for Stevens to drive to Apperfield and back, perhaps longer. Her possessions – hat, gloves, bag – lay here and there on the grass as if dropped at random by a woman who had lost her bearings. She was untidy: all astray. He thought it an improvement. It made her seem more human, less unapproachable. Nor was he slow to connect the apparent distress of Miss Motte with the definite distress of the Trisks, and the shattered looks of the Lincolns when he had taken leave of them after hanging about on his own for a good hour. Not that he had minded: Mrs Bowland had given him ham and

414

eggs in her own room while he waited for Stevens to take him and his gear to the station.

'What's going on?'

The crude approach may have been a relief to one too long inhibited by the need to behave with decorum. At any rate he was impressed by the speed with which she recovered at least some vestige of her extraordinary poise.

'Don't you know?' She straightened her stockings at her ankles. 'They've just found her grave.'

'Whose, for God's sake?'

'The long-lost daughter, Lilla Lincoln.'

Vincent, who had never heard of her, was startled. 'Just today, you mean?'

She nodded. 'They don't want it talked about. It might upset them – and they mustn't be upset, must they?'

'What's all this got to do with—' The Trisks, he had almost asked, but instinct warned him to tread carefully. Clearly a bomb had gone off at Barbarrow and splinters were still flying. Miss Motte must have taken some of the flak, otherwise she would never have come out with the blunt remark about the grave – not to him. They weren't exactly cronies, and besides, it wasn't like her to make an unguarded move or put at risk the slightly weird façade she had seemed to be sheltering behind. It appeared to have cracked. 'What's it got to do with you?' He picked up her scattered possessions. 'It seems to have been a shock to you, too.'

'I haven't been well, that's all. It's the heat. I sat too long in that arbour of theirs. But it's certainly been a shock to them. Apparently someone knew about it all along. They'll try to hush it up of course. Personally I have nothing to conceal. I've been completely open about the whole thing.'

'The whole thing?' He saw that she was still struggling to control an agitation which may have accounted for the outburst that followed. There seemed no other

415

reason why she, who wasn't the type to confide in anybody, should come near to confiding in him, except that he was there, a mere camera, of no interest to her as an individual.

'They knew from the start that Motte isn't my name. I have no name, I made that perfectly clear. It's a disadvantage, I don't mind telling you, not knowing who your parents were, two people who may scarcely have known each other, for that matter. You don't know what may have been passed on to you, what's in you . . . .' She paused, thinking of what there had been in Rodd.

'You seem to have managed quite well on your own.'

'I dare say.' She shrugged. He handed her the hat. She took it mechanically and did not put it on. 'But it isn't just the name. You don't know what to do, because no-one ever told you. You have to find out for yourself, watch other people and make what you can of that. How can you understand? You've never been patronized and treated like a stray cat and washed and put into someone else's clothes and got rid of.' She stopped as if aware that she was behaving unsuitably. Yet she had spoken deliberately, with a coldly suppressed passion.

'What's that got to do with finding Lilla Lincoln's grave?'

'She was lost. They didn't know for sure that she was dead. She could have been alive. She could have come back. No-one could know what she would have looked like after twenty-four years.'

'You were going to pass yourself off as Lincoln's daughter?' And she could have pulled it off. With a few hefty lies and no scruples of any kind, she could have done it. Her appearance? If there was nothing in it to suggest that she was a Lincoln, neither was there anything to suggest that she was not. She had seen to that. He regretted but understood the sacrifice of those marvellously satanic eyebrows and hoped that she would let them grow again. He felt responsible for

416

them, having concentrated on them with such striking effect in that damned photograph.

'It wasn't quite like that. I only wanted them to face the possibility. That's all it was, as things turned out.'

He passed an inward vote of thanks to whoever had come up with news about the grave. The Trisks, obviously. They had saved Esther from having to face the problem of Miss Motte as a step-daughter.

'I had to be careful not to let the feeling grow on me that I had found the place where I belonged, at last.' She had spoken slowly, involuntarily turning to look in the direction of Barbarrow.

He was aware of having underestimated the subtlety of her motives. 'It would be a good place to belong to.'

'I didn't know that a place could matter so much.'

He thought her eyes had softened, moistened even. 'You've fallen in love with Barbarrow?' And as she stared, 'It doesn't have to be a person. You can fall in love with a place.' It might be the saving of her, he thought, to go in for places. Human society was probably not her thing. He sensed in her a possibly damaging effect on defenceless persons. 'There's not a lot of point in trying to be like other people, less still in trying to be someone else. Forget all that about not knowing who you are; at least don't make trying to find out into a way of life. You exaggerate the comfort of knowing one's parentage. Some people would be happier not to know. Take my advice,' she had listened, only half attentive. 'You need to find another interest.'

'What else is there?'

'Plenty.' With a sweep of his arm he indicated the earth and the fullness thereof: the crazy pattern of fields between wandering hedgerows, the soft colours of wayside flowers. 'Nature I loved and after Nature, Art.' He hadn't time to go into all that. It was too high-flown for the occasion. Nor did he care for the next bit, being no longer in a position to warm both hands before the fire of life. 'Look round and see things as they really are. And why don't you find a place of your own to love? Yours and nobody else's. It doesn't have to be a stately home. They've had their day. Sorry, I've a train to catch. Are you coming?'

'Not just yet.'

He looked back as he closed the gate. She raised her hand in an absent-minded gesture of farewell. He had half a mind to go back and tell her that they must have been an interesting couple, her unknown parents. There was certainly nothing commonplace or run-of-the-mill about the assortment of genes they had passed on to their daughter.

'Look round,' he had said, 'and see things as they really are.'

She looked vaguely. There were poppies in the thin soil by the gate. She picked one and glanced, unseeing, into its corolla, then stooped to pick others. She liked the colour. In her hand the flowers served no purpose, were already wilting. She threw them away – and with a sudden change of mood, accepted her destiny, seeing herself as she really was and her future as it might be. The beauty of Nature and Art had no part in her vision. It was her own nature that she contemplated, with a cynical recognition of its advantages. As a slave to her heredity, she could not be held accountable for her conduct. Whatever she did would be done under Rodd's direction and not her own, though it might seem otherwise. Slavery, fully accepted, brought freedom from responsibility.

Knowing the argument to be specious, she smiled, accepting it as a false doctrine she could live by, like all the other false doctrines people chose to follow. She need never feel guilt or remorse (not that she ever had) any more than an automaton need be sorry for its actions. She had never opted for virtue. Now it amused her to think that virtue could not be expected of the likes of her, offspring of a drunken murderer.

Of course he had not been her only parent. He happened to be the one she knew. But whatever she lacked, whatever had been denied her, even she had had a mother. The temptation to think of her as at the very least different from Rodd was momentary. She had pitched her expectations too high in the Barbarrow incident and had learned her lesson. Remembering how belief had come upon her like a flash of lightning, she remembered too that lightning can blind as well as illuminate. She would never believe in anything again. It was no use being sentimental about a woman fool enough to throw in her lot with Rodd. The pair of them must be seen as they really were.

'You need to find another interest . . .'

She eased her shoulders, yawned, stretched and drew herself up to her full height. It was too soon: too soon, she discovered with some impatience, to let go altogether of Barbarrow on which she had lavished so much thought, and to let it slip into the past. There had not been time for it to become another gap in memory, a crevasse into which its inhabitants would fall, out of sight and out of mind. What exactly had happened there? 'An accident,' Esther had said. 'No-one was to blame . . . Lilla is dead. We have seen her grave. Those who buried her acted foolishly from a mistaken impulse to spare her parents', or words to that effect.

Was the nurse dead too? Concealing and failing to register a death was a crime. She ought to know: she'd done much the same thing in keeping quiet about a murder. The Trisks were involved in the concealment. Barney Trisk was a buffoon and not worth bothering about. It was no use bothering about little people. But the Lincolns?

The Lincolns! They returned, to fill her vision and revive a resentment so intense that it almost sickened her. They had made her suffer and had then dared to feel sorry for her. It occurred to her that if ever she should be in a position to inflict pain on them, she now knew their tenderest spot.

The whole affair had centred on a missing child, though her loss had been made good, so to speak, by the arrival of Viola. Two little girls: one buried, one still alive and in the other's place. It was to be hoped – her expression was speculative – that Viola would not share Lilla's fate. She had seen the child once, in March, and had since formed the impression that Viola was being kept out of sight. Over-protected? It would never do to let the same thing happen again, would it? And yet, history was said to repeat itself. Making history repeat itself was quite the sort of thing a person like herself would have no compunction in doing: a person who need feel no compunction about anything.

Any harm she had already done them was nothing to the harm she could do now that she knew how they could be most deeply hurt. Perhaps it was only an idea, not yet an intention, but imperceptibly there grew upon her a conviction that her connection with Barbarrow was not yet at an end, that she could, might – must – come back. Why? The answer was still unformulated, but as it took shape there came with it a darkness in her mind. By contrast, her manipulations so far seemed trivial, a waste of time and thought.

And after all, she told herself, if harm came to a young girl, it was only the redressing of an earlier wrong. Her own ordeal when she was a girl had never been expiated. Justice had never been done on her behalf. She caught her breath in a whisper of self-pity – a weakness so rare that it warned her of how dangerously she had been disturbed by the day's experience. It was all their fault. A throb of sheer hatred rescued her from an unfamiliar mental confusion.

Just suppose . . . The lassitude of despair had left her. She brushed dead leaves and flakes of bark from her skirt, but could not shake off a dark object clinging to the hem. It was a spider, its body the size of a man's fingernail, clamped to the blue silk by its powerful, predatory legs: a loathsome intruder on her very person. She struck at it with her gloves, dislodged it, stamped on it, trampled it to death, crushed it into the ground until it ceased to have shape and lapsed into nothingness. And for the first time she felt the bitter delight of physical cruelty, of destroying a living thing. Nothing existed that could not be destroyed. Life itself could be extinguished as easily as a breath can put out a candle flame. It could be squeezed out in a minute by two hands on a slender throat. It had happened . . . just above her head . . . on a disordered bed . . . in an unlit room. The memory would never leave her. But memory could not account for the surge of destructive energy she had briefly felt: it had come from within, innate, she had not willed it.

She shuddered, but not from weakness, rather from a thought obscurely comforting: that the person she had believed herself to be was dead – and buried no more than half a mile away. Her eyes on the patch of ground where the spider had been, she thought of the unsanctified grave. It was as if she looked down into it and recognized its occupant: not the cherished daughter of wealthy parents but a wretched, flea-bitten girl: an outcast, unwanted, always at the mercy of other people, a creature who no longer existed and certainly unrecognizable in the woman she had become. She pressed and turned the ball of her foot on the ground again, as if treading down earth over a grave: as if trampling into the dust every vestige of her former self.

Was it not a triumph – a miracle – to rise again, transformed, recreated, stronger than ever before and more purposeful? Confidence flowed into her. She exulted in its returning tide. Colour rose to her pale cheeks. She had achieved so much. She had done it all herself. There was nothing she could not do. She had found a new direction, and knew that it demanded a deliberate downward step into dangerous territory, where she had never ventured before. The choice, she would have claimed, was her own. She was in no mood just then to theorize as to the source of her destructive urge, or to wonder if its compulsion was part – a powerful part – of her disastrous inheritance. A new recklessness possessed her. She had no ties, no responsibilities to anyone, no scruples. She would go wherever she liked – and come back when she chose. Meanwhile . . .

'Why don't you find a place of your own?' he had asked.

A cottage, a villa, an apartment? A refuge, a corner of her own in the world's wilderness? Her head cleared. It must be in a town where people shrank to size. In the country people were too few and consequently too significant. They stood out like monuments, demanding attention.

She would need money, needed it now, in fact. Peering in her mirror, she dusted her face with a papier-poudré and consulted a mental list of possible contributors. Most of them she had outgrown: small fry whose help had been secured by means she now despised as crude. It might be necessary to marry. Time – she looked again in the mirror and looked away – was passing her by. Young men worth marrying and sound in wind and limb were in short supply. The others had been slaughtered in their thousands. An older man? A rich widower. If Esther Aumery could find one, so could she.

Then, when she came back to Barbarrow . . . ? Well, there were more ways than one of succeeding where she had so far failed: more direct ways of avenging herself on the Lincolns. And next time it would be different. She would not come as an outsider but with money, possessions, background, status. It would take time. It would take years. But life must have a purpose. She had found hers.

She stood lost in thought, brows knit, teeth clenched, her body stiff with resolution: a figure at odds with the gentle landscape where there were no hard edges, no certainties of outline, only blue-green distances between trees and soft sunlight on leaves and grass. Fortunately she was alone. A sensitive observer happening on the scene – one who loved Barbarrow – might have felt a premonitory chill, as if the place itself were vulnerable.

The feeling of liberation lasted all evening, as she packed and threw out unwanted papers and things she had kept and now found not worth bothering about. One thing, crushed into an old pillowcase, she set aside: a relic, a reminder, a goad on the rare occasion when her courage flagged. It had served a purpose and it was now obsolete, yet it was still so charged with meaning that the mere sight of it threatened her freedom by reviving memories of how she had come by it, and with them the rancour that sharpened her hands into talons as she prepared to tear the thing to pieces.

How to dispose of them? The grate was small, the fire almost out. An alternative solution pleased her. She found paper and string . . .

Mrs Overton was surprised by Miss Motte's abrupt departure, but she had paid to the end of the month and was entitled to go. Clearing the sitting-room grate, she found charred fragments of paper, evidently letters, on one of them a signature: Roland. Love letters? Miss Motte hadn't seemed the type. But after all, it's only human nature, Mrs Overton thought, groping in the ashes: everybody has someone to love.

CHAPTER 28

'I had to bring it,' Esther said, 'to show you. It came this morning, by post.'

He ignored the brown paper parcel she was holding. She was smiling, though not as she had once smiled. Her eyes, once unclouded by any emotion other than rapture in seeing him, were veiled. To have answered a knock and found her on his doorstep brought so swift a pang that he could not speak. He moved the conch shells. She sat down in their place. He sat opposite.

'I told Gervase that I simply had to come and tell you – and show you this – and he agreed that I must come.' This one time, he had said, and for such a very particular reason. Generally speaking, she must decide for herself, there was no need to consult him. Two friends living so near to each other were bound to meet sometimes as neighbours in the normal course of events, he had said, his voice level, his face unsmiling.

'Daniel.' Her lips trembled. 'How . . . how are you?'

'You know.'

'Yes. I know.'

Neighbours, she thought, but always facing in opposite directions. Every time he looks towards Long Rake he'll think of me. I'll look east towards Cat Hill and think of him. It will go on for years and years. We may happen to meet in Hudmorton, at the station, in Unnerstone – not knowing what to say. He'll see me growing older. He'll never hold me in his arms again, and gradually he'll stop wanting to. She knew that she herself was changing. The longing for him, the way she missed him, were becoming part of a deep, incurable nostalgia for a vanished world: for childhood and girlhood, for the innocent lightness of heart she had lost. She saw despair in his eyes as he watched her. Remembering the parcel, she began to fidget with the string.

'How could it happen,' she said, 'what happened to us? Such a terrible thing.'

'Terrible.' He considered the word in all its implications. It was not the right word, but it would serve to describe the limitless gulf that separated them as they sat close enough to hear each other breathe. He reached out and took the parcel. 'You were always hopeless at knots.'

'At tying them. For untying I use scissors. Gervase did those.'

'He meant them to stay knotted.' Daniel plucked at them absently, with no hope of undoing them, no hope of any kind.

'Gervase has had a bad time lately. I don't mean just about us. He's been so good about that.'

'He's a good chap.' And could afford to be, having carried off the prize.

'There's another reason why I came – to tell you. Something else happened. A tremendous thing. Unbelievable, but true. On Friday . . .'

She told him how the mystery of the lost child had been solved, speaking slowly for the pleasure of making it last, of not having to leave him just yet, of behaving for a few minutes as if she would never have to leave him. To watch her as she told the story was all the recompense he had for years starved of the sight of her: a frugal harvest to be stored against the barren years to come.

'How has he taken it?'

With sorrow, she told him, and with a relief that had only sadness in it. A tension so long-lasting and so suddenly released had left him shaken and depressed.

'He needs me more than ever.'

425

'Yes.'

'You haven't asked me how she took it. Clairy.'

'You're going to tell me.'

'I thought she was incapable of feeling, but I was wrong. I was sorry for her. She had believed it – that she was Lilla. Imagine finding what you've been looking for all your life and then having it snatched away. For her it must have been worse than that, to find that, after all, it was only an illusion when she had thought it real. I wonder what she'll do. Where will she go?'

'Back to the underworld.' Daniel could not pity her, but to think of her released, like Eurydice, from the lower world almost into daylight, and then to be forced back to the darkness she had left, gave him a certain satisfaction. He recognized it as unholy. Besides . . . 'She'll rise again,' he said, and wondered if he still cared enough to hate her.

'Well, one good thing has come out of it,' Esther concluded. 'She's gone. We need never see her again.'

'Are you sure?'

'Don't make me doubt it.' She snatched the parcel from him. 'Have you a knife?' But the package was soft, and with some manoeuvring she slipped off the string and parted the brown paper, to reveal a bundle of material the indeterminate colour of seaweed.

'What on earth is it?'

'You don't recognize it? You were always hopeless about clothes.' She shook out the folds.

'A dress of some sort.'

'My green merino. Surely you remember. You made me give it to her.' Naturally he had forgotten. 'Imagine her keeping it all this time. It must have been important to her. It was important to me, too. I didn't want her to have it.'

Nor did she want it close to her in her lap. In sudden distaste she reached up and hung it on the peg where Thomas used to hang his bag. It dangled, distorted but lifelike. Gazed at, it took on a personality distinct from that of either of its wearers.

'I seem to remember some superstition in a book on folk lore.' Daniel had been amused by her reaction. 'It could be unlucky to give a coat to a stranger. It made a bond, and if the stranger happened to come from the other world, the bond would be – let us say – an undesirable one.'

'It's a pity you didn't think of that at the time,' Esther said crisply.

'Sorry, love. I didn't think you'd take it seriously.'

'I don't,' she said untruthfully. 'Only somehow I see it as a sign of how much she hated me, and I don't really understand why. At any rate, she's sent it back. It's a message. It means that she won't be coming back. It's all over.'

'God knows it needs to be.' He was less sure that in the chain of cause and effect a link could be removed. 'Are you going to leave it there as a lasting memorial, like a banner in a church?' As a faded emblem that had changed sides in conflict, it had a certain interest, he thought, until the forlorn droop of the sleeves gave the thing an altogether different character and put an end to his detachment.

'Burn it,' Esther said, her eyes on his thin face, his brow, his lock of dark hair. 'It's the least you can do in the circumstances now that it's all over.'

He took her hands and held and kissed them. 'Between us it will never be over, love. Not for either of us.'

'Never. I knew from the beginning – that it would never end.'

Five minutes more, they agreed, and stayed together, wordless, the flow of time almost arrested until the seconds became an instrument of torture, like water falling drop by drop on a prisoner's brow. There was no future to be shared beyond the next minute and the next, each in its turn slipping into a past no longing could recall.

427

He went with her as far as the stream.

'We had that one perfect summer,' she said, 'to look back on and remember, like old people. It must be so peaceful to be old.'

'A peaceful old age? I shall look forward to that. Time is on our side. It's just a question of waiting – and not dying.'

'You're mocking me.'

'And loving you. My love.' He took her in his arms in the old way.

It could do no harm to let him hold her close, just once more, to remember how it used to be and forget that everything had changed. She dragged herself away. He let her go and watched her cross the stream slowly, step by step, to her own side – the Barbarrow side. She turned to face him across the water, then turned away.

It was worse for him, she thought, as she climbed the hill. She was not alone. Her love for Gervase had grown in response to his need of her. There were different kinds of love. There was sun and there was candlelight. After the blaze of sunset it was the candle that helped one through the darkness. She must think of it like that. She must remember that. Only . . . If only . . .

From the brow of Barrow Hill she waved, a slight figure against a clear sky. But he didn't look at the sky. Instead, walking slowly homeward, head bowed, he saw nothing but his own thick shoes, the shabby brogues of an undistinguished country schoolmaster. Their steady plodding through the lime-grey dust measured, step by step, the distance between his soaring boyhood dreams and his present humdrum state. Through his own weakness and folly – he thought of it as a fit of insanity – he had lost Esther and condemned her to unhappiness equal to his own: a loss all the heavier for his conviction that she would prove the more resilient. Already he had sensed in her the quietness that comes from acceptance. Having made her choice, she was spared the wearisome fret of wondering what to do. Whereas he . . .

Gazing at the sky from the crown of the Aston oak, he had thrilled to the splendour of the universe, believing himself destined to fulfil in it some noble purpose. He had been granted wings and had never taken flight. In the high-flown way he had grown to detest, he had spoken satirically of Clairy's return to the underworld. She had at least risen high enough to fall. From a safer starting point than hers, he had done no more than dream of rising, and remained where he belonged, on the well-trodden earth of a sunken lane.

Hopeless love, failed ambition: either one of them could drive a man to despair. His loss was threefold: he also suffered a failure of vision like an inward blindness. There was nothing to hope for, nothing it was within his power to change, nothing he wanted to do.

Except for one thing. His dusty shoes took him to his own gate and came to rest in his own porch from which he had gone in and out day after day, ever since he could walk. Before that he had been carried in and out. In the fullness of time he would be carried out to his grave. He was sick of the sight of it. The conch shells irritated him to death, as did the green dress hanging limp from the hook. He took it down, rolled it up, shoved it under the seat on the right-hand side and sat down, nudging the bundle further out of sight with his heel. Then he became aware of the ghastly trophy he had always hated, never questioning its right to be there. It snarled down at him, its bared teeth and empty eye sockets an obscene testimony to the agonized hatred of a victim's response to mindless cruelty.

His father's stout cudgel still stood in the corner by the door. He spat on his hands, seized it and took aim. There was not room enough to swing it but two savage upward jabs loosened the nails and a vicious sideways swipe brought the thing down. He left it lying on the floor, found a towel and went down to the river for a swim. Brutal physical violence, of which he deeply disapproved, had had a heartening effect.

As had the change of element from earth to water. Swimming clear of the trees, he turned on his back and saw clouds drift across the clear blue. Rain slanted over the fields as he ran uphill. By the time he reached the Lodge they were moving eastward. The sudden shower was over.

Jake had come back from cricket on the green. He had lugged a stepladder from the shed to the porch and was standing on the top step, wielding an inexpert hammer. He looked down over his shoulder, beaming with pride.

'Don't say a word till you've taken that nail out of your mouth.'

The ladder lurched as Jake complied. 'I'm putting the fox back. I got a shock when I saw it lying there. But don't you worry, Mr Godwain. I've just about managed to get it back.' He dropped a nail to join half a dozen others on the floor tiles. 'You wouldn't think it would fall down, would you, but some of the nails had come out. Two of them were still sticking to the skin.'

'Come down,' Daniel commanded as the ladder lurched again.

'I couldn't leave it on the floor like that. You have to put things right. You said if ever—'

'I say far too much.' Daniel threw down the wet towel. 'Give me the hammer.'

Wryly, without protest, he accepted defeat. The hammer in his hand perversely symbolized his helplessness. He positively felt his breathing space contract as the prison door closed with a slam that echoed down familiar corridors. Once again circumstances hemmed him in. Once again they were of his own making. He was trapped with no means of escape.

It didn't take long to put things right, more or less. The accident had had a mellowing effect on the other victim: the snarl was perceptibly less ferocious; the reason obvious.

'Here's another.' Jake had crawled under both of the seats.

'That's four.' He got up, holding them carefully cupped in his hand. They were narrow, yellow, pointed objects. 'Will we be able to stick them in?'

'You'd better put them in a safe place. Next time I have the glue pot on we'll have a go. Otherwise he'll need a set of false ones.'

The feeble joke was brilliantly successful. Leaving Jake convulsed with laughter, he took the ladder back to the shed and returned to find him groping under one of the seats.

'Were you wanting this green stuff for anything, Mr Godwain? It would do to keep the rain out of the rabbit hutch till I can get hold of a decent bit of felting.'

'No, I don't want it. And look here, it's time you stopped calling me Mr Godwain.'

'You mean – sir?'

'Good Lord, no.' Their eyes met: Daniel's narrowed in thought, Jake's wide in astonished surmise. 'Any ideas?'

'Oh yes. I could call you Governor. There was this boy in "Honour First and Last". He used to talk about his Governor – but that was his father. Perhaps—'

'Never mind. It'll do. When you're eighteen you can shorten it to Gov. Have you got the kettle on?'

When Jake had gone indoors, his face radiant, Daniel walked to the gate. There had been times when this high ground above the Scaur had seemed like a stepping-off point on the rim of the world, and now more than ever, as he faced a spectacular sky of purple clouds gilt-edged with returning sunshine. There was no rainbow to lift the heart, but over Long Rake, clouds were parting to reveal infinite regions of light stretching as far as the eye could reach – and beyond. A solitary crow, small and black against the vast golden chasm, was flying directly towards it as if seeking in its luminous depths a fulfilment not to be found on earth.

Might there still be time? Did there exist a Cause in whose service he could forget self-interest and ignoble dreams of worldly success, a Cause based on ideals a man could live for and – if necessary – die for? Would the time ever come? Was it too late?

CHAPTER 29

'I believe it is already too late.'

Seated on the edge of her chair between Aunt Alice and Mr Auke, Viola shivered in the throes of a fearful sense of urgency. What was it too late for? She sat directly opposite the speaker who was so large that she could not see more than an inch or two of the sideboard behind him. His voice was so tremendous that she felt a breeze issuing from his lips. Everything he said sounded important. He was mighty. When she thought of God, she saw him in the likeness of Mr Krantz. As a very small girl she had believed that he actually was God, and had been disappointed in the way He was dressed.

'To avoid war?' Esther glanced along the table at Gervase, and then at Vincent.

'The League was a noble concept doomed to failure by the ignobility of Nations.' Without being asked, Annie brought Mr Krantz a second large helping of summer pudding and cream. Everyone else had finished. Mrs Baeck, with Eva and Heinrich, had already left the table and gone back to the coach-house. They would be leaving for America the next day and needed to finish their packing, though, having been smuggled out of Germany, they had only one suitcase each. Aunt Alice had lent them money to buy clothes and to pay for the voyage. Viola knew, because Eva had told her, that Mrs Baeck was worried about paying it back. She also knew that it wouldn't matter to Aunt Alice if the money was never paid back: she would simply sell more and more thousands of Skidways' famous Domino Toffees. Father said that Skidways' Domino

Toffees were the only things that hadn't been affected by the Depression.

'When Mussolini went into Abyssinia – that was the time to act. Even last year, when Hitler occupied the Rhineland, there might still have been time. Instead, the free world remained stupefied by indifference to the Fascist threat. You'll tell me that we are re-arming at last, that things are looking up again at the Lincoln Ironworks. But believe me, we've left it very late indeed.'

'Not in Spain,' someone said. 'They're doing something about it there – and a very nasty business it seems to be.'

Mr Auke said something about the Civil War being a dress rehearsal and they went on talking about Spain and Germany and Italy and Russia until it was time for coffee in the drawing-room.

It had been a special occasion, though an informal one. The new table had arrived two days ago and a few intimate friends had been invited to lunch as a celebration. Actually the table was not new: in fact it was very old. Father had been secretly searching for it for years, since before she was born. It had belonged to the Aumerys of Lady Green. When the covers had been taken off and Mother realized what it was, she had burst into tears.

'Oh, Gervase,' she said. 'You remembered. However did you find it? How like you! You spoil me—'

'That would be impossible,' Father said.

'You leave me nothing in the world to wish for.'

They had neither of them paid much attention to the table, and yet they were obviously extremely pleased about it.

While the grown-ups drank their coffee, Viola escaped into the garden. In ten years there had been changes of which she was not aware. So far as she knew, the flagged path beyond the sundial had always led to a white marble statue of a lady holding a sort of flute. She was a Greek Muse. Walking along the path, one saw her intriguingly in the distance, looking towards the house.

'An improvement?' Gervase had sounded dubious when the remains of the arbour had been carted away and the lady raised to her plinth.

'It ought to be.' Esther's first impression had been of a cool stillness reminiscent of another figure. 'Oh, it is. Of course. And she isn't looking at us, is she?'

'Certainly not. She's looking over our heads towards Mount Helicon and thinking of higher things. But if you're not sure, we can take her down and plant a tree – or put a seat here.'

'No. She's beautiful, and Viola will like her . . .'

Viola did like her, and the Muse's domain, with its screen of honeysuckle and clematis, became her favourite place. She also liked the old-fashioned white rose bush at the top of the steps leading down to the shrubbery below William's lawn. Rose bush and shrubs had been planted after some alterations there when she was a year old. In the retaining wall was a spout covered with green moss, as if there had once, long ago, been water flowing into the basin beneath.

To the young man on Barrow Hill the Hall seemed unchanged since he had visited it eleven years before. He paused to look down appreciatively at the old place, still responsive to the glamour it had held for him as an ignorant lad; and now he could see how perfectly the house merged with its setting and could admire the unassuming grace of its proportions. A finger of blue smoke pointed upward from one of its chimneys. The stable bell chimed two o'clock.

He went down slowly, sobered by the thought of his mission. At the bottom of the hill he found a wicket gate, and came to the front of the house. There was no-one about but a girl on the terrace. She had seen him and waited for him to come within speaking distance.

'Good afternoon,' she said.

'Good afternoon.' He had come to a halt at the lowest of the three steps. She was young enough to be still in knee-length socks, and some sort of light dress with bits of very short sleeves like flaps. She had dark, curling hair. 'Would it be possible for me to speak to Mrs Lincoln?'

'She will be pleased to see you, I'm sure,' Viola said in a manner indistinguishable from her mother's at its most formal. 'At the moment she is entertaining visitors, but they'll be leaving soon. Quite soon. Most of them. Do come and sit down.' She perched on one of the chairs and he joined her at the round table.

'You've walked over from Wood Aston, haven't you?' Her manner became rapidly less stately. 'Actually I know who you are. You're Jake. Mother told me once when we were passing the Lodge and you were in the garden.' She did not add that since then she had looked for him every time they drove past. She thought him handsome, and the Lodge was such a pretty little place.

'Jake Hildy,' he said.

'And I'm Viola Lincoln.'

'Yes, I know.'

'Actually I've seen you on the train, going to school.'

'I wish I'd known. I'd have looked out for you. It's too late now. I've left school.'

'People are always saying it's too late. About the Fascists and so on.'

'It's partly about the Fascists that I've come.'

'They seem to be everywhere.' She saw them indistinctly, yellow-faced and mysterious, emerging in groups from the grey map of Europe. 'They're the same as Nazis, aren't they?' He nodded with suitable gravity. She lowered her voice. 'But the Baecks will be leaving tomorrow – for America.' They would get away in time. It would be a relief, though she liked them. But one had to be careful not to upset

436

people who had been through so very upsetting a time.

From the hall came the sounds of leave-taking.

'They're going now. It's been rather a special . . .' 'Luncheon' sounded too grand for summer pudding '. . . lunch.' She told him about the table. 'It's a very old table where six princes have dined. Imagine – all of them meeting. I wonder if any of them knew each other – as friends, you know.'

'Or brothers? George V had five sons, but the eldest, Edward VIII – he's the one who abdicated last year – wasn't born until 1894. How long did the Aumerys have the table? Had all those princes dined at it before or after it came into their possession?'

'I don't know.'

'Before, I should think, wouldn't you?' Jake warmed to the subject, enjoying her anxious concentration. 'Let me see . . . Edward VII was fond of dining, and he had quite a few brothers. But have you considered the possibility that they didn't all dine at the table at the same time? It could have been a series of princes, not a gathering.'

'I hadn't thought of it like that.' She was astonished by his learned grasp of the problem. 'One after another. Yes.'

'We mustn't forget the foreign princes,' he said gravely, 'though there aren't so many of them these days.' He'd better steer clear of the Romanovs. She wouldn't like to know what happened to them. Her eyes would change: they were dark blue, like violets, and wide in respectful attentiveness.

'You won't be travelling on that train any more?' as he paused.

'I'm afraid not.'

'But you'll still be at the Lodge? We pass it fairly often on the way to Miss Angovil's and Mr Horner's.'

'No. The Lodge has been let. I'll be at the University. I'm going up to Oxford in October.' He had learned to say it casually. All the same, his heart thumped in joy and disbelief. With a sudden change to genuine gravity, he remembered who had made it possible – and why he had come to Barbarrow. At the same time a voice called Viola's name.

'Excuse me. I must go and say goodbye to the visitors. I'll tell Mother.'

He got up, suddenly nervous now that the time had come, and knew, despite her smile as she came out to him, that she was nervous too.

'Jake! How very nice to see you!'

She would know on whose behalf he had come, just as he knew why she was nervous. No-one had told him, but he had his own theory based on accumulated scraps of evidence. As a lad he had been a climber of trees and had deciphered the statement carved in the bark of the Aston oak; had sometimes pondered on his governor's long bachelorhood when he had had plenty of encouragement to end it, and marriage would have guaranteed him a headship and improved his prospects beyond that. Above all, he had been impressed by the sadness of the beautiful lady with rings on her fingers who had come to the Lodge one summer afternoon, and by the governor's gloomy silence when he came home that day – unaccountably late – to the meal neither of them could eat.

She was as beautiful as ever and was already trembling on the brink of the sadness he would have to inflict.

'Is anything wrong? Nothing has happened to him? He's not—'

'Oh no.' Not yet, he thought. 'But he asked me to bring you a message. He wanted me to tell you . . .'

She walked to the edge of the terrace, her eyes on the path over the hill.

'There *is* something wrong,' she said.

'He said I was to tell you that there were only two things he had ever wanted. One of them was to find a cause worth devoting his life to.' Or giving his life for? Was that what he had meant? 'He wanted you to know that he has found it. He's gone to Spain, Mrs Lincoln, to join the International Brigade.'

He could not see her face, nor did she move except to glance up quickly at the sky as if to outface the treachery of its unclouded blue.

'He doesn't believe in war,' she said.

'He believes in this one.'

He had never been more certain. They had sat up late, night after night, thrashing it out: the evil of Fascism, its threat to individual liberty, its contempt of human life, the obscenities already perpetrated in its name. It must be stopped while there was still time, he had said, before it spread to the whole of Europe.

'I wanted to go with him.'

She turned to look at him. He was not as tall as Daniel. His build was sturdier, his shoulders were broader. He might be stronger, less easily hurt. He had Daniel's confidence but not his readiness of speech, or his spiritual incandescence. That was unique. All the same, she guessed that his ways and manners were Daniel's; he had absorbed Daniel's ideas, his interests, his standards of conduct. Dark-eyed, dark-haired, perceptive – he could have been . . . In every way but the primal, natural, physical act of begetting, he could be Daniel's son.

'I understand that,' she said. 'The wanting to go with him.'

'But I had to let him go on his own. I had to get out of his way.' The boy's eyes burned with pent-up feeling. 'He's stayed here cooped up on my account when there were plenty of other things he could have done. He wanted me to stay and make something of myself. What I've managed to do has all been due to him. In a way, if this had to happen, it's happened at the right time. I'm eighteen. I can stand on my own feet. He doesn't need to worry about me any more.'

439

'It's the other way round now. Your turn to worry about him?'

'Yes.' Jake hesitated. 'You know what the chances are in the mess-up there is out there.'

'How was he? How was he feeling? Was he – happy to go?'

'Happy?' It wasn't the right word. 'On edge to go. Sure that it was the right thing to do. But,' he looked at her in sudden appeal, 'I wondered . . . There was something about him.' Something in the lingering grasp of his hand when they had parted at Hudmorton station: the long look of affection, the regretful smile broadening into a grin when Jake had said, 'So long, Gov,' using the shortened form for the first time. 'I'm not sure that he intends to come back – ever.'

Esther had come closer. They stood in silence, facing the likelihood that they might not see him again. Esther felt as never before the weight of loneliness, not her own but Daniel's. She seemed to see into his heart, and understood at last the splendour of his ideas, his sense of wasted energy, the dignity of his resignation to and acceptance of a limited duty.

'It's been wonderful,' she said, 'to be loved by him. Hasn't it?' Jake nodded. 'He'll write to you.'

'If it's possible.'

'You'll come and tell me? We're his closest friends, you and I.'

'Yes, I'll come.'

She reached up and kissed his cheek.

'I'll come,' he repeated, overwhelmed and lost for words.

'He looks very serious.' Viola had been hovering just out of earshot. 'All on his own.' They watched him as he went through the wicket gate. 'If we'd been going for a walk, we could have gone with him part of the way.'

'A walk would do us all good. Run and catch him up. We'll follow.'

But Alice had gone back to town with Henry and Flora, and Morgan with Gervase, who had a directors' meeting. There was only Vincent left to accompany her. The day was warm, their walk leisurely. Between two old friends there was no need of conversation. Esther's thoughts were not of her companion.

Had she found tranquillity? The undercurrent of sadness remained, but she had passed through conflict to acceptance of a situation for which there could be no other remedy, schooling herself to think of the fulfilment of happiness as momentary, transformed in an instant to the memory of it or the hope of its return.

Serenity may be more durable than rapture, but it too is constantly under threat. Esther's peace of mind was still not proof against one lurking fear so foolish that she would have been ashamed to speak of it even to Gervase. (Was he sometimes visited by a similar fear?) Clarice Motte had gone – years ago. At first there had been the tiresome possibility that she might find some excuse for coming back – for some practical, if dubious, reason. That had not happened; but the slight feeling of suspense was slow to fade. Where was she? What was she doing? On whom had her shadow fallen? She occupied the mind as if, in defiance of every effort of common sense to keep her at bay, she had actually come to stay.

Time passed; she was no longer expected. She was seldom thought of, relegated in her various guises to a place in Barbarrow's long history. Only now and then Esther would remember with a prick of uneasiness that it was Daniel who had sown the seed of doubt.

'It's all over,' she had told him. 'We need never see her again.'

'Are you sure?'

She would never be sure, though gradually she was able to rationalize the dread as a nervous weakness of her own, unfounded in any likelihood that after such a lapse of time the woman would reappear. But in

the quietness of Barbarrow she had got into the habit
of listening – for a car, for footsteps. After all, one
could never forget the old tragic story or the wildly
colourful local versions of it. They were responsible for
a recurrent dream that Viola was in danger from some
intruder. She would wake in terror, and for a day or
two could scarcely let Viola out of her sight. Even now
she was given to foolish alarms . . .

'That lady you told me about, the one who talked
to you in the train. You said she seemed to know you.
What was she like?'

Viola had been vague. 'Tall, slim. Yes, she knew my
name and where I live. A fur coat. Sealskin, I think.
She seemed to want to talk, but I had to get on with
my geography.' She had been revising for a test.

Who, among their many acquaintances, had a sealskin coat and was also tall and slim? No-one. Simply
no-one . . . But she was reassured by Viola's resistance
to the advances of a stranger. Perhaps a geography test
was as good a way as any of laying a ghost.

That had been months ago, but the episode was
typical of her instinct to keep a constant check on
Viola's whereabouts. Where was she now, for instance?
There was no sign of her.

At the summit of Barrow Hill they stopped. For years
she had made this the limit of her walks. Below lay the
enclosed valley where she had been born. Many a time,
through lowering cloud or sunshine, she had looked
across at the steep rise of Cat Hill and then looked down
to trace the course of the stream as it flowed southward,
sheltered by trees or open to the sky, to Lady Green,
Scaur Crag and Aston Wood. Every familiar feature
– Broom Farm, stepping-stones, ruined barn, meadow
and hedgerow – was a reminder of Daniel.

They had agreed never to meet deliberately. The
walk to the top of Barrow Hill had become a pilgrimage.
It had taken on a devotional quality devoid of any other
intention than to remain in touch, to cling in spirit to an

earlier existence as insubstantial now as a dream and as ineradicable as the memory of youth. A mere sight of him – by the stile, between trees – would have been as longed-for and as disturbing as a visionary presence at a shrine. She would strain her eyes to catch a glimpse of him: he might just happen to be walking along the lane. But he never was. She never saw him there.

They had met elsewhere, perhaps half a dozen times, always by chance, briefly and in the company of others, but never in the very place where they had been together from the beginning, where they had lived and loved and parted with such intensity of feeling that in the place itself there must always linger some trace of it: some sign that it had happened, that it hadn't all been as unremarkable as the fall of leaves and the wearing thin of pebbles in the stream. Year after year she had waited, half expecting to see him on the farther bank, looking up at her as if he had been there for a while, as if he had been led to that very spot at the very time when she happened to be there. But in eleven years it had never happened. He had never come.

And now he was no longer there at all to be glimpsed, even in the far distance. As she stood by the boundary wall and scanned the scene, she felt its emptiness. It was only a view, a place without enchantment from which the vital spirit had departed. The emptiness could not be more vast if he never came back: it would only be longer lasting. It would last as long as she lived; and when she died there would be nothing left of two people whose love for each other had, for one short summer, matched the beauty of its setting. Together the people and the scene had touched perfection.

Voices floated up from the stream: the voices of a young man and a girl. Viola was hesitating on the stepping-stones – on the fifth stone, the awkward one, always inclined to lurch. Jake had gone ahead to his own side, but crossed back again to rescue her. She saw them poised in midstream, hand in hand, as she and Daniel had stood above their own shimmering reflection in the same water. Both constant and ever-changing, it now mirrored another boy and girl. She smiled and was comforted, as if feeling the clasp of a loving hand, as if the beloved place had, after all, grown sentient and signalled a message that the story was not ended. It might go on with different characters, but with the same theme, against the same background of sheltering hills, to the same accompaniment of gently flowing water; and perhaps – it was not impossible – with a happier ending.

She could have shared such a thought only with Daniel. He would understand.

'Yes, yes,' she saw his face light up, the eager movement of his lips, 'and there's another thing . . .'

As he spoke, her faltering idea would take shape, he would raise it to a higher pitch, it would be inspiring. She would listen, spellbound, as she had done many a time when they loitered by the Aston oak, or walked, he a few paces ahead, she lagging behind or running ankle-deep in fallen leaves to catch up with him. He had always been just beyond her reach.

But from the beginning she had warmed to the fire that burned in him. Its flame had set her mind alight. She had tried to understand his ardent longing to dedicate his life to some just cause. Now, as if clouds had parted, the opportunity had come: he had found one of the two things he had most wanted. He had wished she could share it. That was why he had sent Jake.

She longed to tell him that she understood: that if she could not respond as he did to the long-awaited moment, she could with all her heart share the sadness that must have tempered his willingness to go. There was so much that she could have told him if chance had not intervened to separate them, leaving a world of things unsaid.

Perhaps there was still time. Surely there would come a time when she would be able to tell him . . . Some day, somewhere, somehow, she would certainly tell him . . .

She was aware of a movement behind her. 'Vincent!' He had waited, leaning against the wall. 'I'm sorry. For a moment I was far away.'

If only he could catch that look as she turned, not quite returned from wherever she had been. Maturity had heightened her beauty and taken nothing away. Daylight offered no threat to the smoothness of her skin or to the sheen of her hair. But beauty, now at its peak, must fade as all beauty fades. It lay within his power to arrest it at this high point, to fix and keep it to be hung on a wall and looked at. But it was the evanescence of the expression that would defeat him: eyes pensive, lips faintly smiling, the wistful blend of sadness and serenity, and – for a dazzling moment – a mysterious enlightenment.

She felt him looking at her, laughed and pushed back her hair. 'I must look a sight. There wasn't time to tidy up after lunch. It's time we rescued Jake from Viola.' She cupped her hands to her mouth and called, 'Viola!' Her voice drifted down towards the stream and faded on the way.

'Viola!' Vincent bellowed. 'Tea-time.'

'Coming . . .' The response was instant.

'What should I do without you?'

They were at ease together. Theirs had been a long friendship, strengthened perhaps by a similarity of which they were probably unaware. They were alike, each haunted by a longing for the unattainable, for a love idealised and unfulfilled: of all the different kinds of love the most poignant, the most constant, and without end.

THE END